HE
LITTLE
FLOWERS

HER LITTLE FLOWERS

SHANNON MORGAN

KENSINGTON
PUBLISHING CORP.

www.kensingtonbooks.com

KENSINGTON BOOKS are published by

Kensington Publishing Corp.
119 West 40th Street
New York, NY 10018

ISBN: 978-1-4967-4389-3 (ebook)
ISBN: 978-1-4967-4388-6

First Kensington Trade Paperback Printing: August 2023

10 9 8 7 6 5 4 3 2 1

Printed in the United States of America

Anthony: conspirator, collaborator, husband, best friend

25 July, 1969

Time passed too quickly on their last night together.

A fizz of anticipation raced through the sisters as they tipped and toed down the stairs that had creaked for hundreds of years. The girls loved these stolen nights, though they were feared too. Except the eldest, who feared little, as only a seven-year-old with a temperament to match her flaming hair could.

"Shhhh!" Mum hushed with a smile in her voice from the bottom of the stairs.

Through the old manor the sisters crept after Mum, all barefoot, all in nightdresses, all tensing into frozen silhouettes in the shadowy kitchen when the youngest girl whimpered.

"Hush, my flower," Mum murmured, quickly lifting the little one, cradling her in a tight embrace.

The copper pots on the walls of the vast kitchen, unchanged from a bygone era, gleamed in the moonlight, creating a mosaic of patterned light on the flagstones. The scratchy scent of dried rosemary and sage seemed to crinkle time as the girls waited, scarcely breathing. They listened to the house.

A burbling snore broke the waiting silence.

"Move!" whispered Mum, pushing her girls out into the night.

The garden was bathed in a breathless haze of light and shadow where moonbeams danced along every leaf and weaved through petals of sweet-scented honeysuckle and pungent mustard. The hoary old oak tree in the courtyard shivered in prideful glory and swept dappled shadows across the ground in the sighing breeze.

Mum floated across the garden in her white nightdress, ghostlike and so beautiful it hurt to look at her without the tightness of tears. She stopped by the shed smothered in moonflower vines; thick and gnarled with age, their white, tightly furled blooms glowed like tiny barley-twist candles.

Mum held up a hand.

The girls tensed with illicit excitement, yet none of them fidgeted or rustled. The night reclaimed its creeping, expectant silence. Still Mum waited, not moving, not swaying as she sometimes did. Her nightdress pressed against her body, thin and sagged, suggesting a greater age than her twenty-six years, bearing the fatigue of too many pregnancies in too short a time from too young an age.

But even as the girls watched, Mum straightened, sloughing the years of hardship with each deep breath she took, revealing the young woman she should've been had life treated her differently, more kindly.

A frisson of unease stole through the girls, sending gooseflesh up their bare arms, even though the July night still retained the heat of long, lazy summer days. For on that warm air came a murmur of ancient plant lore, a litany from long-dead Thwaite women, older than Thwaite Manor, as old as the surrounding Lonehowe Wood.

"Moonflower, when lit, for fretful vision of thine own death," the girls whispered with Mum, a mere sigh to join those of their

ancestors. *"Moonflower, when lit, for fretful vision of thine own death. Moonflower, when lit . . ."*

The moon watched as the barley-twist blooms unfurled into large, pale trumpets. It was a quick unfurling; a ripple of luminescence that released a cloyingly sweet scent.

The girls copied Mum as she breathed in the moonflowers' freely given perfume, even as shroud-pale moths appeared like will o' the wisps, drawn to the enchanting, deadly nectar.

There was something primeval in their worship of the moonflowers—something witchy and secret and forbidden. In childish innocence, the sisters reveled in the secretiveness, in the conspiracy against Him, in the tickle that danced down their spines that he might at any moment wake from his drunken slumber to find his despised daughters and wife worshipping a plant that could kill him if he pushed Mum too far. There was power in the knowledge of what lay hidden and deadly on the palest of nights.

Time passed too quickly the night before she died.

ONE

❧

Thick, black tea. Teeth-staining tea. Good, strong, Chinese tea, Oolong for preference. The perfect sort for reading the leaves.

Francine Thwaite counted out the last thirty seconds, drank the tea quickly, swung her cup left and right three times, flipped the cup over the saucer to allow the last of the moisture to drain, and peered down at the dregs. Once a white cup, it was now discolored by tannin from countless readings. She couldn't abide those cups with silly symbols she'd seen at the gift shop down in Hawkshead. That was for tourists and idiots, which in her mind were one and the same.

She squinted, searching for symbols. Reading the leaves was a time of quiet contemplation; not for the peace it afforded, but because it was something she had done all her life.

A gust of wind blew in through the open door of the kitchen, setting the Spode horse sliding slowly across the sloping shelf of the old sideboard.

Francine glared at it. "Bree! If I've told you once, I've told you a hundred times: leave the china alone! I don't mind if you muck about with the furniture, but not the ornaments."

The horse stopped mid slide and the air around it took on a note of disgruntlement, like a small child scuffing the floor with her shoe.

She bit her lip to hide her smile as the chair on the opposite side of the kitchen table scraped slowly across the flagstones and the air took on a fascinated concentration. "The leaves aren't saying much," Francine told Bree. "There's what looks like a *C* or a *G* with a pair of scissors near it, a lopsided heart, and a cross . . . What do you make of that? I don't know any- one whose name begins with *C* or *G*."

A teaspoon rose off the table and tapped against the teacup.

"Old Charlie doesn't count," said Francine. "He's a hundred if he's a day, and I've known him all my life. I doubt the leaves are talking about him."

The teaspoon tapped agreement.

"Well, whoever it is, I shall be having a quarrel with them, though probably not a bad one as the scissors aren't that close. Sharp words, maybe?"

The cross made Francine think of graveyards. She hated graveyards to the point of phobia and had never even set foot in the Thwaite graveyard just beyond the garden in Lonehowe Wood. A cross wasn't a good symbol to see in the leaves.

"And there's a letter coming. See the little rectangle here?" She tilted the cup towards Bree. "Should arrive sometime this morning. Bother! I could do without a trip down to Hawks- head." She mock scowled at the chair opposite her. "I wouldn't have to go at all if you hadn't frightened all the postmen so none will venture up here now." She smiled to take the sting out of her irritation that her planned day had been thrown into disarray by her fate in the leaves, adding, "You'd best get over to your tree. And no nonsense while I'm out, understand?"

With one last tap of the spoon, a hiss of warmth brushed past Francine's face like a caress and flew out the open door into the frost-crinkled courtyard enveloped in the jutting arms of the manor.

Francine had been born and raised in Thwaite Manor, though manor was a rather grandiose description. It was too big to be called a house and too small to be called a mansion, which manor tended to imply. It was a U-shaped, triple-story, black-and-white half-timbered building sitting on a hill in the middle of Lonehowe Wood. With twin towers on either side and a defunct clock tower in the center, it seemed curiously asymmetrical, for chimneys sprouted everywhere. Once, the rooms had rung with voices—distant echoing memories, for only Francine and Bree lived here now.

Francine stood up, cleaned and dried her teacup, and walked through to the dark foyer to put on her coat. From a drawer in the table, she grabbed a handful of fennel seeds and shoved them into her pocket before slipping a homemade bracelet made of burdock root onto her thin wrist. It was an automatic action whenever she prepared to venture beyond the boundaries of the garden, for both fennel and burdock were excellent for warding off evil when traveling.

Seething mist rose above the crackling veneer of frost as Francine strode across the garden. She hesitated and glanced over her shoulder, feeling the tug of Thwaite Manor, its safety and warmth. Subdued in a cobweb of mist, the old building sagged wearily, as though Francine's presence was all that kept it from falling into ruin.

Her eyes twitched to the driveway. It was broad, its gravel surface well maintained, but a longer route to Hawkshead. A small track broke off from the road and disappeared into Lonehowe Wood, a dark path, little more than a root-knotted track. But the woods were not a peaceful place. It never had been. Those ancient trees had seen enough human suffering and brutality to create a miasma of creeping spite.

Francine stalked up the gravel road, doubting that any message waiting for her would warrant the shortcut through the woods where she was likely to meet things she'd rather not.

As she drew nearer to Hawkshead, her pace slowed.

The Lake District was an area of outstanding beauty in the county of Cumbria in Northern England, and Hawkshead was its jewel: a tourist mecca nestled in the Vale of Esthwaite, postcard-pretty with its whitewashed houses topped with gray slate roofs clustered around narrow alleys. Francine approved of the lack of traffic; all cars were to remain in the car park provided on the outskirts of the village. No, she had no problem with the village itself; it was its denizens she had long grown to view with a wariness borne of frequent derision received from a young age.

Forcing her shoulders not to hunch under the weight of narrowed eyes peering from every window, Francine strode down a narrow, mist-muddled alley that verged onto the high street.

She glanced at her antiquated watch and stopped abruptly before crossing the road, forcing a man behind her to curse when he barreled into her.

"Dammit, Francine, you still on this jape?" he said, not unkindly, though that didn't stop him from looking along the street uneasily.

"I'll thank you to keep a civil tongue in your head, Gawain Farraday!" snapped Francine as a ghostly carriage passed her right on time, churning the mist, its wheels running below the road's surface before it knocked over an equally ghostly child that darted in front of it.

"I guess you'll be seeing the ghost of the Crellin lassie." Gawain squinted at the spot Francine's eyes were locked on. While the Cumbrians were a superstitious lot and long used to Francine's Sight, most accepted it with a dash of pragmatic disbelief.

Well aware that she was laughed at behind her back, Francine nodded curtly, and with an equally curt, "Good day to you," she marched across the road.

"It's all in your head, y'know!" Gawain shouted after her.

Nostrils flaring with annoyance, she stalked up the high street. Then she smiled with a small vindication, for the leaves had read true as they invariably did: sharp words with the letter C or G.

It took courage for Francine to enter Postlethwaite's and order a pound of bacon. She stood to the back of the butcher's shop while she waited for her order to be weighed and wrapped and watched Guy Postlethwaite out of the corner of her eye. Her loathing of him, of all the people in Hawkshead, was tinged with a lingering fear from her childhood. Only two years older than Francine, he was a stooped, hulking man with a fully bald head and a potbelly that spoke of a penchant for his own wares.

Now, of course, he was a respectable man—the local butcher, as was his father before him, with the Royal Warrant of Appointment not-so-discreetly displayed on the shop window— delivering meat to the queen for decades and very proud of it.

But Francine remembered Guy's taunts all too well. She had been the witch's daughter through primary school, graduating to the slut's sister in secondary school. All that hurtful scorn because of her familial associations. It was sobering to realise that very few people knew anything about her except that she lived in a crumbling Elizabethan manor and kept herself to herself. It was no knowledge at all for people who had known Francine all her life.

Worst of it all, even now Guy Postlethwaite still called her . . .

"Frankie! Your order," holding up the bacon wrapped in wax paper.

To Francine's shame, she scuttled forward, snatched the

package from his outstretched hand and hurried, hunched, out of the shop as though she were still twelve and he fourteen.

It always took some mental adjustment after a trip into Postlethwaite's to remind herself that she was not a child anymore but a grown woman. Francine slipped into a deserted alley and stared unseeingly up at a gable end, calming her ragged breathing and settling her mind. But those unhealed scars of childhood ran deep, the whispered jibes still oozing sores.

It was a good half hour before she felt ready to hurry on to the post office. She waited impatiently in the queue, wanting desperately to go home. Home was safety. Home was free of old hurt and new.

She ensured a wide gap between the person in front of her and behind. She couldn't bear a stranger touching her, even by chance.

"So I told her our Mollie would never do a thing like that. And do you know what that Hillary said? Why, you could've knocked me down with a feather . . ."

"What did she say?"

Francine glared at Marjorie Whitcombe, the postmistress, leaning so far across the counter she was in danger of toppling over the side in her eagerness to hear what this Hillary had said.

The woman being served whispered in Marjorie's ear, whose eyes got bigger and bigger before she pulled back and declared, "She never did!"

"She did! And you know what she can be like. A real firecracker, that one. No wonder . . . And another bout of whispering ensued.

"Ahem!" said Francine loudly, unable to bear the waiting any longer.

The two women turned to the queue, then Marjorie's lips tightened. "It's that Francine Thwaite," she said loud enough for everyone in the post office to hear. "I'd best see to her

quickly lest she sees a ghoulie here again and scares off my customers . . ."

"Hold your wicked tongue, Marjorie Whitcombe," said a
quavery voice behind Francine.

"Oh. Hello, Miss C," said Marjorie, grinning guiltily, like a
naughty schoolgirl.

Miss Cavendish harrumphed. "You always were a frightful
gossip. I remember you in the playground, always whispering
behind your hand to young Kitty here." She frowned disap-
provingly at the luckless Kitty, who looked down at her feet in
embarrassment. "Now, you go about your business, Kitty, so
we can go about ours."

"Yes, Miss Cavendish," muttered Kitty, and she hurried past
the queue with her eyes down.

Francine couldn't resist a smirk, for she had been at school
with Kitty and Marjorie. She had often been the topic of their
gossiping, and occasionally revenge could be a dish served cold
in small portions.

"And you can wipe that smirk off your face, Francine
Thwaite," said Miss Cavendish.

Francine turned to the frail old lady and smiled with genuine
warmth. "Good morning, Miss C, I didn't notice you behind
me. It's good to see you out and about."

"Well, it doesn't do a body any good to laze about, though
my legs aren't what they were."

"I'll be down your way in a couple of days and will bring
you something for the pain."

"You do that, Fran, for my legs burn something awful of a
night. In the day too, to be fair." Miss Cavendish paused then
said, "I've been meaning to come up your way to visit your
mum. I miss her."

"So do I," said Francine.

Miss Cavendish had been the headmistress of the local

school for decades. There wasn't a man, woman, or child in the area who didn't have a dreadful fondness for the old lady and a healthy respect for the sharp edge of her tongue. She had also been Francine's mother's oldest and closest friend and the only person who still came up regularly to visit Eleanor Thwaite's grave.

"Cathedral bells if ever I've met one," muttered Miss Cavendish in a low voice intended only for Francine's ears.

Francine bit her lip to hide her bittersweet smile. Her mum had often spoken in the secret language of flowers that only she and Miss Cavendish had understood. Eleanor had taken that language one step further, believing everyone had a floral equivalent, a totem of sorts, that spoke to their personality. Francine, too, had long thought cathedral bells suited Marjorie Whitcombe; like that incorrigible vine with its frilled, purple trumpets, Marjorie's network of information was fast, unrepentant, and sprouted rumors everywhere.

The queue moved along quickly now that Marjorie was under the baleful eye of Miss Cavendish.

"Any messages?" asked Francine on reaching the counter.

"How'd you know there'd be a message for you?" demanded Marjorie.

Francine shrugged. She had no intention of explaining what she had seen in the tea leaves.

"It's not normal, you know. Coming down here before I've even had a chance to send the message up your way." Marjorie had a matronly figure, with an enormous bosom that lived a secret life all its own. As she turned to the pigeonholes behind her, Francine watched in fascination, especially as she had no bosom to speak of, as those mighty peaks swept majestically to the right before the rest of Marjorie did.

"If you had a phone put in," said Marjorie's young assistant from the other counter, "you wouldn't have to come into the village at all."

"Hush, Emma," said Marjorie, with guilt that sat uncomfortably on a face usually bright with keen interest.

"Just saying," muttered Emma. "She don't want to see us and we don't want to see her."

"Is there a message?" Francine managed to keep her tone civil while ignoring Emma.

Marjorie squinted at the scrap of paper. "It's a tenancy for five months. A carpenter and his apprentice, coming up to work on that new hotel they're building down the way. They'll be arriving today. A Todd Constable made the booking . . . a southerner. London, I think he said," she added with an odd relish, as though London were a distant, exotic country.

"Today? But I haven't spoken to them or made any arrangements."

"There was nowhere else for them to stay, what with it being the low season, so I told them you'd have the space." Marjorie shrugged, unabashed under Francine's glare. "You need the lodgers; your old place must cost a fortune to maintain."

Francine bit down on her retort, for as much as she hated to admit it, she did need the income. A five-month tenancy at this time of year was not to be sneezed at.

"Em's right, you know," continued Marjorie. "If you put in a phone or got yourself a mobile, I wouldn't have to take your bookings for you. And it's not just that, it's the safety aspect. How would anyone know if you were hurt up there in the woods when you're all by your . . . Oh, that reminds me, your sister phoned this morning. She asked that you phone her back as soon as possible. Won't it be nice if Maddie comes to visit? Some company for you. And Maddie was always a good sort."

Francine gave a genteel snort and took the piece of paper handed to her. Her sister was not what she would consider a good sort. Flighty, thoughtless, and irresponsible were far better adjectives to describe Madeleine. She hadn't seen her sister since her last sudden visit about five years ago. Francine wondered if Madeleine was phoning because her last marriage had ended, or if she was about to get married to someone else. It was hard to keep up with her sister's marital disasters.

She nodded goodbye to Miss Cavendish and hurried out of the post office.

TWO

❦

Francine entered the lonely red phone box on the high street. She couldn't abide mobile phones and had never understood why people were so attached to them. Ringing all hours of the day, not giving a body a moment's rest with incessant chatter. Her system of receiving messages from the post office and the public phone was perfectly acceptable for her needs.

Closing the door behind her, she dialed the number on the paper. She wasn't surprised it was different from the one Madeleine had given her the last time she'd phoned. Her sister never stayed in one place for long.

The line rang three times before it was answered.

"Hello, Madeleine," said Francine, unable to keep the reproach from her tone.

"Franny! I'm so glad you called!"

Francine thought to rebuke the use of that hated childhood nickname but refrained, hearing the note of desperation in her sister's voice.

"Are you well?" she asked cautiously.

Sobs echoed down the line, quiet and gut-wrenching. "Oh, Fran. Jonathon died last night. It's been dreadful."

"Which husband is he?" Francine interjected with some caution, well aware it wasn't the best question to ask. On one of Madeleine's infrequent visits home, she had left again almost immediately in a fit of sulks when Francine had mixed up husband three with the then-current . . . possibly husband five? It paid to be sure from the start.

Madeleine sighed in exasperation. "Number seven. The genealogist!"

"Oh . . . What happened to the occultist? When did you marry this Jonathon?"

"I divorced Sebastian ages ago. Haven't you heard a word I've said?" Madeleine cried, dissolving into tears once more. "Jonathon is dead! He lingered for ages, and then we thought he might make a recovery, but last night his heart just gave up. He was the love of my life and now he's gone. I am so utterly lost without him. He was—Francine! Are you still there?" Madeleine's melodrama dampened in the face of Francine's lack of response.

"Yes, of course I'm still here, and I did hear you. I'm, er, condolences. I'm sure it's all been very trying," she added lamely, yet she couldn't suppress the thought that Madeleine had had many loves in her life. Admittedly, one dying made a change from the numerous divorces. "So, why are you phoning me?"

"Because . . ." Madeleine floundered briefly, ". . . because you're my sister and I need you. And—"

Francine imagined her sister biting her lip in hesitation. She pounced on the silence with, "Is something else wrong?"

It was a long time before Madeleine said, "Not wrong exactly. Not now anyway."

"What are you hiding?"

"Nothing!"

She listened to her sister's quiet breathing, sensing a secret, but when the silence grew uncomfortable, she leaned her forehead against the glass of the phone box and stared out at the high street. "Do you want to come home?"

"Yes." Madeleine's relief flooded Francine's ear. "Thank you, Franny. I knew you'd understand. You always know the right thing to say."

Francine shook her head in disbelief. "When will you be arriving?"

"Tomorrow. No, probably the day after next. I need to sort out a few things here first . . . Oh, it's really been too awful. And it's been months since I last saw you . . ."

"Years," Francine interjected in resignation.

"Really? Has it been that long?"

"I'll see you in a couple of days, Madeleine." She disconnected before her sister could continue and let herself out the phone box in a tangle of thoughts.

She loved Madeleine in a perfunctory sort of way because they were sisters, but they had nothing in common. Francine had secretly disagreed when her mum had bestowed *Ranunculus* as Madeleine's flower. While her sister had its attributes of charm, attractiveness, and radiance, Francine thought she was better suited to the frivolity of London pride, or red geraniums for foolishness if she were to be unkind. Even in their floral counterparts the sisters were opposites, for Francine was lantana: thorough, constant, rigid, and an acquired taste, which few had taken the time to acquire.

But though they were night and day, they were all the other had; their father had died when they were both young and neither had any memory of him. Their mother had held their small family together until she died when Francine was twenty and Madeleine sixteen. It wasn't three months after their mother's death that Madeleine ran away to London. Francine had been devastated but, in time, she had realised it was for the best.

Madeleine would have driven her around the twist if she had remained in Cumbria, and it was better they did not see each other often, for drama followed Madeleine around like a bad smell.

No longer having the time to go the cowardly long way round, Francine hurried along the little alleys of Hawkshead. The mist was thicker than before; it eddied around her, twining with the oily smoke spewing from huddled chimneys.

The village fell away as she approached St. Michael and All Angels Church sitting on its lonely hill, the parochial guardian of Hawkshead. Beyond it, Lonehowe Wood played hide-and-seek in the mist. But Francine could have found the little-used path into the woods blindfolded. Once part of the old corpse trail that led to the church, it had a macabre folklore that few in the village wished to acknowledge and was not often used by the locals.

In the woods, Francine slowed, eyes twitching left and right where trapped mist threaded and tangled through the ancient trees like sepulchral fingers. It wasn't quiet in the woods. The constant drip, drip, drip of condensation from winter-bare branches and the crackle and creak of frost in gnarls and boles had Francine whipping around, peering hard into the mist.

The breathless murk took shape around Francine, and the further she went the more crowded it became. The tousle of roots and dead bracken on the sides of the path slowly writhed up into a tight throng of hundreds of specters, silent and watchful as she scurried past. It was not an unusual occurrence; the corpse trail was so called for the coffins that had been carried along the track to St. Michael's in times past. It had never occurred to Francine to question what she saw. Ghosts didn't bother her, but there were some places that felt evil and filled her with an irrational fear.

Fine droplets of moisture clung to her hair and eyelashes; she blinked rapidly, blurring her vision. At a sharp twist in the path, a vile fear scraped up her spine, the fennel seeds gripped so tightly they dug into her palm. She quickened her pace. Deep in the woods, almost disguised by the pitter-patter of condensing mist, came a spine-jangling rasp that chilled Francine to her very marrow.

It was always here, at this bend in the path, that she heard it. The branches of the trees were meshed into a tight tunnel that threshed and chafed against each other, rasping their bloody secrets in a dark litany that the living should never hear.

Breath quickening, Francine forced herself not to flee through this stretch of the gloomy woods. There wasn't a child in the area in the past two hundred years who hadn't been scared stiff by the story of the murdering blacksmith in the eighteenth century who'd used a claw hammer as his weapon of choice, and Francine was no exception. Her eyes flickered to the old scars on the surrounding trees, which, as legend would have it, bore testament to this being his killing ground. There was no breeze in this blackhearted part of the woods, the stagnant mist oozing against her face like cold blood. Francine scurried onwards, eyes narrowed on the meshed boughs above her that abruptly stopped their scraping, the woods growing silent but for the drip of moisture.

With a relieved shudder, she burst out of Lonehowe Wood, her heart lifting with an aching love at the welcome sight of Thwaite Manor trapped in a fogged shimmer of a time long forgotten. The stress of her trip down to Hawkshead deflated in a tremulous sigh as her eyes roved across the crooked crossbeams and blind windows. It was not a proud building; there was humility in its slightly bulging walls, a gentleness to the pitch of its warped roof, a playfulness in its higgledy-piggledy chimneys. And though it wore its years like a tired old woman, it was everything to Francine.

With no idea when her lodgers would arrive, she hurried around the manor to the courtyard, eyes averted to avoid seeing the graveyard. The courtyard walls were covered in ivy, their withered vines bare as they waited for spring. A huge oak tree stood in the center, so gnarled Francine thought it must have been planted when the house was first built. Under it was a walled well with a small slate roof and a wooden pail. The well was defunct, a relic from yesteryear, yet it, like the graveyard, sent a dark shiver up her spine.

She stood under the oak tree and squinted up into its bare branches. "Bree," she called. "Come down. We have work to do."

THREE

❦

The old grandfather clock in the drawing room ticked the waiting hours away. It could be heard throughout the ground floor ... *tick* ... *tick* ... *tick* ... A soothing sound that Francine barely noticed unless, like now, she was waiting. Ten o'clock at night and still no sign of her lodgers. Her furious flurry of activity around the house had been for nothing.

"I don't know when they'll be here," said Francine without lifting her eyes from the book she was poring over as a windowpane rattled in frustration. "Come over here and listen to this."

She waited until a faint flutter of air brushed against her arm. "Now, where was I?" She flicked through the pages of the old tome that crackled with age and smelt like suet on the turn. "Here we are, with Thomas Thwaite ... *The Pilgrimage of Grace of 1536/37 and Bigod's Rebellion of 1537 were in essence a boon to Thomas Thwaite. While a staunch Catholic—* Stop that, Bree," said Francine mildly as dried rosemary rained down on her. "It can't all be interesting, can it? I find it a little worrying that you only prefer the gory bits. Although there hasn't been much gore. Our esteemed literary ancestor Jeremiah Thwaite's writing is as dull as ditchwater."

She skimmed through the next few decades, then, "*Thomas took to wife Eliza Ashburaner, daughter of his rival in Hawkshead, in 1542, thereby consolidating two prosperous ventures into one of the largest in Cumbria. With the birth of their first son, Richard, within the first year of marriage the Thwaite dynasty was assured.*"

Francine flicked through the pages. "I can't be bothered to read all this about the wool industry. It goes on for—goodness! Twenty-seven pages."

Her paging slowed, and she read again. "*As Thomas's business flourished, so too did his family. By 1558, in the year Queen Mary died from the influenza, Eliza had given birth to four sons. Sadly, after nine stillborn daughters, Eliza died in childbirth* . . . Well, at least we know you weren't Thomas Thwaite's child, Bree. He only had boys. How terrible that must've been for Eliza."

She flicked through the pages again, skim reading. "And he died two years later without marrying again. But I'm certain you're a Thwaite. Stands to reason, you being tied to the house . . . alright, the oak tree, if you insist," she agreed when Bree, who had moved to the window, ruffled the curtains in disagreement.

Although Francine rarely saw or heard Bree, the little ghost had Presence. An imaginary friend she had never grown out of, the unkind would say. But she was quite sure in her mind that Bree was a specter attached to the house for a reason she had not yet established. She wasn't even sure if her name was Bree, but it was what Francine had always called her, and through a lifelong familiarity she understood the nuances of Bree's moods, so she could almost visualize the little ghost shrugging, frowning, or sticking her tongue out in a fit of pique.

Bree was Francine's only friend.

A draft tore through the kitchen in a shiver of anticipation. Francine shook her head; she had no chance of reading more when Bree was so restless. She closed the old book of Thwaite history she had found in the manor's library, in which she had been dipping in and out of the centuries as the mood took her, for Bree was not wrong; it was heavy going.

She stood and walked to the window, pushing the curtains aside. The garden sparkled under a pale moon. Frost already littered the lawn, which ran down the slight incline to a rhododendron maze separating the manor from the surrounding Lonehowe Wood. In front of the rhododendron were flower beds that in summer were a riot of color, but with the first prickings of spring lay drab and skeletal.

"I saw my first snowdrop this morning," said Francine to the warm air beside her. "But the crocuses aren't up yet."

The air shrugged its indifference.

"I wonder when these men will arrive," she continued, peering down the driveway. "Marjorie said they were arriving today, but it's past ten already."

She only took lodgers in during summer out of necessity. Her house was much too big for one person and expensive to maintain. Francine was self-sufficient in many aspects. Her vegetable garden provided amply throughout the year. She had good egg-laying hens, a herd of goats, a few beehives on the edge of the woods, and a cow. It was the other things she needed in this modern world, like plumbing, running water, and electricity. Those she couldn't grow, so she had taken on lodgers, just as her mother had before her. She'd never lacked for customers living in the Lake District; tourists by the thousands came to admire the glorious scenery that Francine took for granted.

Gone was the mist from earlier in the day and Esthwaite Water glistened in the moonlight through the naked boughs of Lonehowe Wood. It was an idyllic scene, one suitable for a Wordsworth poem, though Francine did not hold with poetry by that local notable worthy, having always thought he could have chosen a better subject than daffodils if he'd only bothered to learn of their high toxicity.

The window rattled just as the beam of powerful headlights appeared around a corner of the driveway.

"See? Here they come now. There was no need for your impatience, Bree." Francine hurried through to the foyer. The ghost of high-pitched laughter followed her as she opened the door and a white van pulled up to the front of the house.

"And none of your nonsense while they're here," said Francine sternly. "You've scared away enough paying guests with your antics, and we need the money to fix that gable end. So behave or I'll banish you to your oak tree." It was a common threat that she would never carry out, loving Bree far too much to ever cause her harm.

The laughter cut off immediately.

With a fortifying sigh, she said, "Now, make yourself scarce." She waited until she got that empty feeling whenever Bree wasn't around, then stepped out onto the porch. On either side were rowan trees, their branches already covered in large, downy buds.

She stood utterly still, her stomach a knot of anxiety, already wondering what she would say and rather wishing she didn't have to say anything.

"How long does it take to get out of a car?" she grumbled, and absentmindedly took down the wreath of boxwood, blackberry, rowan, and ivy. The leaves were so dry they crackled to dead flakes as she touched them, their protection useless without freshness.

The car doors slammed, breaking the stillness of the frosty night. Francine pulled her shawl tight and hugged her thin chest. A tall Black man walked towards her with an easy, ranging gait. He was followed by an ungainly, rather enormous youth with a shock of red hair.

"Francine Thwaite?" The man's voice was deep, with a melodious whisper of the Caribbean in his accent.

"Yes. I am she."

He smiled. It was a gentle smile that reached his brown eyes. To Francine's surprise, she relaxed her bony shoulders slightly. He wasn't much older than she, possibly mid to late fifties, yet his short dark hair had little grey—unlike hers, which was completely white and held in a bun against the nape of her neck.

"Apologies for arriving so late. I'm Todd Constable, and this is Keefe O'Driscoll."

The redhead grinned shyly.

They all looked at each other.

"May we come in?" asked Todd when the silence became uncomfortable.

"Oh! Yes, of course." Francine stepped aside to allow the men entry to the house.

"Nice place you have here," said Todd, gazing around the foyer. "When was it built?"

Francine was used to the compliments. The foyer had wooden floors, paneled walls, and a high ceiling with black timbers, like a crooked checkerboard. Two staircases at the far end rose to the wings at the back of the house. Against one wall was a long table, black with the patina that comes with serious age. On it sat two pots of garlic. The walls had dark, religious paintings, cracked with age and probably worth something if restored to their original glory, but Francine had never bothered. She was happy for things to remain as they had always been.

"1541. The original part," she said, closing the door. She was pleased to see they traveled light, each carrying only a large overnight bag.

"Sick," said Keefe, which Francine took to be high praise, although she wasn't sure, as she rarely spoke to youngsters.

"When was the rest built?" asked Todd, eyeing the sachets of herbs hanging above the various doors leading off the foyer alongside upside-down bunches of hyssop and yarrow. He turned slowly, taking everything in, his eyes resting on the two pots of dwarf juniper standing on either side of the front door. They were heavy with dusty blue berries, their boughs like spiky feathers hanging so low they swept the floor. His lips twitched to hide a smile when his thoughtful gaze came to rest on Francine.

She shrugged. "Over the last few centuries. This way," she said before there could be any more questions. She led them up the right-hand staircase to the east wing, switching on lights as she went. Opening the first two doors, she stood aside to allow the men in.

She hesitated on the threshold of Todd's room, shy and awkward as the teenager she had never been.

"Er, breakfast is at seven sharp in the morning, and I'll thank you to place your dishes in the sink once done. It'll be bacon and eggs, grown organic." Her lips tightened on the word organic as though it were a sucked lemon, having no truck with these newfangled ideas of organic as something different to what she had always grown naturally.

Sidling just into the room, Francine cast an eye over the huge, oak four-poster bed, thick curtains, and ancient wardrobe with a door that never shut properly. An old ewer and basin rested on the single table, all heirlooms. A quick check ensured the sachets of horehound, agrimony, and betony were where she had placed them in the four corners of the room, protecting her guests without them being aware they needed protection at all. It always paid to double-check, as Bree had a mischievous streak and liked to move things around.

"If that is all," she said while Todd looked around the room. He smiled at her. "Thanks for putting us up at such short notice, love."

Francine nodded, not at all liking being called *love* by a strange man.

She harrumphed in a ladylike manner. "Then I shall leave you to your business, I'm sure," she said, and made her escape.

On the landing she hesitated, wondering if she should have offered them something to eat given it was late and nothing would be open in Hawkshead. Then she shrugged — no good came from creating a pattern of kindness she had no intention of maintaining — and hurried downstairs.

She paused again in the foyer, head cocked to one side. The house had changed with the arrival of her lodgers: a tightness in the air as though the manor was distracted from its world-weariness to focus on the guests.

With a slight shiver, Francine called softly, "Bree."

A tickle of dustiness swept around her, a lightness against her face, her hair, her neck.

"It's time," she whispered, taking a large pouch from the long table in the foyer before heading outside.

It was on diamond-clear nights like these, pulled taut below a gibbous moon with not a breath of liveliness in the air, that Francine caught a glimpse of Bree. A small girl, not much older than seven or eight, her long red hair in two plaits which flapped against her back. She wore a long dress hitched into her knickers as though the length bothered her. Bree glanced over her shoulder, her face a pale reflection of how she had looked in life. A mischievous face, yet strong and full of laughter.

There was another ghost walking alongside Francine on nights like these, for it was in the garden that Francine felt closest to her mum. Memories were in every flower they had planted together and in every bed they had planned. Here, with the moon's light tracing filigreed shadows along each leaf and petal, a darker, older meaning to the language of flowers slunk in. A primordial knowledge that few remembered, from a time when fear was pure and magic was believed.

Francine dug into the pouch and walked along the boundary, scattering powdered angelica root, boneset, and crushed chamomile leaves while Bree stayed well back in the garden and watched.

Francine loved her garden. She had plants from all over the world, which she'd grown from seed. To most people it would appear to be a colourful wilderness in the summer, but there was a distinct method, a strategic placement of certain plants in precise areas for specific reasons. For she understood the darker, older language of flowers.

The flower beds around the boundary she ensured were always maintained. An arch leading into the rhododendron maze had a blackberry vine growing over it; figwort grew beside hawthorn and juniper. A mandrake crept across a bed of St John's wort, adjacent to an elder tree growing incongruously in the middle of a bed of nettles. There were few conventional flowers found in most English gardens, but every single plant, shrub, and tree had been planted for one reason: to ward off evil.

"That should keep any nasty beasties away for another night and keep the good ones safe inside," said Francine when the pouch was empty. She smiled at the hawthorn bushes where the old red berries were being flicked off one by one, as though Bree were playing a game of marbles with herself.

Francine followed in Bree's zipping wake, first rattling the old pods of the carob tree that looked like dried, blackened bananas yet smelled faintly of chocolate, then twisting the long nude fronds of the willow into a snarled tangle. Onwards, she raced to shake the row of *Laburnum* at the edge of the court-yard, waiting for spring to dazzle in yellow. Moments later, the branches of the old oak tree in the courtyard shook slightly, though not a breeze stirred.

Hugging the wall so she wouldn't have to go near the old well, Francine scurried past the herb garden her mother had planted and into the kitchen before scampering upstairs like a frightened child to her private apartments in the west wing.

After a long, soaking bath, Francine put on her long nightie and climbed into bed. She switched off the light and listened to the night.

Small shuffles and creaks filled the old house as it settled down on its foundations as though it, too, was preparing for sleep; its friendly warmth enveloped Francine and smelled comfortingly of dust and the mustiness of old books.

Francine waited, as she did every night. She had learned from a young age not to sleep before the others arrived. They only ever appeared just as she was on the cusp of sleep, in that un-certain place where reality and dreams were neither one thing nor the other.

First came Tibbles—a tabby cat who filled the room with muted purrs before a silky softness brushed against Francine's arm. Next came the old man, the most visible of all the ghosts anchored to Thwaite Manor. He didn't do much, just walked through the bedroom wall and doffed his top hat at Francine before walking through the opposite wall. The ghost of a preg-nant woman followed. She sat at the bedroom window over-looking the courtyard with a wistful expression before a young boy came in and tugged at her skirt. The two left the room as quietly as they had entered.

The only constants were Bree, who sat on the end of Francine's bed, and Tibbles, who curled up beside Francine and slept there until dawn.

Francine did not begrudge the ghosts within Thwaite Manor. They were all harmless. She preferred their company to the living; they didn't expect anything of her except to be remembered each night.

FOUR

Francine sighed as she peered into the teacup. Three cups of tea and the leaves all said the same thing. "A visitor. Definitely female. See that?" She tilted the cup towards Bree, who knocked impatiently on the table. "It must mean Madeleine." Another knock. "No, it can't be the lodgers, they're already here and they're men . . . And there's something that looks like clouds, which means trouble. Close to the figure of the woman . . . a troublesome visitor?"

A ladle fell off a hook on the wall.

Francine smiled. "Yes, that would definitely describe Madeleine." She frowned back at the teacup. "A comb," she murmured. She got up and went to the shelves where she kept her mother's recipe books. She pulled out a well-thumbed book on tea leaf reading and returned to the table.

Though she rarely needed to consult the book, a comb was a new one for her. She found the symbol. It looked almost exactly the same as the one in her teacup. A flutter of disquiet settled in the pit of her stomach. "A comb means an enemy."

"Found it!"

Francine jumped at the sound of a male voice, all thought of enemies evaporating. She whipped around in her chair, eyes wide, then relaxed when the huge, shambling figure of Keefe O'Driscoll came through the door. He gave a low whistle as he looked around the kitchen.

It was impressively large, running almost the length of the west wing's ground floor, with copper pots on the walls. An immense table acted as a central island, with ovens lining the walls and a vast hearth on the far side, blackened by centuries of fires. Drying herbs and vegetables hung from the timbered ceiling, and lead windows allowed diffused light, so the room always had a golden glow during the day. The back door stood open, facing the courtyard, in easy reach of the herb garden.

It was a ridiculously big kitchen for only one person, but it hadn't always been so. The kitchen had fed dozens of huge families over the centuries, and Francine had always liked the room. It was cozy, despite its size, and she had never had the funds or the heart to change it. It held too many fond memories of her mother.

"Phew! What is that godawful pong?" Keefe waved his hand in front of his face. It was the first time he had spoken enough for Francine to pick up an Irish accent.

"Mind your manners, boy," said Todd as he entered the kitchen, shooting an apologetic glance at Francine.

"Cloves." She glanced pointedly at the stick of homemade clove incense burning on a sideboard. "Good for..." She caught herself in time.

"Good for protection," Todd completed quietly, with a thoughtful look at Francine.

Shocked, she stared at him. He smiled back with a raised eyebrow. Feeling like she'd been caught out doing something wrong, she cleared her throat. "So some say," she muttered, and dropped her gaze, confused. She had never met anyone apart from her mum who knew the protective properties of plants. Or was it just cloves this man, Todd Constable, knew of? It was a fairly common spice, but did he know it was also good for attraction?

Where had that thought come from? She peeked at him under her eyelashes to find he was still watching her. She stood up abruptly and put her cup and saucer in the sink, hoping he hadn't seen her reading the leaves. It was one thing to do it with Bree watching, but quite another for strangers to know she did it.

"Anyway, I happen to like the smell," she added, not sure why she needed the justification.

Todd raised his eyebrows at the blatant lie. Francine didn't blame him; it took someone with no sense of smell to tolerate the overpowering odour of burnt cloves, let alone like it. Unless, like Francine, they burnt cloves for a very different reason.

"And what's this?" asked Keefe, peering into the bubbling pot on a stovetop.

"Fig jam," said Francine.

"I hate fig jam," said Keefe amiably.

"So do I," she said, surprising herself by even engaging in conversation with the young man.

"Why do you make it then?"

She shrugged. "I'm not sure ... I just do. Always have done."

"That's enough, Keefe," said Todd with an exasperated shake of his head.

Keefe grinned, then bumbled about the kitchen in the clumsy way of huge young men who were not yet used to their size.

"We're off to Hawkshead," said Todd.

Francine frowned. "Do you not want breakfast?" She nodded at the stovetop, where bacon and eggs sizzled next to the fig jam. One end of the table had been laid for two.

Keefe glanced at Todd hopefully. "Five minutes? I'm half starved."

"You're always half starved," said Todd, sitting at the table in resignation. He glanced at Francine. "We'll be quick, love."

"Don't call me that," she snapped.

His hand paused on its way to the toast rack. "Call you what?" he asked cautiously.

"Love . . . I'm not your love!"

He nodded, and after an awkward moment, said, "Of course, Mrs. Thwaite."

"I'm not Mrs. either. Francine will do."

Todd's lips twitched into a wry half smile. "Very well, Francine. I consider myself told."

"It's so quiet here," said Keefe with his mouth full, oblivious to the snappy tension that filled the kitchen.

"Had Keefe here in my room last night," said Todd, "gibbering like a monkey that someone kept pulling his sheets off."

Francine glanced sharply at the window where the upper branches of the old oak tree were swaying gently in the spot she knew Bree liked best. Muted laughter floated through the back door.

"Next he'll be seeing ghosts," continued Todd, grinning broadly at Keefe's look of horror.

"Wish you hadn't said that," Keefe mumbled. "I hadn't thought of ghosts. Thought there was a kid larking about. And this is an old house; there's bound to be loads of manky old ghosts floating about."

"Bound to be," agreed Todd, winking at Francine, who had started at the mention of ghosts.

Keefe grinned amiably. "Well, a body's bound to think strange things if they're in a creepy old house and don't get any sleep because of the lights flashing into their room all night."

"What lights?" asked Francine sharply.

"From the woods. Your neighbors' place; I can see their chimneys from my window. You should speak to them about it."

"I don't have any neighbors." She frowned at Keefe as unease skittered down her spine, wondering if he hadn't seen the lights from the old asylum in the woods, a dreadful place that had been abandoned decades before. "I, er, I need to see to something," she muttered, and hurried out the back door. "Bree!" she hissed furiously when she reached the oak tree.

Sulky silence greeted her.

"I know you're up there. Get down here now or I'll grow mustard all around your tree so you can't come down again! You know how mustard affects you."

The branches shivered in response.

"Bree! I've told you before not to bother the guests," said Francine, almost pleading. "Now, just behave yourself and don't go near their rooms."

The oak tree shivered again before a warm rush of air tugged at Francine's bun, then flew out into the garden for a good sulk.

Francine shook her head, which unraveled her bun completely. Cursing Bree silently, she curled up her long, white hair back into its customary style, well aware she was delaying her return to the kitchen.

It wasn't long before the sound of scraping chairs forced her back indoors. The men had helped themselves to breakfast and were just getting up from the table.

"Good day to you," she murmured as she passed through to the foyer. Really! Bree was too much sometimes, she thought as she pulled on her coat.

She looked up to find Todd watching her thoughtfully as she shoved fennel seeds into her pocket and slipped the burdock bracelet onto her wrist. Finally, she picked up the covered basket she had left on the table earlier that morning.

"Do you want a lift, Francine?" he asked when Keefe came out the kitchen, shoving a last bit of toast into his mouth.

"I have two perfectly good legs capable of carrying me wherever I need to go," she said with more tartness than intended. The man really was quite unsettling, and once again she felt that she had been caught in some wrongdoing.

"All right then," he said, nonplussed.

Francine nodded and opened the door. She waited until the men had climbed into their van and driven off before setting off at a brisk walk down the road. It was a fine day, one of those early spring days with a crisp snap in the cold air so it hurt just to breathe in.

Down the corpse trail she strode, content in the knowledge that she would avoid the dark heart of the woods today. She stopped with an impatient sigh where the smaller path to Colthouse branched off from the main. "Alfie, if you don't mind moving," she said to the small boy crouched on the path in fascinated absorption of something he'd found. "I'm in no mood for any of your nonsense today."

The little ghost wasn't more than a dappled shadow who wandered off the path, looking so forlorn that Francine almost followed him, as she sometimes did, into the woods to the place where he had died more than a hundred years before. Alfie's had been a short life and a sad death, for he had died of exposure at the age of three when he had wandered into Lonehowe Wood one winter's night. It had been no one's fault, just sad.

Miss Cavendish lived in Colthouse, a hamlet west of Hawkshead, with a view of Lake Windermere and the surrounding fells, as mountains were called in Cumbria, from her little slate-roofed cottage.

After knocking, Francine glanced around the small garden and frowned. Miss Cavendish was a keen gardener, but she hadn't done a winter mulch or pruned the roses she was so proud of. Francine smiled at the pot of oakleaf geraniums her mum had given Miss Cavendish as a memento of their friendship. Every year Miss Cavendish took cuttings to keep the same plant going decades after Eleanor Thwaite's death.

"Fran! How lovely. Come in, come in." Miss Cavendish shuffled aside to allow Francine entry.

A quick glance around the small living room sent a shiver of disquiet along Francine's skin. It was as cluttered as always, but it had an oddly unlived-in feel.

Shaking herself, she handed the old lady a stoppered bottle. "It will taste a bit different; I've added honey to take the willow bark's bitterness away."

"Your honey?"

She nodded. "Collected fresh this morning, and here are some eggs and a couple of pies. I'll put them in the kitchen, shall I?"

"Thank you, Fran. Put the kettle on before you sit yourself down," ordered Miss Cavendish as she made her way arthritically to the chair facing the window.

Once seated with tea, neither woman said anything as they contemplated the view of the crinkled fells tumbling down to Lake Windermere.

"And how is young Maddie these days?" said Miss Cavendish as though she were continuing a conversation.

Francine hid her grin at the rather unsubtle attempt for information. "I'm sure Marjorie has played her town crier role with her usual gusto. And you know very well I spoke to Madeleine yesterday. She said she would be coming up, but she hasn't arrived. One of her husbands has died, and Madeleine was . . . her usual self," she added. It was kinder than airing what she really thought of her sister's melodrama. Francine was not looking forward to more of the same when Madeleine finally decided to come home. And yet now that she thought about it, there had been a catch in Madeleine's voice, a reticence in a situation where histrionics were perfectly acceptable.

"And she always runs home to you when her world falls apart."

Eyebrows raised, Francine nodded. "I suppose she does."

Miss Cavendish chuckled. "Well, she always were a one, that Maddie Thwaite. Didn't half drive the lads mad for her. I have fond memories of all you girls."

"It's only ever been Madeleine and I," said Francine, frowning.

The old lady paused, flustered. "Yes, of course," she murmured. Then she smiled. "Don't you go listening to this silly old woman. Mind's not what it was." But the mind she claimed was not what it was had something on it. "Bree still with you?" she asked in an offhand manner.

Francine smiled. "Of course." Then her lips tightened. "She's taken to frightening our lodgers."

"Our . . . oh yes, yes indeed," said Miss Cavendish vaguely. "Lovely girl, Bree."

Francine's frown returned. Miss Cavendish had never believed in ghosts and had always humored Francine's own beliefs in what she saw. It didn't bother Francine, for Miss Cavendish was the only person in the area who had shown kindness to her, and for that, she would forgive the old lady almost anything. And yet . . .

"You've never believed in Bree." She held up a hand when Miss Cavendish opened her mouth to deny it. "I remember you and mum debating the existence of ghosts, and you were always against."

"That may have had something to do with your mum's fabulous sloe gin. It made us argue something fierce about rather a lot after a few glasses." She sighed and added, "Eleanor was my closest friend, but that didn't mean I agreed with everything she said or did. And I didn't like that Eleanor indulged your . . ." she cast around for a suitable word and settled on, ". . . imaginary friend. It wasn't healthy for a young girl to cling to the past."

"Bree's a ghost; she came with the house."

Miss Cavendish gave an odd sort of shake and nod of her head, as though she were having an internal argument. Allowing a silence to form, Francine frowned at the old lady's bent head, noticing the frailty that seemed more pronounced since her last visit.

Miss Cavendish leaned forward with a conspiratorial twinkle in her faded blue eyes. "Read the leaves for me, Fran, like your mum used to. Good at the leaves was our Eleanor."

Francine nodded stiffly, astonished by the request. Not once in their monthly visits had Miss Cavendish asked her to read the leaves, even though Eleanor Thwaite had done it regularly. The two were silent for a moment, remembering a woman who had lived a small life but cast a long shadow in theirs.

"Drink up and let's have a look."

Miss Cavendish carefully turned the cup left and right three times before tipping it upside-down over her saucer, then handed it to Francine.

A raven, very distinct, connected to a serpent by a wavy line near the handle had Francine's lips tightening, and the sense of unease she'd had on entering the cottage grew.

She didn't need to see any more.

"What do you see?" said Miss Cavendish eagerly.

Francine shook her head, lips so tight they all but disappeared.

"Ah." Miss Cavendish leaned back in her chair. "It'll be soon then?"

"Yes."

Miss Cavendish nodded in a satisfied manner.

"How long have you known?"

"A fair while. Cancer. It's gone to the brain now."

"I'm sorry."

The old lady laughed. "Don't be, marra. It's my time. Death comes to us all eventually. It is the only true certainty in life."

Francine swallowed against the lump constricting her throat. "I've brought the wrong remedy. If I'd known . . ."

Miss Cavendish patted her hand. "You weren't to know. I'm that pleased you came all the same."

Francine's heart cracked with sadness for the dearly loved face that she had watched grow more lined with the passing decades. Their interwoven history was written in every wrinkle of laughter and sorrow shared.

"I hope I fade away in my sleep," said Miss Cavendish with a faraway look, seeing her end already. "Or in this chair so my last sight will be of the lake and the fells. Then I'll go easily." She blinked and smiled at Francine.

Clearing her throat of a grief she would rather deal with in private, Francine said, "I'll do a quick whip around the house, then I'd best be off."

"You're too good to me, Fran."

"It's what Mum would've wanted."

The old lady nodded, but her mind was elsewhere as she gazed out at her beloved fells.

Francine got the cleaning detergents from under the kitchen sink and set about cleaning the house as she did every month. It didn't take long before she returned to the sitting room.

Miss Cavendish hadn't moved.

Francine's brow puckered with worry, and she made a note to herself to check on the old lady more often until she passed on.

"I'll be going now, Miss C—no, don't get up—and I'll come down again with a stronger remedy to help ease your pain."

"Do that, Fran," said Mrs Cavendish vaguely, without turning around. She seemed to have shrunk into her favorite chair, eyes half closed, staring out the window. But whatever she was seeing, Francine was certain it was not Lake Windermere.

With a surge of disquiet Francine let herself out of the cottage, closing the front door softly behind her.

"Bree!" Francine called on entering the house. She hurried through to the kitchen and out into the courtyard. "Bree!" she called again, noting the upper branches of the oak tree swaying in their own little breeze. Sidling along the wall that had no view of the graveyard, she headed to the garden shed that sat beside the chicken coop, goat pen, and the single stall she'd had erected for Maccabee the cow, who had wandered into the woods to graze but would be back by evening, as she always was. All that jumbled domesticity squatted in the stately shadow of a rather beautiful glass Victorian greenhouse that one of the Thwaite ancestors had brought up from London at great expense. And from the distance came the hum of bees on the edge of the woods.

Entering the greenhouse, Francine paused, breathing in the hot, heady miasma of peat, bark, and fertilizer—naturally made, of course. Orchids from far-flung places hung from the glass ceiling; strange ferns fanned out feathery fronds; rare creepers stole across the stone floor; aloes rose spikily beside a *Medinilla magnifica* that had been flowering pinkly for months. It was a private collection of some of the rarest plants in the world that many a collector would kill their grandmother for but was only ever seen by Francine.

On a long trestle table rested hundreds of old jam jars, bowls, a small burner, and pestle and mortar. Half-made straw poppets lay in a pile beside a stack of newly rolled asphodel incense. Essential oils were neatly arranged in front of larger bottles of viscous ointments. Each precious in its own way, each gathered at the correct time and prepared in the ways of the old lore as taught to Francine by her mother.

Picking up a bag from under the table, Francine cast an expert eye over the crushed herbs and roots. A handful here and there were shoved into the bag before she hauled a large sack of compost and another of rock salt into the waiting wheelbarrow.

Leaving the barrow on the edge of the lawn, Francine stomped back to the oak tree in the courtyard.

"Bree!" she called. "Stop playing, we need to feed the plants."

A heavy, reproachful silence greeted her.

"I'm sorry for being cross this morning," she said, shaking her head in exasperation. "Now, stop sulking and come down. Madeleine is arriving soon, and you know how she upsets everyone."

She waited anxiously, hoping Madeleine's name would be enough to force Bree out of her sulk. Bree had been impossible for months after Madeleine last visited—Francine had not been able to take in any lodgers until Bree had calmed down. She needed to protect the house as much as possible now to prevent it happening again.

Francine started walking away, then smiled when a warm gush of air raced past her into the garden. She grasped the handles of the wheelbarrow and pushed it towards the nearest flower bed.

Working feverishly, she scattered rock salt and compost in all the flower beds. Bree frolicked around her, darting hither and thither in her play, and was little help. But Francine didn't need help; she only wanted Bree's company.

The perimeter beds were left to last. She pulled out the bag of herbs and, as she scattered handfuls, she softly chanted a litany of herbal lore passed down to her from generations of Thwaite women, like a verbal *Book of Shadows*.

"*Woodruff be the ruination of a frugal spirit . . . Nut of hazel resists luckless fate in weal or woe . . . Heal the battered soul with bud of loosestrife . . .*"

On the edge of hearing came a shadowy echo of Bree chanting with her. *"Blue vervain to banish those of dreadful humor . . . A scatter of mandrake to foul demonic need . . . Turn the thieving eye with seed of caraway . . ."*

Francine smiled, for apart from the occasional giggle, Bree never spoke. Her ghostly visitors rarely did.

FIVE

The manor closed around Francine like a deep-pressure hug, as though it were trying to lull her to sleep. But sleep was wilful and refused to come. Eyes wide open, she stared up at her bedroom's dark ceiling and worried.

She worried about a great many things. Mostly trifles that grew into big worries in her mind: one of the hens was not laying well, which meant a trip to the nearby farm to buy another hen; a leak in the third-floor bathroom needed seeing to, yet she knew that the recommendation would be to refit the whole house with new plumbing, an impossibility due to her lack of finance.

As the night deepened and darkened, so did her thoughts. Miss Cavendish occupied her mind. She had always been like a favored, though strict, aunt. Francine wanted to bring her up to the house for her final weeks but knew the old lady would refuse. She was a spinster like Francine and through force of habit and circumstance had always relied on herself, rarely accepting the kindness of others.

And what of the comb she had seen in the leaves this morning? It was so rare for her to see something sinister in the leaves, yet she couldn't think of anyone who might wish her harm. She knew so few people as it was. But the very idea scratched at her consciousness like shattered glass under her skin.

So, with all the fretting, the scream that ripped through the house came almost as a relief.

Francine shot out of bed and peered out the window, lips already pursed, sure she would see the village boys larking about in her garden as they sometimes did at night.

Frowning, she cocked her head as another high-pitched shriek flew through the house.

"Bree!" she hissed as she shrugged on the quilted dressing gown that had belonged to her mother. She hurried into the dark hall to the east wing, sensing the manor's alertness, as though leaning inwards to better hear a whispered conversation.

"HAAA!" she cried as she barreled into a dark shape. Then, "Oh, it's you, Mr. Constable," she said, flustered, when he switched on the hall light.

"Evening, Francine," he said, regaining his equilibrium.

"Never mind that, did you hear someone screaming? Your young man, perhaps?"

"I would say it was Keefe winding himself up over nothing. He's been driving me nuts all day, banging on about ghosts . . . I was just about to investigate." With laughter in his voice, he crooked an elbow towards Francine and half bowed. "Care to join me?"

Francine glanced at his elbow. "I think not," she snapped. "Fancy! And in the middle of the night, too." She pushed past him, not liking the way his grin broadened, certain he was making fun of her, and knocked on Keefe's door. Another shriek erupted from within, followed by a loud clattering.

Todd reached past Francine and opened the door when Keefe didn't. Switching on the light, he and Francine gaped at the

Irishman stumbling about the room in a gangly ballet, waving his arms above his head, shrieking, "Get away! Get off me!"

"What *is* the boy doing?" asked Francine, baffled by the eccentricities of youth.

Todd shrugged. "What's got you screaming like a girl, Keefe?"

Keefe turned to them, wild-haired and wild-eyed. His arms dropped to his side, then rose again to hug himself tight. "There's something in here, Todd. I told you yesterday this place is haunted. Something keeps pulling my sheets off. And tonight . . ." He swallowed so hard his Adam's apple spasmed up and down his throat. "Tonight, something was pulling my hair!"

Francine glared around the room for a telltale sign of Bree, then down at the threshold where she scattered powdered bay laurel every morning to stop Bree from entering her lodgers' rooms. The powder was gone.

With exaggerated care, Todd looked around the room and up and down the darkened hall, then said, "There's nothing here." He smiled wryly at Francine as though they were sharing a conspiratorial joke at the expense of the younger man, then frowned when Francine did not return his smile. He cleared his throat. "Anyway, a strapping bloke like you shouldn't be scared of a ghost or two."

"Two?" squeaked Keefe. He leapt into bed as though he expected something to reach out from underneath it. "One was bad enough. I never thought there might be more!" He pulled the sheet up under his chin and shivered. "It's all this talk of ghosts," he quavered. "Us Irish, we're fey. We can see things that aren't here."

Todd shook his head. "You've got that right, there's nothing here."

"There's no such thing as ghosts," Francine lied. It was one thing for herself to be aware of ghosts, but quite another for her lodgers to sense them. She was fiercely protective of her spirit friends.

"Go back to sleep, Keefe," said Todd.

Keefe's wail of, "Don't leave me!" fell on deaf ears as the door was firmly closed.

"Is he always so . . . sensitive?" asked Francine as she and Todd walked the short distance to Todd's room.

"God, no! He usually has as much sensitivity as a brick. I don't know what's got into him."

Francine's lips tightened. She knew exactly who, not what, had got into the Irishman, and when she found Bree she . . . well, she would give the little ghost a perishing talking to. She had a good mind to plant mustard under Bree's oak tree to teach her a lesson.

"Yes, well . . ." Francine smoothed down her dressing gown. "I'll bid you good night then," she said, and turned smartly.

She stopped when Todd said softly behind her, "Why do you live in such fear?"

Francine forced herself to turn and face him. "What a ridiculous thing to say," she muttered. "I fear nothing."

"You've put sachets of agrimony, betony, and horehound in our rooms. I imagine there's one in every room in the house. There's juniper downstairs at the front door, and almost every plant in your garden is said to protect from evil." He smiled. "And you must be the only person I've met, apart from my gran, who cultivates nettles."

Astonished, Francine said, "You know something of gardening?"

"No, but I know something about protection herbs. My grandmother is from Jamaica, and she grows many of the plants you do to keep evil away. She forced me to learn as a kid." He grinned wryly. "To protect me, she said, although she's never been specific about what I needed protection from."

"Is she still alive?" asked Francine, curious in spite of herself.

"Very alive at one hundred and two. She drinks a tea of mistletoe and sage every morning, which she swears is what keeps her alive. So, what are you protecting yourself from?"

Francine shrugged. "You can never be too sure."

Silence hung between them, which she had no intention of breaking. She had used silence all her life to ensure people didn't pry too closely into her life, yet she got the feeling silence did not bother Todd.

"Good night then," he said finally, while Francine stood staring at him silently.

"Good night." She turned on her heel and stalked down the corridor with as much dignity as she could while wearing an ancient dressing gown, wondering why she felt the need for a dignified retreat at all.

In her bedroom, she paused in the act of getting into bed. No point sleeping now; sunrise was not far off. Instead, she got dressed in a tweed skirt and dark-blue blouse before heading downstairs to the kitchen.

She sat at the table and stared at the wall, the manor gently silent in the dead hours of early morning. A flutter settled in the pit of her stomach; she hoped she wasn't coming down with something. "And that's all I need is to fall ill when Madeleine may arrive at any minute," she told Bree, who had started lifting the ladles on the walls and allowing them to fall back with a satisfying clang. "And I want words with you, young lady," she added. "I've told you to leave our guests alone. You scared that boy half to death tonight."

A shadow of laughter came with not a jot of remorse.

Francine hadn't the heart to remonstrate the little ghost further. She found it difficult to stay angry at Bree for long.

After watching the clanging ladles for a while, she said, "I'm not sure I like this Todd Constable. He's unsettling. He's a thoughtful sort of man, and thoughtful people tend to be observant. We don't want him observing things he shouldn't. I think he has already."

The ladles clinked in a rising octave as Bree blew past them at speed, followed by a noise that sounded very much like a blown raspberry.

"And no cheek from you either," scolded Francine, standing up. "Well, we can't sit here idle when Madeleine will be arriving today. May as well give the kitchen a good scrub."

Sunlight crept through the lead-paned windows on a kitchen that sparkled a few hours later when there was movement from upstairs.

Francine cracked eggs and fried up bacon without noticing what she was doing, her eyes scratchy from lack of sleep. Bree was up on the ceiling, pulling at the dried herbs so the brittle leaves rained down on the kitchen.

"I wish Madeleine wasn't coming," said Francine. "I'm not even sure why. She's my sister. I should want her to come home."

Bree drizzled a little dried rosemary on Francine's head in sympathy.

Madeleine wasn't the problem, Francine knew; it was the memories she brought with her. She looked so much like their mother it made Francine's heart ache.

"Something's burning," said Todd.

Francine looked down at the frying pan. The eggs were black around the edges and the bacon beyond crispy.

"I'll do some more," Francine muttered and made to take the frying pan off the stovetop. A warm hand brushed against hers accidentally.

"Don't touch me!" she shrieked as Todd took the frying pan away from her.

She backed away until a comfortable distance separated them.

Todd set the frying pan down and held up his hands. "My apologies," he said, his deep voice soft, like that used to gentle a frightened horse. "I didn't mean to startle you."

Francine nodded, feeling foolish. She couldn't remember the last time a man had touched her; her heart raced as though she'd run up a hill in a dead sprint.

"We'll eat this," said Todd as Keefe lumbered into the room. "I prefer my bacon well done anyway."

Francine nodded again, then blurted out, "Another guest is arriving today. My sister."

Todd stopped serving bacon and eggs onto the two plates laid on the table and looked at her searchingly. "You must be pleased to see her."

"I'm not!" Francine put a hand up to her mouth to prevent anything further escaping. She never gave away personal information. It was so unprecedented she was surprised at the pricking of tears at the back of her eyes. "I need to clean the house," she muttered, and hurried out of the kitchen.

"I think she's a little nuts," Francine heard Keefe say in what passed for a whisper for the boy.

"Hold your tongue and show some respect. There's nothing wrong with her. She's different. Interesting . . ."

Darting into the front parlor to avoid hearing something she wouldn't like, Francine sat down on a chair, erect and tense.

The room was one of her favourites—large yet intimate, with lead-paned windows that provided an airy buoyancy accentuated by lemon-striped wallpaper and the pale-yellow upholstery of the old chairs. But what Francine liked most was the large hearth. It was one of the oldest parts of the manor, and rarely lit; sometimes, like now, when a storm was approaching, it sent draughts down the chimney to ruffle the faded mustard-coloured curtains.

Sensing her anxiety, the old house gathered around her in a tickle of dust motes. Apart from the kitchen, it was in this room that Francine's memories of her mum were strongest. This was where her mum had always done her sewing. Francine could see her now as if it were yesterday, sitting in the chair closest to the windows, her sewing basket on the table beside her, head bent, her tongue sticking out the corner of her mouth as she threaded a needle, using the ungainly dressmaking scissors to snip the thread. She remembered being told many times not to touch those scissors: a long, heavy, lethal-looking pair with a black handle. When young, Francine had been terrified of those scissors and never touched them. It was a simple memory of her mother, but a fond one.

But the room and the memory brought no comfort today. "What is happening to me, Bree?" she whispered when she felt the ghost's warmth perch on the arm of the chair and something soft, as light as a thought, touched her hair.

"Why did Madeleine have to come now? I don't want her here. I like my life as it is, and I don't want . . ." She sighed and rubbed her face hard. "Enough of this. She is my sister. She has as much right to be here as I do."

She stood up, went to the cupboard under the stairs, and pulled out her homemade cleaning materials and linen before going upstairs to her wing of the house.

She touched the door handle of Madeleine's old room and paused. She hadn't entered it for years. Bree fretted beside her, knocking the paintings on the passage walls askew in a fit of agitation.

"Go downstairs, Bree. I'll do this by myself."

Francine was not surprised when Bree fled down the hall, knocking each painting as she went.

Madeleine's room had not been changed since childhood. The wallpaper was ancient, with faded lambs skipping happily through yellow flowers. A narrow bed with a bare mattress stood against one wall while a walnut wardrobe took up most of the opposite wall. A small desk sat under the window. On it was a vase that had a watermark just below the rim and the brittle, blackened remains of flowers that crumbled to dust when Francine touched them. They had once been Madeleine's flower, *Ranunculus*. Those vivid blooms had done little to brighten the room, yet Francine had always placed them in her sister's room when she came home as a reminder of their mother, though she doubted Madeleine had noted the significance.

Of Madeleine, there was nothing. No chosen pictures from

her childhood or books in the small bookcase next to the door. It was exactly how Francine had left the room when Madeleine had left at sixteen. Not even her sister's short, infrequent visits had stamped any personality on it.

When the room was cleaned and the bed made up, Francine placed one of her little protection sachets under the mattress before hurrying out again, not able to bear the lifeless room longer than she had to.

Just as she was putting the cleaning stuff away, she heard a car pull up to the front of the house. She went into the foyer and paused, checking that everything was in place. She wiped half-heartedly at the dust on her skirt and blouse, then took a deep breath. Before she could open the front door, it burst open, and Madeleine blew into the house.

SIX

Madeleine was still beautiful at fifty-one and wore her middle age with hypnotic grace. Her long auburn hair fell down her back in artful waves, makeup disguised the faint lines around her eyes and mouth, but her eyes were still the same. Large, green, ringed by dark lashes and sparkling with vulnerability, as though always on the verge of tears. She wore a leaf-green dress, cut to flatter her voluptuous figure that suggested an irresistible urge to eat too many chocolates.

She paused dramatically on the threshold.

"May I come in?" she asked, her voice deep and husky, a plucked eyebrow raised.

Francine eyed the mound of suitcases the taxi driver was carrying to the porch. With a tight smile, she nodded. "You and all the rest."

Madeleine half ran to Francine and wrapped her arms around her sister.

They were night and day. Few took them to be sisters. Where Madeleine was vibrant color, even if artificially engineered with her advancing years, Francine was pale. Everything was thin about Francine: thin face, thin nose, thin lips, thin shoulders, narrow hips ran down to thin legs, and no bust to speak of—which Madeleine had plenty and to spare.

"It's been too long," Madeleine murmured. "You haven't changed a bit."

"Nor have you," retorted Francine. Close up, she scrutinized her sister's face with concern, for beneath the makeup were dark shadows under Madeleine's eyes that spoke of long, sleepless nights.

Madeleine released Francine and cast a pointed look at the taxi driver waiting to be paid. "Could you? I forgot to bring any cash with me."

Francine glared at her sister before darting into the kitchen where she kept her money in an old biscuit tin at the back of a cupboard. She held no store in banks.

"What's wrong?" she demanded once the driver had departed. "You look dreadful."

"And you always say the nicest things to me," said Madeleine without any tartness.

Francine scowled at the suitcases still sitting on the porch, then dragged them into the foyer before following Madeleine.

Madeleine opened the door to the drawing room that Francine always kept shut and looked around with her hands on her hips.

Francine did not cross the threshold. She had never liked the drawing room, for it faced the graveyard. The huge hearth had not been lit in her memory, and the chairs and side tables scattered over the frayed Persian carpet were never used. It was a dead room, and Francine had never done anything to change it. She didn't like change; change brought complications.

Her nose wrinkled as a strong whiff of stale tobacco emanated from the rarely opened room. It was curious, for she had never smoked and made it clear that smokers were not welcome in her home. She was quite certain her new lodgers did not smoke, for she would have smelled it on their clothes.

"You really could do more to this place," said Madeleine.

"I like it as it is."

Madeleine pirouetted gracefully on one heel and walked to the kitchen. She eyed the teacup sitting on the table alongside a saucer with leaves in it. "And I see you still spend most of your time in the kitchen."

Francine shrugged.

"And still reading tea leaves."

Francine nodded stiffly.

Madeleine put her head to one side and regarded her older sister thoughtfully. "You're uncomfortable with me being here."

"What makes you say that?" She hated when Madeleine said perceptive things like that. It didn't suit her usual airheadedness.

"The way you're holding yourself. So still and erect. You've always done it, as if you're hoping if you keep still enough, no one will notice you."

Francine saw nothing wrong with standing still. It was better than fidgeting. She couldn't abide fidgeters.

Sighing, Madeleine sat down at the table. Francine sat opposite her.

"What happened to your husband, er—?"

"Jonathon," Madeleine supplied, and sighed again. "Lymphatic cancer. Towards the end there was nothing we could do except keep him comfortable. It's been . . . hard." A tear trickled out the corner of her eye. Francine followed its course down the powdered cheek until it plopped onto the table. "It was horrible, Franny. He was such a kind man. He looked after me." She swallowed hard against the deluge of tears that threatened. "I miss him," she whispered.

Clearing her throat in the hope she could distract Madeleine from the full drama Francine knew was close, she said, "What happened to your previous husband? The spiritualist, was it?"

"Sebastian was an occultist. He was a dear, but it didn't work out in the end. And then I met Jonathon." She smiled at the memory that threatened more tears.

"I'm sorry," said Francine lamely, for she could think of nothing else to say in the face of her sister's genuine grief. "This Sebastian," she added quickly as Madeleine's eyes welled up, "was he in the habit of calling up spirits?"

"Of course. He conducted séances all the time. People came from all over the country to get a reading from him. He was famous in his own way," said Madeleine, proud of her ex-husband's dubious fame, as though it reflected on her.

Francine was not surprised by Madeleine's sudden interest in the occult. She had always taken on the interests of her husbands with the same obsession she had for the man in question until she had hooked them and married them, then boredom would set in. Madeleine had the attention span of a mayfly.

"Please tell me you used some protection when you messed with all that . . . nonsense."

Diverted from her misery, Madeleine rolled her eyes. "Of course! Mum taught me all the protection plants too, not just you!"

Slightly mollified, Francine said, "Like what?"

Giving a theatrical sigh of exasperation, Madeleine said in a singsong voice, *"Root of angelica to break the devil's hex . . . For the seer, burnt* Calendula *reaped at noon . . . Sprig of mistletoe will defend kith and kin . . ."*

With a snort, Francine said, "So long as you protected yourself is all I'm saying, though *Calendula* wouldn't have been much good."

"Sebastian swore by it."

"Then the man was a charlatan and an idiot."

Madeleine scowled. "You're still doing it, you know."

"Doing what?"

"If I say the sky is blue, you will always say it's pink or no color."

"I do not!"

"You do."

"Do not!"

"Do!"

Madeleine straightened abruptly and looked around. "And speaking of ghosts, is Bree still with you?"

"You always upset her when you come home, so I sent her to the oak tree until she can behave herself." Francine gave her an old-fashioned look. "You've never believed in Bree. You've never believed in ghosts. I'm rather surprised you bothered with sèances and such with this husband of yours."

Madeleine paused, mouth open to retort, then closed it in a pout. "That's true," she conceded. "But you do, and so did Mum. I suppose I wanted to believe in them too. And Sebastian was so persuasive about it all. He made it seem possible."

An awkward silence filled the kitchen. Madeleine avoided Francine's gaze by staring at the kitchen table.

Certain that Madeleine was hiding something Francine asked, "Why did you come home?"

Madeleine gave a small shrug.

Francine frowned at her sister's bowed head. "Madeleine!" she prompted sharply when the silence stretched beyond awkward. "You haven't been home in five years. Why now?"

"Have you not heard what I've said? My husband just died! Isn't that enough?" She stood up abruptly. "I'm tired. I'll speak to you later." And she hurried out of the kitchen before Francine could say anything further.

Francine listened to her sister's footsteps on the staircase then along the passage on the floor above. She sat at the table for a long while before sighing and going about her chores. She started dinner, before puttering around the house, listening to its quiet breathing, rather at odds with herself. Unsettled, nervy. But that was only to be expected with Madeleine's arrival. Her feet took her upstairs to clean her lodgers' rooms.

Keefe O'Driscoll was rather careless with his belongings—not unduly so, and no more than Francine would expect from a young man. She smiled. There was something childlike in the rough-and-tumble of his room. Keefe, she decided, was a daisy with the unworldliness and simplicity of a child. Making a mental note to put daisies in his room, she hurried on to Todd Constable's room.

Todd, she was pleased to see, was a tidy sort, making his own bed each morning, his few clothes neatly packed away in the wardrobe. She was surprised that he had already imprinted his personality on the room with framed family photographs. Mrs. Constable was a rather lovely woman; at least she assumed the woman in the pictures was his wife. They were laughing together—it was an unaffected picture, captured unawares. A couple of photographs were of two girls who could only have been daughters. A group family photo sat on the bedside table alongside a headshot of his wife. The photos spoke of a love shared, not just through the obligation of a familial link, but because they genuinely liked each other.

She took a last look around before leaving the room. It was all there: thoughtfulness, dedication to his loved ones, and . . . patience. The perfect flower for Todd, Francine decided, was *Astilbe*. She had seen some flowering early near the shed, which she could cut for his room.

Once finished with the bedrooms, she dusted the long corridor that ran the length of the manor, grandiosely called the Lower Gallery. Old, begrimed, and cracked portraits of Thwaite ancestors covered the walls, their names embossed on the frames in small self-important gold mounts. She rarely looked at the paintings; they were part of the furnishings of the house and taken for granted.

Normally, Francine had a lot of patience. But not this evening as she waited for Madeleine to wake up. She longed to peek into her sister's room but resisted the urge. They may be related by blood, but they did not share the sort of familiarity that would allow her to enter her sister's room unannounced.

Instead, she sat on one of the old chairs in the Lower Galley that gave her a view down the west wing's long corridor and waited.

The house ticked quietly around her as it waited with Francine. She always thought the house had its own personality, discreet but watchful over the generations that had lived and died within its walls. Those lives were forgotten by the living, but not by the manor, and there was some comfort in that. Yet, while the house seemed alert, it was laced with a jumpy tension—a sharpness in the air, a brittleness in the walls, an erratic unease that rippled down the gallery and echoed in the gloomy faces of Francine's ancestors peering down at her.

She almost didn't hear Madeleine's bedroom door open before it was too late. She leapt up and darted down the stairs with unseemly haste, then into the kitchen. Dashing to the oven, she titivated about as though she had been busy all the while when Madeleine stepped into the kitchen.

"You are right," Madeleine began without preamble. "I did come home for a reason."

Francine turned from the oven, waiting for her to continue.

"I wanted to come earlier, but we only found out shortly before Jonathon was diagnosed, and then . . ." Madeleine waved a hand about vaguely to express the enormity of her recent heartache.

"Found out what?"

"I think you should sit down before I show you."

Francine almost snapped that she was perfectly fine standing up, thank you very much! But something in Madeleine's tone forced her to sit.

"Well?" she demanded when Madeleine sat slowly, placing a thin folder on the table in front of her that she immediately started fiddling with.

Without raising her eyes, Madeleine said, "Mum lied to us." She held up a hand when Francine's eyes widened with indignation. "Just hear me out," she said quickly. "When I first met Jonathon, he talked a lot about researching family histories and so on. He was fascinated that I knew so little of my family, even though I grew up in all this." She waved a vague hand around. "He started to do some research. I was curious too; there was something quite absorbing about finding out about the people who shaped us and made us who we are. I had always thought our history would be boring, but we have a horrible, dark secret, Franny." She leaned forward, her eyes bright with a twisted excitement. "It was never just the three of us as Mum always said. We had four sisters and a brother."

Francine barely registered her sister's words, for they made no sense in her strictly ordered life. "That's not possible." Shaking her head, lips tight, chest even tighter, she hissed, "No, you're lying!"

"Why would I lie?"

"Then it was your stupid husband. It was the wrong family, or he just made it up. It was always just you and I and Mum. Our father is dead; there was no one else. Mum would've told us. She would have told me!" The last was a plaintive wail.

"I'm sorry, Fran, but it's true." Madeleine paused, eyeing her sister warily, then said, "Have you ever wondered where Bree came from?"

"Of course! I've tried to . . ." Francine shrugged, not wanting to explain her curiosity about Bree or her attempts to find out who the little ghost once was. "She's always been here. She came with the house."

"No, Franny. She died fifty years ago . . . She was our sister."

Curling tendrils of unease tightened across Francine's chest until she could barely breathe. She glanced through the open door to the courtyard and the oak tree, its bare branches swaying above the well without the need of a breeze.

Turning back to Madeleine, she searched for telltale signs that her sister was lying. She had never been a good liar. But her cheeks weren't flushed, and she wasn't holding Francine's gaze in the determined fashion she usually did when lying. Feeling quite dizzy and unable to bear the pity on her sister's face, she looked down at the table. "Tell me," she whispered around the lump that had formed in her throat.

"It's easier if you see for yourself." Madeleine opened the thin folder and slid a few pieces of paper across the table. "We were all registered at the Church of the Sacred Heart in Coniston. I don't remember ever going there with Mum, do you?"

Francine shook her head, though she wasn't surprised, as her mum had never been one for structured religion.

The breath she'd been holding escaped in a gust as she read the names that had been highlighted in yellow on a photocopy from a ledger, all entries written in an old-fashioned scrawl. At the top of each page was the announcement:

Births registered in the parish of Coniston in the County of Cumbria.

30 September 1961, **Bree Elizabeth**, Thwaite Manor, Hawkshead Rural, female, Father—George Robert Thwaite, Mother—Eleanor Mabel Thwaite

13 August 1962, **Agnes Ida**, Thwaite Manor, Hawkshead Rural, female, Father—George Robert Thwaite, Mother—Eleanor Mabel Thwaite

21 December 1963, **Francine Lillian**, Thwaite Manor, Hawkshead Rural, female, Father—George Robert Thwaite, Mother—Eleanor Mabel Thwaite

16 September 1964, **Viola Clementine**, Thwaite Manor, Hawkshead Rural, female, Father—George Robert Thwaite, Mother—Eleanor Mabel Thwaite

1 April 1966, **Rosina Sylvia**, Thwaite Manor, Hawkshead Rural, female, Father—George Robert Thwaite, Mother—Eleanor Mabel Thwaite

26 January 1968, **Madeleine Beatrix**, Thwaite Manor, Hawkshead Rural, female, Father—George Robert Thwaite, Mother—Eleanor Mabel Thwaite

19 November 1968, **Montgomery George**, *Thwaite Manor, Hawkshead Rural, male, Father—George Robert Thwaite, Mother—Eleanor Mabel Thwaite*

Francine read the names over and over, shaking her head . . . *Bree. Agnes. Viola. Rosina. Montgomery . . .* She had no memory of the names, except Bree, and that was simply a name she had made up as a child. It didn't mean that her little ghost was the *same* Bree. There was no jolt of familiarity, no sudden gasp of remembrance, and yet there should've been, for based on the birth dates, they had all been born close together; they should've grown up together.

"These must've been stillbirths," she said, thankful for the logical reason she presented.

"There's a separate register for stillbirths," said Madeleine softly, as though raising her voice even slightly would send Francine over the edge. "And I have the records of our baptisms too, all in Coniston." She slipped another two pages across the table. "These are the only death records." She was crying silently.

Francine's throat convulsed. She didn't touch the pages at first, merely stared at them in horror. Her hands shook as she picked them up and read the stark words. Bree Elizabeth Thwaite and Montgomery George Thwaite, both recorded as dead by drowning on the 26th of July, 1969. The oldest and the youngest of the Thwaite siblings.

"They both drowned," said Francine dully. "Like our father."

But Madeleine was shaking her head. "Mum lied to us about that too. There's no record of his death anywhere."

Francine came over all cold. "Our father is dead," she insisted. "He drowned in Esthwaite Water on his way back from the pub when you were little more than a baby. Mum told us—"

"There was no accident, Francine! Mum lied to us."

Francine shook her head, every nerve wanting to disbelieve her sister. "What happened to him then? You have all the answers. You tell me what happened to him!"

"I can't. He may be dead now, but he didn't die here. His death would've been recorded here if he had. I don't know what happened to him."

A hard seed of trepidation settled in Francine's stomach and sent tendrils spreading throughout her body until her skin rippled with goosebumps. She didn't want to hear anymore. She had adored her mother, the one person she had trusted implicitly, who had always been there for her.

"Why would Mum lie about our father's death?"

"I don't know, Francine!" said Madeleine, frustrated by her sister's stubborn refusal to accept the truth. She breathed deeply through her nose, then said in a calmer tone, "I thought you might remember something. You would've been five when Montgomery and Bree drowned."

Hollow-eyed, Francine shook her head.

"You don't remember anything?"

"No. I certainly don't remember any siblings except you, and I would have remembered Bree." A pricking of tears formed at the back of her eyes. "Bree was our sister, and I don't remember her!"

Madeleine reached a hand across the table to comfort Francine but withdrew it when the action wasn't reciprocated. "I knew you would take this hard. I think you must have been close to Bree when she was alive. Maybe that's why you . . ." She paused, then said, "Why you remember her the way you do, as an imaginary friend."

Francine ignored the doubtful suggestion that Bree was only a figment of a fractured memory. "What happened to our other sisters?" she asked, her voice gruff from contained emotion.

Agnes. Viola. Rosina. The names didn't sound familiar, and yet now that they were forced into her mind, she thought, just possibly, there was a distant echo of a memory, elusive as a cloud's shadow. Her brow puckered as she tried to conjure anything of her early childhood.

There was nothing. Not a single memory she could grasp. She couldn't remember Bree, yet Bree had always been with her.

Madeleine shook her head. "I never found out what happened to them either. The only mention of them is the birth records and the baptism. There's nothing else."

Sitting utterly still, mind racing, Francine tried to make sense of it all. But she couldn't. It was all too sudden, too disruptive. Too impossible. "How long have you known?"

Madeleine shifted uncomfortably in her chair. "A few months," she admitted.

Aghast, Francine stared at her sister. "Why didn't you tell me sooner?"

Madeleine hesitated, then said, "Because I knew you would react like this. To be honest, I wasn't even sure you'd believe me."

"Rubbish! You couldn't be bothered to tear yourself away from your chaotic life in London!"

Another hesitation. Madeleine nodded. "That is partly true," she conceded. She glanced around the kitchen and shivered. "I know you love it here, but I've always hated it. And I *was* planning to make a trip up here to tell you, but then Jonathon fell ill."

Mollified, Francine nodded stiffly, though she couldn't resist adding, "You could've phoned or written."

"Give me some credit, Franny. This is not exactly something you tell someone over the phone or put in a letter."

The prickle of tears scraped the back of Francine's throat. She couldn't, wouldn't cry in front of her sister. Standing up abruptly, she darted towards the door leading to the courtyard.

"I've seen their graves," Madeleine said.

Francine paused on the threshold. "What?"

Madeleine wore an expression of surprise, as though she'd just had a revelation. "Bree and Montgomery. They're buried in our graveyard. I wasn't scared of it like you; I used to go in there when I was small. I remember seeing their names on the gravestones, but they had no meaning to me, not then."

Francine nodded, though she had no intention of setting foot in the graveyard, and hurried out to the oak tree in the courtyard.

"Bree!" she called, her voice shrill.

The bare branches rustled faintly.

"Bree, please come down." She swallowed, wondering how to tell the little ghost she knew they were sisters and yet remembered nothing of her when she'd been alive.

Francine waited a full five minutes under the oak tree. Bree didn't come down, yet Francine knew she was there, watching.

26 July, 1969

Bree crept down the stairs, knowing full well she should be out in the garden with her sisters and baby brother. She paused on the landing, head cocked, listening intently.

Below her, the foyer stretched to the front door, shadowed and gloomy, the wood-paneled walls lined with age-raddled paintings of Thwaite ancestors who had never done anything interesting that Bree could tell.

Certain the house was empty, she slunk down the last few steps and peeked into the drawing room. Her nostrils twitched at the tobacco that hung in a blue mist over the room. Though the scent was not unpleasant, the associations it conjured were— a permanent stamp of His personality over, not just this room, but the whole house.

Almost giddy with racing adrenaline at her daring, Bree paused on the threshold, her attention caught by movement through the window where her siblings were restoring the old chamomile seats and lawn with Mum.

It should've been a lovely scene. Not for Bree. All she saw was the undercurrent of unease with each tilt of a head, the flicker of eyes towards the house. All waiting for the moment He set off down the path through the woods leading to Hawkshead, and everyone, even the house itself, would breathe a sigh of relief.

Agnes, only a year younger than Bree, stood next to Mum as she knelt beside one of the chamomile seats. Agnes held her blue-and-white dog close to her chest with one hand and pointed in hard little jabs with the other. Bree's eyes narrowed. She didn't need to hear to know Agnes was telling Mum what to plant where, while Mum ignored her in patient silence. But even as she bossed, Agnes's thin shoulders were set straight and wary, her eyes traveling here and there, always waiting in dread for a cry of being found out, always needing a story to tell Him to avoid a beating.

Maddie, always crying, always needy, clung to Mum's skirt, face crumpled around large green eyes that had a perpetually luminous, haunted expression, even when she was happy. Happiness was not something she'd known often in her eighteen months of life.

A burst of laughter was trapped in the sunlight that filtered through the closed window to dance on the sunrays with the dust motes. Bree smiled. It was hard not to when Rosie laughed. She had a deep laugh for a three-year-old girl that swelled up from her belly. It was one of the most joyous sounds in Bree's life. Rosie had fallen flat on her face, but unlike other children who would've cried, she simply laughed so hard she got hiccups. She got up, hiccupped, and promptly fell on her bum, only to laugh all the harder for it.

Viola was the one to go to Rosie's aid. Only a year older than Rosie, Viola was the quiet one, the dreamy one, a giver and a caring little soul, yet she never asked anything for herself.

Bree's eyes were drawn to her favourite, Figjam, sitting beside Monty, who sprawled open-legged and swaying on a blan-

ket nearby, a red toy tractor in his hands that he kept pulling close to his face before pushing it away, fascinated by the play of light at different distances. Figjam was scowling unhappily at her baby brother, no doubt having been told by Mum to watch him.

Sensing she was being watched, Figjam looked up at the manor, her face pinched into a worried frown before reverting back to scowling at Monty.

Dragging her eyes away from the summer sunshine Bree had every intention of enjoying once she had done what she needed to do, she spied the purse on the small table beside His chair. She wouldn't take much—just enough to add to her filched pile without being noticed, but not so little as to be pointless for the danger and the severe repercussions if she were caught. Perhaps three shillings this time. Yes, three should be little enough.

Bree slipped into the room, tiptoeing to miss the floorboards that creaked. It was the work of seconds to open the purse . . . she paused in surprise. Never had she seen so much money; pound notes in a tight roll filled the purse to bulging. He'd never had more than coins before.

A creak in the foyer.

Bree's head whipped round so hard her long plaits slapped her face. Turning, with the purse behind her back, her fingers furiously twisting, she glanced out at the darkened foyer, her heart racing.

The notes were smooth against Bree's seeking fingers. She peeled off a few by feel alone and snapped the purse shut quietly before placing it back on the table. Then she tiptoed to the doorway to gain a better view of the foyer.

Not even dust motes stirred lazily in that shadowed darkness. She moved towards the doorway, tensed to run.

Squinting around the doorway then up the stairway, blood rushing into her ears with a roar, she frowned. Was this a game? It wasn't usually His way; He was more direct, with bluster and bruises. But someone was there. She sensed that occupied feeling when someone was trying to breathe shallowly to avoid discovery.

Frown deepening, she crept out and edged along the paneled wall of the foyer, her eyes darting into each secretive corner, each stain on the wall that appeared almost human in shape, each shadowed crack and crevice. Old houses were wonderful in their way with unexpected nooks, an abundance of rooms to hide in, and long corridors for young swift feet to run away down. But the same could be said for someone in hiding, waiting to pounce.

Her neck stiff with spooked panic, Bree stumbled into the warmth and light of the kitchen. Slipping the stolen notes into the pocket of her dress, she hurried past the immense central table.

She skidded to a stop, turned, and grabbed two handfuls of small cakes cooling on trays. They were still warm and smelled of ginger. Feeling guilty that Mum would blame Figjam for taking them, for Figjam loved ginger, Bree shoved the cakes into her pockets alongside the notes. With a last look back at the silent house, she darted out into the courtyard.

The sunshine was glorious after the gloom. Bree hurtled into the garden before forcing herself to walk. Agnes caught sight of her and frowned that annoying, knowing little frown of hers.

With a nonchalance she didn't feel, Bree approached Figjam and Monty, her shoes sinking into the chamomile lawn like a plush carpet, releasing the scent of bruised apples.

Monty gurgled happily when he spied Bree. He was a happy baby; there was no reason for him to be anything else. His would be a charmed life, for he was the son that had always been desired, not another daughter to be despised.

"Where have you been?" whispered Figjam, her freckled face clearing of the worried frown at the sight of her sister.

Bree put a finger to her lips, opening her eyes wide to convey the strictest of secrets that could only be shared in the safety of their hiding place. She sat down and turned her face to the sun, allowing the heat to drain away the cold alarm she'd felt in the house. Now, she could revel in her own daring that she had managed to filch more money than she'd ever held.

Viola rushed up to her crying, "Look what I made!" and thrusting a daisy chain into Bree's hands. "It's for you, Bree. I made it for you," she added breathlessly.

Grateful for the distraction, Bree put the daisies on her head. "Now, I'm your princess," she said in lordly tones. "You have to do what I say."

"You can't be a princess if you're wearing daisies," said Figjam. "It needs to be asters. That's for kings and queens. Mum said so."

Viola's face fell. "Sorry," she whispered. "I'll make another one with asters."

With a glare for Figjam, Bree said, "No! I don't like purple anyway. And daisies are for children, and I am a child. So I shall be a child princess. Now . . ." She looked around thoughtfully.

Viola's hazel eyes widened with excitement now that a game was in the offing. Bree could make a game out of nothing that could last for hours.

"Run to the graveyard and pick some asphodel for me."

"Yes, your majesty," said Viola. She dipped into a crooked curtsey before dashing across the lawn, hitching her skirt into her knickers as she had seen Bree do when running.

The moment Viola was out of earshot, and with a quick glance to ensure the others were too, Bree whispered, "Have you seen Him? He wasn't in the house."

Figjam shook her head. "I've been watching the path like you said. He hasn't gone out."

A quiver of misgiving ratcheted up Bree's spine. "He wasn't in his room either. I checked."

"Are you sure about this, Bree? If he catches you . . ."

Even though she was twitchy as a startled hare, Bree did what she always did. She smiled at Figjam's worried face and took her hand, always the protector, always the comforter. "It will be all right. Everything will be all right," she lied so convincingly, she almost believed herself.

SEVEN

Francine's long, furious strides took her through Lonehowe Wood along a carpet of gold and green, where the late afternoon sun filtered through the trees.

It had to be a cruel trick. The records could've been falsified. It was impossible she would forget something so intrinsically part of her life as four sisters and a brother. Impossible she could ever forget Bree living or dead.

Except Madeleine wasn't cruel. She was ditzy, self-absorbed, and irritating, but never cruel. And as much as Francine longed not to believe it, she knew Madeleine had not been lying... But their mother had.

It was such a shocking blow to all Francine's rigid conceptions. She stopped in the middle of the path and clutched her stomach as it spasmed with tight dread.

Though her throat still prickled with tears, she wouldn't allow them to flow. She straightened and stood utterly still, trying to remember anything from her early childhood to back up what Madeleine had said. But not a single recollection surfaced. Her mind was blank, as though she had emerged fully formed at the age of five.

It only now occurred to Francine that she had never thought of her father at all, having trusted implicitly the story her mum had told her of his drowning. She had no vague image of what he looked like, no random recall of how he smelled. There wasn't a single photo of him in the house. There were no family photos at all.

The long shadows merged with dusk and still Francine stood, lost in thought. It was some time before something, not a memory as such, more a sense of atmosphere, started tickling the back of her mind. She turned the sensation over slowly: a tenseness, an alertness, an underlying agitation muted through long exposure. But the source of the atmosphere was impossible to tell.

Had it come from Mum? No, definitely not. Her father? Apart from Madeleine asking about him when they were young—and it had always been Madeleine who asked—their mother had never spoken of him.

Francine growled with self-directed anger, not sure if it was a genuine recollection or her imagination stressing the impression because she was overwrought.

As she strode unseeingly through the woods, dusk darkened to night and the diurnal birds settled down while nocturnal animals slowly crept from burrows and nests. Never silent, nature was a creeping murmur of thousands of creatures going about their lives of eat or be eaten.

With a startled gasp, Francine stopped in her tracks, jolted from her dark thoughts, and stared up at the building that rose out of the woods like a diseased pustule. While the corpse trail had an ancient darkness, there were other places in the woods with a rivaling aura that was a wholly human evil and far more recent.

Hemmed in by vast ancient oak and beech trees squatted Nonsuch Asylum for the Criminally Insane, as it proudly proclaimed on the sign stretching over the huge stone gateway. It was a gloriously hideous confection of lions, gryphons, dragons, and giant eagles, as though the architect had been unable to decide which monster would best protect the world from those locked inside.

Francine had always hated the old asylum. It had been the north of England's answer to Bedlam and just as notorious in its day, with the added mystery that its location had largely been kept secret. A secret Francine was determined it remain. But once it had been the palatial home built by one of her ancestors, though it was not as old as the manor. According to the Thwaite Histories, it had been leased to the government in the eighteenth century, but when the lease expired in the 1980s, Francine's mum had refused to renew it. The horrible place had since been reclaimed by the woods. Francine had never needed the warning not to venture into these parts as a child, and now, apart from the occasional teen from Hawkshead thinking it would be a lark to spend a night in what was locally believed to be a haunted house, no one came this way.

She turned on her heel, her skin crawling with the need to put distance between herself and the asylum, certain she could hear the lost cries of the old inmates, even though she had never seen a soul in the grounds, living or dead, on the few occasions she had walked on this path.

She stopped when the lights of Thwaite Manor appeared through the trees. The house was a beacon of beckoning warmth, offering sanctuary within its walls. But not even her beloved home could untangle her knot of unresolved dread.

Francine forced her eyes to flicker towards the graveyard.

It menaced in the gloom. There was no symmetry to the tombstones, no neat lines hemmed within the wrought iron fence. Weeds encroached onto the mouldering stones, and trees crouched over the mortal remains of Thwaites going back five hundred years.

Clenched hands sweating at the mere thought of entering the graveyard, Francine shut her eyes. Even when her mum had died, she hadn't been able to force herself to step through the gates. Yet it was because of her mum that she hated it, for that was the only place she had ever seen her mother cry.

She unclenched her hands. Small crescents scored her palms where her short, practical nails had dug into the flesh.

She needed confirmation. Needed something more solid than a couple of photocopied pages from parish records. And she could do it . . . for Bree.

Francine set off down the path to the house, then paused once more when she reached the fork. Right led to light and the warmth of her home, left led to terror of the graveyard and answers.

Blood rushed to her head so hard she thought she might faint. She shut her eyes again. Without opening them, she turned to face left.

A deep breath . . . eyes open quickly . . .

If she stepped through the rusting gate her rigidly routine life would change forever. She took one step forward, then another, until she stood in front of the gate.

No maintenance had been done on the graveyard in thirty years, not since her mother had died. She had always tended the graves, even the ones that were so old their etched names had long since faded.

Francine put her hand on the latch. The cold metal bit into her skin. She turned and fled down the path to the house, through the courtyard, and bolted into the kitchen, slamming the door shut behind her.

She leaned against it, her heart hammering fit to burst. Her skin was cold, yet she was sweating as though she had a fever.

Slowly she became aware of three pairs of eyes staring at her. Straightening, and with as much dignity as she could muster after her undignified entrance, Francine said, "Good evening."

She walked stiffly through the kitchen and up the stairs to seek sanctuary in her bedroom. She got ready for bed, ignoring the early hour, and lay between the cold sheets staring up at the ceiling. The house hunkered over her, suffocating in its closeness, its tense stillness.

Bree did not come.

The old manor hummed with a thousand little nighttime noises: a rustle of the curtain, a faint scratching along the skirting, a creaking rasp when the bathroom door swung slightly for no apparent reason.

Francine kept watch through the night, desperate to see one of her ghostly friends. She needed their presence, their constancy, and the comfort they had always brought. Never had they not come at night when all was quiet, even when Madeleine was here.

And yet, as the night lengthened, Tibbles did not leap onto her bed, the man in the top hat did not pass through the wall, and the pregnant woman did not sit at the window to wait for her little boy.

Francine's ghosts had forsaken her.

Light streamed in through the window when Francine woke. It was late morning. With the guilt of an early riser, she leapt out of bed and got dressed.

Downstairs was quiet. The foyer lay tenebrous and silent but for the grandfather clock in the drawing room ticking time away. And over the shadowed gloom the odor of tobacco leached out in sullen, stubborn tendrils, so faintly Francine was certain she imagined it.

Tensed, head cocked to one side, she listened to the long tick of the grandfather clock and sought the other rhythms of the building. All the little hums and beats that were so much a part of the background noise were still except the slow *tick* . . . *tick* . . . *tick* . . . She had always had a special affinity to the atmosphere of Thwaite Manor and sometimes felt like a barometer to its moods.

The house felt different, off-kilter.

The house felt uneasy.

Shaking herself free of fanciful notions, she darted into the kitchen. Everything was neat and tidy. There was no sign of Madeleine, and she assumed Todd and his apprentice had long since gone to work on the new hotel. She picked up the stoppered bottle she had left on the sideboard the day before and smiled grimly. There was someone she needed to speak to.

One hand clenched tightly around the glass bottle, the other clutching fennel seeds, Francine stalked through Lonehowe Wood. She ignored the silent ghosts lining the corpse trail. So wound up in her own thoughts was she, it was only once she headed down the small fork towards Colthouse did she realise that Alfie, the youngest of the ghosts in the woods, had not been in her way as he usually was.

The weather suited her mood. One of those gloomy, heavy days when it seemed the sun would never shine again, with a persistent drizzle that frizzled hair and created damp but no real wetness. By the time she reached Colthouse, she was walking in a cloud.

A knock on Miss Cavendish's door, a shuffle from within.

"Fran!" said Miss Cavendish. Her lined face lit up with happy surprise, then fell when she took in Francine's tight expression. "What's happened?" she asked, moving to allow Francine entry.

Once in the small sitting room, Francine turned to the old lady but didn't sit when Miss Cavendish gestured for her to do so. She needed to be standing and in control for this conversation.

Without preamble, she said, "Madeleine is home." She paused, swallowed, shook her head. "She told me . . . she told me . . . Bree . . ." The last word was a whisper, for now in the warmth and familiarity of Miss Cavendish's sitting room, she couldn't continue.

"Sit down, Fran," said Miss Cavendish quietly.

Francine perched on the edge of a chair, half turning to face the old lady, whose sympathetic expression hurt to look at.

"What did Maddie tell you?"

"That there were seven of us. She showed me our birth records, and—" a dry sob, "—and two death records. I didn't know Bree was my sister!" Francine burst out. "My own sister, and I forgot about her!"

"Ah." Miss Cavendish leaned back in her chair. "You truly don't remember anything?" she said after a long moment.

"No . . . What happened to them? All the death records say is that Bree and Montgomery drowned. There's nothing else. No mention of my other three sisters, and Madeleine said Mum lied to us, that our father didn't drown in Esthwaite, that there's no record of him dying here at all," she said, words tangling together in her rush to get them out. "I need to know the truth about Bree."

Miss Cavendish gazed out at the blanketing drizzle before she sighed and said, "There is no easy way to tell you this, but I shall tell you the facts as I know them, not the rumors that circled at the time." Her lined face creased with crucifying sadness. "Bree and Monty drowned in that well in the courtyard of the manor some fifty years back. And the same night, George— your father—he ran away, taking those other three mites with him. That is the short of it. As to the longer, who can tell?"

Francine shivered. She had always hated the well in the courtyard. "That's it? That's all you know?"

Miss Cavendish was quiet for so long, Francine thought she

wasn't going to answer. When she did, it was in a soft voice edged with grief. "No one really knows what happened that night . . . except your mum, and she wasn't telling. I was closer to her than anyone, but she never spoke of it. Never mentioned Bree or Monty or the younger girls, not once after the tragedy. Not even when you started talking about Bree as though she were right beside you; gave me a right turn that did, I don't mind telling you. I tried to speak to Eleanor then, but all she said was to leave you be if you gained some comfort believing Bree was still with you, even as an imaginary friend. Eleanor took her secrets to the grave . . . But I remember the search as though it were yesterday. Your mum sent up the hue and cry when she couldn't find some of you . . ."

Miss Cavendish's forehead puckered into a frown. "Can't rightly remember now which of you we were looking for . . . Bree and Monty for certain, and one of the other girls, I think."

With a shrug, she continued, "Whole village turned out, and we searched all night. Through Lonehowe and down to Esthwaite Water, up to Grizedale Forest. We even tried to get into the old asylum in the woods, though they weren't having any of it; that's how it was in those days, they had nowt to do with us and we them. Don't think I ever saw the inmates, much less the doctors and nurses and such . . . But, all that time, Monty and Bree had been down the well. They were found the next morning. I had been searching up in Grizedale and heard the cries. When I got there, Bree and Monty were lying beside the well. And George—" her lips tightened with disapproval "—your father had already scarpered long before then with the younger girls, and good riddance, I say. Not the girls, of course, but that George Thwaite was a mean piece of work, and lazy to boot."

"What do you think happened?"

"I don't know, marra. The story made the nationals, though

they all said the same thing, just talk of the drowning. There was an inquest; the verdict was an accident. An awful accident, but an accident all the same . . . There was talk, of course. There were some as thought George had a hand in the drowning of Bree and Monty."

"But you didn't think so?" asked Francine, pouncing on the old lady's hesitation.

Miss Cavendish frowned, then shook her head. "George would never have harmed Monty. Worshiped the boy. You'd think the second Messiah had been born in Thwaite Manor the way he carried on." Her face wrinkled into a grimace of angry remembrance. "That George didn't care a jot for any of you girls. Cruel he was, and filled with hatred, especially for Eleanor. But he didn't cow our Eleanor, though Lord knows he tried. She was a strong woman."

"If he was so terrible, why didn't she leave him?"

Miss Cavendish raised her sparse eyebrows in surprise. "Why would she? The house was hers, more so with the death of Monty, sad to say." She peered at Francine, then shook her head. "Lord, you really don't know anything. Your mum never mentioned the deal Old Man Thwaite set up with your father?"

"My grandfather? He died when I was a baby. I never knew him."

Miss Cavendish was silent for a long while, then said, "It was no great secret what happened there. He was a difficult man, was Old Man Thwaite, especially after your gran died. Eleanor wasn't older than twelve or so then. He had old-fashioned views and was mad for the manor, as all you Thwaites are. Wanted to keep it in the family, carry on the family name. And that was a problem with only a daughter. So the old man hit on the idea of marrying Eleanor off to a distant cousin, one of the Ullswater Thwaites."

"My father?" Francine clarified, trying to keep up with a family history she had never been aware of.

Miss Cavendish nodded. "George had the right surname and was a distant relation. Who knew a name could be so valuable? But it was to Old Man Thwaite. And George jumped at the chance; there he was at thirty-odd years and naught to show for it, and along comes Old Man Thwaite with a proposition that would see that layabout married and with a manor.

"But he was a crafty old bastard, and I think he had George's measure. He set up a contract that George would only get the manor if he and Eleanor produced a male heir, and even then, the manor would only pass to George once that heir turned five."

Horrified, Francine cried, "Why didn't Mum say no?"

The old woman shrugged. "George had his eye on the prize, and he could be charming when the mood took him. They got married when Eleanor was just seventeen. And George certainly made every effort to uphold his end of the bargain, for Eleanor was pregnant year in and year out. But as girl after girl was born, George's manner to her turned hostile. He blamed her for all the girls, but he never laid a hand on her until Old Man Thwaite died."

She paused and swallowed with a grimace, as though merely telling the tale was poison on her tongue.

Francine was horrified that she had known so little about her mother. To think the two men closest to her had hatched a scheme all for the sake of a name, while her mum had borne the brunt with a wretched life.

Miss Cavendish cleared her throat and half smiled at Francine. "It got a bit better after Monty was born, of course, but by then Eleanor and George hated each other so much they could never come back from that." She sighed. "And when Monty died, George's plans were in tatters. I think he'd had every intention of selling the manor once Monty turned five."

"Tell me about Bree," whispered Francine, her voice breaking along with her heart. "What was she like?"

Miss Cavendish's smile was one of genuine fondness. "A wild one. And tough, too. She had this great length of flaming hair and a temperament to match, I don't mind telling you. But she took a lot of flak from your father. It worried your mum something terrible, for Bree would bait him to take his attention away from the younger girls . . . You were very close to Bree. Thick as thieves, the two of you. Made Agnes that mad. Jealous she was, for you all wanted to be Bree's special person. But Bree chose you. She had a special name for you. Can't recall it now. Odd name, really, because she couldn't say your name when you were born—"

"Figjam." The name came unbidden to Francine's lips, bypassing any conscious thought or memory, surprising both herself and Miss Cavendish.

"That was it. Odd name."

"What were the others like? Rosina, Agnes, and Viola."

Miss Cavendish smiled fondly again. "Pretty things they were. You all were, with the reddest hair. You always knew a Thwaite from the hair. I had a soft spot for little Rosie. She had just started at school and was the sweetest thing; I swear she came out the womb laughing. Agnes was a real bossy boots, and Violet was the shy one, a gentle child. You were all so different." She smiled at Francine. "You were the serious one. Ever so serious and too clever by half. You still are, and much too serious sometimes."

Her chest tight with emotions she dared not release for fear of falling apart, Francine opened her mouth a couple of times, but found her throat constricted with horror. It finally burst from her with, "Why don't I remember, Miss C? There's this huge chunk ripped from my life. A tragedy," she said, for she could not bring herself to speak of this cruel event in her past in broader terms, "that should be indelibly imprinted in my memories, but there is nothing. And why did Mum lie to me? I trusted her—" Her voice broke, her face ravaged by confusion. "You were Mum's closest friend. Surely—"

"I'm sorry, marra. I tried to speak to Eleanor afterwards, get her to open up. She never did. She never spoke of your sisters or little Monty. She would walk away if I even mentioned your father's name. Afterwards, all that was left in Eleanor for that man was a fierce hatred."

She shook her head, jaw clenching with a remembered loathing of her own. "It didn't stop there; she took all the photos down, took all the clothing away. Took away every trace of her children and husband as though she couldn't bear to be reminded." Miss Cavendish leaned forward to rest a hand on Francine's arm. "A piece of your mum died that night, Fran. She was never the same afterwards, and who could blame her? To lose five children in the space of a night is too much for any parent to endure. But she was a good mum to you and Maddie. She lived for the two of you. You should take comfort in that."

"Did she ever try find Agnes, Rosina, and Violet?"

"She kept on at the police to find George. She was that desperate to find him so she could get her girls back. There wasn't much more she could've done that the police couldn't. And they tried, I know that . . ." Miss Cavendish broke off, frowning.

"What?" said Francine. "Have you remembered something?"

"No, not remembered, more an impression I had at the time." She paused, then said, "I think Eleanor knew she wouldn't see those girls again after a time. In those first weeks she still hoped George and the girls would be found, but as time passed, she lost that hope. We all wondered what had happened to them, of course. Plenty of rumors and ridiculous stories. Sightings and such . . . Tosh and nonsense, I say. George took them far away, though where, who can say?" Miss Cavendish patted Francine's arm. "Now, we can only hope George is dead and buried where he can't harm anyone. He'd have been in his nineties now, for he was a fair bit older than our Eleanor. But the girls would still be very much alive today."

Even now, talking about her siblings felt odd. It didn't make the girls any more real—more like people in someone else's life. Bree was the only one who was real to Francine, merely in an unreal way. Yet, by the same token, talking about the girls like real people gave her a small sense of what she had lost: the sisters she had never known, and a little brother who would forever be a baby. A lost and forgotten family.

The two women sat in quiet contemplation of that dreadful time fifty years ago before Miss Cavendish said, "I'm tired now, Fran." She did look frailer than when Francine had first arrived, as though talking about the past had sapped what little was left inside her.

"That reminds me." Francine pulled out the bottle and handed it to the old lady. "It's strong smelling, that'll be the turmeric and ginger, but it will help ease some of your pain as the end nears."

"Thank you, Fran." She looked at Francine for a long moment. "You'll be searching for your sisters then?"

Startled, Francine stared back at the old lady, for she had been thinking exactly that; she hoped that if her sisters were, indeed, still alive, they had had happy lives. She hoped they remembered her even though she had utterly forgotten them.

She nodded slowly. "I think so. I will try anyway." She shrugged. "I'm not even sure where to start. It all happened so long ago."

"Find Sam Woodall; he'll know more about it than I do. He was a young man at the time, bit wet behind the ears, but not a bad lad for all that. He was the constable who first arrived after your mum got onto the police. Later, another lot arrived from Kendal and took over, but young Sam was a local lad; he understood our ways."

"Is he still with the police?"

"No, marra. He'll be on pension now. Last I heard he'd moved out Seatoller way."

EIGHT

❧

By the time Francine got home, the wind had picked up into spiteful gusts before a looming storm. The front door slammed behind her, cutting off the banshee gale, and the silence of the house hit her like an unopened tomb. Airless and stale, as though the windows hadn't been opened in decades. Yet, the silence was electric and tasted of ozone.

Putting it down to the approaching storm, Francine whipped through the empty rooms. "Bree," she called. "You can come out. Madeleine has gone out."

The house remained silent.

She went into the courtyard to the oak tree. Its gnarled branches whipped about, shaking the slanting drizzle into Francine's face.

"Please, Bree," she said. "I need to do something, and I don't think I can do it by myself."

The branches lashed around so that it was impossible to see the telltale movement when Bree was up in her oak tree.

Francine was really worrying now. Bree had never disappeared like this before; for a couple of hours at most, never for twenty-four hours. Not even Madeleine's presence would keep her away that long.

Dejected, she turned to the well.

It was a rather pretty well; a conical slate roof covered a circular stone wall and a bucket on a chain. A long metal handle with a fine patina of rust from years of disuse poked out one side.

A shiver of suppressed horror ran through her, but not a single recollection of the drowning of Bree and Montgomery pushed through her barricaded subconscious. Yet, she had always hated the well. Perhaps some part of her did remember, emerging as a peculiar fear rather than a tangible memory.

Pulling her shoulders back, Francine walked up to the well and forced herself to peer down the long shaft, the wind at her back pushing her so she had to clutch the encircling wall for support. A dank odor wafted up to her, accompanied by the faint slap and splash of dark water against stone. How had a baby and a seven-year-old girl ended up in the well? She glanced up at the oak tree thrashing above her. Bree loved that tree. She always went there when upset. Was that because it was near where she had died?

Sighing, Francine stepped back. "Bree?" she called again, without much hope. The oak tree remained lashing and dripping.

She hoped Bree would come back when she went out to protect the garden tonight . . .

Francine's eyes widened. Clamping a hand over her mouth, she whispered, "Oh no!" through her fingers. She had forgotten to protect the house last night! She had been so overwrought by Madeleine's revelation that she had lost her routine. No wonder her ghosts hadn't come to her last night.

She ran to the greenhouse. Grabbing a bag of rock salt and

another of dried herbs she kept stocked, she put them in the wheelbarrow and dashed into the garden.

"Please come back, Bree," she muttered as she scattered the herbs around the boundary; they blew far and wide with the gusting wind. *"Please, please, please . . ."* was a whisper of need that enveloped her as she worked furiously, hoping against hope that her lapse had not caused irrevocable harm. She worked her way around the garden to the back of the house, tossing rock salt with a heavy hand.

A spiked gust sent a spatter of drizzle into Francine's face. She straightened, searching for any activity to indicate Bree was nearby. She swung round to catch a blur of movement, the sway of a branch not in keeping with the wind's direction, or a shadow where no shadow should be.

The wind dropped inexplicably, and a false calm settled as she turned to the graveyard. Her throat tightened with dread. Gloomy and unloved under a bruised sky; the surrounding trees didn't so much shelter the tombstones as hunker over them like vultures over carrion.

She turned away, unable to force herself towards those gates. She faced the rhododendron instead, her heart beating unpleasantly. Erratic, too fast.

Stepping into the maze so she couldn't see the graveyard, she slipped left, then right, down the narrow, darkly green pathways surrounded by towering walls of tightly knit leafiness.

Her feet led her to the center, where an old stone bench, clad in moss, sat before a defunct fountain. A statue of Neptune had once vomited water into its surrounding stone basin, thick with lotus. But the lotus had long since died, the water in the basin was a rusty veneer that stank of rot.

Francine sat on the moss-shrouded bench and stared at Neptune. For all its neglect, it was a peaceful place and . . . happy.

The memory came with the vivid clarity of a snapshot. A birthday party on a summery day . . . blue-and-white-checkered cloth next to the fountain . . . cake on the cloth. Around it lay a woven garland of chrysanthemums. Bree knelt beside it. Bree as Francine had never remembered her. So real, tucking the last chrysanthemum into the garland before staring expectantly down the path that led from the center of the maze.

Heavy footsteps . . . not in the maze. The rasp of boots on gravel . . .

Francine turned her head, squinting as though she could see through the walls of rhododendron to the driveway beyond.

Bree standing up, a finger to her lips, head cocked, listening to the footsteps. Then she was off, scampering left and right through the narrow pathways with fleet-footed certainty.

Francine, following the memory of Bree, traveled those same paths. Everything was from a younger vantage point; the walls of the maze were the walls of a castle where the monsters and fairies of a child's imagination lurked. Bree was ahead of her, standing at the maze's shadowed entrance, staring up at the house that shimmered in the intense sunshine, its edges softened with the distance of time, as though viewed through a soap bubble.

Francine stepped out of the maze, desperate to hold on to the memory and allow it to follow its course. Bree running across the lawn . . .

"Francine."

Francine almost screamed in terror. She whipped around, the memory tattering like a dream on waking. She swallowed her wail of frustration as Todd strode across the lawn towards her.

"You startled me," she said accusingly.

"Sorry," he said, smiling so his eyes crinkled. "I came to pick something up and saw you standing here. I've never known anyone stand as still as you do."

She blinked and dusted off her soil-stained skirt, flustered. Apart from passing pleasantries dictated by society if they met accidentally, Francine had barely spoken to the man since he'd arrived. She looked around to avoid Todd's gaze, until her eyes alighted on the graveyard. Tensing, having forgotten what she had planned to do, she quickly tossed the rock salt still clasped in her hand into the nearest flower bed before looking up to find him watching her with a curious expression. His gaze moved to the bag of rock salt in the wheelbarrow.

Ignoring his raised eyebrow, Francine waited for him to say something. They both stared at the manor. Todd appeared as lost for words as Francine was.

"I, er, I noticed your clock tower is leaning slightly," he began.

"It's been leaning like that for years," said Francine, not at all pleased with his criticism of her home.

"I think the footing may have given way, which is causing subsidence." He cleared his throat when Francine said nothing, then rushed on with, "It's not just the clock tower; the porch is about to fall down where the mortise and tenon joint has failed and needs to be replaced. And there's the staircase; it's rather dire with dry rot. And then there's the gable end . . ." He nodded at the gable end in question.

Francine followed his gaze. It bulged in the center and the exposed timbers were badly cracked.

"The house needs a little work," she conceded, trying to see the manor through Todd's eyes. She couldn't. Like anything truly loved, the old building's faults were invisible to her. "Though I don't see what concern it is of yours."

"I could fix some of it for you, if you like."

Francine blinked at the generous offer. "Why?"

"Because it needs to be fixed."

"I'm well aware it needs to be fixed, but why do *you* want to fix it?"

Taken aback, Todd shook his head in confusion. "Because your house is becoming a death trap. If you don't fix the gable end soon, that whole side of the house will fall down. The drawing room is below it; if anyone should be in there, they'll be killed. And if the clock tower falls over it could jeopardize the integrity of the second floor and possibly the facade. Those are the most structurally unsound areas; there are other smaller issues, but those are needing urgent attention."

"It's an old house; of course there will be issues. But I don't need your help," said Francine briskly. "There's a perfectly acceptable builder in Hawkshead."

It was a lie, of course. The only builder Francine knew was in his eighties and could barely get up a ladder, let alone fix a five-hundred-year-old house.

Todd nodded and glanced about as though searching for another conversation opener, one less likely to set Francine on edge. She saw his indecision and wished she hadn't been so abrupt. He seemed to genuinely want to help her. That alone confused her, but what confused her more was that she wanted his help.

She relented. "I was about to go to the graveyard." She felt a lot braver with Todd beside her, and uttering her intention aloud forced her into an action she was dreading.

"I've seen it. I rather like graveyards. They have a melancholic peacefulness."

"You *like* them?"

He grinned. "The dead can't harm you, and they're quiet. I often go to our local cemetery in London, just to get away from the madness of the city."

Intrigued by this man who went to graveyards to find solitude, she blurted out, "Who've you buried there?"

Todd didn't respond at first, then said, "My wife. She died four years ago . . . a brain tumor."

"Oh, I'm sorry." Photographs of the smiling woman in Todd's room entered Francine's thoughts. Those photos spoke of the memory of love beyond death. She rather liked him for it.

He sighed. "There was nothing more to be done for her. Death was a release in the end."

Francine was never sure what to say in these circumstances. Usually, she avoided talking to people, so the dilemma rarely arose. Yet she felt an enormous pity for this man whom she barely knew.

"Would you mind if I came with you into the graveyard before I go back to work?" said Todd when she didn't add to the already awkward conversation. "I've been curious about it but didn't want to enter without your permission. A family graveyard is a personal space."

Relief flooded through her. She would've been too proud to ask, but an offer she could just about swallow.

"If you like." She waited until he started walking down the path and followed slowly, her feet growing heavier the closer she got to the gates. Her skin tingled with panic, and she almost turned back.

But Todd was already pushing open the gates. They creaked horribly. He glanced over his shoulder and grinned. "Nice spooky gates . . . Are you alright?" he asked when he saw her ashen face.

"Fine, fine," she muttered. "Unlike you, I don't care much for graveyards."

"You look terrified."

"I most certainly am not!" Her hands bunching into fists, she marched past him until she was just within the gates, surprised at her own daring.

"All your family is buried here?"

Francine nodded, her throat so tight with terror she couldn't manage a verbal answer.

Todd hunkered down in front of the nearest headstone. Francine stared at him, wide-eyed, terrified that, if she looked away, she would run out of the graveyard and never have the courage to come back again.

"Jeremiah Desmond Thwaite," Todd read aloud. "Born 1823, died 1876. RIP." He traced a finger over the fading letters.

Surprised by a name she recognized, Francine found her voice and said hoarsely, "He wrote the Thwaite Histories."

Todd laughed. "You have Histories too?" He shook his head. "How far do the graves go back?"

"Five hundred years." She took a step closer to him. His calm presence was reassuring, and some of her panic receded. "My family have lived here from birth to death since the first Thwaite. Thomas Thwaite bought the land in 1538, after the Dissolution of the Monasteries."

Todd smiled up at her. "What an amazing heritage to have. My family come from Jamaica, but the furthest I can go back is my grandmother. I have no idea where the other side came from. Somewhere in England is all I know."

Francine took a deep breath. She had come this far, and as she had no plans to ever set foot in the graveyard again, she had to find Bree and Montgomery's graves as soon as possible.

She took a step up one of the overgrown paths, then froze when Todd said, "Eleanor Mabel Thwaite, 23 December, 1943 — 13 June, 1984. RIP. The gravestone's fairly new . . . Is this your mum?"

"Yes."

"She died young, only forty-one."

"I was twenty when she died. Madeleine was sixteen." Francine swallowed convulsively. It was the first time she had seen her mum's grave. "She just faded away." Impressions of her mum from her earliest memories surged into her mind that, with hindsight and recent knowledge, formed a different image from the juvenile one she had retained. "I think after my father . . ." She paused, re-evaluating what she had been about to say. "After he left, a part of her left with him, or perhaps he killed something in her." She blinked at this new insight. "I think she only stayed alive long enough to see Madeleine and I to adulthood."

"You were close?"

Francine nodded. "She was my best friend." Her eyes prickled. She cleared her throat, uncomfortable that she had divulged so much to a virtual stranger.

"And Madeleine?" he asked. "Are you close to her?"

"No. We've grown apart." The corner of her mouth dimpled in an effort to stem her emotions. "To be fair, we've never been close, even as children."

She took off down the higgledy-piggledy rows rather than face more of Todd's questions. There was some order to the graves. Twentieth-century rested beside eighteenth, seventeenth ran up one side of the fence, as though that century's Thwaites had decided the other centuries were beneath them and the separation had followed in death. At the very back of the graveyard were the earliest graves. Small headstones keeled over like crooked, pocked teeth, grass almost hiding them from view.

Distracted from her search, Francine paused between the rows of Victorian graves and tomb chests to stare in astonishment. They were covered in a tangle of hibernating plants that had run wild over the decades into a Gordian knot of remembrance, love, and sadness. While none bloomed at this time of year, each plant spoke to her in the secret language she understood: celandine for family reunited in the afterlife, bluebells and daffodils for grief, dandelion for the fragility of life, *Amaranthus* for endless love. A lonely willow, stunted and dwarfed, wept over the tombs in earthly sorrow.

Except one. Hate. Francine recoiled in shock. It was the simplest of the graves, little more than a mound of earth and without a headstone. But every plant on it shrieked a terrible hatred. Monkshood thrust up amongst the dahlias; Francine didn't need to see a bloom to know they would be black, as would the skeletal rosebush. Tansy and St John's wort revealed hostility and animosity. She had no doubt that basil and lobelia would be in there too. Whoever was buried in that unmarked grave had been truly hated—a loathing that had endured and flourished through time in a dark floral chronicle.

With a shiver, Francine picked her way through the snarl of thick vines and prickled stems stretching across the path. But with each row she grew more agitated, lips moving silently as she read each name. In her anxiety, she lost some of her fear of the graveyard. She was barely aware of Todd moving to a corner, where he watched her with a puzzled expression.

She stopped at the last headstone, her stomach hurting from holding herself so stiffly, and shook her head in confusion.

"They're not here," she said.

"Who isn't here?" asked Todd, keeping a careful, neutral tone.

"Bree and Montgomery. They should be here!" she cried, shrill and distressed. "Madeleine said they'd be here, and they aren't!"

"They're right there," he said, nodding at an alcove off to one side, where two small tombstones huddled together. "Bree, Elizabeth Thwaite, born 30 September, 1961, died 26 July, 1969; and Montgomery, George Thwaite, born 19 November, 1968, died 26 July, 1969 . . . So young. And they both died on the same day."

Francine stumbled to the graves and dropped to her knees. She reached out a hesitant finger and traced the names.

Todd moved farther into the graveyard, leaving her alone with the dead. Her dead. Her brother and sister had been here all the time, a few hundred feet from the house.

A lovely old dogwood crouched above the two graves. It was one of Francine's favorite trees; in summer it was an eye-catching blaze of white. Montgomery's grave was a small, prickled field of crocuses that were just pushing their spring stems up through the soil.

A tear traced down her cheek unchecked. She hadn't cried in so long she wasn't sure how. A silent sob wracked her thin body as the walls she had built so carefully around herself started to crumble, swept away by a dam of overwhelming emotion.

"I am so sorry, Bree," she whispered.

She knelt before the graves for a long time, her heart withering with bittersweet sorrow that if not for Bree's presence in her life and the gravestones in front of her, it would have been as though her brother and sister had never existed.

26 July, 1969

"You're doing it wrong, Rosie!" scolded Agnes.

"Wrong?" Rosie, a smear of soil across her cheek, her plaited red hair a wild mess of leaves and twigs, looked down at her patch of the chamomile lawn in consternation. "The flowers are in the ground."

"They're the wrong way up!" snapped Agnes.

Rosie's mouth formed an O of understanding, then she squatted on her haunches and giggled to herself. "Silly, silly Rosie."

"Not silly Rosie," said Mummy with a warning glance at Agnes. "Just a young Rosie. I'll show you so you'll know next time." And even though she had shown Rosie how to plant seedlings many times before, Mummy carefully dug up the chamomile, their daisy-like flowers bent and soil laden, releasing their bruised scent of overripe apples. "Now, my flower, what can you tell me about chamomile?"

Rosie scrunched up her face. "Chamommomomile is a baboon?" she hazarded.

"Try again," said Mum. When it came to teaching her daugh-

ters the many properties of plants, she had the patience of a saint. The girls knew more about plants than was strictly healthy at their young ages—knowing that, while many were healing, so many could kill, and many did both.

"Chamommomomile is a baboo . . . a bab . . . ? Bree? What's that lucky word?"

"A boon," said Bree, drawing her attention away from her vigil of the manor to her little sister's fiercely concentrating face.

"Chamommomomile is a boon?" Rosie tried again.

"Almost," said Mummy, smiling. "A boon is chamomile to divert black curses . . . Now, say it three times so you remember."

With her hands behind her back, face screwed up and lifted to the sun as though it would supply the answers, Rosie dutifully recited the old litany.

It was just one of many that had passed down through the Thwaite women, all written in the vast old book kept in the kitchen, watermarked, annotated, added to by countless hands, and so heavy Bree could barely lift it. Mummy called it the Book of Shadows. Bree liked the sound of it. It spoke of secrets, and if there was one thing Bree loved, it was keeping secrets. But not as much as she loved wriggling secrets out of others.

"Now, tell me three things about chamomile," said Mum.

"Um . . ." began Rosie, biting her lip. She glanced at Bree, then at Agnes for help. Agnes's eyes narrowed, noticing that Rosie had first looked to Bree. Lips tight, she turned back to fiercely weeding the low border of St John's wort.

"Helps you sleep," Figjam supplied. Of all the girls, Figjam had a natural affinity for plants. If it had been any of her other sisters, Bree would've been jealous. Figjam's diligence in the garden and hanging on to Mum's every word had lent her an extraordinary knowledge of plant lore for a five-year-old girl. Personally, Bree found plants boring and only learnt what she had to.

"And it's good for allergies," Agnes threw over her shoulder, not to be outdone by a younger sister.

"*Let's get moving, Figjam,*" *whispered Bree, who was rarely able to sit still for more than a few minutes. She wanted to run and never stop. Run away from the cloying atmosphere that not even the sun could dispel. Leave her life behind if only for a few hours of stolen freedom.*

"*No! Mummy's going to let me plant the fennel. And I want to.*" *Her tone was almost defiant. It was rare for Figjam not to fall in with Bree's plans.*

Lips tight, a quick glance at the house, Bree quelled her nerves and nodded. She knew she ran a narrow second only to Mum in Figjam's affection. It was not something she begrudged her little sister, for Mum and Figjam were so similar in character and nature that it would've been impossible for them not to share a tighter bond than the ones Mum shared with her other children.

"*One more, Rosie . . . No, Fran. I know you know the answer, but you must let Rosie have a go otherwise she will never learn,*" *said Mum when Figjam opened her mouth to answer.*

"*This is going to take forever,*" *muttered Bree as Rosie stood in front of Mum, obviously clueless.*

"*Helps with pain,*" *muttered Figjam under her breath, "protects against curses, strengthens bones, helps with swelling." She said them over and over again in some vain hope that Rosie would hear her.*

"*Helps with swelling,*" *Bree called out when Rosie started to swish her skirt about, losing interest.*

Rosie beamed at Bree, then darted off across the lawn to Viola.

"*Mummy?*" *said Viola, who was happily turning circles and watching her dress balloon around her, having completely forgotten about finding asphodel in the graveyard. "Is Rosie still a crocus?"*

Rosie looked at her sister in surprise. "I am not a crocus. I am a rose because I'm Rosie."

Mum smiled. "You're still too young to be anything other than a crocus."

"I'm old! I'm three!"

Mum put her head to one side and regarded her daughter thoughtfully. "Well, perhaps . . ."

A breathlessness entered the garden, for there was a solemnity in the bestowment of a flower, and all the girls stopped what they were doing and turned to Rosie. Even the manor leaned in expectantly so it, too, would be part of the private ceremony.

Bree released the breath she'd been holding in a sigh when the hush was broken by Rosie's fit of nervous giggles.

"She should be a delphy," said Viola. "It's a happy flower and Rosie is always happy."

"Or she can be the same as me," said Agnes.

Bree smirked, gleefully noting that Agnes still avoided naming her flower aloud because she couldn't pronounce chrysanthemum properly. Secretly, she thought Agnes should've been a thistle, for she was prickly and mistrustful. She was sure Mum had just been kind when she gave chrysanthemums to Agnes; they symbolized honesty and truthfulness.

Mum appeared not to hear Agnes's suggestion. "Yes, I think delphiniums will be perfect for you, for you are always cheerful and you have a big heart."

Rosie grinned, allowing Viola to hug her before she, too, started turning circles to watch her skirt billow out like a twirling umbrella.

"I think He's out," Figjam whispered to Bree. "Mummy is always happier when he's not here," she added with that odd perceptiveness children have of their parents' relationship.

Bree glanced at the house again. Perhaps it had been her imagination after all that someone had been watching her while she'd been in the drawing room. She should've been relieved, but her stomach remained tight with disquiet.

She had to be sure. "Mum? Where is . . ." she began at the same time Agnes said, "What flower is Father?"

The spell of lazy sunlight and deep-scented plants broke with that simple question. Mum stiffened. It took a long moment before she half turned to Agnes with a strained, secretive expression. "Asclepias tuberosa," she murmured, as though to herself.

Bree frowned at Figjam. "What does Asclepias tuberosa *mean?" she whispered, as Figjam knew all the meanings of the flowers.*

"It's milkweed," she whispered back. She looked up at Mum with a serious frown. "It means 'leave me.'"

Bree nodded, her expression dark and fierce. "I wish he would."

"So does Mummy, I think."

The strain did not leave Mum's face when she turned to her daughters, noting their anxiety. "Keep at your chores, my flowers," she said, then hurried over to Monty and gathered him up in her arms when he chose that moment to wail his frustration. Maddie started crying too, her small fists bunching into Mum's skirt.

But it was too late to worry about chores. Rosie and Viola left their twisting game, and seeing Mummy was occupied with Monty and Maddie, they gravitated towards Bree. Agnes ran towards Bree too, then stopped, surprised by her natural reaction to run to her sister, not Mum.

"Calm down, all of you," said Mum. "He's not here; there's no need to get into a tizzy. The best thing is to keep busy."

And by degrees they all did calm, but it was a calmness which came from a shared proximity providing false security.

NINE

❧❀❧

"You're still here?" said Francine.

Todd sat on a tombstone a short distance away. She had completely forgotten about him.

He nodded, searching her face. "You ready to go?"

She nodded, relieved he hadn't asked her why she was sitting in front of a couple of headstones crying. She couldn't have borne questions. Numb from a grief she hadn't known she carried, she stumbled after Todd.

"I have to get back to work," he said when they walked into the garden. He cleared his throat, then shook his head and smiled at himself. "I, er, I . . . Will you be in this evening?"

Surprised by the question, Francine nodded. "I am always in."

"Good. I'll see you later then." He strode away across the lawn.

Picking up the handles of the forgotten wheelbarrow, Francine pushed it towards the back of the manor. There she stopped and peeked around the corner to see if Todd had definitely left. He had.

Still drained from her emotional outpouring, she added confusion to the list of emotions she would rather not be feeling right now. For Todd Constable did confuse her, in ways she had never been confused before.

Maccabee the cow strolled in from the woods and nudged Francine in the back, jolting her from her deliberations.

"You can wait," she said curtly, and trundled her wheelbarrow across the garden, followed by a single-minded Maccabee. She placed the empty bags back in the shed, cleaned the wheelbarrow, and leaned it against the wall without any awareness of what she was doing. Then she fed Maccabee, who was lowing grumpily.

Still lost in confused thought, she walked into the house. She stopped in the foyer. It was there again, that off-kilter sensation. Stronger than this morning, but not silent. A humming from the walls . . . no, not humming. Muttering, low and deep.

Francine put her ear to the nearest paneled wall. The age-darkened wood was oddly warm against her skin. She turned her head and frowned at the wall. Was the house talking to her? Certainly, she had always had an affinity to the house, but she was quite aware it was inanimate, and its moods were more . . . atmosphere; talking houses were in the realms of psychosis.

The muttering moved farther down the wall. Francine followed it to the drawing room. She stopped at the closed door, filled with that cobwebby sensation of fear that something dreadful lurked beyond. The muttering was louder here, more an argument in hushed, furious tones, though Francine couldn't make out the words.

She put her hand on the handle and turned it slowly. The faint odor of tobacco leached through the door, stale yet cloying.

Stepping back, heart beating too fast, Francine pressed herself against the wall opposite the drawing room, not taking her eyes off its closed door. The hushed argument retreated to a creeping susurration.

Unable to bear it any longer, Francine darted into the warmth of the kitchen. She shook herself mentally but couldn't shake the oppressive mood that trailed her like a shadow. It was probably just the ancient heating system making its presence felt; she only ever put it on when she had lodgers, as the oil was so expensive.

The best thing to stop her desperately swirling mind from exploding was to keep busy. She put a chicken in the oven and cut up a few potatoes. She went out to the vegetable garden to pull up a few late parsnips and the last of the leeks before heading back.

Francine paused on the threshold, then walked back slowly to stand under the oak tree. "Bree," she called softly.

The branches thrashed about in the wind that had risen again. Whether the little ghost was there or not, Francine couldn't tell.

"I know what happened to you," she said. "I know about you and Montgomery. I know that we are sisters . . . Why did you stay? Why have you not gone on to wherever the dead go?"

The oak tree continued to sway; there was no response from Bree.

Francine waited a full minute, then sighed and took the vegetables into the kitchen. She took her worries out on the leeks, cutting them into slivers as she ran everything through her head. But she was no nearer to understanding anything when she shoved the parsnips in with the chicken and the leeks into a pot of boiling water.

"Dinner ready?" asked Madeleine, coming into the kitchen.

Francine whipped around. "In a while," she said, her voice harsh. She cleared her throat. "I thought you'd gone out," she added, hoping her face had lost the blotchiness from her tear storm.

"I did. I needed to get out . . ."

"In this weather?"

Madeleine shrugged. "It's this house. I've had this wretched feeling ever since I arrived that the house doesn't want me here." She smiled self-consciously when Francine snorted in disbelief. "So I went into Hawkshead to see if anything had changed. Nothing had, as usual."

"What did you expect? That the world would change to spite you?"

"Change never harmed anyone. You could do with changing yourself, Franny. You could blunt that sharp tongue of yours for a start!"

Ignoring the barb, Francine moved to the kettle rather than face her sister. She put it on the stovetop and waited for it to boil before pouring two cups of tea without asking if Madeleine wanted one or not.

After placing a cup in front of her sister, who had seated herself at the table, Francine sat down opposite her. She took a deep breath. "I went to the graveyard earlier."

Madeleine's eyebrows rose. "You're full of surprises today. I'm amazed you listened to me and went there at all. You've always been terrified of graveyards."

"I'm not terrified of anything!" Francine glared at her sister. "I saw their graves," she added through gritted teeth.

"So now you know I was telling the truth."

"As far as the deaths of Bree and Montgomery are concerned." She swallowed hard before continuing. "And I spoke to Miss Cavendish this morning."

Madeleine frowned. "Why?"

"She was Mum's closest friend."

"Apart from you."

The bitterness in her sister's tone gave Francine pause. "Well . . . yes, I suppose. But what I'm trying to tell you is that Miss C was there on the night Bree and Montgomery drowned. She was part of the search." She looked out the window where the gale tugged at the dormant ivy on the courtyard walls. "They drowned in the well."

"What? Our well? That well?" Madeleine paled. "I had thought . . . I thought they'd drowned in Esthwaite."

"What made you think that?"

It was a long moment before Madeleine shook her head and said, "I suppose because Mum told us our father had drowned there."

"And you put two and two together and made five."

"There's no need to be nasty," snapped Madeleine.

An apology hovered on Francine's lips. She swallowed it, for she was angry . . . yes, angry with Madeleine. If she hadn't come home, Francine's life would still be nicely ordered, as she liked it. There was something to be said for the adage that ignorance was bliss; she wished she could turn back the last twenty-four hours and still be in blissful ignorance. She sighed, knowing she was being unreasonable. She wanted to blame someone for her scattered thoughts and broken heart, and Madeleine was an easy target.

"What did Miss C say?" asked Madeleine when the silence stretched.

Francine told her everything, though she couldn't look at her sister for fear that her reproachful thoughts were plastered across her face.

"Six girls for one boy. He must've really hated us," said Madeleine in a small voice. "And when Montgomery died, his claim to the manor was gone."

"They could've had more children."

"True. Why didn't they?"

"Hatred," said Francine softly. "Miss C said they hated each other by the time Montgomery was born."

"It doesn't sound like that would've stopped a man like him . . . I wonder what happened to him?" Madeleine spoke of their father with the remoteness one would for a stranger. But that's what he was. No more than a title for a man neither could remember.

"I only know what Miss C told me, and that was little enough. No one seems to know what happened to him and our sisters . . . She really didn't like him. He sounded like an utterly horrible man. Poor Mum."

"Poor Mum who lied to us," muttered Madeleine.

Francine scowled. She had thought long and hard about her mum today, until she got to the point where she decided to trust her mum's decision to keep quiet until she knew more of what had happened. "Maybe she lied to protect us," she said, feeling her way around the tentative idea. "From something so terrible she kept it secret, knowing the knowledge would damage us."

Madeleine's green eyes widened with horror. She leaned across the table and whispered, "What if he killed them?"

"Mrs C doesn't think—" Francine began, but was waved off by Madeleine, who had an idea in her head she was determined to run with.

"That could've been Mum's secret! Think about it, Franny! Five children to die or disappear in the space of one night—it can't be an accident. Maybe Mum saw him do it, or knew he did it, and she couldn't bear to tell us that our father was a murderer. And you said Miss C said he was an utter bastard. What if he killed Montgomery and Bree, then ran away in a fit of remorse?"

Francine rubbed a hand across her face. She was deathly tired, drained of all emotion, so it was hard to deal with Madeleine hatching dramatic theories. The sum of their knowledge was a few scratched names in the parish records, two tombstones, and secondhand memories from Miss Cavendish. It wasn't enough to form even the vaguest of theories.

"You don't know that he killed anyone," said Francine her tone dampening. "And there was an inquest that said the drowning was an accident. Why would he run away if it was an accident? Even Miss C doesn't think he had anything to do with it. And he would never have harmed Montgomery if he wanted to claim the manor."

"Well, I think he killed them."

"Enough!" Francine cried. "Neither of us has any idea what happened. There is no point in speculating. All it will do is wind us both up."

Madeleine glared at her mutinously. But she relented almost immediately, no match for Francine's returning cool gaze.

"You're right. Of course, you're right, and . . ." She smiled suddenly. "You realize we have three sisters out there somewhere?"

"I know, but how will we find them after all this time?" Her jaw hurt from holding it so tight, holding herself together so Madeleine didn't see the cracks that had formed today. She dropped her gaze to her teacup. The leaves had stewed just long enough. Thankful for the distraction, she gulped down her tea, scalding her throat.

Oblivious to her sister's watchful eyes, she tipped the dregs of tea into the saucer and looked for symbols in the leaves left in the cup.

"What do you see?" asked Madeleine when Francine frowned in consternation.

"A ship, a closed book, a heart, and . . ." She tilted the saucer slightly and gasped. "A comb."

"So you'll be going on a journey where you won't be able to read, and maybe find love as long as you brush your hair," said Madeleine blithely.

Francine ignored her. "A ship does mean a journey," she said slowly, "and a heart can mean love or trust. An open book is good news, and I think a closed book is . . ." She frowned. "I think a closed book means I need to investigate something." Her eyes were drawn to the comb, a symbol she had seen earlier in the leaves, not long before Madeleine had arrived. "A comb means an enemy," she said, her tone bleak with apprehension.

Madeleine leaned forward with ghoulish interest. "I can't imagine you know enough people to have an enemy."

She was right, of course. Francine knew very few people, and no one she knew was likely to be an enemy. A love interest, ditto. But that did nothing to alleviate the quiver of disquiet streaking through her veins.

She peered at the ship shaped in the tea leaves and shook her head. She had no intention of going on a journey. She hadn't been further than Kendal, not twenty miles away. The only symbol that might have any bearing on her future was the closed book. She did want to investigate something. She wanted to know what had happened the night Bree and Montgomery drowned in the well. In the hope of finding her sisters, she needed to find out where her father run to.

Francine and Madeleine had an early dinner in the kitchen. The wind careered around the house; it wouldn't be long before the storm broke. They said little; Francine had never mastered the art of idle chitchat, and Madeleine was too lost in her own thoughts. But they were both thinking of their family's fractured history. It was impossible not to.

After dinner, with the plates washed up, Francine moved to the front parlor with Madeleine tagging along behind her.

Most nights, when she was alone, Francine read or played a game of cards with Bree. But she could not be bothered to read, and Bree had made it obvious she wouldn't come back into the house.

"Would you like to play a game?" she asked Madeleine half-heartedly.

Madeleine shrugged, just as reluctant to spend time with her sister as Francine was.

Francine went to a small cabinet tucked in the corner and pulled out a tattered box of Monopoly.

Both women perked up when they heard a car drive up to the house. Doors slammed before heavy footsteps sounded in the foyer.

Todd's head appeared around the door. "Evening, ladies," he said, a little startled by their expressions of relief at the sight of him. Keefe hulked in the background. Todd spied the box of Monopoly Francine had clasped to her chest like a shield. "I wondered how you passed the time in the evenings," he said, coming into the room.

"Would you like a game?" Madeleine asked with a winsome smile and a lot more enthusiasm than she'd shown a few minutes before.

Francine's eyebrows shot up. Her sister's demeanor had changed from boredom to a vivacious hostess, like a split personality. She shook her head in disbelief. Madeleine was impossible around men.

"Sounds good." Todd grabbed Keefe's arm and pulled him into the room.

Francine took out a folding table from beside the cabinet, surprised by how angry she was at her sister.

"I'll take that," said Todd and placed the table in the center of the room. He winked at Francine.

She frowned at him. No one had ever winked at her before, and she wasn't sure how to interpret it.

They sat down and began to play.

"How are you enjoying the Lake District?" asked Madeleine, her voice dropping to a husky breathiness as though she were bestowing an intimate confidence, which made Francine scowl at the board.

"It's been surprisingly interesting," said Todd and began dealing out the money. He smiled at Francine conspiratorially.

"But you must miss London. I love seeing Franny, of course, but I miss the bustle of a big city. It's so quiet here." Madeleine laughed huskily for no apparent reason.

Francine's scowl deepened. No one laughed like that unless they'd smoked all their lives, and Madeleine had never smoked, as far as she knew.

"Can't say I miss London at all."

"There's no TV here," interjected Keefe moodily. "And I've never really played board games. That's for old people."

"We *are* old people," said Todd. "If you don't want to play, go read a book. It will do you good."

"If there was decent reception, I could use my tablet," said Keefe, unable to let a good grouch go.

"Who are you calling old?" said Madeleine, horrified at being categorized as one of the old people. "I'm only . . ." a slight hesitation ". . . forty-seven!"

Francine hid her grin and muttered, "Fifty-one."

With Madeleine glaring daggers at her, Francine decided she might enjoy the game after all and set out to win.

She didn't say much but concentrated on the game, trying to ignore Madeleine flirting with Todd. She wasn't even sure why it bothered her. Her sister was a flirt and always had been, yet she wished Madeleine wouldn't flirt with him. He was her lodger, not a guest. It wasn't seemly.

Todd threw his hands up in defeat when Francine won. "You are too good, Francine."

"I'll put on some coffee," said Madeleine, standing up gracefully.

"Not for us. Keefe and I are off to bed. Early start tomorrow."

Keefe's chair almost toppled over as he leapt up in his haste not to endure another game, and he was out the door with a mumbled goodnight.

"Oh, so soon?" said Madeleine with a pout. "We can't entice you with one more game?"

"I've had enough too," said Francine firmly, and began packing away the pieces. "But I will have a coffee if it's still on offer."

Madeleine hesitated, then flounced off to the kitchen.

"How are you feeling now?" asked Todd the moment Madeleine was out of earshot.

Francine blinked. "I'm fine. Why wouldn't I be?"

"I was a little worried about leaving you this afternoon."

Mortified that her lack of emotional restraint was being brought up, Francine hid her face by shoving the last few pieces in the box before getting up and stashing it back in the cabinet.

"You seem . . . different."

"I'm fine," she said, her back to him. "It was nothing."

She tensed when she heard him move behind her. "Do you want to talk about it?"

"I don't want to talk about anything!" she snapped, turning to face him. She shut her eyes briefly when he backed off, startled by her fierceness. "Sorry, that was uncalled for."

Todd eyed her warily, then gave her a hesitant smile. "Well, I do. I was, er, going to ask if you would like to have dinner with me one evening, but perhaps now is not the time."

"Pardon?" she said, not sure she had heard correctly.

He cleared his throat and half turned away. "I feel like a teenager, it's ridiculous," he muttered to himself. Then he looked Francine in the eye. "Francine, would you please go out to dinner with me?"

"What on earth for?" she asked, bemused as a blush crept up her throat.

He threw his head back and laughed. It was a wonderful sound; deep, melodious, contagious peals filled the parlor with warmth.

Francine didn't see what was so funny. She glared at Todd until he stopped laughing.

"You truly are the most unusual woman I've met," he said. "I'm asking you out on a date!"

"Oh," she said, nonplussed, then, "Ohhh!" with belated understanding. "But I've never been on a date before."

"What? Never?" He shook his head and laughed again.

"What's so funny about that?" she demanded, her blush creeping up to her face, flattered in spite of herself.

"Why have you never been on a date?"

She shrugged. "No one asked me. Anyway, I'm not one for all that sort of thing. You're best off asking Madeleine to dinner. She would know what to do."

"I know exactly which sister I wish to have dinner with, and you don't have to do anything, just be yourself . . . Think about it." Todd strode out the room and was gone before Francine could respond.

Dazed, she put her hands to her cheeks. They were warm; she was blushing furiously. Her body was giving her away in a most unseemly fashion. Granted, Todd Constable was attractive, and he had surprised her with his request to dine with him. But to blush like a schoolgirl at the age of fifty-five?

She shook her head, then stopped. And what would be so terrible about dinner with an attractive man? It was only dinner, not a marriage proposal. Except . . . Todd made her feel comfortable and uncomfortable at the same time. She wasn't sure if she liked the sensation or not, whether she liked *him* or not.

No, that was a lie. She did like him, but it was more than that. A bond had formed between them this afternoon. Something had broken inside Francine in the graveyard. Her heart, perhaps. Shattered childhood impressions. But there had also been a melting of the ironclad defences she had built around herself. And Todd had witnessed the breaking and melting.

Madeleine returned, carrying a tray. "Where has Todd gone?"

"Todd?" echoed Francine, confused.

"Todd Constable. Your lodger."

"I know his name," said Francine waspishly. "But when did you start being on first-name terms with him?"

Madeleine shrugged. "He asked me to call him Todd yesterday when you went off into the woods."

Francine gritted her teeth. "I'm going out," she muttered.

"In this?" said Madeleine. "There's a gale blowing out there."

Francine shrugged and left the room. She grabbed her mum's old Barbour and picked up a pouch of herbs before wrestling the door open. "Bree," she called once in the garden. It was a half-hearted call, for the devil himself wouldn't have heard her above the screaming gale that crashed and thrashed through Lonehowe Wood.

She had just started scattering herbs around the boundary of the garden when she froze, eyes wide. The flicker of light came again, from the woods, the briefest glint that was quickly overwhelmed by a tremendous gust of wind that screeched past her, so fierce it blew her bunned hair free to tangle wildly around her face. She could *see* the wind. Dead leaves, twigs, and hissing sleet slashed and dashed about in a frenetic dance. The deafening eruption rushed past her and hit the manor in an explosion of breaking glass. The leaning clocktower swayed alarmingly. Francine held her breath, waiting for it to topple over as the wind crashed into it. The tower tilted, then righted itself as the devilish wind tore through to the other side of Lonehowe Wood.

A muffled crash from inside the house.

Francine broke into a run, wrenched the front door open and dashed through the foyer, crying, "Madeleine?"

Another crash sent her rushing into the front parlor. Exploding destruction greeted her horrified eyes.

In the middle of it all Madeleine cowered, her arms protecting her head from flying glass as a tremendous downdraft from the chimney battered the parlor, clashing with the wind streaming in through the shattered windows that set the curtains flapping madly.

"Madeleine!" Francine cried, pulling her sister to her feet.

The downdraft strengthened, blowing up glass splinters. The sisters scuttled to the doorway to watch, dumbfounded, as the howling wind battered the room like a bedeviled dervish.

"I've never seen anything like this before," whispered Madeleine, gripping Francine's arm hard.

"Nor have I." Eyes darting between snarls and tearing crooks of air, a horrible realization slid into Francine's mind. This wasn't natural.

Her lips tightened with fury. "Bree!" she shouted. "Stop making this racket right now!"

"Are you insane?" hissed Madeleine, gripping Francine's arm tighter. "This is not Bree! It's the storm!"

Francine shook off her sister's restraining hand and stepped just into the parlor. The furious air spun around her until her unpinned hair swept around her face like seaweed in a storm.

"Bree?" she shouted again, the quaver of doubt in her voice quelled by her anger. She could sense the little ghost's presence. But Bree was mischievous and playful, never destructive. A pinching cold shuddered through her. Something else was here, something malicious and malevolent, something that didn't belong.

She turned wide, frightened eyes to Madeleine and allowed her sister to drag her back to the temporary safety of the doorway.

"It's not Bree. She isn't real!" cried Madeleine. "You know this isn't Bree. It's just a freak wind."

Francine shook her head violently. "Bree *is* here, but she's not alone."

Madeleine expression creased in confusion, then in dismay. "Francine . . ." she began, then whipped around at a crash from the kitchen as a blast of cold air flung through the open back door.

Lips tight against the fear tingling in every pore, Francine cried, "Get behind me!"

Madeleine didn't hesitate and got behind Francine, who felt her tremble before realizing she was trembling just as hard.

The cold air twisted into a funnel and reached out towards the women.

The pouch was still clasped tightly in Francine's hand. She pulled out a handful of herbs and threw them at the cold air.

A horrible, unearthly shriek ripped through the parlor and the ethereal whirlwind writhed away. The herbs snaked and mixed with the shattered glass still flying about the room, gouging the yellow wallpaper.

"What was that?" Madeleine whispered.

"Agrimony and horehound."

"It won't work!" Madeleine wailed just as a shaft of warm air flung itself down the chimney and smashed into the cold, pushing it towards the center of the room. "It's a storm, Francine! Just a storm."

"Bree's trying to protect us!" cried Francine, her eyes flickering from hot to cold, a terrible gusting of invisible violence. Above the clash came an awful high-pitched scream that grated on frayed nerves.

"We must help her!" Francine pushed Madeleine into the foyer, then half turned as the ghastly scream followed them. For a few seconds, the image of a man materialized amid the raging cold tempest—mouth open, face contorted with hatred before the warm air smashed into him.

"Keep it together," Francine snapped at Madeleine, who was sobbing with terror, then she marched through to the kitchen with Madeleine hard on her heels. She was not having any of it. This was *her* home! Her mum had taught her how to deal with evil. She shut the back door, which had been forced open by the storm.

Opening drawers, Francine pulled out a few pouches, then reached up to the dried herbs hanging from the ceiling and pulled them all down.

Back to the foyer she scattered a thick pile of herbs along the threshold of the dining room.

"What are you doing?" Madeleine asked, watching Francine in bemusement.

"We must protect ourselves. Protect the house."

"With what? Your stupid herbs?" hissed Madeleine, scuttling after her sister, who tore from room to room, pouring herbs along each doorway, then scattering them all over the stairs that led to the upper floors.

Ignoring the jibe, she snapped, "Shut up and get ready."

"Ready for what?" It was a fearful whisper and a more fearful glance that Madeleine gave Francine's tight expression, as though concerned for her sister's sanity.

"I don't know."

Francine cautiously approached the parlor. The colliding air kinked and curled. A fixed shelf was wrenched away from the wall and flew at the twist of cold air that whipped up then dove towards the fireplace. Bree's small image appeared, flickering on the mantelpiece, her lips drawn back in a feral snarl.

"Bree!" Francine shrieked as the little ghost leapt onto the screaming specter.

Bree was absorbed into the writhing air that emitted a shriek that almost burst Francine's eardrums, followed by a dreadful whimpering that broke her heart.

"Bree!" she shouted. "Get into the fireplace right now!" And she rushed into the parlor, throwing up a cloud of herbs.

Yarrow . . . Betony . . . Figwort . . . Vervain . . . It rained down as a flash of warmth brushed against Francine and disappeared into the fireplace.

A tormented screech stabbed the darkest part of Francine's soul. Frantic. Wild. A frenzied coil of cold air rose to the ceiling, then bolted down, pushing against her.

Francine stood her ground and yelled, "Get out of my house!" Then she ran from the room, grabbing an openly gaping Madeleine as she passed.

They raced across the foyer, a bitter, cold fury on their heels.

"Open the front door, then follow me!" cried Francine, releasing Madeleine before darting into the dining room.

Madeleine didn't dare disobey her sister. She yanked the door open and pelted into the dining room as the cold air launched itself after them, then shrieked as it slammed against the open doorway as though something physical barred its entry to the dining room.

Francine's protection held.

"It's angry," whispered Francine, ignoring Madeleine's nails digging into her arm.

The blaze of cold rage smashed and crashed about the foyer, searching for entry and finding none. A beseeching wail of thwarted fury ripped through the old building before it blasted through the open front door, out into the night.

The manor sagged into a breathing silence. There was no proud elation in victory, merely exhaustion.

Tapping came from the roof, lightly at first, then harder, as the wind gave way to rain.

Francine pulled away from Madeleine and raced to the front parlour.

"Bree?" she whispered. "It's alright. It's gone. You can come out now."

A quiet sobbing came from the fireplace. It faded as a warm draft of air shot up the chimney when feet thundered down the stairs.

Francine and Madeleine, their faces equally white with shock, turned to Todd and Keefe as they screeched into the parlor.

"Holy shit!" breathed Keefe, surveying the destruction created in only a few minutes with deep admiration.

An explanation was needed, but Francine's throat convulsed so hard she couldn't speak. All the fear she had restrained flooded in, and she started to shiver. She glanced at her sister pleadingly.

"It was the storm," Madeleine offered without needing a question asked, a quaver of terror still in her voice. "The wind shattered all the windows. Look!" She jabbed a finger at the windows that even now allowed the slanting rain to leave puddles on the wooden floor. "We get really severe storms here," she added. "Something to do with the geological formation of the lake system and the fells."

Francine glanced at her sister, gobsmacked, then at Todd. He was frowning at the sodden herbs lying amidst the fragmented glass.

"Did you hear that god-awful racket upstairs?" said Keefe. "Sounded like demons from hell were screaming from the walls."

"That was the central heating system," said Todd. His gaze rose to Francine, his frown deepening. "Didn't you hear it?"

"The central . . ." Francine broke off and glanced at Madeleine, who shrugged.

"Is that what it was?" said Keefe. "I thought it was the ghosts again. Making one helluva noise."

Todd shook his head in exasperation.

"I'm telling you, there's ghosts here, Todd. I can *feel* them. Especially on nights like these. They're made for all sorts of nasty ghoulies to come out and scare the living bejesus out of folk. And did you see the lights? Just before the storm? The woods were flickering like crazy." He shivered. "Like jack-o'-lanterns," he added darkly.

Francine's eyebrows rose in surprise. She had forgotten about seeing the lights in the woods before the storm. It had been a brief sighting and had completely slipped her mind. It was years since she'd seen them herself, and she wasn't sure what to make of their reappearance.

With another shake of his head, this time in exasperation, Todd smiled at Madeleine and Francine. "Ladies, you've both had a bit of a fright. Why don't you go to bed and leave this to Keefe and I? I'm sure there's something we can use to board up the windows for tonight to stop any further damage from the storm. I'll sort out replacement glass tomorrow."

"That's very kind of you," said Madeleine before Francine had even opened her mouth to reject his offer.

Francine seemed incapable of moving and Madeleine pulled at her arm. Francine took one last look around the room. It still had a pressurized feeling, as though the storm had not yet broken, yet it was otherwise empty.

Madeleine smiled at the men as she forced Francine out into the foyer and led the way upstairs.

TEN

The sisters went to Francine's room. Neither wanted to be alone, and for Francine, this was the biggest shock after so many. She needed the presence of another living human, and she was glad it was her sister; Madeleine would understand what had just happened.

"Did you see anything?" Francine said the moment the door closed.

"See what?"

Francine frowned. "There was something in the parlor."

Madeleine's face grew uncharacteristically shuttered. "It was just the wind, Franny. There's always been downdrafts in that room. It was just the storm."

"No! Something was in there with Bree! She was fighting it. Something—something evil." She stared at her sister, then her lips tightened. "What have you brought home with you?"

Madeleine gaped at her. "Have you lost your mind?"

"Ever since you came home the house has felt different, and tonight . . ." She sat on the bed and tried to remember the moment Madeleine had entered the house yesterday. Then she closed her eyes in dismay. Madeleine had asked to come in, and she had responded: *You and all the rest.* How could she have been so stupid?

She looked at her sister, who was watching her with concern. "You've somehow managed to attract an evil spirit and brought it home with you," she said calmly, though she felt anything but calm. "You'll have to leave. You can't stay here. I will have no truck with evil."

Madeleine's eyes widened, then glistened with tears. "You're kicking me out?"

"Yes . . . no!" Francine tried to gather her scattered thoughts. "I'm sorry, Maddie," she said quietly, using the diminutive she hadn't used in years. "This is your home too. That was uncalled for."

Astonished, Madeleine said, "I don't think I've ever had an apology from you before."

"That's because you haven't deserved one before," Francine snapped.

"Aren't your ridiculous herbs meant to keep evil out?" Madeleine snapped back, even as a tear rolled down her cheek.

"The herbs won't keep out a spirit that's been invited in." Francine rubbed her face, bone weary. Madeleine was wrong. They did keep evil out, but if an evil spirit had been invited in, no amount of protection in the world could stop it from entering.

She stood abruptly. "You need to get rid of this spirit you've brought here."

"And how am I supposed to do that?"

"Ask your husband. You said he conducted sèances and such."

"Sebastian? He's my *ex*-husband." Madeleine pulled a face, then shrugged. "Anyway, I just went along with it to humor him. And I haven't seen Sebastian in four years! Surely this spirit of yours wouldn't wait four years before making an appearance."

This gave Francine pause. Why *would* a spirit wait so long to manifest?

"I think you should see someone," said Madeleine, her voice low and calm into the silence that formed.

"What?"

"I was married to a psychiatrist for a while . . ." Madeleine began.

Francine rolled her eyes. "Of course you were."

"And I think he would say that you had some sort of psychotic episode during the storm."

"Couldn't you feel it?" Francine hissed. "The menace? It was here in our home, using the storm to get in."

"It was just a storm, Francine! Just a storm, nothing else. There were no ghosts, menacing or otherwise. Just a terrible storm."

"Why are you being so stubborn?" Francine cried with unnecessary vehemence to counteract the smidge of doubt creeping into her mind.

Madeleine stared at her sister with haunted eyes. "Because none of this makes sense. I don't believe in ghosts. I never have." Then in a whisper, "And because I can't bear for you to be right."

Francine rubbed her face hard. It had been a long day; she had cried for the first time since a child, been terrified out of her wits, and she was filled with sadness, belatedly grieving for Montgomery and Bree.

She avoided her sister's expression of concern, then said, "Bree was here. She was protecting us."

Madeleine rolled her eyes at the ceiling in frustration. "So, just for the sake of argument, why would she do that?"

"I don't know, and I can't even ask her because she won't come near me."

Madeleine plopped down on the bed beside Francine. "I'm sleeping with you tonight," she said with a small shiver. "There is no way I am going back to my room after all this talk of ghosts."

Francine nodded.

She loaned a nightdress to her sister, who eyed its vintage with disdain, shared Francine's toothbrush, then climbed into her narrow bed.

It was a tight fit, but neither complained, each taking comfort in their proximity.

Madeleine was a fidgeter. She wrestled with the quilt for a while, then quieted. Francine thought she had fallen asleep when she whispered, "Just for the sake of argument, why didn't you use asafoetida? Even I know it's supposed to totally destroy a spirit . . . *Burnt stench of asafoetida to wreck black souls.*"

"You have to burn asafoetida, otherwise it won't work, and it clears all energies, good and bad. It would've destroyed Bree too."

Madeleine was quiet for a moment; Francine could almost hear her sister's mind mulling things over. "What about asphodel? *A path to the hereafter asphodel will reveal.*"

"It would've sent Bree into the afterlife too."

Madeleine sighed. "It's always about Bree for you, isn't it?"

"Yes," said Francine slowly. "I think it always has been, even when she was alive."

"I hate her sometimes."

Francine wriggled around so they were nose to nose. "Why?" she whispered, hurt. "Bree's never done you any harm."

It was a long time before Madeleine whispered back, "Because I wanted you to be *my* sister. Just mine. But it was always you and Bree . . . It's hard to take second place to an imaginary friend. When we were small, you were always off in the woods with Bree, doing whatever you two did, and I always wanted to join in, but you wouldn't let me. I-I wanted Bree to be my imaginary friend, too, so you would spend time with me."

It was Francine's turn to pause before answering. "I didn't know you felt like that."

The pillow shifted with Madeleine's shrug. "Would it have made a difference if you had?"

Another pause, then, "No, probably not."

Francine lay still, squinting at her sister's shadowed features, waiting for her to say something else. Instead, all she got were quiet snores a few minutes later.

Rolling onto her back, Francine listened to the rain, hoping it would lull her to sleep. She played over what had happened in the parlor again and again, and with each replay, Madeleine's skepticism colored Francine's certainty. Perhaps nothing unnatural *had* occurred and she had imagined it all. Except Bree. Her only certainty was that Bree had been there, and she had been terrified.

The night deepened and slowly the storm abated, leaving the outside world sodden and silent. The night noises of the house reclaimed the darkness. Dull creaks, furtive scratching, and a persistent low muttering from the walls. The manor crouched over Francine, heavy, shuttered, and oppressive.

Francine pretended sleep until she felt Madeleine get out of bed and leave the room. When dressed, she hurried downstairs and stopped in the foyer, frowning. Light through the stained-glass door patterned the dark floor, and she could just make out a wisp of smoke as it crept from below the drawing room's closed door.

The faint odor of tobacco roamed around the foyer. Not stale, but fresh, and from a pipe. Cherry and maple. A pleasant fragrance, yet it sent a twitching shiver through her. She stared hard at the drawing room door, even took a step towards it, hand outstretched.

A noise from within the house startled her. A gasp. Her own. She whipped around, a hand to her chest, heart beating too fast.

Silence wrapped around her, a spiteful silence. Tight. Tense. It squeezed with the sensation that someone was watching her from the shadows, yet she knew if she turned around, no one would be there.

She forced herself to calm down by degrees, with deep breaths. When she felt able, she glanced at the drawing room door again, then called herself every kind of stupid. There was nothing there. No smoke leaked underneath the door, it was merely dust motes dancing on the patterned light.

Taking herself and her unruly imagination in hand, Francine straightened her shoulders and stalked through to the parlor . . . and stared.

The parlor was spotless: chairs and tables back in their places, the shelf back on the wall, a box stood in the corner, filled with glass and broken ornaments that no amount of glue could fix. All that remained to show for last night's violence were the scratch marks in the wallpaper and the boarded windows, which left the room in an unlovely gloom.

And in that unlovely gloom, Francine's certainty from last night that something malevolent had stormed into the house shriveled to nothing but doubtful whispers.

"Amazing, isn't it?" said Madeleine, peering in through the doorway.

Francine nodded. "Mr. Constable did this?"

"Yes. He must really like you to go to all that effort."

"What makes you say that? He's only just met me."

"Which you could say about almost everyone you've met in your life. No one *knows* you, even when they've known you for years. You're the most restrained, self-contained person I know." Madeleine sounded almost sad.

Francine didn't know what to say.

"Take it from me. I know men, and Todd would not have done this if he didn't like you."

"Oh." Warmth spread from Francine's chest to her face. She turned away, lest Madeleine see.

"Maybe it's time to let someone get close to you," said Madeleine softly.

"I'm perfectly fine by myself," Francine retorted. "I'm going out," she added, already marching towards the foyer.

"Where are you going?"

"Out!" Francine grabbed her coat, a handful of fennel seeds, and her burdock bracelet, then stalked out, slamming the door behind her.

She stopped, startled by the sight of Todd on the lawn, gazing up at the roof of the manor with a worried frown. He saw Francine and his frown dissolved into a warm smile. "Good morning."

Francine nodded and came to stand beside him. She, too, looked up at the manor, her heart sinking. The old building cringed like a whipped dog. The many windows reflected the hurrying clouds with a sullen watchfulness and the expectation of another beating.

"You lost a few tiles during the storm," said Todd. "I should be able to find replacements at a reclamation yard that will be in keeping with the age of the house. But the clock tower, as you can see, has subsided even more." He glanced at Francine out the corner of his eye to gauge her reaction.

She kept her eyes firmly on the house.

"And your central heating needs urgent attention. There's a strong possibility you have leaks in the piping and that could create all sorts of problems. . . . Do you know how old it is?"

Francine shrugged and hazarded, "A hundred years, more or less." She sighed deeply. "Look, Mr. Constable. As you have pointed out, there are a great many things that need fixing, but every repair you've mentioned needs a great deal of money and that's something I don't have a lot of. So, I shall add the central heating to the list and get around to it when my finances permit."

Todd rubbed his chin. "I could help you there. I have a mate who could do it for the cost of the materials if you put him up here while he's doing the work."

He grinned broadly when Francine's jaw dropped at his generous offer. "You get to know a lot of other trades in my line of work."

"I—" At a loss for words, Francine found herself nodding when she knew she should be shaking her head. She didn't want his charity, and yet her head was still nodding. "Well, perhaps the central heating," she conceded. She gave him a tight smile. "That is most kind of you."

"No problem." He took in the coat draped over her arm. "Are you going down to Hawkshead? We were just about to leave. Would you like a lift?"

"No, I think you've offered quite enough already, and I prefer to walk." And with that, she nodded at Todd and strode past him.

She hesitated at the path through Lonehowe Wood. She didn't want to take the shortcut but knew Todd would drive right past her on the road; it would make her look like a stubborn idiot for not accepting his offer of a lift.

Gripping the fennel seeds tightly in her hand, she took the path.

The moment the trees closed around her, her thoughts turned to more pressing problems than central heating and collapsing clock towers. She had spent all night thinking and was no nearer an answer. Doubt strode beside her, jabbing its elbows into her side every few meters. Perhaps Madeleine was right and she'd been insane last night, seeing things that weren't there. And what had she seen? Nothing but air . . . air shaped like . . . something almost physical. No, it was probably all in her head. And yet . . . And yet something was wrong with Thwaite Manor. For the first time in her memory, the manor felt imbued with a brooding bitterness, an atmosphere so unfamiliar that her friendly ghosts would no longer come into the house.

There was a queue of tourists waiting for the bus to Ambleside. Waiting impatiently with them, Francine scowled at the flood of yet more tourists who got off the bus when it arrived before she could climb on board. Paying for a return ticket, she took the single seat at the front so she wouldn't be bothered by the other passengers.

Sam Woodall, she pondered as the bus lumbered along the banks of Lake Windermere. She didn't remember a Sam Woodall. He would probably be about eighty or more now.

Another bus and through the forbidding, scree-strewn fells towards Keswick, where Francine took to fretting. She had never had any dealings with the police before and wasn't sure how one spoke to a policeman, albeit a retired one. Could she ask a policeman questions? Usually, it was the other way around. And what if they had some sort of confidentiality code, like lawyers and doctors?

It was only when she arrived in Keswick that she realized the tea leaves had read true once more; she was on a journey, the farthest she'd ever been from Thwaite Manor. It wasn't more than twenty-five miles, but she could've been in a foreign country for the anxiety it caused. It didn't help that Francine hated Keswick on sight. It was modern and big: two things she couldn't stand in most things.

Resigned to a day of buses, Francine climbed onto one bound for Seatoller. The weather had turned to drizzle and mist, which rather suited her gloomy mood. She peered out at the passing houses of Keswick that gave way to the shrouded fells of Cat Bells around Derwent Water; the peaks loomed in and out of the gloom like islands that no longer existed on maps.

It was easy to find the address for Sam Woodall after a quick query at the pub, as Seatoller village consisted of one street under the watchful eye of the mighty Honister Pass. His was a small slate house with a neat garden Francine approved of and a bright red door.

The door opened almost as soon as Francine knocked, as though her approach had been noted from a twitch of a curtain.

Sam Woodall had a gentle face under a shock of white, wind-blown hair, which widened into a smile and a crisscross of wrinkles indicating a life spent mostly outdoors.

"Good morning," said Francine stiffly. "I am Francine Thwaite."

"One of the Hawkshead Thwaites?" he asked, eyeing her with interest.

She nodded.

"And why would a Thwaite come all the way to Seatoller?"

"I believe you were the policeman called out when my brother and sister drowned."

"Ah. So, it's come to that, has it? Well, I was that." He gazed at Francine for a moment before he stepped aside, waving a hand for her to enter.

Sam Woodall led the way down a short, dark corridor, through a small kitchen, and into a conservatory attached to the back of the house.

And there Francine stood transfixed.

Orchids. They were everywhere. On the floor, on windowsills, on shelves along the walls, and hung suspended from the ceiling so they appeared to float. Two worn leather chairs with a table between them stood in the center of the room.

She turned on the spot, marveling at the sheer magnificence. "What a wonderful secret garden."

Woodall smiled in delight. "It's strange you should say that. I have always considered this my secret place . . . Take a seat."

Francine sat primly on the edge of one of the leather chairs.

"I had just put the kettle on," said Woodall. "Would you care for a cup of tea?"

"Bags or leaves?"

"Leaves."

"Yes, please."

As soon as he disappeared into the kitchen, Francine leapt up to have a better look at the orchids. Woodall had a wonderful collection. Some of the blooms she had only seen in books, and she felt a deep envy, having never managed to grow orchids with the same success her mum had achieved.

"Here you go." Woodall came into the room with a small tray. He placed it on the table. "So, Ms. Thwaite . . ."

"Francine will do," she said, taking the proffered cup, wishing now she hadn't accepted the offer of tea. The humidity in the conservatory was stifling.

"Francine. Why do you wish to speak to me?"

Clearing her throat, she said, "I'll come straight to the point. I want to know what happened to my brother and sister. I *need* to know."

To give Sam Woodall his due, he wasn't even slightly taken aback by her brisk tone. "Why now? They drowned fifty years ago."

Francine stared down at her teacup, marshaling her thoughts. "I've only just learned about it, but I don't remember what happened. I don't think I was there at the time."

"You were there," said Woodall. "But it's not surprising you don't remember; you couldn't have been older than five or six."

"I was five."

He regarded his orchids for a moment, rubbing a finger under his nose, then said, "I remember that night, clear as day. Your mum called me out because she couldn't find three of you. There was the baby boy and the eldest girl . . . can't remember her name now. A live wire, that one. Great girl with red hair and freckles."

"Bree," said Francine, her chest tightening with sadness. "Her name was Bree."

"And there was you, of course."

"What?" Francine gaped at the old man. "There must be some mistake."

"No mistake. Your mum couldn't find you or your brother and sister. We searched high and low, but it was only the next morning we found the three of you in the well."

"*I* was in the well? No! That's not possible. I would never forget something like that!"

"But it's true all the same," said Woodall, his lined face creasing. "Saddest thing I've ever seen. You and your little brother were in the bucket. Your arms were clenched so tight around him, it was a job to get the two of you apart. It was only when we brought up the bucket that we saw Bree . . . just this tangle of red hair in the water below."

He paused, cleared his throat, and continued, "We thought you were all dead at first. You were sitting that still in the bucket with your eyes closed. It was dead cold in that well, too, even in the middle of summer. Yet, you survived . . . Your mum was white as a ghost when we pulled you and the baby out, but she held it together. It was almost as though she had already expected the worst and dealt with it. But when we found Bree, she broke." He shook his head, throat convulsing with remembered sorrow. "Just broke in front of us all with a dreadful wail I shall never forget."

Shivering with cold horror, Francine forced herself to say, "My sister, Madeleine, came up with a rather ludicrous theory that our father killed them."

"It's possible," Woodall conceded. "It was certainly a line of inquiry we pursued, but I could only go on the evidence at the scene, and the verdict at the inquest was that it had been an accident."

Francine pounced on the note of uncertainty in his tone. "But you don't think so."

Woodall shook his head slowly. "Something happened at Thwaite Manor that night that was larger than the drownings." He took a sip of tea, then leaned forward with his arms on his knees and gazed at his orchids with narrowed eyes of memory. He seemed unaffected by the humidity in the conservatory.

Francine waited, tense as a bowstring. "What made you think it wasn't an accident?" she finally asked.

"A number of things, and none that made much sense. It was a very strange night. At first, it appeared we had two little bodies and a missing father. But it was only after we found you three in the well and your mum went to fetch the other girls that we realised they were missing. So, we searched again, all through the house and back through the woods." He sighed, then shrugged. "The most logical explanation was that your father had killed Bree and Montgomery, then run away with the other three, and that's exactly what we thought, until the verdict came back as accidental drowning.

"It made sense, for your father had adored that boy; he wouldn't have harmed him intentionally. But it was common knowledge that he hated you girls, so why had he taken three of the girls with him? For spite? It was no secret that theirs was an unhappy marriage, and they must've had a blazing row that night, for Eleanor was bruised something terrible."

He glanced at Francine to see how she was taking the information that would be painful to hear. She stared back at him, ashen and haunted.

"Are you alright?" he asked gently.

Francine nodded stiffly, not sure she could speak without vomiting.

When he was certain she was coping, he continued. "Another niggle was why George had left in such a hurry if he were innocent of the drownings. He had packed a bag for himself, but nothing for his daughters. Except for a toy. One of the girls . . ."

Sam Woodall frowned. "Aggie . . . Agnes! That was it. She had this stuffed dog; Eleanor said she carried it about wherever she went. It struck me as odd at the time that that was the only thing missing . . . Under the circumstances, I suppose it's not that strange. If your father had drowned your brother and sister, whether by accident or not, he would have been in a highly stressed state and not thinking clearly. He had taken all the money in the house, too, so he could have planned to buy whatever the girls needed when they were safely away . . . In the early days of the investigation, we thought George would turn up of his own accord to return the girls, as he was not the sort of man who would have lasted long looking after three small children. But he never did."

"Did you know my father well?" Francine asked, voice hoarse from trying to restrain a scream lodged in her throat. The thought that it was a real possibility her own father might have had something to do with Bree's death was too big to comprehend. Too hurtful.

"As well as anyone else in the village. I won't lie to you: George Thwaite was a right bastard." Woodall's tone was harsh, causing Francine to flinch. "First time I met him, I'd not been long on the force." His lips tightened with anger. "He was dragging your mum down the high street of Hawkshead by her hair. I got him off her, but I was that close to beating the living daylights out of him then and there. Only thing that prevented me was my uniform . . . I wanted your mum to press charges, but she wouldn't. And I can't say he ever did anything to raise my opinion of him."

He glanced at Francine with kind eyes. "Your mum was better off without him. He'd lay into her week in and week out. Probably laid into you and your sisters too. And the times I threw that man out of the pub come closing time, blind drunk and ready for a fight . . . Almost every brawl I broke up, George Thwaite was involved. He was at it the night of the drowning. Had a huge bust-up down the pub, broke a bloke's arm in the fracas . . . After he ran away, I hardly ever had a brawl there."

"Did you search for him afterwards? Even though the drowning was considered an accident?"

Woodall nodded. "Of course. He was the girls' father, but he had taken them without their mum's consent. There was a nationwide hunt. Every station across the country was on the lookout. There were sightings, of course, but they amounted to nowt. We never caught a sniff of any of them. They just vanished. He probably went abroad before we even started to look." He opened his mouth, then seemed to think better of whatever he'd been about to say.

"What is it?" Francine demanded, her voice harder than she'd intended.

Woodall gave her a wry smile. "I've always thought your mother took a long time before she called us. I think she wanted him to get away." At her look of surprise, he added, "You have to remember the type of man your father was: abusive, arrogant, a bully. Your mum wanted him out of her life. I think she only called us when she was sure he'd had enough time to get far away. That's what I would've done." He paused and took a sip of tea before continuing. "Of course, when we all realized he had taken the girls, she was desperate to find him."

Francine snorted in frustration. She had hoped to get some clarity from the old policeman, but all she had was more questions.

"What happened after he disappeared?" she asked when a silence stretched between them that Woodall seemed disinclined to break.

"In the first weeks afterwards, your mum would come down to the station three or four times a day for news of the girls." He frowned at his orchids. "Then, from one day to the next, she stopped coming. I don't think she could bear any longer to be told we had no news, and she lost hope of us finding them. Then . . . life went on. We still searched for your father but, as time went by, other crimes took precedence. There wasn't much more we could do without a genuine sighting of him.

"Afterwards, your mum started taking in lodgers to make ends meet. She was a fine woman, your mum. She raised the two of you by herself. Never married again, but that was no surprise." He hesitated, mouth twisting on a sour thought. "It wasn't easy for her. Hawkshead can be a funny place. There was sympathy at first for Eleanor, but that disappeared, as your mother made no effort to be part of the community. I think there were those who resented that their sympathy wasn't acknowledged. You and your sister attended the local schools, but otherwise you all kept yourselves to yourselves." He grinned. "Until your sister hit adolescence, of course; then every boy from miles around was hanging about her. Caused your mum a few headaches, that one."

Francine glanced sharply at the old man. "You sound as though you knew my mother well."

He smiled shyly. "She was kind to me, and I made a point of going up the hill to check on her every week. She always had time for a cuppa and a chat. Nice woman was Ellie Thwaite. It's something I can't say about everyone in Hawkshead. There were those who resented my presence." He shrugged. "Times were changing. The police were viewed as the enemy, and the local bobby was disappearing. Then my station was closed down, and I was stationed at Windermere. I didn't see much of your mum after that—maybe twice a year if I was in the area . . . I was saddened when I heard of her death."

"I don't remember you," said Francine wonderingly, alarmed by the black holes in her life that she hadn't been aware of a few days ago. People and events had vanished from her memory.

"You were hardly ever there when I came around. If you weren't at school, you were in the woods. You were a quiet little thing. Hardly knew you were about even if you were in the house. But your mum worried about you."

Francine blinked. "She did? Madeleine was the troublemaker, not me!"

"Oh, your sister was a handful, but you were unnaturally quiet, and you could stand still for hours at a time without moving a muscle. It wasn't normal in a child. I . . ." He petered off and shook his head.

"You what?" said Francine, intrigued by this outside view of herself from a stranger.

He smiled apologetically. "I wondered if perhaps your quietness wasn't because of the time you'd spent in the well."

"I'm not sure what you mean."

He chuckled. "I'm not sure what I mean either. It's just a passing thought."

Francine slumped slightly. "Why don't I remember any of this?"

Woodall peered at her kindly. "It was a traumatic experience for a little girl. It happens sometimes when people have been through something horrific. The mind blocks it out because it can't handle it. A bit like shell shock in a way. It's your brain's way of protecting you."

Francine bit her lip. She wanted to cry, then chastized herself. She never cried—apart from in the graveyard yesterday, and that would never happen again. It was a weakness, and she had no intention of crying in front of another man.

"Is there anything else you wish to know?" asked Woodall when the silence stretched into long minutes as Francine stared unseeingly at the orchids, trying to remember anything with the new information.

"I'm sure there is, but I don't know what because I can't remember anything."

Woodall opened a small drawer in the table and pulled out a notepad and pencil. He quickly scribbled a number, tore off the sheet, and handed it to her. "Here's my mobile number. If you think of anything, phone me."

Francine took the paper gratefully.

"Now, I think we should talk of happier things," said Woodall, standing up. "It's not often I get a chance to show off my beauties."

Francine smiled; it was a bribe if ever she'd heard one—information for company. "I would like that."

"Excellent!" Woodall rubbed his hands together and, in a gallant fashion, held out a crooked arm to Francine.

She glanced at his arm in consternation then gingerly took it, feeling a little odd.

Woodall patted her hand and led her around the conservatory, showing her each bloom before moving out to the garden.

Francine remained with the old man for a few hours, surprised by how much she enjoyed his company. It was amidst the refined beauty of his orchids that she decided Sam Woodall was more suited to a different flower. He was not beautiful, so-phisticated, or majestic like his orchids. He was something far more special: thoughtful, modest, and compassionate. All the traits of the shy, often-overlooked pansy. And as they talked—about plants mainly—she realized she had been wrong in her first impressions. Sam Woodall did not want or need company. He wasn't lonely; he was selective with the company he chose to keep. She was flattered he had chosen to spend time with her.

26 July, 1969

Rosie curled up against Bree, content to lean against her oldest sister and watch Mummy croon to Monty and Maddie in turns.

"Tell me a secret," Bree whispered. Rosie was still the easiest one; she hadn't yet learned how to keep secrets.

The little girl looked down at her hands, then up at Bree. She smiled as rosily as her name, then clambered to her chubby knees. With cupped hands hot around Bree's ear, she breathed, "I do have a secret."

She leaned back to gauge Bree's reaction with wide-eyed anticipation.

Bree turned to see that Agnes was out of whispered earshot before cupping her hands around Rosie's ear. "What secret?"

"Agnes said I was not to tell you."

Bree looked down at Rosie sternly until the little girl squirmed with delicious anticipation of soon releasing a secret she was bursting to tell.

"See my crown?" said Bree, pointing to her head. "I am your

princess today. So, as your princess, I command you to tell me your secret!"

Rosie reached up with delicate fingers to touch the daisies on Bree's head as though they were spun from filigreed gold. She caved as easily as Bree knew she would. The little girl's breath was hot on Bree's ear as she whispered, "A secret place."

Bree's stern look grew sterner as her curiosity burned to almost consume her. She had known for weeks that Agnes, Rosie, and Viola had a new hiding place. Their old one had been lame, and Bree had sussed it out quickly: under the table in Mummy's greenhouse, where the hot-pink blooms of Medinilla magnifica grew so low they swept the floor. Bree was desperate to find their new hiding place, for she had a horrible, sneaking suspicion it was better than Figjam and hers.

"Do you know where it is?"

"Of course!" giggled Rosie as Bree changed tactic, leaving her sternness to tickle her sister instead.

"What are you doing?" Agnes's shadow fell across Bree and Rosie.

Rosie's eyes grew wide in horror. "I didn't say anything! Promise, Aggie. I didn't tell her where . . ."

"Rosina!" Agnes yelled. She turned to Bree, who was staring up at her sister with a calmness she knew would infuriate Agnes. "You leave Rosie alone!"

"Why? She's my sister too. I can speak to her if I want."

"Bree!" Figjam grabbed Bree's arm, then nodded to the path leading from Hawkshead.

The girls all turned, arguments forgotten in an instant.

He stomped up the dusty path, mopping his brow as he left the last of the trees behind him. On spying the womenfolk of his family, he scowled.

Bree stared hard at him. He had been drinking; she had learned to read the telltale signs: flushed face, eyes too bright, a looseness to his limbs. The trick was to gauge which degree of *drunkenness he was in. She glanced at Mum, saw her narrowed eyes, and knew Mum was trying to gauge it too, hoping he was still in the early stages, where he was manageable and could be manipulated. What came after always ended in bruises and anguish.*

Without a greeting or acknowledgement of their existence, he stomped into the manor.

The money was hot with guilt in Bree's pocket. She stood up abruptly. "Figjam and me are going into the woods, Mum," she said, eyes darting to the house.

Mum frowned at her daughter's agitation. "What have you done, Bree?"

"Nothing! Why do you always think I've done something?" But the notes were burning in Bree's pocket, hiding her barefaced lie.

Mum glanced at the house. She swallowed, then turned and smiled brightly at her daughters. "I won't let anyone hurt you, my flowers." She glanced at Bree. "And if you've done nothing wrong, then you've nothing to worry about." It was another barefaced lie. The Thwaite family had spun a web of lies they told each other and themselves. It took less than nothing to upset Him.

"Maybe we should leave, Mummy?" said Agnes nervously. "Father looks angry."

Surprised by this unusual show of solidarity, Bree half smiled at Agnes. But Agnes didn't see. She was staring at the house, hugging her blue-and-white dog so tight, it was a wonder the stuffing didn't burst out of its crisscross of scarred stitching.

"Who took it?" The roar echoed around the manor, then fled into the garden.

Everyone froze.

A thundering stomp. He was in the courtyard.

"George?" said Mummy, stiff, straight, and severe in the face of his fury as he stormed across the lawn. She hurried towards

him, hampered by Monty in her arms and Maddie clinging to her skirt.

The broken veins on his face bulged like tiny worms under his skin. "Who took it?" he roared again. "Which of you devil's spawn took my winnings?"

"What are you talking about, George?" asked Mum, hugging Monty close as he started to wail in earnest at the raised voices. Not to be outdone, Maddie started screaming, too, burying her face into Mummy's skirt. "Everyone's been in the garden with me the entire morning."

Agnes's eyes flickered between Bree and Him. Bree sent a silent plea to her sister, but knew it was in vain when Agnes's eyes narrowed. She pointed at Bree. "It was Bree, Father! I saw her coming out of the house earlier. It was her!"

"Tattletale-tit, your tongue will be split," hissed Bree just loud enough so Agnes would hear, "and all the little puppies will have a little bit!"

Agnes's expression wavered between defiance and guilt, then crumpled at the corner of her mouth as she tried not to cry.

Mum stood between her daughters and her husband like a shield. He stopped and eyed her warily. "Don't, George," said Mum, with a hand up that was both placatory and defensive.

"Don't what, woman?" he yelled.

Mum said nothing. She stared at him. Just stared, even as Monty and Maddie's shrieks cooled to whimpers, then silence. It was a battle of wills that Mum rarely won. Bree only noted the tremble in her hands because she was looking for it.

The girls all held their breath, eyes flickering between Mum and Him, waiting for the signal to run.

"Out of my way," he muttered. "I'll deal with your brats as I see fit."

Yet, he didn't move, anchored to the spot, almost hypnotized by Mum's gaze.

Bree thought her chest would explode from the tension that fizzled around the garden. They all stood like statues, frozen under the sun in a jittery tableau, with the manor leaning in towards them, tense and watchful.

He made the first move. A narrowing of his eyes, lips pulled back in a snarl, shoulders hunched like a clenched fist. He snapped his head down until it was inches away from Mum's.

"Do you want me to hurt them?" he hissed. "Don't make me hurt your flowers.*" There was a sneer in the word, twisting Mum's special name for her children into something ugly. "You know what happens when you defy me, and you will only have yourself to blame."*

Mum had not judged well. She dropped her hand and her eyes, huddling into herself.

She had lost.

Monty suddenly wailed, as though the unbearable tension in the garden was physically hurting him.

He paused, focused on his son, then pushed past Mum roughly.

"George!" she cried, hurrying after him. "No one's taken anything. They've all been here with me the entire morning!"

Bree leapt to her feet. Flight or fight? She wanted to fight, but one look at her younger sisters sent her down the course of flight. She glanced longingly at the oak tree in the courtyard. It was her place of safety, with the added advantage that it drove Him mad, as He couldn't reach her in the highest branches.

She glanced at Mum, saw the slight nod. There was an unspoken agreement between Bree and Mum when He went further than Mum could control: she looked after Monty and Maddie, and Bree looked after the older girls.

Bree grabbed Figjam's hand, hoisting her to her feet in a rough jerk, and took off.

As she passed Agnes, she hissed, "Run! Take Vee and Rosie and run into the woods!" The warning felt stale on her tongue, for she would rather have slapped her sister for yet another betrayal.

Agnes nodded without protest. She grabbed Viola and Rosina's hands, both girls on the verge of tears, and raced across the lawn towards the church.

Bree glanced over her shoulder, her heart clenching at the sight of Mum standing in front of Him—so small against the might of his wrath, now placating and fearful, with nervous twitches of her head to ensure her older children were out of harm's way.

"I'll kill you this time, Bree!" came His roar as Bree and Figjam tore past the graveyard and raced up the incline towards Lonehowe Wood. "So help me, I'll kill the lot of you!"

ELEVEN

❧

Like fireflies, the lights of Thwaite Manor flickered through Lonehowe Wood as Francine made her weary way up the drive. She paused in the garden and faced the old building, reluctant to enter. There was a melancholic droop to the eaves, emanating an unbearable yearning during Francine's absence and conflicting reproach for her late return.

She let herself in, then scowled when her sister's throaty laughter floated from the dining room. She considered sneaking upstairs to continue reading the Thwaite histories. Not to find out who Bree was now, of course, but because she had always read aloud to the little ghost. She had finally got to an interesting section with Queen Elizabeth's scourge of the Catholics, which the Thwaite family had not survived unscathed, and knew it would've interested Bree, for there was gore aplenty.

She turned in resignation towards the dining room, but instead found herself in front of the drawing room with no recollection of walking the few extra paces.

Her breath caught in her throat. The manor's attention was

focused on a single point within its walls with the intensity of a nervous deer in the sights of a hunter. A small voice in her head hissed, *Get out of here! Leave before you discover something that will destroy you.*

"There you are!" cried Madeleine, poking her head out of the dining room, startling Francine.

She whipped her hand off the handle of the drawing room door guiltily, her chest still tight with an overwhelming dread.

"You're late." Madeleine took her arm firmly and drew her into the dining room.

Francine blinked in astonishment. The dining room had been transformed into an intimate candlelit room. Red and white roses, which Francine knew had not been taken from her garden, as she didn't grow them, filled vases on every available surface and the air with their overpowering scent. She doubted Madeleine remembered their significance; respectively, red and white roses were for eternal love and young love—together they represented unity. A unity Francine had never felt with her sister.

Todd and Keefe stood when she entered; they had cleaned up for the night. Todd had gone to the effort of wearing a suit, and she was surprised how attractive she thought he looked.

"What's going on?" she hissed at her sister while eyeing Todd, who was smiling at her.

"I told you this morning," said Madeleine in exasperation.

"Told me what?"

"That I'd invited Todd and Keefe to dinner, to say thank you for fixing the windows."

"You never said anything of the sort!"

Madeleine shrugged. "Well, I thought I did, so the thought counts."

Francine counted to five, wanting to slap her sister. She didn't want to have dinner with anyone, and certainly not with her lodgers. She wanted peace and quiet. She wanted her quiet, orderly life back.

Madeleine led her to the table. "I've cooked," she added proudly. "I was married to a chef once, if you remember."

"I don't," said Francine sourly as she was forced into a chair opposite Todd.

"And he taught me a few easy dishes," continued Madeleine blithely. "So, tonight we shall start with asparagus gratin."

Francine twisted around in her chair. "Asparagus from *my* garden?"

"Where else am I likely to get asparagus at this time of year?" countered Madeleine before sashaying out the room.

"How are you?" asked Todd when Madeleine was out of earshot. "You were white as a sheet when you came in."

"I'm fine." Francine looked down at the tablecloth, wondering where Madeleine had dug it up from. She hadn't seen it since her mother died and had forgotten where she'd packed it away. She peeked at Todd. He was watching her with a thoughtful expression.

"That was some storm last night," said Keefe when the silence stretched until even he picked up on the undercurrent. "And the noise from the central heating . . ." He shook his head and leaned forward in a conspiratorial fashion. "It sounded like voices in the wall . . . You know," he added when Todd and Francine looked at him sharply, "like a weird murmuring. It didn't half do my head in."

Todd rubbed a hand over his mouth to hide his smile and winked at Francine. "Perhaps it's a poltergeist?" he teased. "You keep saying the Irish are fey."

Keefe started as the wind chose that moment to sweep through the open window, ruffled the tablecloth, and set the candles to flicker and cringe before it fled through the door.

"That's not funny, Todd. This old place is already giving me the creeps."

Todd gave Francine a smile of complicity, which faded when she didn't return it. She was gazing solemnly at the spot where the cold wind had departed.

She turned back to Todd. He raised an eyebrow, wearing the same thoughtful expression he seemed to wear whenever he looked at her. It made her feel like a gauche schoolgirl.

"I am not staying here if there are ghosts and ghoulies about," said Keefe with a visible shudder. "Me mam's house is haunted, I swear it. Weird noises at night and things being moved about."

Madeleine came into the dining room, precariously laden with four plates. Todd leapt to his feet, grabbed a couple before they crashed to the floor, and placed one in front of Francine.

She peered at the dish, surprised by the artful presentation. She tasted it and her surprise grew. "This is quite good, Madeleine," she said.

Madeleine preened. Once she was seated, she took over the conversation, which immediately turned from awkward to flowing in her expert hands.

The main meal and dessert passed quickly. Francine contributed little to the conversation. Silence was safer, her refuge. Instead, she listened while Madeleine asked Todd and Keefe questions. Questions that Francine would never have dreamed of asking, and it was then she understood why Madeleine fascinated men. She had the ability to make men feel like they were the most interesting people in the world, so even Keefe blossomed under her gentle interrogation.

Until it got personal. Francine's head jerked up when Madeleine asked Todd, "And you aren't married?"

"Madeleine, that's enough!" she snapped.

"What's wrong with asking if someone is married or not?"

"I'm widowed," said Todd, with a wry glance at Francine.

"Oh, I'm sorry . . ." said Madeleine, with a smirk at her sister. "When did your wife die?"

"Four years ago."

"You must miss her terribly. Do you have any children?"

"Two girls. They're grown up now."

"They must be proud of you."

"I'm sure they are," said Todd in resignation.

Francine rolled her eyes in disbelief. "I think we need some coffee," she said, standing. She paused when the windows rattled again, and a gust of cold air rushed into the room.

Madeleine swallowed her next question, her mouth snapping shut as she glanced around the dining room nervously.

"The wind does that a lot in this house," said Keefe.

Stomach tight with trepidation, Francine thought quickly and said, "We're probably in for another storm . . . I'll get that coffee," before hurrying into the kitchen.

She paused and searched for a sign that something otherworldly was there, hoping for a sign of Bree. Yet, Bree's presence had never made the hairs on her nape prickle with disquiet, had never made her whip around in fear of her own shadow.

The kitchen was hot and humid, cloying, oppressive. She opened all the windows and the door leading to the courtyard, then picked up the flashlight hanging from a hook by the door and darted outside. She didn't want to be in the house. It no longer felt as it should, like a home should, and she had the awful feeling that as she didn't want to be in the house, so the house didn't want her either and was pushing her out.

She walked to the oak tree. "Bree!" she called. "Bree, please come down."

The branches rustled dryly in response.

"Please, Bree."

The sound of sobbing came down from the boughs and broke Francine's heart.

"Oh, Bree," she sighed. "What happened to us, to our family?"

The sobbing breeze increased, then faded as though Bree was running away.

Francine's eyes slid to the well. The chain clanked slightly in the breeze that had slunk into the courtyard.

She took a step back, fetching up against the oak tree, eyes darting about the courtyard. Someone . . . no, *something* was watching her. Or perhaps it was the house. The blind windows stared down at her. They had always appeared bright and welcoming; now they were darkly edged with malevolence.

Buck up, Francine, she scolded herself. *It's a well, nothing more.*

She stepped up to the well and held her breath as she peered into it. A black circular hole gaped below her like a throat. Francine tensed and listened to the night. The silence was absolute; not even the murmur of voices from the house.

Without thinking about what she was doing, she turned the handle, lowering the bucket until a splash of water sounded. The well was a lot deeper than she had realized, surprised there was any water at all, as she had no idea what source was feeding it.

Taking a deep breath, she leaned over the wall and switched on the torch. But even with the light, she couldn't see the water.

Pressure on her back . . . Cold, with the strength of icy fingers . . .

Francine half screamed. The torch fell into the well, clunking against the sides before a loud splash echoed up to her.

The pressure increased.

Flailing, she grabbed the supporting wooden pillars holding up the roof. "Get away from me!" she shouted, pushing backwards.

She twisted and fell to the flagstones.

A cold wind howled around the courtyard, with a high-pitched wail in its depths. It wrapped around Francine and the well, battering against them in fury.

Unsteady breathing—her own—filled Francine's ears, echoing the erratic beat of her heart, until it was all she could hear. She shut her eyes and held absolutely still. A heaviness to her limbs, the pressure all around her, pushing against her until the stone wall dug into her back. Blood roared in her head. She squeezed her eyes shut harder. Visions of being dropped into the well flooded her mind until she thought her head would burst. The wind pushed against her, forcing her to her feet.

"No!" she moaned, trying to keep low to the ground. "I'm not going in there again." A memory picked at the corners of her mind . . .

Darkness . . . water slapping against stone . . .

Keep still . . . Keep still . . . I'm right here . . .

The flash of memory was as bright as the well was dark.

Keep still . . . Don't make a sound . . . Stay alive . . .

It wasn't her voice. A whisper in her ear, on the edge of hearing, giving comfort where there was none to be had.

"Francine?"

Keep still . . .

"Francine!"

Don't make a sound . . .

A hand shook her shoulder. A large, warm, human hand.

"Francine! Open your eyes." Urgency in the voice. A familiar voice that didn't belong in the well.

Her breath came in short, hard gasps as she forced herself to open her eyes.

Todd's face was inches from hers. She noticed fine laughter lines around his eyes. She had never had a man's face so close to hers before.

She tried to back away, a small moan escaping her lips.

"What is going on here?" Todd demanded.

Shaking her head, she got unsteadily to her feet with Todd's hand under her elbow. Shadowed images rushed through her mind faster than she could grasp them, leaving only a residue of coldness, darkness, and whispering silence.

"I'm fine," she muttered hoarsely, shaking off his helping hand. "I fell, that's all."

"Bullshit!"

Francine flinched as though physically hit.

"You were cowering beside the well, terrified." He took her arm again firmly and drew her into the kitchen.

Forcing Francine into a chair, he put the kettle on the stovetop before searching for a couple of mugs. She glanced around with fearful eyes, feeling like an intruder in her own home as the manor enveloped her in a suffocating fug.

"So, this is where you two got to," said Madeleine from the doorway.

"I would like to speak to your sister in private," said Todd. It wasn't a request.

Madeleine took one look at Francine's ashen face and nodded before turning back into the dining room.

Todd placed a steaming cup in front of Francine and poured in a healthy dollop of cooking sherry from a bottle he had unearthed from one of the cupboards. He sat down opposite her.

"Drink!" he commanded when Francine made no move towards the laced tea.

Like an automaton, she gulped down the boiling liquid, barely feeling it scald her throat, completely numb as she replayed the darkness over and over in her head.

It was a peculiar memory: a whisper in the darkness and a sense of terror that made her stomach spasm with nausea. But now she wondered if it wasn't because Sam Woodall had told her she had been in the well and her imagination was filling in the blanks.

The sherry hit her then. It rushed through her veins, warming her so she gasped.

"What happened?" she whispered.

"According to you, you fell."

"Oh." She touched the back of her head. No bump. Physically, she felt fine; emotionally, she was shattered with the last vestiges of the dark memory receding. She had a headache.

"What is happening here, Francine?" asked Todd, his tone gentle.

"I don't know," she said truthfully. "I'm not usually clumsy . . . Why do you care anyway?"

He smiled. "I'm not too sure. There is something about you, though . . ." He seemed about to say something else, then thought better of it. "What were you doing out in the courtyard?"

"Talking to stubborn ghosts."

Todd frowned. "Are we talking figuratively or literally?"

"Both. Neither." Francine stood up, her head pounding so hard her vision blurred. "I'm going to bed." She turned to go, then stopped. "If you aren't happy here, I am sure you will find alternative accommodation in Hawkshead that will be more to your liking."

Todd's chair scraped as he, too, stood. "I have no intention of going anywhere." He came around the table and barred Francine's way. "I don't generally care what other people do with their lives, but I do care when it impacts me. You've obviously had a fright tonight, so I'll leave it for now. But I won't let this rest. Not now."

Francine nodded, too numb to argue, and turned to go, then stopped again as an idea penetrated the pounding in her head. "Do you know how I can find someone?"

"What do you mean?"

"Someone who went missing fifty years ago."

Confused, Todd said, "Is it someone you knew?"

"Yes, sort of . . . My father ran away when I was small, and I want to find out what happened to him."

He frowned. "Why do you want to find him after all this time? He'll probably be dead now."

"Probably, but I want to know what happened to him. The type of life he led after he left us."

He nodded thoughtfully. "We could try the internet."

"The internet?" cried Francine, horrified. She'd rather curl up with a venomous snake. "I don't even own a radio. I'm not even sure what the internet is!"

Todd's laughter filled the kitchen. "I can't say I'm an expert, but I know someone who may be able to help us."

Francine's face grew warm at his casual reference to *us*. It was a friendly word—intimate without being overly familiar. She almost blurted out everything then, but a life ruled by self-restraint reined her in and she kept quiet.

"I'll speak to Keefe," said Todd. "He's always on his sodding iPad. If nothing else, he'll be able to steer us in the right direction."

Francine nodded gratefully and turned for the third time to leave the kitchen.

TWELVE

Francine woke with the headache she'd gone to bed with. The Thwaite Histories lay open on her stomach, though she had read little the night before. She didn't often get headaches, and she lay back on her pillow. She couldn't summon the energy to do anything. She needed to think, but there were so many things to think about she didn't know where to begin.

Ten minutes later, she was still in bed, shivering with a terrible fear, her eyes on the ceiling curving in at the sides as though the house were trying to swallow her.

She could remember quite clearly what had happened the night before. Every little detail, from the spiteful coldness trying to push her into the well to the memory of whispers in the darkness. She hugged herself tightly and tried to force all thoughts from her head. She had to do something, but she wasn't sure where to begin when she wasn't sure what had forced its way into her home.

Swinging her feet over the edge of the bed slowly, she stood up. It was an effort to finish her morning ablutions before making her way downstairs.

Pausing on the landing, she heard muffled voices drifting up from below. It sounded like an argument. Blowing out a breath of frustration and wondering what Madeleine had done to annoy one of her lodgers, she made her way down to the foyer.

"Madeleine?" she called.

Frowning when she got no answer, she hurried into the front parlor to find it empty. She peered out the window, but the garden was empty too. Back across the foyer to the dining room, then a quick peek into the kitchen. All empty. A quick dash upstairs, opening and closing doors as she went. She didn't bother with the third floor, as no one went up there, and she was sure the voices had come from downstairs.

Making her way back down to the foyer, Francine slowed, then stopped. The house was sullen and stifling in its emptiness. Yet, she was sure she had heard raised voices.

Shaking her head with the thought that perhaps she still lingered in a dream, she stepped into the kitchen and put the kettle on. It was then she noticed the vase of *Astilbe* on the table. Pinned beneath it was a note and a small pile of printed pages. She picked up the note and frowned.

Francine.

I got your father's name from Madeleine and had Keefe look up what he could on the internet last night. He didn't find much apart from a few old articles about a drowning.

I'll see you this evening.

Yours,

Todd

Francine was not sure what to make of *Yours, Todd*. Was that the normal way Todd ended his notes, or had it some deeper significance? She had been rather successful ignoring any thought of his dinner invitation and was relieved she was alone so no one could see her blushing furiously.

She touched the stiff plumes of pink *Astilbe*, fluffy as candyfloss on a stick, not sure what to make of them either. Her blush deepened, for it was the flower she had thought most characterized Todd. But *Astilbe* meant more than patience and devotion to loved ones. There was a secret message if given as a gift: *I will wait for you.*

The kettle whistled insistently, intruding on her baffled musings. She made herself a cup of tea, then sat down at the table and picked up the printed pages. How had he managed to print everything during the night when she hadn't a printer in the house? She hadn't heard his van leave—but then, she had been sleeping like the dead.

The first read:

27 July, 1969
A WELL OF TRAGEDY

HAWKSHEAD—Bree, Elizabeth Thwaite, 7, and her little brother, Montgomery George Thwaite, 8 months, drowned last night in an old well at their home, Thwaite Manor in Lonehowe Wood near Hawkshead, Cumbria.

The children of Mr and Mrs George Thwaite were discovered in the early hours of this morning. Just how the accident occurred was not clear at press time.

The local constabulary was called out by the children's mother, Eleanor Thwaite, 26, last night when the children went missing.

Residents of nearby Hawkshead joined the search through Lonehowe Wood, but the children's bodies were not found until 6:15 this morning. The police are searching for George Thwaite, father of the deceased, who vanished during the night with three of his daughters: Agnes Thwaite, 6; Viola Thwaite, 4; and Rosina Thwaite, 3; and they urge anyone with information of their whereabouts to come forward.

*Funeral arrangements are pending at the Church
of the Sacred Heart, Coniston.*

A sob caught in Francine's throat; she was unprepared for the
sudden shock of seeing Bree's face staring back at her from the
photo at the top of the article. She had thought her recollection
of her sister had blurred with the passing of time, preserved as
glimpses on moonlit nights. But Francine had unknowingly
kept Bree sharply alive in her memories, for it was this face she
had retained in that single solid memory she had had of Bree in
the rhododendrons: a strong face with wide eyes and a defiant
expression.

The black-and-white photograph was grainy and rather
small. A family group photo. One she had certainly never seen
before. Her mother appeared tiny next to the large, bearded
figure of her father, George Thwaite. The girls were arranged
by size in front of their parents, with Montgomery and Madeleine sitting on Mum's lap. No one smiled. It wasn't a Happy
Families sort of portrait.

Three of the faces had been circled. Francine liked to think
she recognized the faces, but really, she was guessing that
Agnes, aged six, was the girl with a thin face that scowled at the
camera, holding a stuffed toy that superficially resembled a
dog. Viola, at four, had two long, neat braids hanging over her
shoulders, and stared solemnly ahead of her. Little Rosina,
holding Bree's hand, was the only one whose lips were slightly
quirked, as though she had been told not to smile but couldn't
help herself. On the other side of Bree stood a young Francine,
the most serious of all, staring at the camera.

With a last long look at Bree's face, Francine cleared her
tight throat and turned to the other articles. But they all said
the same thing, some more sensational depending on the slant
of the newspaper. The accident hadn't made it to the front page

of the nationals, which were taken up with stories of the moon landing of Apollo 11 and its recent safe return to earth.

She was no further in gaining new information about what happened that night. There was no mention that she had also been in the well, as Sam Woodall had said.

A dour silence settled around Francine like a scratchy, frayed shawl that gave little comfort. She was aware of the manor as she hadn't been before, of echoing rooms and long, dark hallways just beyond the walls of the kitchen. Yet, the space was oppressive, stuffy, and weighed down on her unpleasantly until she sat hunched over the news reports, startling at the slightest sound.

In that heightened state, a movement through the window brought her to her feet. It was a relief to leave the stifling atmosphere of the kitchen and step out into what promised to be a sunny day—one of those gorgeous February days where the sun took the edge off the frosty air.

She hurried across the garden; early crocuses had come up during the night to add bright splashes of color against the green of the lawn. She stopped a good, comfortable distance from the graveyard. While she had entered it once, she felt no inclination to ever do so again.

"Miss Cavendish?" she said, squinting in the sharp sunlight.

"It's alright, Fran. You don't need to come any closer. I won't be long, just popped in to say hello to Eleanor."

Francine nodded and waited, frankly astonished the old lady had managed to walk all the way from Colthouse in her condition.

Miss Cavendish stood for a long time in front of Eleanor Thwaite's grave, leaning heavily on her walking stick. There was neither sadness nor joy in her expression, merely resignation of the inevitable. Miss Cavendish's visit was not a greeting, Francine decided. It was a farewell.

Miss Cavendish walked stiffly and slowly to the two small graves in the alcove dappled by the old dogwood tree, and bowed her head. Francine was shaken to see the old lady wipe her face as though she had been crying before she opened the graveyard's creaking gate and made her way down the slight incline to Francine.

The two women gazed at the graveyard. Even in the sunshine its menace was palpable under the crouching trees.

Miss Cavendish turned to Francine with a slight frown. "Maddie came down to visit yesterday. She's worried about you. Says you've taken it into your head that she dragged an evil spirit into the house."

"Something *did* come home with her," said Francine, lips tight with annoyance.

"Grief is a funny thing, marra."

"Funny is not how I would describe grief," she said, glancing askance at Miss Cavendish at the abrupt change of topic.

The old lady smiled. "It takes people differently. I look at you—who has forgotten everything that happened to your family, to our Eleanor—who couldn't bear to hear a word of what she had lost, and Maddie, who's never been able to settle to one thing or the other all her life.'

"I can't see how it would've affected Madeleine. She was little more than a baby when—" Francine cleared her throat, surprised how hard it was to even speak her siblings' names out loud. "When the tragedy occurred."

Miss Cavendish turned to face the manor. It looked peaceful in the frost-sharpened sunshine, like something from an old book. It didn't look real; it didn't fit in the modern world. Rather like Francine.

"Perhaps, but she lived in a house of tragedy, and that taints a person without their knowing. Taints and saddens their soul. It gets under your skin like an itch that cannot be scratched because you don't know where to scratch. It doesn't make her grief any less real . . . Treat her with kindness, marra. She doesn't have your strength."

"I'm not strong."

"You have your mother's strength, and our Eleanor was the strongest person I've known." She squinted up at the sky, then said, "It's a beautiful day; walk with me to the road, Fran," and she started her slow way across the lawn without waiting for an answer.

"You don't want to come in for a cup of tea?" said Francine, catching up in two long steps.

"Not today, marra."

Francine's throat clenched with the sad thought that this might be one of the last times she'd see the old lady. To stave off future grief and prolong what little time they had left, she said gruffly, "I'll walk you home."

They walked in silence for a long while before Miss Cavendish flourished her walking stick at the wide verges that kept Lonehowe Wood from encroaching on the manor's driveway. "Don't the crocuses look a treat? Not long now and the daffodils will be up. Though I don't think I'll be around this year to see the bluebells."

Francine nodded. There was no point in trite denials.

With an odd expression, Miss Cavendish added quietly, "Eleanor said all young children were crocuses until their personalities matured to suit their true flower."

"Youthful happiness," said Francine, surprised and rather relieved that Miss Cavendish had brought her mum into the conversation, as she had been wondering how to broach the subject. "Makes sense."

"She set great store in flowers, did our Eleanor."

With a wry smile, Francine said, "I've always hated that I'm lantana. It's considered a weed by many."

"But she wasn't wrong. You are rigid and severe. But there's a positive side too: you are constant and loyal."

From anyone else, Francine would've been wounded by this analysis of her personality. She swallowed the bitter bile rising in her throat. "Do you remember what flowers my sisters were given?" she asked, hopeful that, through the language of flowers, she might gain some insight into who her sisters might have been.

Raising her sparse eyebrows, Miss Cavendish said, "Not all of them. Viola was peony. . . ."

"She was shy?"

"Yes, but compassionate. A lovely girl was Viola." Miss Cavendish frowned, then brightened. "Now, Agnes was a right little madam, bit of a tattletale; she was chrysanthemum."

"Which color?"

"Lord, I can't remember after all this time. Eleanor said she was honest, though. Too honest sometimes."

Francine nodded. "She would've been white chrysanthemum."

Miss Cavendish shrugged. "You'd know better than I. Rosie hadn't moved on from crocus yet, I don't think, and you'll know Maddie's flower."

"*Ranunculus* . . . And Bree?" said Francine quietly, her chest tightening with anticipation at even a crumb of information about her sister when she was alive.

"A tree, I think. Can't remember which one now."

It came to Francine unbidden and was out her mouth before she'd had a chance to turn it over in the privacy of her mind. "Dogwood."

Miss Cavendish stopped walking and leaned heavily on her cane in the shade of the woods, then nodded. "Yes, that could be it."

"I have two growing in the garden." Francine shut her eyes,

the tightness in her chest increasing until it felt like her heart was too big to fit within her rib cage. "One's growing over Bree's grave." She flickered through the meanings for dogwood: reliability, endurance, love unbroken in adversity. But there was another meaning: rebirth. She wondered if that had crossed her mum's mind when she had planted the dogwood beside Bree's grave. For Bree had had a rebirth . . . after death.

"Why didn't you tell me before?" burst from Francine. "You knew I couldn't remember anything of the drownings, so why not just tell me? You were there and you never said anything."

Miss Cavendish started making her slow way down the road again before saying, "Relationships are complicated and Eleanor . . ." She sighed. "Eleanor was the person I was closest to in the world. I loved her dearly, like a sister. But to maintain that level of closeness in a friendship there has to be utter trust, and that is especially true with secrets shared and promises kept."

Relationships were a closed book to Francine. Her closest relationship was to a ghost. It made for as uncomplicated a relationship as you could get.

"Mum made you promise not to speak of it," she said dully.

Miss Cavendish nodded. "Even when you were at school, I made sure not a breath of it reached you or Maddie, at your mum's insistence." She glanced sideways at Francine. "Don't think harshly of her, marra. She loved you and Maddie so much. Everything she did, no matter how misguided, she did to protect you two. Never forget that, but also remember that Eleanor never recovered from that night. She was a broken woman until the day she died."

The women walked in silence until they reached the main road to Hawkshead. It was only when they were on the dry-walled lane on the other side that Miss Cavendish said, "Maddie is not alone in her worry of you, marra."

Francine scowled. "Maddie's wrong. Something has entered

the manor, but I don't know what it is. I've never seen anything like it."

With a surprisingly angry shake of her head, Miss Cavendish said, "I always warned Eleanor that she would create a pattern of fear in you because of her own fears. All that nonsense with those protection herbs—"

"They're not nonsense!" Francine interrupted. "Mum was clear that they kept evil out, especially in the days leading to her death. She never stopped going on about it. I've never missed a night . . ." She faltered, realizing her lie even as the words left her lips.

"And what sort of evil would that be?"

"I-I don't know," Francine conceded. "Mum never said, and I don't think I ever asked."

Miss Cavendish stopped, rested heavily on her cane, and peered down the dry-walled lane to the narrow view of the fells in the distance. "Well, I won't say it didn't give me a start when Maddie told me of that storm. It sounded like . . ." Her lips tightened, and she turned away from Francine's questioning glance.

"You saw something!" Francine cried triumphantly. "Something with Mum."

"Let's just say I've had my lack of belief tested on occasion, but it won't do you any good to dwell on such things." Miss Cavendish started walking slowly again.

"Please tell me, Miss C," said Francine after they'd walked some way in a silence the old lady seemed disinclined to break. She thought Miss Cavendish wouldn't respond until she sighed and gave a half nod, half shake of her head.

"Now, you're to take this in context," warned Miss Cavendish. "For your mum and I had been drinking heavily, so I cannot swear that what I saw wasn't down to that." Another sigh when Francine nodded. "It wasn't long after Bree and Monty drowned, maybe a couple of weeks or so. I was up visiting with

Eleanor; I was up there a lot in those early days after the tragedy. To be honest, I was that worried about our Eleanor's state of mind. She was destroying everything that belonged to that George—though that's to be expected, I suppose. There were memories everywhere . . . But I digress," she said, smiling at Francine. "I was helping your mum burn George's clothing down near the greenhouse. A great bonfire we had raging that night. Eleanor was pensive, and I was that glad there were no tears, for I think she must've cried an ocean since that night—understandably so. That is the problem when confronted by intense grief: there is only so much one can say, yet knowing that whatever you say will not be heeded.

"What happened next . . ." Miss Cavendish shook her head, frowning down the long years to focus on a single moment in time. "It came out of the woods. I've always likened it to a freak wind of sorts, but it did not act as nature intended. Hissed around like it was trying to attack us. Darting out, then back again. And so forceful it scraped against our skin.

"But our Eleanor, she dealt with it. I'd heard your mum called a witch before—though never to her face, mind. It made us laugh that hard at the very idea. But that night, I wondered if everyone else wasn't right. Your mum looked . . . other-worldly. She barely flinched as that ghastly wind weaved around us. Then she headed for the greenhouse and came out with all manner of herbs; your mum set great store in her herbs. She took to muttering and tossing them out, and damn me for a devil if that wind didn't back off. She pushed it right past the graveyard and into Lonehowe."

They had reached Colthouse. Miss Cavendish stopped at her gate and turned to Francine. "The next morning common sense and logic prevailed, and I put it down to all manner of things—mainly your mum's sloe gin. But it was when I looked in the mirror that I saw my face had been rubbed raw, like the skin had been grated off. I don't mind telling you, I was that shaken."

She shook her head. "That is the long and the short of it, marra. What happened that night has puzzled me over the years, and I still can't make head nor tail of it. I know what I saw, and all I am utterly sure of is that a foul wind entered the garden that night that scared me half to death. And I don't mind saying that Maddie talking of something similar in the manor kept me up all night with the worry of it."

"A foul wind," Francine murmured. "It was there all the time, this . . ." She had no name for what had entered her house. It didn't behave like the ghosts in her home. It didn't behave like those in the woods or in Hawkshead. Yet, it had always been there, in the woods, biding its time after her mum had banished it there. And now it had found a way back into the manor. "Who is it? This spirit?"

It was a long time before Miss Cavendish said, "While I don't hold with that sort of thing, I'm fairly certain your mum thought it was George, though she never said as much."

Francine paled. "My father? But he ran away."

"So he did."

"But . . ." Francine stared around wildly, her thoughts scattering and merging in new patterns that were perfectly logical but made no sense either. "There was only one way she could have known that. My father *did* come home, but after he died." Ashen and shivering with horror, she said, "He's been there all this time. In the woods. I've been protecting the house from my father."

The old lady shrugged. "It's what Eleanor believed." She opened the gate and walked slowly towards her front door. "The only reason I feel able to tell you all this is because your mum and I never spoke of what happened that night, and she never . . ."

"Never made you promise not to tell," Francine interjected.

Miss Cavendish smiled. "She knew me too well. Knew I would never breathe a word of it to a soul. Couldn't have the headmistress of the school sprouting nonsense about ghoulies using the wind to suit themselves, could we?"

"But . . . wait! That means he must've died just weeks after he disappeared. If he died, what happened to the girls?" said Francine, eyes wide with horror.

"Probably in social care would be my guess."

"Then I'll never find them," Francine whispered, her heart breaking for her little sisters, who had been left to the four winds, probably ending up in some social institution because of her father's need to spite Eleanor. They would have been so loved at home if only he hadn't taken them.

Miss Cavendish gave Francine a long, appraising look. "That doesn't mean you must give up, Fran."

But the horror of what her little sisters might have been subjected to shriveled any hope that she would find them after all this time. Those despairing thoughts kept her quiet as she settled the old lady in her favorite chair, where she closed her eyes immediately. It was with deep sorrow that Francine turned to leave, then stopped at the door when Miss Cavendish mumbled something. Francine hurried back and crouched down next to her chair. "I thought you were asleep."

"I probably was. The curse of old age, dropping off at inappropriate moments." Her paper-dry hand rested on Francine's arm, and she peered kindly at her. "We have talked of strange things more often than not."

Francine nodded.

"You know I loved Eleanor, but there were some things I believe she did, in desperation, that set her on a path none should take. And you know I've loved you like the daughter I never had, not just for Eleanor's sake, but my own."

Francine frowned in confusion. "What are you trying to tell me?"

"Not telling, warning you. You wish to know what happened that night of the drowning, and I wish I could tell you more, but I can't, for I know so little. But if you are determined to discover the truth, rather than looking to your ghosts for answers, perhaps look to another more logical, human possibility. Don't let your mum's fears destroy your life." She patted Francine's hand and leaned back in her chair, closing her eyes. "Go now, marra, and ponder that a while.'

26 July, 1969

"GET BACK HERE, YOU LITTLE BUGGERS!"
His roar rang in Bree's ears as she gripped her little sister's hand, and they ran deeper into the woods.

"You're a curse! A wicked curse sent to test us. God will punish . . ." was but a whisper as the trees closed in around the two in leafy silence.

"Come on, Figjam!" Bree cried, letting go of her sister and running ahead. She glanced over her shoulder and laughed as Figjam tried to keep up, her little legs peddling like mad as their flying feet led them down paths of long familiarity.

Their laughter was flung up into the canopy of trees and captured by the beaming sun as though everything around them sensed the girls' elation at their stolen freedom.

For stolen it was. There would be retribution when they returned home. But not now, and now could stretch into eternity if Bree wanted it enough.

Their swift feet led them deep into the woods to the stream running beside a piled jumble of boulders that looked strangely man-made. Perhaps a dolmen once, or a burial chamber. It was a sacred place, a place of safety, then and now.

Slithering between the boulders through an opening that was the perfect size for seven- and five-year-old girls, Bree nearly burst with happiness as she entered their secret hideout.

Sitting at one of the stones that served as chairs around a larger stone embedded into the soil, flat and table-like, she lit the stub of candle while she waited for Figjam to pull herself into the small grotto and seat herself with an air of expectation.

"Well?" said Bree. "What did you bring?"

"Two things," said Figjam, and shyly pulled out a small pink button. She placed it with reverence on the stone table then grinned, gap-toothed. "I found it near the church."

Bree picked it up and marveled at the sheer pinkness of the button. "It's perfect," she declared. "This is why you are my favourite sister; because you always find the best stuff."

Figjam beamed, her usually pale cheeks twin red spots of pleasure.

Bree stepped over to the natural ledge on the side of a boulder that served as a shelf. A small rag doll leaned against a couple of favorite books and a couple of protection sachets she had filched from Mum's greenhouse at Figjam's insistence. A tattered board game rested on two tin boxes, slightly rusted, one with a picture of a happily smiling family at a carnival, the other of a Christmas tree with another happily smiling family around it. False pictures of happiness. It wasn't much but, to Bree and Figjam, it represented all their carefully hoarded treasures.

She pulled down the Christmas tin and placed the new button inside. Then she brought down the other tin and sat opposite Figjam. Reaching into the pocket of her dress, she pulled out the ginger cakes, still warm, and placed them in the tin alongside a couple of lemon sherbet candies and a stick of licorice.

"These are for us to share," said Bree sternly. "I know how you love ginger, but you have to share, Figjam. Understand?"

The younger girl nodded, her hazel eyes locked firmly on the ginger cakes. Figjam knew she would get more than her share, for Bree always gave her more.

"Now," said Bree, "what else did you bring?"

Figjam's thin lips twisted with hesitation.

"No secrets," said Bree, leaning across the table and frowning. "No secrets between you and me."

"No secrets," agreed Figjam, *though still hesitant as she pulled out a small red tractor. Guilt was written all over her face.*

"That's Monty's. We agreed not to take anything from the others, only stuff we've picked up."

Her sister shrugged and turned the tractor over in her fingers. "He gets everything," *she muttered.*

"Monty's only a baby. He can't help who he is."

Figjam nodded, her hazel eyes growing large in an effort not to cry. "Why does He hate us?"

They weren't talking about Monty anymore. Bree had hoped they could have an afternoon where He didn't darken their happiness. His name was not allowed in their secret place. It was theirs. Free of hurt. Free of bruises. Free of unhappiness.

"Because we're not boys."

"I can be a boy," *Figjam said earnestly.*

"No you can't. Doesn't work like that." *Bree handed her sister a cake while thinking of something to change the subject.*

But Figjam continued in a low voice, "I do everything He asks. I keep quiet, I keep still, I don't make a mess, I try so hard, Bree!"

"Eat your cake," *said Bree, not unkindly, for there was no response to her little sister's heartfelt plea; nothing she said would change their lives.* "Remember, we need to make a decision," *she added before Figjam could say anything else.*

Figjam ate her cake as tears trickled down her cheeks.

"So," *said Bree, raising her hand.* "I say we let Agnes, Rosina, and Viola join us. But not Maddie yet, because she's too small."

"And she cries too much. Maddie is always crying."

Bree nodded. *Their youngest sister could cry for hours until Mummy looked drawn from lack of sleep. It affected the other girls, of course: less attention, given more responsibility, Mummy's weary distractedness, until they all turned to Bree for their small life triumphs and tragedies.*

"Why?" said Figjam.

"Why what?"

"Why do you want them here? This is our special place. You've always said so."

Bree hesitated, then pouted, knowing Figjam would wheedle the truth out of her eventually. *"Because they have a secret place, and they won't tell me where it is."*

"Good. Then let them have theirs and we'll have ours."

"But I want to know where it is!" Bree burst out.

Figjam scowled. *"Fine. But not Agnes. She'll tell-tale to Fath—To Him, then He gives her a sweet. I've seen her."*

Figjam wasn't wrong. *Each of the girls had their own way of dealing with Him: Figjam kept quiet as a shadow; Viola and Rosina, being younger, hid behind their mother or Bree; Agnes told tales on her sisters in the hope of winning His favor; and Bree—she always fought back.*

THIRTEEN

Francine stood in the gloomy foyer and allowed the silence of the house to settle around her, hoping it would settle her jangled nerves and muddled thoughts. Instead, the air pressed close, tight and cloying, broken only by the faint ticks of the grandfather clock slicing time in the drawing room like the heartbeat of the manor. But that stately beat was uncertain, ever so slightly out of step, and between each tick was a murmuration, like the distant beating of a thousand birds' wings in unison.

With a shivery sense that the slightest noise would be punishable, she stepped towards the drawing room's closed door. The murmuring was stronger here, rising to a hiss of spiteful whispers behind cupped hands. Francine stared at the dark woods with the same fear Bluebeard's last wife must've felt standing in front of the door that, if opened, would reveal a dreadful, bloody secret.

She started guiltily at a creak, as though she'd been caught snooping in her own house, and dashed across the foyer, then stopped on the threshold of the parlor.

Madeleine sat curled in a seat overlooking the front garden with a pensive expression.

Francine's eyes ran around the room, her eyebrows raised. The smashed windowpanes from the storm had all been replaced; Todd had done the repairs while she was out.

She turned to leave before she disturbed her sister. But, sensing Francine's presence, Madeleine twisted around, then quickly turned back to the window.

"I thought you'd gone out," said Francine, unable to keep the sour note from her voice.

"I slept in. I had the most terrible night. I kept waking up thinking I was being watched."

It was a barefaced lie, for Francine had peeked into her sister's room that morning when she'd heard the raised voices, and Madeleine had not been there. She didn't bother to contradict her sister as she entered the parlor and sat down, her back so straight her spine could've passed for a ruler.

She frowned at Madeleine's turned head. "Look at me!" she said, her voice low.

"I have looked at you," said Madeleine sulkily, feigning an increased interest in the view of the garden.

"No, you haven't." Francine stood abruptly, strode across the room, pulled her sister around, grabbed her chin, and scrutinized her face. Her eyes widened with horror, for beneath the makeup were shadows along Madeleine's jawline and around one eye.

"Happy now?" Madeleine demanded, wrenching her face away from her sister's grip.

"Who hit you?" Francine hissed.

Madeleine's usually soft face was brittle and tight. "I don't know. When I got up this morning the bruises were there when I looked in the mirror . . . Maybe it was this malicious spirit you say I brought home with me," she hissed back. But there was genuine fear in her eyes.

Francine sat down, her shoulders sagging. "You didn't bring it home; it was already here. I was the one to let it into the house when I forgot to protect the garden the night you arrived."

"Already here? What are you talking about? Oh god." Madeleine put her hands to her face. "I can't believe I'm even considering that a ghost hurt me during the night. I didn't even feel it, Franny!"

"What other alternative is there?"

Madeleine's green eyes glistened with unshed tears. "I don't want you to be right. There has to be another explanation."

"I think I know who it is," said Francine gently, for she couldn't handle tears now, not when she felt on the verge herself. "Miss C was here . . ."

"I know. I saw you leave with her earlier." She smiled ruefully at Francine's raised eyebrow. "I've been here for a while. I needed to think, try and find a solution to all"—she waved a vague hand around—"this so it made sense."

"She said you went and saw her yesterday, that you were worried about me."

"I am. Though now . . ." Madeleine shifted irritably, as though she weren't comfortable in her own skin.

Before a sullen silence formed, Francine told her all she had learnt from Miss Cavendish.

"She thinks this . . . this spirit is our father, and that he's been here all the time?" said Madeleine doubtfully. "And Mum somehow banished it to the woods?"

"I don't think Miss C believes that, but she thinks Mum did."

"That's insane," Madeleine muttered.

Francine looked at her sister's bruised face. "Is it?"

"Yes! And what's scary is you believe it too."

"Of course! How can you not believe when the proof is on your face?"

Silence stretched between them, filled with horror and the *tick . . . tick . . . tick . . .* from the drawing room.

"I have something for the bruises." Francine stood and walked through to the kitchen. Madeleine followed close behind, fearful to be alone.

On entering, Francine spied the note from Todd and the printouts lying forgotten on the kitchen table. She gathered them up quickly and put them in a drawer to read again when she was alone. She wasn't ready to let her sister know she was doing her own research into their family history. Not until she found something concrete.

She rummaged around in a cupboard, then handed a large tub to Madeleine, who had seated herself at the table.

Madeleine opened the tub and gave a cautious sniff. "Smells quite nice. Is it pineapple?"

"Partly, and *Arnica*. Both are good for inflammation.'

Madeleine dabbed the ointment onto her face while Francine made some tea. She placed a cup in front of Madeleine, then sat opposite her reluctantly, not wanting to continue the conversation for fear of ridicule.

"Let's assume for the sake of argument," began Madeleine, "that our father is haunting the house."

Francine's eyes snapped to her sister warily. "Yes?"

Madeleine bit her lip, then sighed. "How did Mum know he was dead in order to banish him?"

"He must've found his way home after he died."

"Why?"

Francine pondered the question, then shrugged. "This was his home." But her response sounded trite even to her own ears.

"If he died, what happened to our sisters?"

"Miss C thought they would've ended up in social care."

Madeleine rubbed her face, wincing as she touched a bruise. "Then we'll never find them."

"We have to try. If we can find out what happened to our father, where he ended up, that will give us some clue to find them. Maybe speak to the local authority."

With a small hopeless nod, Madeleine lapsed into silence. It was a long time before she said, "Sebastian said all spirits have a reason for staying beyond death."

"What's your point?" asked Francine, frowning.

"I've been speaking to a few of the older villagers down in Hawkshead, and our father was an utter bastard. They all knew he was beating Mum, and not one of them did a thing about it. If I were Mum, I would have killed him."

Francine glared at her sister, jaw clenched with fury. "Take that back! Mum was a darling. She couldn't have hurt a fly. I can't believe you would even think that of her!"

"This is all hypothetical, Francine!"

Still glowering, Francine swallowed the bile rising in her throat, then nodded stiffly, trying to think along lines that were so utterly impossible. "Fine!" she snapped. "Hypothetically, she murdered him. So what would she have done with his body?"

Madeleine shrugged. "Buried him in the garden somewhere. Maybe under the hyacinths. They've always grown beautifully."

"More likely under the thistles," said Francine tartly. "Hyacinths know better than to grow beautifully for a horrible brute like him. Anyway, your conjecture is skewed. If he didn't run away, where are our three sisters? Did Mum kill them too? And all on the same night that Bree and Monty drowned?

"What?" she said when Madeleine looked at her oddly.

"Why did you call our brother Monty when you can't remember him?"

Nonplussed, Francine shook her head. "I don't know. It's a logical nickname for Montgomery, I suppose."

"Maybe your memory is coming back."

Francine didn't think so and reverted to their conjecture. "The whole idea that Mum killed anyone, even our horrible father, is ridiculous."

"There's no need to take that tone with me, Francine!"

"I'm not taking any tone."

"You are so bloody self-righteous! You know I don't *believe* Mum hurt anyone, let alone killed them. This is all conjecture, but you always think you're right! I always hated that about you. You were like that when we were children too. It drove me mad!"

Francine snorted. "If you want to pick an argument with me, you'll have to come up with something better than that." She laughed a brittle, shrill laugh, knowing it would infuriate Madeleine, even though she had never felt less like laughing. But she wanted a fight. Her nerves were frayed, and her head ached. The kitchen shrank around her, pressing against her skin with clammy fingers.

Madeleine glared at her. "And I've always hated it when you did that." She stood up so fast her chair fell with a crash. She stomped towards the door, then turned around. "I'm leaving and I'm never coming back to this ghastly house."

"You do as you must, Madeleine," said Francine with false calmness, knowing her sister would do no such thing. "And you can take that evil spirit with you!"

"And you always have to have the last word!" shouted Madeleine shrilly. "Well, not today! I can't live like this." She waved her hands about. "I'm not like you. I don't like living with the dead. They should stay dead!" She spun on her heel and stormed upstairs.

"Good riddance," Francine muttered, but she didn't mean it. She was sorry she had allowed her anger to get the better of her, but Madeleine was so maddening. She sat for a long while, staring down at her teacup, intensely aware of the prickly atmosphere edged with the sour glee of the unkind words still hanging in the air.

Unable to bear the tension both in herself and the house, Francine stalked outside, needing to speak to someone, but the only person she had ever felt comfortable speaking to was Bree. She missed her ghosts. It wasn't just Bree, whom she missed most of all; she hadn't seen any of her other ghosts since Madeleine's arrival.

She turned to Thwaite Manor. Dressed in sunlight, its mullioned windows reflected the mild warmth like stars. And though seconds before she had been desperate to get out of the house, from outside it looked lovelier than ever. With its edges blurred like a fading memory, it was too beautiful to contain evil within. For the first time in her life, Francine feared her home. It no longer felt like a safe haven.

Francine turned when a movement caught her eye. The trees of Lonehowe Wood waved wildly as though a whirlwind were passing through. She tilted her head to one side. There was a pattern to the wind, moving from tree to tree, not gusting freely.

"Bree?" she called hopefully.

The wind darted from one tree to another, whipping up the boughs with their newly formed buds before leaping to the next.

Francine followed the wind, determined not to lose sight of it. She was distracted by another gust that followed the first as though they were playing hide-and-seek with each other around the trees.

A coldness wrapped around Francine's heart. "Bree!" she shouted, and ran to the edge of the garden. "Bree!"

A wild sobbing broke the sunlit day, followed by a low, building howl.

"RUN, BREE!" Francine yelled as she raced after the first gusting breeze into the woods.

Through the speckled shade she caught a glimmer of the little girl racing along a path. Bree turned a terrified face towards Francine before she fled deeper into Lonehowe Wood.

"Bree!" Francine shrieked as the second wind ripped after the little ghost. She ran after them, deep into the dappled shadows. In shafts of sunlight, she spied the man she had seen in the drawing room a couple of nights back. He was flying after Bree, his face contorted with rage, chasing her away from the house, deep into Lonehowe Wood, away from the little ghost's home.

Francine raced after them, but soon the wind outdistanced her.

Chest burning, gasping for breath, she kept running in the direction they had taken.

She stopped finally and bent over with her hands on her knees, panting hard. Slowly, she became aware of the silence of the woods. A dark, brooding silence.

She knew the woods well, had traversed its paths all her life. It was a place that had brought her happiness. Now, it menaced. Sunlight mottled the ground, each shadow holding secrets and watchful eyes. She hadn't been in this part of the woods for ages. With no idea where Bree had gone, she started up a small animal track, calling Bree softly. She kept looking over her shoulder, sure something was following her. Each time she turned, she thought she caught a flicker of movement, as though someone had just stepped behind a tree.

Shaking herself, Francine tramped down one path after another. There were no ghosts in this area apart from a lonely hiker who had turned up a few years before. In the middle of winter, he had trekked through the woods alone and broken his leg during a snowstorm. He had died from hypothermia in the end, trapped and alone in the woods. He was always curled up between the roots of a big tree just off the path.

The sun passed overhead, shadows shifting into new positions, so the woods changed shape and took on a deeper hue. The air was damp and clammy. Tendrils of hair stuck to Francine's nape as she continued down the path that felt like a forgotten memory.

She was just about to turn back to the house when she heard sobbing coming from up ahead. She picked up her pace.

A glade opened up, with a stream running through it, bubbling happily on its downward journey. A couple of weeping willows trailed in the water and over a collection of large, tumbled boulders on the edge of the far bank.

The sobbing was louder.

Francine scrambled across the stream where the half-submerged stones acted as a natural bridge.

"Bree?"

The sobbing ceased abruptly.

"Bree!" Francine's relief was so intense her throat constricted. "It's only me. Please don't go."

She gingerly made her way to the boulders. To her surprise, she found a narrow opening, just big enough for a child to creep through—or a thin fifty-five-year-old woman on her hands and knees.

Francine crawled in, her narrow shoulders scraping against the rocks, then stopped when it opened into a cavity. She peered around the gloom in wonder. The air was dank, not unpleasantly so, and smelt of moss and lichen, and stale . . . something familiar, something that tickled her blocked banks of memory.

She crawled in further. "Bree?" she whispered, sensing the little ghost's presence.

Francine's eyes roved around the enclosed space. It was big enough that she could sit cross-legged in the middle. A couple of skylights cast patches on the ground. Two mossy rocks sat on either side of a larger one, like a small table and chairs. It all felt . . . familiar. Without thinking, Francine reached up to a natural shelf cut into one boulder just above her head and patted about until her fingers touched something soft and damp. She pulled it down and studied the little doll, shaking her head in disbelief.

Another foray revealed other childish treasures: a Beatrix Potter book of Mrs. Tiggywinkle, the pages stuck together from damp, the drawing of the mop-capped hedgehog still discernible on the cover; a candle stub; a tin box of brightly colored buttons and pins, now rusty; an old biscuit tin, the paint long since flaked off, containing what might have been food but was now a layer of acid-green mold on the bottom that still smelled of sugar.

The last item was a small tractor. It was incongruous amongst the more girly items. It looked new; the red paint had not a single scratch on it.

Francine placed all the items on the natural table and sat on one of the rock chairs with difficulty.

A pricking of memory forced its way to the front of her mind. She had been here before.

The tractor moved slowly across the stone's uneven surface and came to rest against the biscuit tin.

Francine sighed tremulously, quite teary with relief. "Hello, Bree."

Something brushed lightly against her hair. Francine smiled. She gestured around the hollow amidst the boulders and said, "We used to come here when you were alive. We used to play here." It wasn't a question. "It's strange, but it's almost as though I walked here from a memory I don't remember." She squinted through the half-light at the opposite side of the table, wishing she could see Bree. "It was . . . important to us," she said, feeling her way through tangled emotions and suppositions. "Our secret place."

Francine sat quietly for a long while. There were so many things she wanted to ask Bree, even knowing it was impossible to get much of an answer. Bree, who had always been a part of her life, going from a living sister to a dead one—a transition that had not impeded their relationship.

The silence stretched, broken only by the scratchy sound of the tractor being pushed back and forth by Bree.

"I know you're my sister," Francine began, "and I know you drowned in the well. Why were we in the well, Bree?" The air tickled her neck unhelpfully. "Was it truly an accident?"

She thought back to a couple of evenings ago when she'd

been peering into the well and something had tried to push her into it. It had felt so real.

"Did our father drown you and Montgomery?"

The sun shifted position overhead, casting a shaft of light into the tiny chamber lighting up the dust motes like floating diamonds.

She shook her head. "That doesn't make sense; everyone I've spoken to said he adored Montgomery . . . but not us. Not his daughters. He hated us." She tried to catch a fragment of an idea that was frustratingly just out of reach. Then she smiled grimly at herself. Subconsciously, she had accepted Madeleine's suspicions that George Thwaite had killed his children.

"I hope it was an accident, just a dreadful accident." Bree had taken to stroking Francine's hair as a soft breeze entered the small hollow. Her mind raced with possibilities, which were quickly discarded. "If you weren't pushed into the well, did you fall in?" She stiffened as another horrible suspicion crept over her. "Did Montgomery fall into the well and we climbed down to get him? No, that doesn't make sense. He couldn't have been old enough to be walking yet. He was only eight months old." But as the tickling breeze wound about Francine's nape, a horrible suspicion grew into another unfounded theory. "Bree? Did you have something to do with it?"

The little breeze gusted to the far end of the cavity in an instant and was replaced by sullen coldness.

Francine held herself utterly still lest Bree should leave because she was asking the wrong questions. It was a while before she felt a reproachful breeze slink back to ruffle the tendrils of hair around her temple.

Worried she may have been on the right track with her last question, but any further delving would send Bree fleeing, she changed tack.

"Is our father haunting our home, Bree?" She was almost too scared to speak the words out loud, fearing a man she couldn't remember. But she desperately needed some sort of confirmation, even a ghostly one. The slanting sunlight shifted over the mossy table, spotlighting the little red tractor.

It rolled over the uneven surface of the table and nudged the tin again.

Francine let out the breath she hadn't been aware she was holding. It was all the confirmation she needed. "Why did he run away? What happened that night?"

Enveloped in Bree's silence, Francine wasn't even sure what questions to ask, and even more unsure that she wanted the answers. She had too little information, too little memory to puzzle it out without confusing herself more than she was already.

FOURTEEN

꒰ꕤ꒱

Francine's shoulders tightened the moment she stepped inside the manor, sensing a resentful tension that pressed down on her until she stooped under the weight of unsaid truths and false memory.

Grimacing, she forced herself to straighten, then hurried upstairs to check Madeleine's room. All her clothes were still there, strewn about in typical Madeleine fashion. Francine wasn't sure if her sister would carry out her threat to leave, for she tended to live in the heat of the moment. Francine hoped she would stay and was sorry they had argued. She needed someone, a living someone, and Madeleine was the only family she had left.

She went back downstairs, grabbed her tray of cleaning detergents, and set to scrubbing the house vigorously in an effort to clear her mind, which was twisted into a jigsaw of broken thoughts, dark suppositions, and uneasy ideas. But no amount of cleaning could rid the air of its edgy sharpness or the brittle hostility leaching from the walls.

Francine put the cleaning stuff away and escaped into the

garden to take out her disquiet on the plants she hadn't got around to pruning yet. Grabbing a pair of pruning shears, she stalked up to the maze of rhododendrons and came over all cold.

She held her breath lest the wisp of memory disappear of Bree as she had once been, alive and vital with youth, intent on something Francine couldn't see.

Bree turned and pressed a finger to her lips, then she darted out into the sunlight and ran across the wide lawn to the house. Francine hurried after her. Bree opened the front door, then closed it softly behind them.

A murmuring . . . Mum's voice. Strained, tightly controlled . . . fearful.

Bree took five-year-old Francine's hand and tiptoed across the foyer. They stopped in front of the closed door of the drawing room, their breath tight and shallow.

A sibilance of wordless whispers . . .

Bree pressed her ear to the door, her face scrunched with concentration . . .

A sharp pain broke Francine's absorption of the drawing room door, the whispers fading back into the walls as reality righted itself.

She glanced down at her hand; the tip of her pruning shears was rusty with a drop of her blood where she'd gripped them too hard in her fist.

With a tremulous sigh, she tried to grasp the memory again, but it was already fracturing into nothing more than tattered, untethered threads, leaving only a residual impression of trepidation.

She became aware of the quiet ticks and creaks of the manor, its attention turned elsewhere, inwards, away from the drawing room, away from Francine. With a visceral feeling that her home was turning its back on her, she almost cried with the agonizing sense of alienation, overwhelming in its intensity.

Francine fled outside, to the far end of the garden before turning to face her beloved home. Was the manor trying to tell her something? A secret within its walls. A secret so dreadful . . .

"Stop this, Francine!" she shouted to the wide sky and the long shadows creeping across the lawn.

Snorting with frustration, she turned away from the manor and with some effort returned to the memory, trying to place it against some sort of framework that made sense. Bree was there, but seen from a different perspective, of a five-year-old girl looking up at her older, taller sister. It must've been before Bree had died. By why this memory? It felt like a loose end, detached and unmoored.

With her newfound supposition, Francine started towards the rhododendrons, hoping to trigger the memory again. She rounded the house, then stopped in consternation in front of the withered clematis vine lining one wall. The wisteria growing above it had a new trellis. A trellis she had never seen before.

"Todd Constable!" she hissed.

"When you say my name like that, I am thinking I should take it out again."

Francine whipped around. "Why did you put it in when I didn't ask for it?"

"Your wisteria was trailing across the clematis, and I've always liked clematis. It should be on full display when it starts flowering, not hidden. Even by something as lovely as wisteria."

Francine eyed him, wondering if he was making fun of her.

"You could say thank you," he added mildly.

"Thank you," Francine muttered, unable to keep the ungracious note from her voice. "And thank you for fixing the glass in the parlor," she added. Thanking people didn't come easily; the occasion rarely arose where she needed to.

"That was actually Keefe. He's coming on nicely and did a good job."

"Where's your van?" she asked, not having heard the engine. She could have done with the warning.

"It's a beautiful evening, so I walked. Keefe is working a bit later, then driving back. He needs the practice." He smiled. "Would you like to go for a walk?"

"I've been for a walk already." And an unexpected run, but she wasn't about to tell Todd how and where she'd spent her day.

"Then perhaps you'd like to show me your garden."

Francine started to make an excuse, then nodded. She was proud of her garden and rarely got the opportunity to show it off.

They walked together in silence before Todd said, "I read the newspaper articles Keefe found." It was a leading statement, but his deep voice was gentle and invited confidences. "It must have been an awful time for you and your family."

Francine shrugged with a nonchalance she didn't feel. "I don't remember any of it. I was five at the time."

They walked again in silence. Francine wasn't sure she was ready to speak to anyone about her family tragedy. It was all too personal, too confusing . . . and Todd was her lodger, after all. Even if she felt the need to bare all, which she didn't, not really, she didn't want Todd to think she was insane.

"But some things are coming back to you, aren't they?" he said gently. "That night when you were by the well . . . I'm assuming it's the same well?"

Francine hesitated, then nodded. "Little things. I'm not even sure if they're really memories. I remember being in the well, except all I remember is it was dark and Bree was telling me to keep still." The words were out before she could stop them.

Todd stopped dead. "You were in the well too? That wasn't in the papers."

"I know. I found the policeman who was first on the scene. They fished me out along with Bree and Montgomery. I have no idea why I'm not mentioned in the papers. I can only assume my mum insisted, perhaps to protect my identity."

"What were you doing in the well?"

Francine hesitated again. How did she explain that the little she knew was mere supposition, confirmed only by Bree, a ghost? "I don't know. The only thing I can think of is Montgomery fell in and Bree and I climbed in after him."

"So, why was Bree telling you to keep still?"

Francine paused. It felt peculiar hearing someone mention Bree as casually as if she were a real person. "I don't know. It *is* strange, now you mention it. We could have been playing a game, I suppose."

"A game in a well with a baby," he scoffed. "Children have a remarkable degree of self-preservation from a young age. My kids would have been screaming bloody murder if they'd been trapped in a well."

Francine caught her lip between her teeth, trying to stretch the tentative memory of that time in the well. It had been dark and quiet. Bree had been with her, whispering in her ear.

She shook her head in frustration, aware Todd was watching her. She smiled ruefully. "I can't remember anything else. Just silence and the dark . . . I've always been frightened of the well," she admitted. "At least now I know why. I just wish I could remember more."

He nodded his understanding. "Why have you decided to look for your father now, when you must know he's probably dead?"

The abrupt tangent startled Francine. She opened her mouth to tell Todd her father certainly was dead because he was haunting the house, then she snapped her mouth shut. She was surprised to find she didn't want to lie to him. But while she knew she came across as eccentric to most, the truth was too strange, and she doubted he would believe her . . . Or worse, he would believe her and pack his bags immediately. For a reason she couldn't explain, she didn't want Todd to leave.

"I'm curious," she said instead. "My mother told us he had died in an accident, then Madeleine told me he hadn't died here at all." She shrugged. "I have this skeleton in the closet I had never known about, and I want to learn more. What sort of man he was, why he ran away . . ."

"Why your mother lied to you?" Todd interjected softly.

Francine nodded. "That too. She had no reason to lie."

"Unless she was trying to protect you."

"From what?"

"She was your mother; it's what mothers do . . . Could she have protected you from something one of you girls did?"

"Like what? We were little girls, and Monty wasn't even a year old."

Todd nodded, walking with his head down in thought. "The papers said they wanted to find your father," he said after they had done almost a complete circuit of the garden. "There wasn't much information, but it's odd he disappeared on the same night two of his children drowned. The fact that the police were searching for him and had asked for the public's help makes me think they thought he may have had something to do with the drowning. Is it possible he drowned your brother and sister then ran away?"

"I hope not. I hope it was just a tragic accident." She was about to add more, then thought better of it. "But I understand he was a brutal man, and it was for the best that he left."

"But not the best for your three sisters, whom he took with him."

"Yes," said Francine sadly. "That's why I want to find out what happened to him. I am hoping I might be able to find my sisters too. We were only a few years apart, so they should still be alive."

"I would want to find them too. I—" He stopped and frowned in surprise. "Why is there a cow in the garden?"

Francine laughed. "That's Maccabee. She'll be wanting her dinner."

Todd gazed at the cow coming towards them, then at Francine. "You really are the most intriguing woman I've met in a long time."

"Most think I'm batty or barking mad. Those are the kinder names I've been called."

He smiled. "But never dull."

Maccabee lumbered up to Francine and nudged a velvety muzzle against her stomach in a bovine play for attention.

"She won't leave me alone unless I feed her," she said, and started walking around the side of the house. She quickly fed Maccabee and the chickens. Todd followed without saying a word, but she was aware of his eyes on her all the time.

"Don't touch that!" she cried as he moved towards the bed of moonflowers, their new shoots already creeping up the side of the shed with a single early bloom, a testament to the plant's sheltered spot. That single furled trumpet quivered as Todd nearly touched it, before jerking his hand away. "Why not?"

"It's highly toxic."

Todd frowned. "My wife grew these in our garden. I doubt she would have done so if she'd known it was toxic."

"Most gardens have poisonous plants people aren't aware of," Francine said as she put the feed back in the shed and moved into the courtyard. She nodded at the ivy covering the walls of Thwaite Manor. "Even ivy. You see it everywhere because people aren't aware of what's poisonous. It's grown because it's pretty. People really should be more aware."

"And yet you have all these nasty plants growing in your garden."

Francine shrugged. "My mother planted many of them. She loved the moonflower and I've never had the heart to rip it out. Anyway, there's just me, Maccabee, the goats, and the hens. The animals know not to touch what will harm them. They're surprisingly clever that way."

Todd laughed. "Your garden is a veritable death trap to the unwary."

Francine gave him a small smile. "My mother taught me what was toxic and what wasn't. Moonflower is one of the worst, part of the nightshade family. It can cause hallucinations, unreasonable violence or, at worst, death." She nodded at the maze of rhododendron. "That's just as bad, except it will just kill you without the hallucinations. Hydrangea is pretty deadly too, as is foxglove, and that grows everywhere."

"And don't forget the nettles," said Todd dryly.

"True, yet they can be beneficial, and all they do is give you a bit of a rash. There are far worse things than nettles."

Todd threw his head back and laughed.

Francine watched him doubtfully, not sure what he had found so funny and hoped he wasn't laughing at her.

He sobered up when she paused by the herb garden through habit. "You were very close, you and your mum. You talk about her a lot," he said.

"We were. She was wonderful. Always busy. She couldn't stand still for two minutes, but she was always there when we needed her. She taught me everything I know about gardening. We spent a lot of time out here." Francine smiled at the memory of herself and her mum, bent over the beds. There had never been much need for conversation; it had been enough that they were together.

"So where was Madeleine while you and your mum were busy in the garden?"

Francine looked at him in surprise. "With her friends. She was never interested in the garden. She spent most of her time down in the village."

"That must have been lonely for Madeleine."

"Why? She had her friends."

"And you had your mother."

"Yes," said Francine slowly, staring at the ivy draped over

the walls of the courtyard like the skeleton of a tapestry waiting to be woven with leaves. Barely aware of Todd's curious expression, she walked up to the ivy and peered at it intently. A death trap garden. Until now, she had never given much thought to the poisonous plants. There were the usual suspects found in most gardens: English ivy, moonflower, foxglove, hydrangea, rhododendron, oleander, poinsettia, even wisteria was toxic enough to cause vomiting. It was the others, those growing in the greenhouse or in sheltered spots, that were rarely found in an English garden.

Shaking her head, Francine walked past Todd into the garden again. She stood there, hands on her hips, and frowned. Almost every single plant in her garden had some form of toxicity. She glanced at the moonflower vines. Her mother's flower. Like all the flowers in their secret language, moonflower had suited Eleanor Thwaite almost too aptly: *to bloom in dark times*. It was only now Francine understood how dark those times had been for her mum.

"What is it?" asked Todd. "Have you remembered something?"

She snapped out of her reverie. "Not remembered exactly. Just noticed something I hadn't before." She turned abruptly and stalked into the house.

In the parlor was a bookcase filled with gardening books Francine rarely used. She pulled out a few and flipped through them.

Todd sat down in a chair opposite her and picked up one of the books, opening it at a random page.

"So many poisonous plants," continued Francine, as though Todd had asked a question. "I . . ." She shook her head, unable to form the vague idea into something more solid.

"What are you thinking?" asked Todd softly.

"I don't know . . . something in the garden . . ." She shut a book hard, so it snapped the air. "I wish I could remember!

Why don't I remember? I've got all these random facts and theories banging about my head but no matter how I try to put them together, they never make any sense."

"You were a small child when all this happened," said Todd, his tone gentle. "It was traumatic, so it's not surprising you don't remember." He studied her pale, taut face, then said, "Let's think about this logically. There are a number of possibilities: first the drowning was an accident, and your father ran away with the girls—which I am inclined to believe, as the police would not have sent up a hue and cry to find him otherwise. Second, there were two accidents that night: Bree and Montgomery drowned, and on the same night, your father and the other three girls died too. Though I think it is too coincidental to have two accidents on the same night . . . There is another possibility. It's tenuous, but still a possibility, and something you have mentioned before."

"Yes," said Francine, not taking her eyes off Todd's face.

"You said that while you were in the well, Bree was telling you to keep still."

Francine nodded.

"So maybe you and Bree *were* playing a game. Hide-and-seek. You hid down in the well, taking Montgomery with you because you were hiding from your sisters. It might have been something you'd done before."

"Except you said earlier that children had a remarkable degree of self-preservation and were unlikely to do something as dangerous as that."

Todd smiled. "I could be wrong. Maybe you and your siblings didn't inherit a self-preservation gene . . . To continue my rather tenuous reasoning, maybe Bree and Montgomery drowned, your sisters saw what happened and ran away. How old were they?"

"Agnes was six, Viola four, and Rosina would only have been three."

"Which scuppers that theory altogether. They would've been too young to think of running away." He paused, then added, "Well, maybe not Agnes. She could've been old enough to think about it and lead her younger sisters, but they would've been found fairly quickly. Even Agnes would've been too young to have the organizational skills necessary for a successful attempt at running away . . . And that doesn't explain what happened to George."

Francine bit her lip. Todd was thinking of his own children, whom she thought had been raised in a loving home, from the little she knew of him. From all she had learned of her own family, theirs hadn't been a loving home, and their reactions might have been different from other children's. If their father was beating them, maybe the first thing they would do in any situation was run away.

They both looked up when the sound of a car engine came through the window.

"That boy!" sighed Todd, standing up. "He's riding the clutch . . . I'll speak to you later." He walked out of the room, leaving Francine to her plant books.

26 July, 1969

Time passed too quickly when she and Figjam were in the woods, away from the reality of their lives.

It was a glorious day, one of those summer days that shouldn't be allowed to end. Hide-and-seek in the woods, their own version of hopscotch across the stones in the stream, which devolved into a splashing fight, then back to their secret place to eat the last of the ginger cakes. It was a happy day, and there was a lot to be said for short bursts of happiness. That happiness needed to be stored up to see them through the bad.

As the sun began its slow descent, the shadows lengthened, signaling the end of their freedom.

"We'd best get home, or we'll be in trouble," said Bree reluctantly.

Figjam stopped in mid swirl; she had been trying to catch motes on the slanted sunrays dappling the forest floor in a quilt of light and shadow.

Her radiant face creased into a worried frown. "Don't want to go home." Her bottom lip trembled as she tried not to cry.

"Let's live here, Bree. Let's never go back. We can live in the woods."

Bree crouched down in front of Figjam and took her face in her hands. "I won't let Him hurt you," she whispered fiercely. "I won't let anyone hurt you."

The worried frown didn't leave her little sister's face, but Figjam nodded and took Bree's hand, and the two started off down the narrow path.

"Wait!" cried Bree. She tugged on Figjam's hand and went back to their secret place. She hunkered down beside a hollow at the base of one of the boulders at the entrance, which Bree had told Figjam was a fairy door and therefore the safest place to hide their most valuable possessions. Digging in the moist earth, she took out a tin box that clattered with buried treasure.

Figjam crouched down beside her as Bree opened the tin, then gasped in shock as Bree pulled the pound notes from her pocket and put them in the tin with the few coins already within.

"What have you done, Bree? You said only coins."

Bree shrugged. "We need lots so we can take the others with us."

Figjam nodded, then her brow creased once more with worry. "What about Mummy? We can't leave Mummy behind."

"Of course she's coming with! We would never leave Mummy behind."

"But Mummy doesn't know about our secret place."

"Of course, she does," scoffed Bree. "Mum knows everything . . . Come on, let's go." She placed the tin box back in its hiding place and took her little sister's hand once more.

The sun moved too quickly as they retraced their steps along the path leading home. Little was said, neither wanting to voice their trepidation over what the evening would bring. As the trees thinned, their steps got shorter, slower, delaying the inevitable.

"Bree! Francine!"

"*That's Mummy,*" *said Bree, taking Figjam's hand more firmly and dragging her along.* "*We'll come back tomorrow. Really early, before breakfast.*"

"*Can we do that?*"

"*Of course!*" *said Bree with a confidence she didn't feel, but she would've said anything to remove the sad expression from Figjam's face.*

Just before they left the shelter of the trees, Bree stopped and crouched in front of Figjam. "*Remember what I said,*" *she said, her tone intense.* "*You must remember.*"

"*Make myself small,*" *Figjam whispered, touching Bree's red hair, which was tied into two long braids.* "*Don't make any noise. Keep still as a mouse even when—*" *She broke off, then wailed,* "*But I don't want Him to hurt you either, Bree!*"

"*Bree! Francine!*"

Bree smiled a small smile. "*We'd best go, or Mummy will get into trouble too.*"

They broke into a sprint.

Mummy stood in the garden with Monty on one hip, her thin, pale face anxiously scanning the woods. Relief then, with a heartfelt, "*Girls!*" *as Bree and Figjam burst through the trees and ran down the hill.*

As the girls reached her, she said, "*You're cutting it fine today. He'll be back any minute. Bree, round up your sisters and get them bathed. They were playing near the church . . . Not you, Francine,*" *she added when Figjam made to follow Bree.*

"*Aw, Mummy,*" *moaned Figjam.* "*I want to go with Bree.*"

"*No, you come with me,*" *said Mummy, distracted as she glanced down the path leading to Hawkshead.* "*What are you still doing here, Bree? Get a move on and we can all hope for a peaceful night.*"

Bree winked at a crestfallen Figjam, mouthed, "*I'll be back soon,*" *and took off around the corner of the house and down the hill on the path leading to the church.*

FIFTEEN

As the night drew in, Francine could not leave her suspicions alone. She went to bed early and lay in the dark thinking incoherent thoughts that weighed heavily, sucking the air from her lungs. Not even the breeze hushing and shushing through the open window eased her tangled burden; instead, it teased the curtains into fretful sighs and undulated along the walls like silk on glass.

A muted purr filled the room.

"Tibbles?" she whispered, not daring to hope her friendly ghosts were coming back to her.

Tibbles leapt onto the bed. A lump formed in her throat as the cat rubbed against her arm, then curled up beside her. Slowly, a sense of normality settled on Francine, her thoughts clearer than they had been since Madeleine had come home.

It all centered on her father . . . No. George Thwaite. She would not give that title to a stranger for whom she had no memory or love. She had only two indisputable facts: Bree and Montgomery had drowned in the well fifty years ago, and her father and three sisters had vanished that same night . . . and a third: her mum never spoke of the tragedy, not even on her deathbed.

Francine sat up abruptly. Why had her mother never spoken of the drowning? She could understand the grief and horror her mum had lived with, but to never speak of it again, to take away all reminders of her husband and children? It was extreme. What had Mum seen that night that was so terrible she took away everything to keep it a secret?

Eyes darting around the room with the speed of her leaping thoughts, Francine tried to put the tragic jigsaw together—George had run away, and Mum couldn't find three of her children; she phoned the police; Francine, Montgomery, and Bree were found in the well.

Francine frowned. Was she looking at this back to front? If she put the drowning to one side, she was left with the disappearance of her three sisters. Why *had* George taken the girls?

The kindly face of Sam Woodall loomed large in her mind, and her frown vanished with new insight...Mum hadn't known the girls were missing! Sam had said there was another search *after* Bree and Montgomery were found. They had searched again, through the house, the garden, the woods. It was heart-wrenching to imagine Mum running through the house, frantic, searching all those little hiding places only a mum would know about...But they were nowhere to be found, and only then was it believed that George had taken them.

Fingers drumming against her lips, Francine's mind circled around and around but kept coming back to the same question: why would a man who had hated his daughters take them with him?

Unless he hadn't ...

"Oh god!" Francine whispered, running ahead with the

sheer horror of it all, taking a leap in conjecture that made perfect, terrible sense . . . Had George killed the girls then run away?

The idea was a terrified scream percolating around her head until it seeped into her marrow with the certainty that it was the only plausible explanation.

But Mum must've suspected. She knew George, knew his nature, knew he hated the girls, knew he would never have taken them with him . . . Yet, she had clung to a desperate hope. Sam had said Mum had constantly gone down to the station, demanding news of George and the girls in the early days of the investigation, then stopped coming . . . Was that when she had given up hope?

Shivering, Francine hugged herself tight. "Poor Mum," she whispered to the stillness of the night, unable to imagine the desperate despair and helplessness her mother had endured, first losing two children, then three who were missing but whom she must have suspected she would never see again.

Unable to bear even thinking of her mum's intense anguish, Francine paused in her deliberations and backtracked a bit. If her father had killed the three girls, where had he put them?

Francine mulled this over, trying to put herself into her father's position without recoiling with horror, yet unable to keep her distance from the image of his shadowy form lifting each small, lifeless body . . .

Shaking herself free of that heartbreak, she concentrated on the practicalities. It would've needed to be somewhere they couldn't be found easily . . . The woods? No. He wouldn't have had long, and the woods were too far away . . . Not the house, for Mum would've been there, with a strong possibility that she would've caught him in the act or found the bodies before George had a chance to get far enough away.

The solution hit Francine so hard she gasped at the daring,

yet simplicity, of the only possible place. The garden! It had to be the garden. Mum had forever been changing the flower beds around, planting something new. There was always a bed of freshly turned soil, which would have made it easy to hide three small bodies, and no one, not even Mum, would have suspected.

Francine couldn't help but note the terrible, hidden symmetry—George concealing his terrible crime by burying the girls he had hated in the garden that Mum had loved.

There was one thing she could do, though the very idea broke her heart. The mere thought of finding three little skeletons was too much to bear . . .

Tibbles suddenly sat up and stared at the bedroom door, eyes glowing with an unearthly light.

Surprised, Francine watched the cat. Tibbles's routine had never varied: she had always hopped on the bed and rubbed against Francine's arm before curling up and going to sleep.

"What is it, Tibbles?" she whispered. Scalp tingling, she followed the cat's stare.

A faint rumble echoed around the room. A low growl from Tibbles, then she leapt off the bed and disappeared through the wardrobe.

Something had frightened the ghost of a cat.

The bedroom door vibrated as though frantic moths were trapped inside.

Francine watched the door handle, wide-eyed. It turned slowly.

Skin crawling, Francine felt about in the drawer of her bedside table. Her fingers grasped the heavy torch she kept there.

A tiny creak. The door opened slowly . . .

"Franny?"

"AHHH!" Francine cried, and almost fell out of bed. "Madeleine! You scared the life out of me!"

Sheepishly, Madeleine came into the room.

Francine switched on the bedside light and regarded her sister.

"Sorry." She sat on the edge of the bed, ill at ease.

"Where have you been all afternoon?" asked Francine while looking into the shadows, shivering so hard she pulled the covers up to hide it.

"I caught a ferry to Windermere and went down to Kendal. I've only just got back."

"Oh," said Francine because she could think of nothing else to say. Alarmed, she noted bruises along Madeleine's chin that hadn't been there yesterday.

A breathing silence filled the room with stuffy staleness even though the window was open. It pressed down on the sisters until even Madeleine sensed it and edged closer to Francine.

"I'm . . ." said Madeleine at the same time Francine said, "Have . . ."

"You first," said Francine.

"I just wanted to say I was sorry . . . for everything." She looked down at her sandals. Francine noted the mud on them. Madeleine had lied. She hadn't been to Kendal at all but for a long walk, and in the most inappropriate shoes. "I needed a little time away from the house."

"And me," said Francine, not unkindly.

Madeleine nodded.

CRASH!

A shiver of shock coursed through the subsequent hush, electric in its watchful intensity.

"That came from the bathroom," whispered Francine.

The sisters glanced at each other uneasily.

"Should I go and check?" asked Madeleine, pulling her legs up onto the bed as though she expected a hand to reach up and grab her ankle.

Francine shook her head, shivering so hard her teeth chattered. "I probably left the window open. There's a bit of wind building up." It was a lie; there was only a tickling breeze outside.

They watched the dark doorway leading to the bathroom.

"I think we should check," whispered Madeleine. "It might be nothing."

"In this house?" said Francine, then she brightened. "Maybe it's Bree."

"That's hardly better than . . ." Madeleine paused, not wanting to voice her fears aloud, ". . . the alternative."

Francine glanced at her sister in surprise. That had almost sounded like an admission that she was starting to accept the manor was haunted.

"I'll go." Francine got out of bed, gripping the torch, though not even a wrecking ball would help against a ghostly apparition.

"I'm coming with you." Madeleine darted off the bed and crept behind Francine as closely as she could.

Their breathing was loud in the still night air as they stopped at the door. Madeleine took Francine's hand and squeezed so hard Francine winced.

Throats tight, stomachs spasming with dread, the two peered into the dark bathroom. Everything looked the same in the gloom: a functional lavatory, ball-and-claw bath with a pale shower curtain, a basin with a mirrored cupboard above it. The cupboard door was ajar, reflecting the dim light from the bedroom.

A soft whistle came from behind the shower curtain. Muted. Tuneless.

Francine froze. "Did you hear that? He's in there," she hissed.

"I didn't hear anything," Madeleine said with a tremor in her voice.

Francine noted her sister didn't need to be told who *He* was.

Swallowing against the urge to scream, she felt along the wall for the light switch, revealing the stark utility of the bathroom.

"GET OUT OF MY HOUSE!" Francine yelled, unable to bear the creeping tension any longer. "Go away! You are not welcome here!"

A long, slow hiss of air sounded from the bath. The shower curtain flew out and flailed wildly before a slap of coldness bowled past the women and fled through the open window of the bedroom.

Deep, pulsing silence returned to the room . . . then *drip, drip, drip . . .*

A giggle broke the silence.

"Stop that!" Francine cried, staring at her sister in horror as the giggle crescendoed into manic laughter.

Madeleine shook her head, unable to stop, and pointed into the bathroom.

Francine turned. In the reflection of the mirror, she saw Bree sitting on her bedroom window.

"Bree!" Francine whipped around just as the little ghost grinned and vanished. "Stop that, Maddie!" she exclaimed.

Madeleine had tears streaming down her cheeks. "I thought . . . I thought—" She gasped between laughter, then erupted into another bout of hysterical mirth.

Francine slapped her.

"Enough of that!" she snapped.

Madeleine stared at her wide-eyed, laughter gone. "Sorry," she whispered. "I don't know what came over me."

Then Francine did something unprecedented. She hugged her sister.

"We'll get through this," she murmured as Madeleine started to cry. Francine felt her sister's shivering match her own. Over Madeleine's shoulder, eyes twitching left and right, she was aware that something was still watching them. Spine crawling with fear that it was the malicious spirit of George Thwaite, she knew she could not go on as she was. She needed to find out what he wanted and get rid of him, and she knew where to make a start.

It was a long minute before Madeleine pulled away and wiped her face. "I'm sorry for not believing you. I never thought Bree was real, but now with the bruises and . . . and . . ." She waved a hand in the direction of the bathroom as fresh tears trickled down her face. "I keep feeling I need to apologize to you all the time. Everything I thought, everything I do seems to be wrong."

"You haven't done anything wrong." Francine led Madeleine back to the bed and sat beside her, trying not to wince as Madeleine gripped her hand, her long, painted nails digging into Francine's palm. She glanced at her sister with a rush of fondness she rarely felt; her flighty, scatterbrained, vague sister.

"Would you like a cup of tea?" she asked.

Francine stayed awake long after she had settled Madeleine in her own room. The moment she got into bed Tibbles leapt onto it, but instead of her customary nuzzle and settling down, the cat sat on the edge of the bed and stared at the bathroom.

The shadows in the room vacillated, creating nighttime terrors Francine couldn't shake: the hook on the bedroom door cruelly speared her dressing gown, clothing in her open wardrobe hung like flayed skin, an ancient water stain on the ceiling spread like a vicious bruise.

The night deepened and so, too, did the sensation that she was being watched. Her attention kept returning to the old portrait facing her bed of some Thwaite ancestor who'd traveled to the Middle East. Francine had always liked the portrait; it seemed so very exotic, a contradiction to her staid life. Now, the eyes of that Victorian traveler seemed trained on her, two burning holes in the canvas filled with spite.

Tibbles sat on the edge of the bed the whole night like a sentinel, her eyes fixed on the bathroom, seeing something Francine was glad she could not.

When she finally fell asleep, she thrashed and turned, struggling to breathe as though something was sitting on her chest, squeezing the life out of her.

SIXTEEN

The moment Francine heard the engine of Todd's van start, she leapt into action. After a quick peek into Madeleine's room to ensure her sister still slept, she hurried downstairs and out of the house without stopping for breakfast. Shovels, pitchforks, and shears were cast into the wheelbarrow and pushed into the garden.

It was an overcast day with the promise of rain later. The perfect weather for digging up a garden.

Francine stood with her arms akimbo and frowned. Her deductions in the stillness of the night before had seemed quite logical. Now, with a spade in her hand, doubt crept in. She bit her lip, then shook her head; she would not be able to rest easily if she didn't check every bed in the garden. If nothing else, she would be able to eliminate one theory.

With sorrow she started digging up the purple nightshade.

A monotonous rhythm of digging and pulling formed. Her arms and back ached with the repetition as the bed of St. John's wort was ripped apart and the chamomile lawn desecrated before Francine turned to the moonflowers.

She looked down at the plants she had pulled up, their roots bare, like begrimed skeletal hands, the heart-shaped leaves already wilting. Her nose wrinkled at the foul odor emanating from the damaged roots.

Eleanor Thwaite's flower. On every full moon she had woken Francine in the dead of night so they could watch the blooms unfurl to worship the moonlight. It had been their secret ritual. Francine had kept a secret log of the moon in anticipation. On those nights, she had pretended to sleep until her door opened and her mum would shake her gently. It was perhaps her favorite memory of her mum. The stillness of those nights, the scent from a hundred flowers filling the air. She still did it every full moon, in silent tribute to her mum.

Francine turned, seeing her mum's slight figure in a white nightdress in her mind's eye, walking alongside the moonflower vines that covered one side of the shed, brushing her hand against the pale trumpets, and with a small, distant smile saying, "Botanical and common names, Fran."

"*Ipomoea alba*," said the much younger Francine. The garden was her classroom and there was always a test. "Commonly known as moonflower, morning glory, and moon vine . . . Why do you call them moonflowers when most people call them morning glory?"

"Because they are at their best in the moonlight and past their prime in the morning." Her mum had stopped walking and gazed down at a bed of smaller plants, their purple trumpets open and erect. "Now, *Datura*."

"Devil's snare, devil's trumpet . . . um . . . jimsonweed, devil's weed . . ."

"So many devils," her mum had murmured. "*Beautiful, baneful* Datura *for trance and death.*" She smiled at Francine. "It's curious that so many of the trumpet flowers are poisonous."

Francine had shrugged. "From the same family?"

"You know better than that, Fran! *Datura* is *Solanaceae*, or nightshade, as is *Brugmansia,* and my beautiful moonflowers are *Convolvulaceae*, of course." She had clapped her hands softly. "Give me the flowering families of . . ."

Shaking the memory away, Francine tackled a bed of daffodils and narcissus, their green stems poking through the ground, topped with nodding buds. It was a pity to rip the bulbs up before they had bloomed, but at least she could save these and replant them. The bulbs were flung onto the lawn. Francine dug deep, sweating as she worked without pause.

No bodies were revealed.

A light drizzle fell as she ripped her garden apart until it looked like a newly dug graveyard. The very idea made her shudder.

Francine began on the bed encircling an old dogwood tree that was just starting to burst into its white spring splendor. She buried the pitchfork deep in the bed, then stopped and stared at the plants. Francine vividly remembered planting this bed with her mum when she hadn't been much older than ten; Eleanor had cried as she had placed each plant into their holes, gentling the earth with the hands of a mother smoothing tears away from a child's cheeks.

Sinking to her knees, Francine ran her hands over the tight knot of peony bushes, their long, darkly green leaves hiding stems tipped with balled buds. "Viola," Francine whispered. Her hand swept above the stalks of chrysanthemums that would bloom pure and white in July. "Agnes."

Madeleine's *Ranunculus* was there too, as was Francine's own lantana. A low thicket of purple crocuses cozied right up to the trunk of the dogwood for Monty—little Monty who hadn't lived long enough to have his own flower. Lining the far edge of the bed, delphiniums were already pushing through the soil, though still a long way off from flowering in long spikes of blue, white, and pink. "Rosina?" Francine murmured, for it was the only plant that Miss Cavendish had not mentioned, and she assumed her mum had given the little girl a flower post-humously.

And over the flower bed, Bree's dogwood crouched protectively, its branches sweeping low, so they caressed the plants encircling it.

It was the closest Francine would come to guessing at the personalities of her lost siblings, but it was all here in the language of flowers, left by Eleanor Thwaite in memory of her children, and more personal and descriptive than any photograph could have been.

With a lump in her throat that threatened tears, Francine turned away from the flower bed, one she could not bring herself to dig up, and started on the next.

For five days she ripped her garden apart, starting at first light and working until it was dark. She was so obsessed with finding her sisters' bodies that she barely ate, hardly noticed the time or the weather, and stared blankly at Madeleine and Todd when they approached her. They soon learned to leave her alone, and a strange pall of silence settled over Thwaite Manor. No one knew how to deal with Francine when she came in late at night, begrimed and staggering from exhaustion. She wouldn't accept the help offered by Todd, who looked bewildered by the devastation in the garden. Francine did not answer his questions but walked upstairs without really seeing him and collapsed into bed.

Yet, even in her exhausted state, Francine was aware of the menace emanating from the old house, convinced it was imbued with the spirit of George Thwaite watching her every move. It was there when she woke up, stiff and unrefreshed. A spiteful whispering from the walls, silences where no silence should be, a mysterious knocking at night. In the garden, she constantly sensed being watched and kept looking over her shoulder at the lead windows of the house. They stared back at her blankly, but occasionally she thought she saw a flicker of movement in one of the upstairs windows.

It wasn't just the constant uneasy aura, but the fresh bruises she noticed on Madeleine every day. Madeleine didn't once complain, but her gaze would meet Francine's and a moment of understanding passed between them.

In time, Francine realized she had gone mad during those days of demonic activity, and in some small way it was cleansing. As though destroying her garden was clearing awful fears and repairing her fractured soul. With each plant tossed out, she felt cleaner, purer, without understanding why she needed to be cleansed.

It was almost evening on the fifth day when she finally confronted the maze of rhododendron. She was numb with exhaustion. Hundreds of plants were strewn about, roots in the air, flowers drooping, and newly formed spring leaves wilting. Even her border of protective plants was gone. Their protection was unnecessary now, for evil had entered her house and would not leave.

She peered into the high walls of rhododendron, thinking of all the hours she had spent in there—usually hiding from Madeleine. Bree had always been with her. The maze had been created centuries before, filled with secret corners. She willed that wisp of memory of a living Bree to come forth. But nothing came except what Francine had already remembered.

With a sigh, she set about the nearest wall, snipping and cutting into the deep growth.

"Francine?"

Francine dropped her shears in fright and whipped around. Brushing stray strands of hair from her brow, she regarded

Madeleine, who was twisting her fingers into a knot of uncertainty, her eyes darting between Francine and the mangled garden.

"What's wrong?" she asked tiredly.

"Nothing's wrong exactly. I wanted to tell you something."

"Well?" she demanded when her sister continued to gaze around the garden, bewildered by the destruction.

"I phoned Sebastian. I wanted his advice . . . about our ghostly problem," she added when Francine stared at her blankly.

"And?"

"He said there's a misconception that ghosts haunt the areas they were familiar with in life. Most ghosts usually remain because their death was traumatic and haunt the areas where they died. He said that's why there are so many ghosts in hospitals—because most people die there—and also why there are so many sightings around accident or murder sites."

"And we have no idea where George died," said Francine. She picked up her dropped shears and started snipping at the rhododendron, aware Madeleine had not left and was dithering with something else on her mind.

"I think he is wrong," said Madeleine.

With a deliberate sigh, Francine turned around again. "About what?"

"I know Father—George—is here." She blinked in surprise at the firmness of her tone. "I know it's Him."

"If your ex-husband is correct, then it can't be," said Francine, still being contrary, though she agreed wholeheartedly with Madeleine.

"Think about it, Francine! You've only had Bree here, and there's been no other ghosts, friendly or otherwise, in the house."

"There are. I have a cat called Tibbles that sleeps on my bed every night. An old man walks through my bedroom walls, and there's a pregnant woman with a little boy. I saw them every night before you arrived."

"Tibbles?" said Madeleine, bewildered.

Francine frowned. "Yes. That's just the name I gave her."

"Tibbles was a boy. He was *my* cat. He disappeared when I was eight."

"What?" Francine stared at her sister in confusion. "We've never had a cat. We've never had any animals at all apart from Maccabee and the goats and hens." She would have been twelve when Madeleine was eight, so there was no way she would have forgotten a cat.

"I found him in the woods. Someone had hurt him, and I looked after him, but he never came in the house. He lived in the graveyard, then he disappeared one day and never came back. I thought someone had taken him home." Her face crumbled. "I hadn't thought he could be dead. Poor Tibbles."

"How would I know his name?" asked Francine.

"I told you about him. I wanted you to help me feed him, but you refused to go near the graveyard."

Francine digested this. "I wonder what happened to him."

"Probably got eaten by a fox or something." Madeleine sighed sadly, then shook her head at the uprooted garden. "Mum would be so angry with you for doing this to her garden."

"It's *my* garden," Francine retorted. "I shall do whatever I like with it."

"Why? Have you had an infestation of moles or something?"

"No, I . . ." She paused and sought a realistic explanation. There wasn't one. "I noticed how many poisonous plants there were, so I'm taking them all out," she lied out of sheer stubbornness. It was almost plausible, and she congratulated herself on her quick thinking.

Madeleine's eyes narrowed. "Rubbish. You're looking for

something. I know you think I'm stupid, but I've been watching you. You've even dug up the lawn, which I refuse to believe is toxic."

"It's not."

"You're looking for their bodies, aren't you? You think George killed our sisters." She sounded gleeful. Francine almost expected her to clap her hands in delight and crow, "I told you so!"

Francine snorted and started hacking at the nearest rhododendron, the dismissal clear.

Madeleine's cell phone rang, then cut off almost immediately. She looked at the screen and smiled like a cat with cream. "I have to take this," she said, distracted, and walked carefully though the uprooted plants and out of earshot.

Francine turned and stared after her sister, then around at what was left of her garden. She had found absolutely nothing. She was no nearer the truth of what happened that night, yet she was unable to shake the certainty that George had killed the girls. All she had managed to establish was he hadn't buried them in the garden. She was tired of being in a permanent state of confusion with crazy theories of what might have happened based on almost no factual evidence. There was a key to the mystery, yet she had no idea which lock the key fit, for there seemed to be a great many locks in her head.

A hand touched her arm, startling her out of her gloomy thoughts. She turned to face Todd, her eyes bloodshot and staring.

"I think you've gone far enough," he said. "I have no idea why you are destroying your garden, but it can't go on."

Really! First Madeleine, then Todd, when all she wanted was to be left alone.

"Who are you to tell me what I may or may not do with my garden?" she snapped. "I shall do as I please."

Todd raised an eyebrow. "Why would you dig up an entire garden?"

Francine shrugged, deciding to stick with the lie she'd fed Madeleine. "I realized how many poisonous plants there were. It was only when we were talking about it the other day that I really noticed it."

"So you decided to rip them out all at once?"

The note of incredulity in Todd's voice rankled Francine. "It's the right thing to do."

"Bollocks! And if you're wanting to do the right thing, something that is genuinely a health hazard, I suggest you fix your house."

Francine glanced at the gable end. It seemed to be bulging worse than before. One more storm and it would crumble. The same went for the clock tower that she was almost certain was leaning more precariously. "It will have to wait."

"Let me do it," he said, his tone soft. "I've spoken to my mate about the central heating. He said he could come up from London next month to take a look at it. But I can fix the gable end and the clock tower."

Francine hesitated. He already knew her financial situation did not permit major renovation projects.

As though he had read her mind, he added, "All you'd have to pay for is the materials, and I can get you mate's rates on everything. Keefe and I can do the work in our spare time."

Francine eyed him doubtfully, then sighed in resignation. Todd Constable confused her; she simply couldn't understand why someone she barely knew would do her such a kindness. Yet, she couldn't refuse his offer either. The decrepit builder in Hawkshead was more likely to bring the whole house down than fix it.

"Why do you want to help me?" she asked. "You don't know me at all. You're my lodger, for heaven's sake!"

"I know you well enough, and it's not so much for you, but for the building itself. It would be a shame to see such a lovely place fall to wrack and ruin."

"Very well," she said ungraciously. "You'd best give me a list of the materials you need."

"No need. I'll sort that out."

Francine's retort hovered on her lips, but didn't escape. She had no idea what sort of materials she would need. She was quite handy around the house, but her level of building competence involved a hammer and a couple of nails.

She nodded. "Thank you."

He eyed her warily with something on his mind.

Francine frowned at him. "There's something else?" she queried.

"No – Yes – That is . . ." He half smiled. "You make me feel like a schoolboy sometimes," he said ruefully.

Flustered—for that was how he always made her feel—she muttered, "Sorry."

"I was—er—" He took a deep breath. "I'm not in the habit of asking a woman twice if they've said no, but I thought, now we know each other a little better, that you might reconsider having dinner with me?"

Francine blushed. Though she hadn't wanted to admit it to herself, she had been hoping he would ask again. She watched him out the corner of her eye. He was wincing in anticipation of her refusal. "I would like that."

"You would?" he said, blinking in surprise.

Francine bit her lip and smiled. "Yes, I think I would like that very much."

"Okay." He beamed. "Whenever's convenient for you."

"Any night's convenient." Francine started walking up to the manor to hide her flaming face.

"There's something else," said Todd, falling in step beside

her. "I've been doing some research." He faltered and looked almost guilty.

Francine eyed him inquiringly.

"I was curious about your father and your desire to find him—and your sisters, of course."

Francine stopped walking abruptly. "Well?" she said, her tone hard.

"I think I may have found him."

26 July, 1969

"What do you want?" Agnes demanded when Bree raced through the church gates, red braids flying out behind her, before skidding to a stop in front of them. She crossed her arms around her tatty blue-and-white dog and scowled. Viola and Rosina stopped putting flowers on the old graves and hurried over to Agnes.

Bree frowned at her sisters. "Did you pick those from Mum's garden?"

Viola looked guilty and hid the pale-blue flowers behind her back. "Mum said forget-me-nots are for remembering dead people. And no one is remembering the old ones here." She nodded at the pitted headstones, the names long since weathered away.

Shaking her head, Bree said as bossily as she could, "Mum says you're to come home right now. Father will be home soon."

"Shan't," said Agnes, narrowing her eyes. "Father doesn't scare me."

"He scares me," whispered Viola, her large, green eyes gazing up at Agnes with awe at her older sister's bravery.

"That's because you're a tell-tale," snapped Bree. She glanced at the younger girls. "Vee, Rosie, go on up to the house. We'll leave Agnes here if she's not scared." She grinned slyly. "You can stay with the ghosts."

"What ghosts?" said Viola with a nervous glance around the old graveyard, which had suddenly taken on a sinister air. She took Rosina's hand and hurried over to Bree, who as the eldest seemed the one most able to brave any ghosts.

Agnes glared at her little sisters for their betrayal, until they shrank behind Bree.

Bree grinned victoriously. "You coming or not?"

"Not." Agnes turned away to hide the tears of hurt collecting in the corners of her eyes. This was a battle of wills she would never win. No one won against Bree.

"Come on, Aggie. Stop being silly. We need to get on be-fore Father gets back from the pub. You know what he's like when he . . ."

"Don't Bree," said Viola, tugging at her arm. "I want to go home."

Bree didn't move. She eyed Agnes, who made a great play of placing another forget-me-not on an old grave to hide her face.

"If we aren't all home by the time Father gets back," said Bree, "we'll all get into trouble. Please, Aggie. Come with us; we haven't much time."

Agnes, now more composed, turned to her older sister. "Only if you tell me where your hiding place is. I know you have one." Her hands balled into fists at her daring to stand up to Bree. "And if you don't tell, then I'll find it and tell Father. So there!"

"I'll only tell if you tell me where yours is first!" Bree cried, with a quick glance over her shoulder at the Hawkshead's path. It was empty.

"You tell first." A cunning expression marred Agnes's face, which would've been pleasant if she weren't always scowling. "And if you won't let us join your secret place, we won't let you *join ours," she said, angling a warning look at her younger sisters.*

"I don't think you have one," said Bree with a hard stare at Rosina, whom she knew was close to giving up the secret.

"Yes, we do," said Viola, lisping slightly. "It's in the . . ."

"Shut up, Vee!" Agnes shouted.

Bree bit her lip, then sighed in resignation. "Fine! But I'll only tell you once you're all bathed, otherwise I'll never tell."

Agnes glanced at Viola and Rosina, who were both fidgeting in their anxiety to be on their way before Father came back from the pub.

"Fine!" she snapped. "But you better keep your word, Bree, or I really will tell Father."

Rolling her eyes, Bree took Viola and Rosina's hands and marched up the hill to the house without waiting to see if Agnes followed.

SEVENTEEN

"Alive?"

Todd threw his hands up in the air. "And now I finally have your attention!'

Francine eyed him warily. "Have you found him or not?"

"I may have found a way to find him," Todd admitted.

"Tell me."

"I . . . er . . . Keefe, that is, has scoured the internet and not found anything new apart from those old newspapers. So I thought that if your father was a violent man as you and Maddie say . . ."

"Madeleine!" snapped Francine.

"Madeleine then," said Todd, holding up his hands and laughing in the face of Francine's fury at his familiarity with her sister. "I've been talking to her a bit about your father . . ."

"George," she muttered. "George will do."

"As you wish . . . My reasoning was that a violent man will stay true to form and your . . . George probably came into contact with the police at some stage after he ran away. I have a friend on the police force. I spoke to him a few days ago and asked him to look for a George Thwaite in their national records. He is still wanted for questioning, you know. The deaths of Bree and Montgomery were closed and archived after the inquest came back with a verdict of accident, but the police still want to speak to him."

"And your police friend found him?"

"Not exactly," Todd conceded. "They have nothing new, but he did say that if George had had any sense, he would've changed his name. Which is likely, considering he was never found. But as this happened so long ago, and if George had come up in front of one of the courts for violence, then there's a chance it may be recorded in the National Archives."

"That's quite an undertaking," said Francine. The logistics were huge: an entire country with who knew how many forty-year-old men fifty years ago, and no idea what name he could've assumed. Of course, it was all based on the assumption that George Thwaite had remained in England.

Her mind raced along new tangents. Where would a man go who didn't want to be found? Into a wilderness, somewhere like the Scottish Highlands. It's where she would've headed.

"Have you thought of something?" Todd's deep voice cut through Francine's conjectures.

"No." She regarded Todd. "You're a man . . ."

"Thank you for noticing," he said dryly.

Ignoring his interjection, Francine said, "If this had been you, where would you have run to?"

"London," he said promptly. Then he squinted slightly as he considered the possibilities more thoroughly. "That would be my first inclination, as I'm a Londoner born and raised; George wasn't. But I still think a big city would've been his best bet. A man could lose himself in a big city: get a new identity, start a new life, be another nameless face in the crowds. From here, Liverpool would've been his best option. There's a port; I could get passage on a ship, possibly even work for my passage if I hadn't any money."

Francine was glad she had asked, for a big city was the last place she would have run to. And George could have done as Todd said: changed his life completely. The only thing he couldn't change was his character—a deeply flawed, violent character with a tendency to drink.

"Even with three young girls with him?"

After a moment, Todd nodded. "Yes. He would've needed things for them—clothes, food—and even with children in tow, he could've made up some story. But he might've headed inland instead. Manchester or Leeds. Both big cities."

Francine rubbed her face in an effort to concentrate. Perhaps Todd was right, a big city . . .

"What are you doing?" she demanded as Todd's hand came towards her and moved a damp tendril of hair that had escaped her bun from her shoulder.

His lips tightened. "Someone's hurt you."

"Nonsense! No one has hurt me." She glanced down at her shoulder and swallowed hard. On her pale skin, plain to see where the shirt had fallen away, was a livid bruise shaped like finger marks.

"Who has been hurting you?" he hissed. "Madeleine?"

"Really!" said Francine sternly to stop her voice from shaking. She glanced up at the house. Was he in there now, watching her? Her stomach twisted with a terrible fear. It must have happened during the night, but she had no recollection of it. Just like Madeleine.

Her attention snapped back to Todd. "Madeleine and I may argue occasionally, but we are never violent."

"What is going on here, Francine?"

"Nothing!"

Todd gazed at her with hooded eyes. Then he turned abruptly and stalked towards the house.

Nonplussed, Francine hurried after him. "Where are the National Archives?"

"Online."

"Pardon?"

"You won't have to go to some stuffy old building to do any research, Francine. Everything is on the internet now."

Her face fell; visions of a vast building crammed to the ceiling with files were replaced by an insurmountable sea of technology.

She looked around her devastated garden, her heart aching. It had all been for nothing. She had been so sure her sisters had been buried here.

"I'll show you what to do," said Todd reassuringly as he led the way into the dining room where Keefe sat absorbed by a tiny screen. He smiled shyly when they entered.

"It's all ready," he said to Todd. "But I can only get 4G reception in this room and the kitchen."

Francine's eyes darted between the men and the small screen, her heart sinking. She allowed Todd to lead her to the chair that Keefe quickly vacated.

"I've connected a wireless mouse for you," Keefe explained. "I think you'll find it easier to start with than the touch screen."

Francine looked at him blankly.

"Would you prefer to use the screen?" he asked with an anxious glance at Todd.

"I have no idea what you're talking about, young man," said Francine.

"I'll show her what to do," said Todd. "You can get on."

Keefe scuttled out of the room faster than a rat up a drainpipe.

"Keefe is terrified of you," said Todd, pulling up a chair.

"Why?"

"You can be intimidating."

"You don't seem intimidated," she grouched. "And I've actually tried to be!"

He laughed. It rolled over Francine in velvety waves until she smiled properly for the first time in days.

"Ready?" he said, nodding at the tablet.

In the next hour Francine learned a lot more about computers than she wanted to. Many of the terms flew over her head, but she got the gist of some of it and was soon absorbed in the little screen, pulling up one document after another of old Crown Court records.

Cases of violence, murder, assault, and all manner of horrible crimes from 1969 swam before her eyes. There were thousands—hundreds of thousands. And all she had was George Thwaite's age of forty-three.

She wasn't aware of Todd leaving the room, or the cup of tea placed at her side by Madeleine. The night wore on as she scrolled through one case after another. She got quite good at saving files she thought bore a closer look into a folder, and soon the folder was metaphorically bulging.

It was close to midnight when Madeleine came in carrying an iPad. "Todd told me what you were doing," she said, and sat at the table. "I can't sleep, so I thought I'd help."

Francine smiled at her gratefully, then her smile faltered. "How do I make the archives get into your thingamabob?"

Madeleine grinned. "You don't. I just need the address."

"How would I know the address? I've never been there!"

"The website." Shaking her head, Madeleine took the borrowed tablet from her sister, had a quick look at the screen, and handed it back to her.

"I have to say," said Madeleine as her fingers hovered over the screen, "I never thought I'd see you enter the twenty-first century."

Francine snorted in response, but she couldn't help a buzz of pride.

The sisters worked in companionable silence late into the night. And though the house creaked and rustled about them irritably, they both felt they were doing something positive for a change, and they were doing it together.

Bleary-eyed, Francine and Madeleine sat at the kitchen table staring into early morning cups of tea. They had found nothing in the old court cases, and their enthusiasm had dwindled as the night wore on. And yet something had happened last night that Francine was trying to analyze. A bond had formed that they'd never had as children. She was quite fond of her sister this morning.

Todd and Keefe walked into the kitchen.

"How did you get on?" asked Todd. He looked hopeful.

"Not well," said Francine, stifling a yawn.

"Terrible," said Madeleine. "Never realized there were so many violent men in England. Makes me sick to think of it." She stood up. "I'm off to bed."

Todd placed a card in front of Francine. "See you tonight," he said, and, grinning like a schoolboy, he walked out, grabbing Keefe, who had been staring longingly at the stovetop where Francine had put the frying pan in preparation for breakfast.

Francine frowned down at the card in a stupor of fatigue. It was gilt-edged, with the words, *You are cordially invited to dinner with Todd Constable at the Holbeck Ghyll restaurant.* Handwritten on the back was, *Be ready at 8pm.*

A fluttery sensation Francine was beginning to associate with Todd Constable tickled her stomach. Her face flamed red as she read the card three times.

She had changed her mind; she wouldn't go. It wasn't seemly. What would they talk about? She lay her head on the table and shut her eyes. She needed to sleep, but her mind was tangled up like a snake's wedding. Her life wasn't her own anymore, and Todd just complicated everything. She needed to get her life back. She wanted Bree to come home. She needed to get rid of George. She needed to fix her garden. She needed to sleep . . .

A door slammed shut.

Francine awoke with a gasp and sat bolt upright. Her throat was sore, as though she had been sleeping with her mouth open. Still half asleep, she called, "Hello?" Then, "Madeleine?"

A cold susurration came from the walls that set Francine's scalp tingling. She wasn't alone.

Now wide awake, she glanced at the murmuring walls, heart pounding. "Bree?" she whispered hopefully.

Francine wasn't prepared for the sudden iciness that gusted around the kitchen, rattling the pots and utensils on the walls before flinging itself against the table. An awful, tortured howling followed, as frigid tendrils wrapped around Francine's throat, lifting her from the chair, garrotting her.

As quickly as it happened, Francine was released so she slammed back into her seat, her head whipping forward with the violence.

Shivering, eyes darting about the kitchen, waiting for another attack, terrified in her vulnerability, she listened as the howling mutated to a sly croon that sidled out of the kitchen and into the foyer.

For a long time, Francine didn't move. She stared at the doorway, ears straining for a sound from the foyer, knowing the evil that had been her father had not left the house. He was waiting for her in the darkness.

Unable to bear the tension any longer, she stood up quietly and on soft feet entered the foyer.

The walls were silent even as the air withered around her.

Light shone through the opaque glass of the front door, creating kaleidoscopic patterns on the dark floor.

She turned slightly, nose wrinkling at the odor of tobacco that spilled out of nowhere and spun with the dust motes. Drawn to the drawing room, in her mind's eye she could see Bree with her ear pressed to the closed door, squinting with concentration, a finger to her lips.

Desperate to take the threadbare memory further, Francine took a step forward.

Voices beyond . . . Dark whispers . . . The furious undertone of adults arguing . . .

A hand on the door handle, a child's hand. Hers or Bree's? A quickening in Francine's chest, a childhood fear, no less terrible with the distance of decades.

Whispers rising . . . a terrible anger . . . No, hatred . . .

Words filtering through the small crack that Francine peered through. Words with little meaning but fury . . .

The stifling airlessness of a room rarely opened tightened around Francine.

Mum's back towards her . . . Mum's sewing basket on the table . . . Someone else was there . . . Him. Home earlier than usual . . .

An indrawn breath of horror . . . Hers or Bree's . . . ? Or Mum's . . . ? And a scream. A shrieked name: Bree . . .

Running away, trailing fear . . . Bree ahead of her, darting through the kitchen into the sunshine . . .

Rain splattered onto Francine's face, dissipating the memory of sunshine to torn cobwebs, but not the remembered terror.

Chest heaving, she closed her eyes and lifted her face to the rain that mingled with tears she hadn't been aware she had shed. Wrapping her arms tightly around her thin chest, she rocked on the spot, lulling herself into a sense of calm.

It was a long time before she'd gained enough composure to open her eyes. The louring clouds wept over Thwaite Manor, creating a false gloom. Rain collected around the crooked chimneys and ran down the valleys of the roof to the mullioned windows like oily tears.

As though it were as fragile as a broken eggshell, she cradled the fractured memory in her mind, viewing it carefully from side to side for a crack she could delicately lever open more fully. She considered her childhood terror, still lingering like a shiver in the dark. She didn't think it was a new fear, but one she had experienced many times; no doubt her parents had argued mightily, and there were times when she would have overheard them. They had been arguing about Bree... What had Bree done that was so terrible it had warranted a shriek like that?

Something jarred. Something was wrong with the memory, something out of place. Try as she might, Francine couldn't put her finger on what that something was.

With a shuddering sigh, she became aware of something gripped tightly in her hand. She uncurled her fingers: Todd's note, which she had fallen asleep holding, was crumpled and sodden.

She snorted and marched into the kitchen to throw it in the bin, then paused.

Why not? What would it hurt to go out to dinner with a man? She had said yes, after all, and she wasn't in the habit of going back on her word. And it would get her out of the house. She *needed* to get out of the house. Perhaps if she were in a different environment she would think more clearly, away from the sickly vacuum her home had become.

She welcomed her decision for all of two seconds before the logistics hit her. At the age of fifty-five she would be going on her first date.

All of a-dither she sat down abruptly, then stood up again. What would she wear? She had nothing but tweed skirts; sensible, rather masculine shirts; and trousers, most of which had once belonged to her mum. What did one wear on a date? Oh god! Makeup! She'd never worn it before and didn't own any.

Then her sinking heart rose slightly; she knew someone who did.

Scuttling upstairs, she knocked on Madeleine's door and burst in without waiting for a response.

Madeleine sat up, pulling the bedsheets up to her chin, and stared at her sister owlishly. "What's wrong?" she asked, voice croaky with sleep. "Has something happened? And why are you so red in the face?"

"I need your help," Francine blurted out.

Madeleine's expression sagged with astonishment. "My help? You never need help from anyone."

"Please, Maddie. I'm . . ." Francine hesitated, then all in a rush said, "I need—I'm going on a date tonight."

Madeleine's mouth formed a perfect O of amazement, then she burst out laughing. "You? On a date? You're the quintessential spinster. You don't even know any men under a hundred!"

Francine gritted her teeth and turned to go. "Never mind," she muttered, hurt curdling in her chest.

"Wait! I'm sorry." Madeleine leapt out of bed, all laughter gone.

Francine stopped, hand on the door. She turned and nodded. "You're right, of course. It's ludicrous to even contemplate doing something so silly at my age."

Madeleine smiled. "It's never too late." Her smile stretched into a broad grin. "It will be fun! You'll be a blank canvas. And I have the perfect dress for you. It will go beautifully with your eyes."

"What's wrong with my eyes?"

Madeleine laughed. "Nothing! I've always thought they were rather pretty, a mix of green and gold."

"Hazel."

Madeleine pouted. "Green and gold. Hazel sounds so boring. Who is it then?"

"Mr. Constable," Francine said shyly, sure her ears would catch fire they were so hot.

"Todd Constable?"

"Yes! What's wrong with that?"

Nonplussed, Madeleine shook her head. "But he's your lodger."

"So? He's a decent man."

"And good looking," Madeleine grouched. "I was rather hoping he would ask me out."

Francine kept silent. What was she thinking? Men didn't show an interest in other women when Madeleine was around. She couldn't go to dinner with Todd. "Leave it," she said. "I'm not going after all. You're right, I'm being silly."

"Oh, stop it!" Madeleine pulled her towards the bed and pushed her down, then opened the wardrobe.

An explosion of color spilled from the tightly packed space in silks, cottons, and other fabrics Francine couldn't have named if she tried.

"What time is he picking you up?"

"Eight."

"Damn! That doesn't give us much time. It's gone four already," said Madeleine, looking at her watch.

"Four? It's only morning." Francine peered out the window but was unable to tell the sun's position, for the clouds covered it. Had she really slept so long in the kitchen?

"We need to go to Windermere," said Madeleine.

"What on earth for?" Francine nodded at the stuffed wardrobe. "I should be able to fit something in there."

"The dress is not even half of it. We need to tart you up. Pluck your eyebrows for one. Have you ever had them plucked?"

"No." Francine felt her eyebrows. "There's nothing wrong with them. Perfectly good eyebrows."

Madeleine rolled her eyes. "They need shaping, so your eyes look bigger."

"No!" snapped Francine. She had no intention of parting with her eyebrows. "We'll make do with what you've got here."

"But you need a manicure. Have you seen the state of your hands?"

Francine sat on the offending appendages, well aware they were so ingrained with dirt from the garden she could no longer scrub it out of the little creases. She glared at her sister mutinously.

"Oh, you are no fun, Francine!" Madeleine cried. She tapped a finger on her lips thoughtfully as she regarded her sister in a way Francine would've found insulting if she didn't urgently need Madeleine's help. "Go and have a bath. I need to think about this."

"About what?" asked Francine, bewildered. "All I need is a dress."

Madeleine turned back to the wardrobe. "Go, Francine! And make sure you scrub well. I want you to sparkle when you come back." She paused and peered closely at her sister, eyes narrowed. "He's hurting you too," she murmured. "When did that start?"

Fingers to her shoulder, Francine felt the bruise. It didn't hurt, merely a slight tenderness.

"Have you seen your throat?"

Francine shook her head in horror at the mirror Madeleine held up to her. A thin, red welt traced around her neck.

"I can't go out, can I?" she said dully, not daring to tell her sister what had happened in the kitchen not long before. "I can't leave you here alone with that—that thing."

"You can, and you will. We'll cover the bruises so no one

will be any the wiser, and Keefe can keep me company. Father never tries anything when anyone else is around. A coward in life and a coward in death."

"Don't call him that! He was no father to us."

Madeleine swallowed visibly, then smiled with false brightness. "Stop worrying and go take your bath! Forget about Fa— Him tonight and have fun for a change."

EIGHTEEN

❧❀☙

A few minutes before eight, squirming inwardly and outwardly, Francine glared down at the dark-green dress. Her knees peeped out just under the hem! No one had seen her knees before . . . and the neckline! Madeleine had somehow managed to give her a cleavage with a padded bra and makeup. Francine hadn't known one used makeup on one's chest.

Oh, and the makeup. She cringed, sure she looked like a clown. The face staring back in the mirror was not her own. Her eyes were longer and bigger, ringed with thick lashes. Her pale skin looked almost creamy; her lips were no longer thin but had a plump bottom lip.

"Take it off," she cried. "I don't look normal."

"Shut up," said Madeleine through a mouthful of pins as she took Francine's long white hair and did it up in a chignon. "There!" She stepped back to admire her handiwork, her head to one side before nodding. "You'll do."

"I will not do! I'm not going!"

Madeleine ignored her, gripped her sister's arm, and frog-marched her downstairs.

"Now," she said when they reached the foyer, and adjusted a tendril so it curled over Francine's shoulder. "Remember to smile often and laugh at his jokes even if they're not funny. Men love to think they're amusing, so let them think it. And it won't hurt to compliment him; not too often—just enough to make him feel good about himself. And don't order soup."

"Why not?" asked Francine, bewildered.

"You'll mess over yourself. And don't order everything he does. Todd strikes me as a man who likes a woman with her own mind."

"I *do* have my own mind!"

"And don't dominate the conversation. You don't have to listen when he's talking, but you must look as if you are."

"Why wouldn't I? He may have something interesting to say."

"And ask him about work, but not too much. Men love to talk shop. And try to steer any conversation away from sport . . ."

Francine nodded helplessly, her stomach so tight with nerves she thought she might throw up all over Madeleine's lovely frock. Having Todd speak all the time would be a blessing.

"And you must linger over coffee at the end. You don't want to rush home, or he'll think you don't want to be there with him," continued Madeleine.

There was a clang from outside.

The sisters looked at each other, trepidation mirrored on their faces.

"It's nothing," said Francine, but she was already hurrying into the dining room with Madeleine hard on her heels, peering through each window as she went. She reached the far window and frowned.

Keefe stood in her devastated garden, surrounded by long metal poles. He gave the sisters a thumbs-up when he saw them.

"Sorry!" he shouted. "Just putting the scaffolding up. Shouldn't take long."

"It really is nothing," said Madeleine, her relief palpable. "For a second I thought . . ." She trailed off and smiled at Francine. "They've been clanking about on the third floor too. I can't remember the last time I was even up there. The library always gave me the creeps."

Francine frowned. "That will be for the clock tower. Mr. Constable said the footing is giving away . . . And I like the library."

"You would. And for god's sake *do not* call him Mr. Constable. Call him Todd; we are not Victorians. Now, where was I?" said Madeleine as they hurried back to the foyer. "Oh yes. Coffee . . . The end is when a date is at its most intimate, it's the time to ask personal questions . . . and you could try to flirt a little."

"Flirt?" Francine stared at her sister in horror. "I don't know how!" she wailed.

Madeleine bit her lip. "Yes. Well. Never mind the flirting then, but at least try and make yourself appear interesting. Don't talk about gardening all the time, or . . . do you have any other interests?"

"Books."

"Excellent! Books will make you seem intelligent, but don't be too forceful in your opinions."

"I hope she is very forceful in her opinions," said Todd as he came down the stairs, rather dashing in a dark suit and white shirt that contrasted perfectly with the dusky skin of his throat. Francine was relieved he wasn't wearing a tie; it made his attire less formal.

"I'll make myself scarce," said Madeleine. She kissed Francine on the cheek and darted into the kitchen.

"You look lovely," said Todd.

Taken aback, Francine eyed him cautiously. No one had ever said she was lovely before. She cast around frantically for a return compliment but came up empty; her tongue wasn't working.

He led her to the passenger door of his van, opened it, and held out a hand to help her in. Francine stared at it helplessly, then got in by herself. She heard Todd chuckling as he walked around to the driver's side.

The drive through Ambleside and around Lake Windermere was torture. Not a single opening sentence sprang to Francine's mind. This was wrong, uncomfortable. She shouldn't have come.

She peeked sideways at Todd. He didn't seem at all uncomfortable; his long fingers rested lightly on the steering wheel, and he wore a small, unreadable smile.

The road wound round the lake before Todd turned off and drove up a steep, winding lane. A brook bubbled down the hill beside it. It ended in a sumptuous, wisteria-clad, Victorian building, all slate brick and slate roofs that screamed expensive to Francine's sinking heart; the money she had brought with her wouldn't even cover the bowl of soup Madeleine said she shouldn't order.

They were ushered into the paneled dining room with a magnificent view across the lake to the crinkled fells beyond.

"I've booked a table on the terrace," said Todd as they followed the maître d' through a glass door. "I thought you might prefer to be outside."

Francine nodded, touched by his thoughtfulness.

Once seated and their drink order taken, Francine regarded the view rather than look at Todd. She knew every fell zigzagging across the horizon. They were friends.

"Are you going to talk to me at all tonight?" asked Todd with a wry smile when the silence had stretched into long minutes.

With brutal honesty Francine said, "I don't know what to say."

"Francine." He leaned across the table. "There is no need to be so nervous. I have been living in your house for the past few weeks. I've seen you every day. Just relax. You might actually enjoy yourself if you allow it."

"I don't know how to do chitchat. Madeleine said I was to let you do all the talking and talk of sport and not talk about work—no, the other way round—but not too much and a million other things."

"We won't be talking about sport or work," said Todd firmly. He leaned back and smiled. "Tell me anything you like. Your favorite book. What was your best subject at school? Do you like the color blue? Do you prefer dogs or cats?"

"*The Old Man and the Sea.* Biology. Yes. Both," said Francine promptly, as though it were a test.

Todd laughed. "Let's try that again."

There was something about Todd Constable that invited confidences. It was that quality Francine had been resisting since she'd met him. For he was one of those rare people who actually listened and seemed genuinely interested in what he was listening to. It took a couple of false starts and gentle prompts from him before Francine started to talk freely about herself. The courses placed in front of her were tiny explosions of color and taste, and not at all filling.

Coffee and petits fours had arrived at the table when it occurred to Francine she had monopolized the conversation and not taken a single bit of Madeleine's rushed advice.

"What were you searching for in your garden?" asked Todd.

Thrown by the change in subject, Francine stilled, then said, "I don't know what you mean. I told you I was taking out all the poisonous plants."

"You were searching. Tell me what's going on in that house, Francine."

She shook her head, wanting to tell him, but not wanting to sound like a dotty old woman.

"You live in fear. I noticed all the herbs you placed around the house. I saw you talking to the oak tree in the courtyard too." He sighed. "Is the house haunted?"

Francine's eyes locked with his. She couldn't look away.

"Why are you searching for your father fifty years after he ran away?" he continued when Francine didn't speak. "Why are you so terrified of the graveyard? And that night during the storm? There was something..."—he searched for a word—"...odd going on that night."

"It was just a terrible storm," said Francine, her excuse weak even to her own ears. "The parlor's always been prone to down draughts from the chimney, and with the wind—"

"I think the house is haunted and you're trying to hide it," Todd interjected.

Francine gave up. She closed her eyes with a dreadful feeling that her first date was about to end in disaster. She nodded. "It is. It's always been haunted."

"So you can see ghosts." His face was expressionless.

She nodded, not sure if he believed her or not. "There are a few I see often in or around the house; at least, I did until George ... my father's spirit entered. They're scared of him ... Oh, and in Hawkshead, of course, and in the woods; there are thousands along the corpse trail."

"It can't be easy."

With a shrug, and rather amazed he was taking her seriously, Francine said, "I didn't realize it wasn't normal until I was in my teens."

"And it's not just the ghosts that are scared of your father." Todd wore that thoughtful expression she was coming to know too well. "Is he the one who's been hurting you?"

"Yes. Madeleine was bruised shortly after she arrived home; I was a few days later."

And then, as she had already started, she kept talking, telling Todd everything she had gleaned since Madeleine had arrived home with the dreadful news that the Thwaite family had once been much larger.

He stared off into space, nodding occasionally. It was dark now; they were the last diners on the terrace. "Don't take this the wrong way," he said when Francine petered to a stop, "but is it possible these ghosts are all in your head?"

Francine grew very still. He didn't believe her. There was no point wishing all her words back. She looked down at her lap, her chest tight with hurt.

"They are more real to me than the living." She looked up at him. "You don't believe me," she said, her tone harsh.

Todd raised his eyebrows. "I do. I've always believed in ghosts. It's hard not to in my family. But I've never seen one; I rather wish I could . . . I should speak to my grandmother. She used to scare us when we were kids, always going on about the other side. But she might have some ideas how to get rid of your father's spirit."

"She might?" said Francine hopefully.

He nodded. "She's always said ghosts remain for a reason, but once that reason has been taken away, they will rest. So we need to discover why your father has remained here."

"That's what I've been trying to do. Not very well, I'll admit. I thought if I found out where he had ended up, I'd be able to discover why he stayed, possibly because of something that happened when he died. I am sure it has something to do with the night Bree and Montgomery died. George is at the center of everything, and now he's in my house, and he's getting stronger." She swallowed and touched her throat. She was relieved that Madeleine had covered the welt with makeup; she didn't want Todd to know just how bad it was getting.

"Do you think your other three sisters are alive?"

Francine paused, then shook her head. "I think they died the night Bree and Monty did. They are the reason I dug up the garden. I was so sure they were buried there."

Todd took a sip of coffee, hesitant to speak his mind. "What an extraordinary love Bree must've had for you," he said finally.

Francine frowned, for she could tell he was choosing his words with care. "Of course she did. She was my sister."

"That means nothing. There are siblings everywhere who have nothing to do with each other. Your relationship when Bree was alive must've been extremely strong for her love for you to go beyond death. I can't think of a greater devotion than remaining to protect the ones you love."

Francine swallowed against the threat of unwanted tears. "I've never thought of it like that."

"Why would you?" said Todd, not unkindly. "You were so young when Bree died, yet you loved Bree so much, too. You still do." He smiled crookedly. "I almost envy you that bond. I don't think I've ever experienced a love as deep as that except for my children."

"Not even for your wife?" said Francine, surprised.

"I loved her deeply. I still do, and I always will. But love between a man and woman is very different to that between a parent and their children, or between siblings."

Francine sighed. For the first time in her life, she almost regretted not forming more intimate bonds to create a legacy to leave behind.

Sensing Todd's continued hesitancy, she said, "What are you trying to say?"

He took another sip of coffee before answering. "Have you ever wondered *why* Bree remained with you?"

Of course, Francine had wondered about Bree before she knew they were sisters, but afterwards . . . "No," she said slowly. "I'd rather assumed it was because her death had been traumatic."

"Perhaps she had a hand in the drowning." Todd's tone was cautious, worried about how she might react to any criticism of her ghostly sister.

Francine eyed him warily.

"And perhaps your mother knew what Bree had done," he continued. "Which may be why she never spoke of the drowning, to protect your memory of Bree."

Francine's frown deepened, then softened with sadness. "She was only a little girl. If she had been the cause of Monty's death, it could only have been an accident. And she drowned too! And I was in the well with them. I—" She shook her head in mute denial, feeling a treacherous prickle of tears.

"You truly remember nothing of that night apart from that one memory of being down the well?"

Francine started to nod, then shook her head. "I remember them fighting," she whispered.

"Who?"

"My parents . . . They were in the drawing room. They were arguing . . ."

"On the night Bree and Montgomery drowned?" Todd verified.

"I'm not sure. It could've been, but maybe it was from before. I think they fought a lot, but I keep coming back to this particular memory."

"Maybe because of something you saw." Todd leaned across the table and gazed at Francine intently. "There could have been someone else there that night. Perhaps your father killed this third party, then ran away with your sisters, possibly to protect them."

"Where are you going with this?"

"I don't really know. It just occurred to me that your father is being seen as the villain, when he could have been the good guy. He could have killed the person who killed your siblings."

"That doesn't make sense. I have it on good authority that he hated us, his daughters, and he was abusive."

"I'm not saying he wasn't, and I don't condone his behavior. I'm merely suggesting that, on that particular night, perhaps he tried to protect you all as a father is supposed to . . . And maybe you saw who killed your brother and Bree and your mind is protecting you from the horror you witnessed."

26 July, 1969

"Hurry!" Bree cried, herding Agnes, Rosina, and Viola up the stairs and into the bathroom. "Agnes, keep watch at the window. Vee and Rosie into the bath now!" she commanded, already pulling Rosina's dress over her head.

"Stop bossing us around!" snapped Agnes, but she did as Bree said and kept watch at the bathroom window, sucking the ear of her tatty dog nervously.

"Maddie's crying," said Rosina as she climbed into the bath beside Viola and allowed Bree to wash her hurriedly and none too gently. "Is she sick?"

"I don't know," said Bree, trying to block out Madeleine's screams down the hall. "She's a baby, so she can't tell us what's wrong . . . Vee, use the flannel and wash your bits. You're big enough to do it yourself."

Obediently Viola took up the flannel, long used to doing whatever her sisters told her to.

"Hurry up!" cried Agnes, climbing down from the chair she'd been standing on to see out the window. "He's coming!"

"How far?" Bree pulled Rosina out the bath and patted her dry with a towel.

"Just coming through the trees." Agnes jumped into the bath before she had fully taken her dress off.

"Does he look scaredy?" whispered Rosina. *"Will he shout?"*

Agnes and Bree shared a fearful look over their younger sister's head. Shouting was a certainty; it was what came after that terrified the older girls.

"What about Franny?" said Viola. *"Father will shout at us all if she doesn't bathe before he's back."*

"Rats!" Bree turned to Agnes. *"Stay with Vee and Rosie. I'll go get her."*

Agnes scowled. *"Go and look after your favorite. Just like you always do."*

Bree stuck out her tongue at her sister and charged from the room as Agnes said to the younger girls, *"She's always so bossy."*

"So are you, Aggie," Bree heard Viola say before she hurtled down the hall, peeking into Figjam's room. It was empty.

Calling Figjam softly, Bree raced down the stairs and through the kitchen.

She skidded to a stop in the courtyard. A surge of fright set her heart to a frantic patter; she could hear Him stomping up the path, muttering under his breath.

NINETEEN

❧

"I'm off to London," said Madeleine.

Francine stared at her owlishly over the top of the tablet. "Why?"

"I, er, have things to see to," said Madeleine, eyes wide. "Jonathon's effects and the will, and—and . . ."

"You're lying. I can always tell when you're lying. No one actually looks as innocent as you are trying to look right now."

"Really!" Madeleine flopped down in the chair on the other side of the kitchen table, her expression of innocence dropping into a scowl. "I do have a life, you know!"

"You mean you're bored and have probably found yourself another fancy man, and in a couple of months I will get a message that you are married yet again."

Madeleine's scowl deepened into a pout. "Fine! If you must know, I need to get out of this house! I am sick of searching through boring old records about people I am so pleased I never have to meet. And yes, I am bored, and no, I don't have a fancy man. Where did you even come up with that term? Anyway, the only one with a *fancy man* is you!"

"I do not."

"Todd Constable?"

"We only went on one date, which hardly constitutes . . . well, not very much at all." Francine didn't want to think of Todd Constable. In the three days since their date, and Francine was counting, she had actively avoided him. She thought their date had gone well, but she wasn't sure, and she certainly wasn't going to ask Todd, and even if she did, and it had, what then? What happened next? Avoidance was far simpler. And to be fair to herself, she hadn't seen Todd since. Perhaps he was avoiding her, too, for only late at night did she hear heavy boots on the stairs, long after she had gone to bed.

Madeleine rolled her eyes. "Look, I just need a break. I need lights and people and perfume and dinner in a restaurant that serves up food in pretty little portions. I need to breathe! And I can't breathe here. It's stifling and I need to get out!"

"Then go," said Francine coldly, and turned back to the tablet, dragging the mouse violently across the table so the curser on the screen zigzagged with equal violence and disappeared.

Madeleine dithered in the doorway. Francine didn't look up; she wasn't going to make this easy for her sister. Finally, there was a sigh before Madeleine's footsteps echoed through the foyer and up the stairs, even as Francine's stomach cramped with hurt that her sister was leaving.

That had been a week ago, and she had not heard a word from Madeleine since. That she regretted fighting with her sister was a given. She always did. That she hadn't heard from Madeleine was no great surprise. It was Madeleine all over. Running away when life got too difficult.

And with every day that passed, the manor contracted around Francine, pressing her deep within its murmuring walls. It played on her mind, tricked her eyes, and frazzled her sense of perception. She found herself hesitating before turning a corner, or quickly turning her head to a blur of movement. She found windows open she was sure she had shut and small items she hadn't seen in years suddenly appearing in the kitchen or foyer. But that was nothing to the fresh bruises that appeared every morning when she woke up.

That intense, constant awareness wore her down until she escaped to Colthouse to check on Miss Cavendish or buried herself in the old court cases until her brain was as squelchy as a pudding and with as much intelligence. She tried not to look at the empty chair on the opposite side of the kitchen table. The truth was, she missed her sister. She missed the bond and emerging camaraderie that had formed as they concentrated on solving their ghostly problem.

The weather took a turn for the worse. All week the wind howled around the house like a vengeful fury. A gust of cold air would have Francine jumping in fright, only to find a window had blown open in the squall. She kept thinking it was George Thwaite's fury until the gale died down and rain splattered against the windows. Her garden became a sodden mess, and muddy boot prints became a regular sight through the foyer and upstairs.

It was Saturday night. Francine went upstairs late. She didn't want to admit she had been waiting up for Todd to return.

Her bedroom was cold and dark. The window was open, and the air shivered with a heavy, occupied feeling.

Francine switched on the light. "Is anyone here?" she whispered.

Not a twitch of the curtain, not a creak from the bathroom door whose hinges were loose and swung easily, not a rustle along the skirting that for years Francine had thought was plagued by mice before realizing it was another of Bree's forms of communication.

"Who's there?" she said in a louder, stronger voice that belied the tremble in her hands. "Bree? Is that you?"

The window slammed shut so hard the whole wall shuddered. It flew open again, and an icy breeze tore around the room before flying out into the night.

Francine followed it with fear-wide eyes. She swallowed hard, then straightened her shoulders. She would not be chased from her own bedroom by anyone or anything!

She marched into the bathroom, completed her ablutions in record time, scampered with unseemly haste across the room to switch off the main light, and leapt into bed, pulling the covers up to her chin. In the dim light of the bedside lamp, she watched the shadows on the wall opposite, wishing she had thought to close the window. A breeze frolicked around the courtyard her room overlooked, twisting the curtains and the shadows to dance in grotesquely human shapes.

Shutting her eyes tight, Francine concentrated on the back of her eyelids to stop the shadows coming alive in her head. It was enough that she lived in a house full of ghosts without seeing horrors in the shadows.

Sleep would not come. Sighing, she opened her eyes and reached out to the tome of Thwaite history that had been relegated to her bedside table while she spent most of her time searching through old court cases. If nothing else, it would bore her to sleep.

In the hope that Bree was nearby and could hear her, Francine cleared her throat and read aloud, *"In 1564, Richard Thwaite took to wife Joan Longrigg, and quickly had two daughters in two years. Richard was a devout Catholic and grew increasingly concerned by the restrictions placed on Catholics..."* Francine paused with her finger on *Catholics* and peered, narrow-eyed, around the room. There it was again. A faint scratching.

"Bree?" she whispered.

There was no swish of the curtains, no bump to indicate the

little ghost was in the room. The scratching paused . . . then *scritch, scritch, scritch* . . .

Spine prickling with unease, Francine continued reading, loudly now, almost shouting the words to override the horrible scratching. "*Life grew increasingly fraught for Catholics after the Rising of the North in 1569. Though Richard Thwaite had no hand in the rebellion itself, there is evidence that he made a significant contribution to . . .*"

Hours crept by and still Francine shouted out the details of the Rising of the North, and still the *scritch, scritch, scritch* was there whenever she paused for breath. "*In 1571, Richard Thwaite brought to Thwaite Manor a Jesuit priest, one Thomas Beckett, to further his children's spiritual education. As his family grew, so too did Thwaite Manor. Richard added towers on the east and west front facade and a library for his wife, Joan, who was an avid reader of religious texts.*"

Bolt upright in bed, Francine barely took in the words she was yelling, thankful her lodgers were in the east wing and couldn't hear her as the night gained the thick, lonely texture that came with the small hours of morning.

Scritch, scritch, scritch . . .

"*As recusant Catholics, the Thwaites were fined heavily for refusing to attend Church of England services,*" she bellowed. "*But as Queen Elizabeth's pursuivants grew shrewder and more punitive in their hunt for Jesuit priests, Richard commissioned a secret room to be built into the fabric of Thwaite Manor for his family to continue practicing mass in secret . . .*"

The words caught up with Francine's brain. She reread them, skimming excitedly through the tightly written lines.

"A priest hole," she breathed, then gasped as she turned the page to a plan detailing the location of the secret chamber. She lifted her face, mind racing, barely registering the subversive scratching. How had she never known there was a priest hole in Thwaite Manor?

Closing the tome with none of her usual care, she leapt out of bed and hurried out into the sleeping silence of the house. The passage was dimly lit from the couple of wall lamps Francine always kept burning at night when she had lodgers.

She hurried through the dappled shadows pooling between each light, then took the stairs two at a time to the foyer smothered in midnight black.

She opened the cupboard under the stairs and fumbled about for the light cord.

The cupboard was tiny—barely a meter square—with wood paneling covering the walls as in the foyer.

Squeezing inside, she closed the door behind her and opened the volume of Thwaite history with difficulty in the confined space.

She scrutinized the plan of the priest hole, which detailed how to open it, then surveyed the cupboard. It appeared too small to hold any secrets. Putting the tome down, she bent to view the paneled walls. They were in pristine condition. Not a single crack had formed, yet the walls had been installed centuries before. She felt along the panels.

She nearly missed the slight indents on the last panel. Placing her fingertips in the indents, she pushed hard to the left . . . and leapt back with a small, startled scream when the entire back wall slid to the side with an audible grating creak and disappeared into a recess, releasing a cloud of age-old dust.

"Oh my," she breathed, then coughed in the dust. Her stomach in a knot of anticipation, Francine reached for the spare heavy-duty torch she kept in the cupboard, having no intention of heading into the bowels of the manor in the pitch dark. The torchlight revealed seven narrow, dusty, wooden steps right below the staircase Francine had walked up and down every day of her entire life. At the very bottom was a room.

She pulled herself onto the top step and, half crouching, made her way awkwardly down the narrow stairs. Five hundred years of accumulated dust rose around her; on the peripheries of the torchlight, it curled and spiraled, creating shapes where no shapes should be. A quick flick of the torch revealed the tiny chamber was empty but for a single spider in one corner casting its web. No adornments, no embellishments. The room had been designed for one thing only: to hide.

Francine's breath was loud in the withered silence pooling around her like a shroud. It was a silence that stole into her very marrow.

Then an echo came from everywhere and nowhere—whispery, musty, and as dry as a tomb. It bypassed Francine's ears and hit her primeval nerve of fear. She whipped around, torchlight flailing wildly, almost falling in her haste to get her back against the wall, stirring up dust so it swirled up into a cloud that clung to the stale air.

Ever so slowly, the dust floated down, shaping, curving, and merging into a little girl in braids with a finger raised to her lips. On the very edge of hearing came *shhh*.

"Bree! You scared the life out of me," cried Francine, her hand to her chest above her galloping heart. "I was having visions of ghostly priests trapped down here." Then she flicked the torch around the priest hole. "When I first read about this place, I thought . . ." She tried to smile as tears filled her eyes. "I thought our sisters might've been down here."

A sob sighed around the secret chamber before a rush of warm air, as soft as a moth's powdery wings, caressed Francine's cheek then flew up the stairs.

"No! Wait! Please don't leave," she cried, and hurried after Bree, stepping out of the cupboard in time to see her shadowy form vanish up the stairs.

Francine dashed after the little ghost to the third floor.

A fluttering, like a bird trapped in a closed room, sent Francine hurrying to the library in the West Tower. Her bare feet left prints in the dust that had accumulated over the years, for she rarely ventured up here.

She paused on the threshold to switch on the lights.

The geriatric candelabra in the center of the circular room sent out soft, glowing fingers to brush against leather-bound volumes in bookcases wrapped around the walls from floor to ceiling.

"Bree," she called softly.

A distressed sob whispered on the stale air. In the dim light, a darting mirage quivered about the library, hither and thither, a fretful brushing against the book spines, a swooping graze against the floor, then up to the chandelier to set it swinging alarmingly on the old chains, frightening the spiders from their webs.

"Bree! What are you doing? What is upsetting you so?"

The lightest of touches, the merest caress against Francine's cheek and a warmth against the crook of her neck, as though Bree had rested her head there.

"What are you trying to tell me, Bree?" she whispered, scarcely daring to move lest she upset the little ghost even further.

Criiik . . . criiik . . . criiik . . .

Turning her head fearfully, Francine looked down the long gallery behind her, lined with yet more portraits of Thwaite ancestors. Poles and planks lay against one wall, in neat preparation for their erection around the clock tower.

The scratching faded to a fractious mutter.

"Is that Him, Bree?" she murmured, the hair on her nape prickling unpleasantly.

A whimper rippled into Francine's ear like the softest of rumors. Bree's warmth slid from her neck and flitted into the passage.

Francine chased after her, eyes on the walls that muttered and whispered as she took the stairs down two at a time, desperate to keep sight of Bree. The foyer still lay shrouded in midnight as Bree flittered through the front door.

Grabbing her coat off the rack, Francine opened the door and slipped outside.

It was still dark out, made all the darker by a veil of clouds, crowding the garden with shadows. Bree ran ahead, little more than a glimmer of moonlight on a moonless night.

"Bree!" Francine called, desperate not to lose sight of her. Then her pace lagged when the little ghost disappeared into the graveyard. The surrounding trees were mere vulpine shadows, twisted and still, expectant and watchful.

She approached the graveyard cautiously, but her love for Bree overrode her fear. Somewhat fortified that Bree had not vanished into Lonehowe Wood beyond, she opened the creaking gate and walked down the rows of her dead.

Treading quietly so as not to alarm Bree into flight once more, she passed the Victorian Thwaites, whose graves were a knot of color, each announcing anew their floral messages of remembrance, love, and sorrow, marred only by that single dark warning of hatred on the nameless grave that Bree flitted around for a moment before dashing away. Francine passed the sagging yew tree where the earliest Thwaites were buried. Their headstones were not as grand as those of later centuries; they were humble, moss-encroached, and pitted.

She stopped beside Bree, now a still shadow amidst shadows, in front of her own grave. Beside hers, Montgomery's grave was ensconced in a cheerful mantle of purple crocus.

"I'm so sorry, Bree," she whispered, not knowing what else to say to the sadness that filled the air between them. Bree was a trapped soul, a ghost with the gentle paradox of fearing what lay beyond yet yearning for it, too.

There were so many reasons a soul might remain: a debt that needed paying, vengeance, guilt over earthly actions and their subsequent consequences. Yet, Francine couldn't imagine what unfinished business Bree might have with the living, and she desperately didn't want to know, unable to bear the thought of life without her.

Not so George Thwaite. He, too, was a trapped soul, saturating the very walls of her home like an evil disease. Something had happened at his death that had bound him to this world. Was it for an unpaid debt, vengeance, or guilt? Or perhaps something else altogether? She needed to figure out what he needed to rest.

Firming her resolution to discover what had happened to George Thwaite, Francine sighed when she realized Bree was no longer beside her. She looked around the graveyard, but her sister was gone.

Francine's sigh scurried around the sepulchral shadows, the tree above seeming to draw closer as she hunkered down to weed around the two small graves. She sat back on her haunches and looked up at the silhouette of the drooping dogwood.

A sob caught in her throat as the memory of her mum rose unbidden in her mind. It swept over her like displaced déjà vu, as though she was inside someone else's memory.

Standing up slowly, lest an abrupt movement dislodge the memory, Francine stepped back from the graves. Her mum, digging with a shovel . . . It was night . . . She was digging in the graveyard.

A moan of anguish escaped Francine's lips at the thought of her mum digging the graves of her own children. Alone. An intensely private burial.

Yet the perspective felt all wrong, distorted. The memory from a much younger age, through a kaleidoscope filled with clear, cut glass. Francine walked out of the graveyard, then turned to face it when on the dug-up lawn.

It still felt wrong. She could remember her mum kneeling, head bent, shoulders shuddering with a terrible grief. Guilt swept over Francine, feeling like a sneak viewing another's intense grief that should never have been witnessed in a place she was not supposed to be.

Fifty years on, Francine stood staring at the graveyard she had feared all her life, until the sky quickened in the east with a pearl-edged cast.

26 July, 1969

"Figjam," Bree called softly, her stomach clenched into a fist of dread as His heavy tread drew nearer.

She glanced at Lonehowe Wood, then discarded the idea that Figjam would've gone in there by herself. The oak tree?

Bree hurried to the vast oak tree and hissed, "Figjam! Are you up there?"

No answer.

"If you're up there, then don't come down now. He's nearly here."

She turned at the sound of a rattle over the thud of His heavy footsteps.

Standing still, Bree cocked her head, listening.

There it was again. The rattle of a chain.

Frowning, she hurried over to the well.

The bucket was just visible in the gloom, nearly at the bottom of the well, and sitting in it, fast asleep with his head resting on his chest, was, "Monty?" Bree whispered to the little boy. "How did you get down there?"

Back tensed, conscious that at any moment He would come round the corner into the courtyard, Bree cranked the handle and quickly hoisted Monty up. Tears streamed down her face. A beating would come. There was nothing she could do to avoid it. Monty was down the well, no sign of Figjam, and herself not even bathed yet. There was no time to hide. No time to run to her oak tree until He had calmed down.

Trying hard to staunch her tears, she pulled the bucket towards her and hauled out her little brother. His body was heavy, a dead weight as he slept.

She held Monty tight against her chest, barely conscious he was wet, but very conscious that the heavy footsteps had been replaced by heavy breathing behind her.

She turned slowly. He loomed over her, red hair sticking up in all directions, hazel eyes bloodshot and furious as He glared down at his eldest daughter.

"What are you doing out here?" he shouted, whiskery face close to Bree's, stale alcoholic fumes hitting her nose. "How many times have I told you little brats to stay away from the well?" Then His eyes drifted down to Monty clutched to Bree's chest. "And with my boy!"

"Father," she began, backing up against the well until the old stones dug into her back.

He snatched Monty from Bree's arms with one hand as the other came around in a wide arc and struck her on the side of the face.

Bree went flying across the courtyard.

Hurt, winded, she lay very still, eyes shut.

TWENTY

There was no point going to bed now. Francine sat at the kitchen table with the borrowed tablet, staring blankly at the screen filled with lists of court cases, pushing the mouse back and forth without noticing what she was doing.

Secrets. So many secrets in Thwaite Manor. They murmured in the walls, hid in slyly built rooms and whispered down the chimneys. Francine's abstract thoughts tied her mind into knots of ghosts, emotions, life, and death. She could feel the past weighing down on her, stretching out clammy fingers to brush roughly against her . . .

"Francine?"

Francine awoke from the brown study she had fallen into and gazed stupidly at her sister.

"God! You look terrible," said Madeleine, entering the kitchen cautiously, as though expecting something to be thrown at her. "Have you actually slept since I left?" She glanced around and shivered. "And this house! I don't know how you can stand it. My skin started crawling the moment I stepped inside."

"It's not the house," said Francine finding her tongue. "It's Him. He's infected it. I can feel Him everywhere . . . What are you *doing* here?"

Madeleine took the seat across from Francine. "I hadn't left for good." She placed a thin file on the table in front of her. "I was doing research."

"Why? We were already doing research. I'm *still* doing research." Francine scowled at the tablet, loathing it more than before she had learned to use it.

"I got bored with the court cases, so I read some blogs on how to find information. It was mainly for researching ancestry and . . . What?"

"You lost me at blogs. What are blogs?"

"It's like an online diary. Anyway, I got to reading, and then thought perhaps we were looking in the wrong place. We've been looking at major crimes in Crown Courts, but all crimes first go to the local magistrate's court. And we don't know that George committed a murder or anything like that, but he was a violent man and, well, I thought perhaps he'd been in another pub brawl or some sort of public disturbance that wasn't serious enough to go to a Crown Court. So I got to thinking some more, and I realized I know a lot of people who could help. Lord knows I've been married to most of them. So I figured—"

"You're gabbling. Get to the point."

"Well, you make me nervous when you stare at me like that! Now, where was I?" Madeleine said, with every intention of enjoying her moment. "Oh, yes! As you know Jonathon was a genealogist, so I phoned some of his colleagues. One of them always had a thing for me and, oh, Franny, you and I hadn't a clue where to look; there are these databases! It was actually quite exciting. I wanted to phone you, except you don't have a bloody phone, which is really inconvenient, I might add."

"Just tell me what you found!" said Francine, exasperated.

HER LITTLE FLOWERS 263

"Nothing! At least, not then, because there was nothing in the magistrates' court cases that we could find. So Jonathon's friend suggested I speak to someone at the police. So I spoke to Mason—"

"You say that as though I should know who Mason is," said Francine, resigning herself to listening to Madeleine's ramble.

"He was my second husband—no, I lie—my third. He was in the police force. Gone private now. He has his own security firm, which was no real surprise, as I always suspected he was a bit bent, and I'm sure he was kicked out the force for something underhanded."

"Madeleine! Just tell me what you've found!"

"Montgomery!"

"What?" Francine cried, bewildered. "What has he got to do with anything? He was dead when George ran away."

"But his name came up in an old police report." With a triumphant flourish, Madeleine pulled out a couple of pieces of paper from the file and slid them across the table. "This happened a week after Bree and Montgomery died," she said, her voice breathless with excitement.

Shivering under the smothering weight of the house's narrowed attention on herself and Madeleine, Francine focused on the pages.

Lancaster and Morecambe Constabulary: Lancaster County
Case number: MWH 4/71 – 58973
Date: 4 August, 1969
Reporting Officer: PS Havens
Prepared by: PC Disciple

Incident Type: Public Disturbance
Address of Occurrence: Williamson Park, Quernmore Road, Lancaster.

Witness:
Mrs. Eliza Winthorpe of 21 Wyresdale Road, Lancaster.
Mr. and Mrs. Geoffrey Clements of 22 Wyresdale Road, Lancaster.

On 4 August, 1969, at approximately 20:45, a middle-aged man created a public disturbance in Williamson Park. After complaints from Mrs. Eliza Winthorpe, PC Disciple and PS Havens were dispatched, and arrived on the scene at 21:23. The suspect had climbed into the fountain and was laughing hysterically as he splashed the small crowd that had gathered.

The suspect was of medium build with red hair. His face was noticeably red. He was clearly intoxicated.

PS Havens approached the suspect and asked him to come out of the fountain. He was sworn and screamed at.

The suspect climbed to the top of the fountain, carrying a bag with him. There he sat, hugging the bag and muttering, "My boy. My Montgomery. My big, brave boy," over and over again, before he started screaming, "He's dead! My boy is dead!"

Francine's head jerked up to her sister who was watching her anxiously.

"He actually mentions Montgomery," said Madeleine. "I had to read it five times because I thought I was reading the name wrong."

"But he sounds like he was insane."

"He probably was."

Francine shook her head and returned to the report.

The suspect refused to come down. PS Havens climbed into the fountain and spoke to the suspect to calm him. The suspect burst into tears and vomited over PS Havens before launching himself off the fountain, screaming, "I can fly!"

He hit the ground hard yet seemed unharmed. He rose to his feet, screaming, and swung at PS Havens.

PS Havens and DC Disciple wrestled the suspect to the ground. PS Havens read the caution and was in the process of handcuffing the suspect when he vomited over PC Disciple. In the confusion, the suspect managed to escape the officers' grasp and ran across the park.

PS Havens and DC Disciple pursued the suspect and cornered him at the edge of the park. The suspect turned violent again, and struck PC Disciple in the eye, before charging into PS Havens. The officers put some distance between themselves and the suspect. The suspect lost all interest and walked in a circle, muttering to himself, "So many flowers." Then he grew agitated, shouting, "All her flowers for one boy." He continued in a similar vein for some time.

The suspect became subdued, and the officers were able to handcuff him. Once detained, he said to the officers, "I must go home. I made a pact with the devil, and it is mine. That witch shan't take it away from me."

He was taken to the holding cells at the station. On arrival, his bag was removed from him, which caused a bout of violence.

The suspect was held for twenty-four hours in the hope he could be questioned once sober. He did not sleep in that time nor did his behavior change. He swung between extreme euphoria, wild rages, manic giggling, and bouts of depression, which led to longer bouts of tears. He muttered to himself constantly, appeared confused by his surroundings.

The suspect had no personal papers or identification on him, and when questioned would not give his name or any personal particulars. After twenty-four hours, when there was no change in his behavior, a doctor was called for. Dr Robert Lapino's report is attached.

On the doctor's recommendation, the suspect was remanded in custody to Nonsuch Hospital for further observation before his hearing in front of the Magistrates.

"Is this all you found?" asked Francine.

Madeleine nodded.

"Where's the doctor's report and the witness statements?"

"I don't know. That was it, and after that, I hit a dead end. There was no hearing and no other reports that I could find."

"What about this hospital? Did you go there and speak to someone? I'm sure you've been married to someone in the medical field at some stage who could've helped you."

"That hurts, Francine! Anyway, I couldn't find any mention of a hospital called Nonsuch in Lancaster."

"There must be!" snapped Francine. "You didn't look hard enough. It's probably closed now. Did you think of that?"

"Yes, I did! Where do you think I've been these past two days? In Lancaster itself! And there is and has never been anywhere called Nonsuch Hospital in Lancaster. Lord, Francine! I found our father and that's all you can say? No thank you or well done or anything!"

"Thank you and well done," grouched Francine. She gazed at her sister's woebegone face and sighed. "Why didn't you just tell me what you were up to? I would've gone with you."

Madeleine burst out laughing. "You? In London? Even Lancaster would've terrified you. You hate going down to Hawkshead!"

Francine scowled, for her sister was right, though the laughter rankled. It murmured fractiously around her, taking on a spiteful edge until she knew she was no longer hearing Madeleine's laughter.

Madeleine hiccupped into silence, feeling the echo of whispering malice. She was quiet for a long moment, then shrugged. "I knew you would've said I was being foolish," she said in a small voice. "I wanted to do something right for once. Something that would make you proud of me."

Francine bit back a retort. Madeleine looked so anxious and so like a younger version of herself in need of a kind word, which she had rarely received from her older sister.

"I *am* proud of you," Francine said gruffly. "I've always been proud of you."

"Now you're lying through your teeth. I've been an embarrassment to you all my life."

"No," said Francine, feeling her way through a home truth she had never admitted to herself. She swallowed against a desire to snap something cruel and said, "Well, perhaps a bit. But I was . . . I've always been envious. You're good with people. You always know what to say and people like you. I'm not like that."

"It would help if you actually *liked* people." An uncomfortable silence hung between them that Madeleine finally broke with, "It *is* Father, isn't it?"

"I think so. There's the connection to Montgomery."

"And Mum used to call us her flowers," added Madeleine.

"Yes, she did." Francine read the report again. "There's no mention of Viola, Agnes, and Rosina." But even as the words left her lips, she knew the answer before Madeleine said, "You and I both know he killed them."

The words hung between them with an awful conviction. And on the edge of hearing came raspy, nasty laughter.

"Lancaster." She stared at her sister dully. "He didn't get very far. Lancaster can't be more than an hour away."

"Yes. I had thought he would've ended in one of the big cities. Lancaster's not that big."

"But he wanted to come home. Why would he want to come home? Everyone said he and Mum hated each other. And what is this nonsense about devils and witches?"

Madeleine shrugged. "All our family was in Cumbria. George was the last of the Ullswater Thwaites, and we're the last of the Hawkshead branch. We're the only Thwaites left."

Francine hit the table with her fist, causing Madeleine to jump. "I wish I could remember!" she cried. "Why can't I remember what happened? It's all there in my head, I'm sure of it!"

"Calm down, Franny," said Madeleine nervously. "I doubt you saw anything. You were only five at the time."

Francine stood up, unable to bear the creeping, skulking atmosphere of the manor. "I'm going out. I need to think."

She stalked out through the courtyard to the garden and grew angry with herself for the destruction she had wrought on the vaguest notion that her sisters were buried there.

She glared at the scaffolding running up the side of the building like a praying mantis, surprised to see Todd and Keefe working on the gable end. Todd usually took Sundays off, he and Keefe disappearing for the day, returning late in the evening. Francine had never thought to ask where they went and assumed they were sightseeing.

Old timbers lay below the scaffold alongside an assortment of tools and machinery.

Todd waved down to her.

Francine turned away, flushing with embarrassment, not sure how to end the silence between them. She started towards the woods . . . and froze in shock, a hand to her mouth.

"He thought he could fly," she murmured. Head to one side, she ticked off the plants that lay strewn across the remnants of the lawn: withered, browning clumps with roots clawing the air like giant insects in a death dance.

The symptoms were all there in the police report: nausea, delusions, confusion, mood swings, red face—blood pressure possibly. Sick to her stomach, Francine's whole world shriveled with horror.

He had been poisoned.

It took all of two seconds to jump to the obvious conclusion because there was only one person who had hated George enough and knew enough about poisons . . . Her mother. She had been poisoning George *before* he had run away, *before* Bree and Montgomery had died.

TWENTY-ONE

Francine didn't notice Todd until he was walking towards her.

"You've been ignoring me," he said, a teasing note in his voice.

Disconcerted, her mind too full of revelations, she simply stared at him, then found her tongue, and said, "I—well, you're never here."

"Yeah. Sorry. I've been . . ." He frowned, taking in her ashen face. "What's wrong? Has something happened?"

"I've been looking at this the wrong way," said Francine distantly.

"Looking at what the wrong way?"

"All this time I've seen George as this sort of demon who had destroyed our lives. I dug up my whole garden because I managed to convince myself he had killed my sisters and buried them here before running away. When I found nothing, I thought I'd been wrong."

"You haven't quite managed to destroy your garden entirely," said Todd dryly. "There's still the rhododendron you can butcher."

Francine barely heard him. "But I was wrong."

Todd frowned. "You've lost me."

She dropped her voice to a hurried whisper, conscious that Keefe was on the scaffold in listening distance. "I think my mum was poisoning my father. Long before that night. Everything is here in the garden."

"You've remembered something?"

Hazy echoes swirled around the edges of her mind; forgotten feelings from before the tragedy. More fleeting inklings that were based on other people's recollections.

"No, not as such. Just a sense of . . . atmosphere. Of fear and awful expectation. And she could've done it easily too. Slipping small doses in his meals. It would explain so much, especially when I read that report. The symptoms were there, if you know what to look for."

"What report?"

It was still in Francine's hand, crumpled and forgotten. She shoved it at Todd.

"Are you sure it's about your father?" he said once he'd finished reading.

"No. Yes. I don't know . . . It could be."

"Okay," said Todd slowly. "And you think his behavior was due to poisoning. So which one?" He waved a hand around the mutilated garden.

"Moonflower." Francine didn't need to think about it. "It was my mum's flower, her favorite. Killing someone she hated with something she loved. It makes a rather ghastly symmetry."

"To me he sounds like a man crazed with grief who had drowned his sorrows in too many pints. Even the cops thought he was drunk as a lord."

Flummoxed, Francine grabbed the report and reread it. "Do intoxicated people think they can fly?"

"On little pink elephants if they've drunk enough."

"Oh . . . I don't know much about the effects of alcohol. Perhaps you're right." Francine half smiled with shame that she'd even considered her mum could do something so dreadful. "For a moment I thought I was onto something."

"Even if your mum had been poisoning him, it doesn't mean your father didn't kill your sisters." Todd looked at the scaffolding, then at the ravaged garden, before turning back to her. "How far are you willing to take this?"

"As far as I can. I want to know what happened. I *need* to know."

"You have a starting point. This Nonsuch Hospital . . ."

But Francine was already shaking her head. "According to Madeleine, it doesn't exist and never has. And the chances are, even if it had existed, it's probably closed now otherwise . . ." She petered off, her eyes flying to Lonehowe Wood.

"What is it?" said Todd, watching her with a worried frown.

"It's not a hospital." She closed her eyes at her stupidity. "It's an asylum."

She grabbed Todd's arm excitedly. "It's not Nonsuch Hospital, it's Nonsuch Asylum! I knew the name, but I couldn't place it. And it all makes sense. If this report is really about George and he appeared of unsound mind, it makes sense he would've ended up at Nonsuch, as the closest mental institution to Lancaster."

"*The* Nonsuch Asylum?" Todd's eyebrows rose in surprise. "I thought it was an urban myth. You know where it is?"

"It's in there, but it closed decades ago." Francine nodded at Lonehowe Wood, her skin crawling at the mere idea of that terrible place hidden amidst the ancient trees. Even from a distance she could feel it mouldering quietly, biding its time to unleash its leprous poison. It was the most unloved place in the world. Where nightmares come from.

"There could still be records. It should be fairly simple to find out where those records ended up."

"On the internet?" said Francine hopefully.

"I doubt anyone would've bothered to put the records of an abandoned asylum online. But . . ." Todd's eyes narrowed with thought, then he smiled at Francine. "Give me a minute." He pulled out his cell phone and tapped on it.

"What are you doing?" said Francine.

He smiled apologetically. "Googling the number for Bethlem Museum of the Mind. I went there once—They might have an idea where the records have gone, seeing as Bethlem was the worst of asylums . . ." A tinny voice interrupted him and he held up a finger and walked away. For a long while he spoke low, so Francine couldn't hear him. "Well, that's that," he said as he walked back, putting his phone into the back pocket of his trousers.

"And?" said Francine.

He grimaced ruefully. "Nothing encouraging. The woman I spoke to said if George had been alive when Nonsuch closed then his records would've gone to the institution he was transferred to."

"I *know* he's dead."

"But not if he died at Nonsuch. And I imagine, if it's anything like the size of Bethlem, then it will probably have its own graveyard. I know you are terrified of graveyards but a quick scout around the graves might turn something up."

"They didn't know his name."

"You can't go on the basis of one report, Francine. He may have given his name later." Todd threw up his hands in exasperation. "You have a date and place on the report where you could start looking. Something tangible, and the answer could be in walking distance."

Francine's throat tightened with dread. It wasn't just graveyards she feared; it was the asylum itself. All her life she had feared it, had avoided it. But to walk inside on purpose . . .

"What if I came with you?"

She blinked at Todd. "Why?" she whispered.

He smiled that slow, easy smile that crinkled his eyes. "Because I want to."

"But what about your work down in Hawkshead?"

"It's Sunday and Keefe can get on with the gable for the afternoon. Will do him good to work on his own and hopefully use some initiative." His smile broadened into a grin. "And who wouldn't want to visit a creepy old asylum in a creepy old wood?"

Flustered by Todd's grin, Francine realized, not for the first time, what an attractive man he was. Why did she always feel like a giddy schoolgirl around him?

Even then she hesitated, fearful she was on the cusp of discovering something she would regret knowing. She took a deep breath, then another, intensely aware of the watching silence from Thwaite Manor. It was there in the echo of whispers from times past, there in the fretful shudders of the branches of Bree's oak tree, though not a breath of air stirred, but mostly it was there in the shiver running down her back that George Thwaite was consuming her home like a cancer. It was folly, really, this fear of what might not be, knowing she had to find out the truth. Before she could think about it too much, she turned towards the path leading into Lonehowe Wood without waiting to see if Todd followed her.

Francine and Todd gazed at the grotesque gateway with *Nonsuch Asylum for the Criminally Insane* emblazoned in black lettering above it. The wrought iron gates were unlocked; a cut padlock hung uselessly from a chain, courtesy of previous intruders. Todd pushed open the gates, which creaked with a spine-tingling grating along the gravel path.

They glanced at each other, then wordlessly stepped through the gateway with the caution of stepping through a magical portal to a horror-filled dimension.

The asylum looked more like a garish palace, with too many towers and turrets. Gargoyles leered down from the roof. Bay windows peered blindly through the overgrowth and a broad balcony wrapped around the entire third floor. There had been extensive gardens once. Now, they garrotted the old asylum in weeds and ivy left to run wild. There was this to be said about ivy: it hid much of the building and was probably all that kept the walls from collapsing completely. The entrance, however, was rather lovely: a zigzagging double stairway of pale stone that glowed in the gloom of the woods. Every meter up both stairways were robed statues staring stolidly at their counterparts on the opposite side like somber sentinels.

"Jesus," whispered Todd, rubbing his arms as though chilled. "This place gives me the creeps. It's probably haunted."

"Probably." Francine inched closer to him, his shivering unease matching her own. Something was off, odd. She kept twisting her head to check if something was behind her. Nothing was.

Just beyond the strangled garden was an equally strangled graveyard of plain wooden crosses at the end of one of the weed-choked paths.

It was an unbearably lonely place, a wild, secret garden for the forgotten dead. Hedged in by high walls on three sides and Nonsuch Asylum on the fourth, the long grass was combed by a gentle breeze into ripples that did nothing to dispel its wretchedness. *Laburnum* had thrived and self-seeded freely, and their newly golden racemes wept over the crosses below. Francine doubted the first *Laburnum* had been planted in memory of those who lay mouldering beneath the sighing grass, yet the tree was apt for the many who'd died here in obscurity, with only a number crudely etched onto wooden crosses to remember them.

Todd frowned at the crosses. "No names?"

Francine shook her head.

"What do you want to do?" he asked when she didn't respond.

Francine bit her lip. "I'm not sure."

"Is this the part where you tell me we're going in there?" He nodded at the throttled building. He wasn't smiling.

It was what Francine had been thinking. It wasn't as though she was trespassing, as the asylum still belonged to her, even though she had never thought of it as hers. She was here now, and more importantly, she wasn't alone. She would not have got through the gateway if she'd been by herself, for she could sense eyes everywhere, watching from the undergrowth, from the blind, broken windows. Even the gargoyles appeared so lifelike that they might leap off the roof and take flight on bat wings.

Stamping down on the primordial terror racing through her veins, she said, "Yes. As you said, there could still be records, and no one has been in here since the place closed. It would be foolish not to go in and at least check."

Todd opened his mouth, then shut it again and nodded. "I just hope to Christ I don't see anything," he muttered, and hurried after Francine as she marched up the beautiful stairway, ignoring the solemn gazes of the hooded statues.

The front doors stood slightly ajar, another cut chain swinging loosely to one side, next to a faded yellow sign claiming, "Private Property. Do Not Enter." Pushing at one of the doors, Francine stepped into a vestibule, already tensing for what she might see.

"Oh god!" she whispered.

A long corridor stretched out before them. The walls bulged and buckled in waves that disappeared into the middle distance, with a bench running the length of one wall.

There was an odor of stale sweat, disinfectant, and fear that had not dissipated in the decades since the asylum had been abandoned, and so visceral it leached from the walls like a fungus. If madness were ever to have an odor it was this, combined with a deep, black, sticky despair that got into the tightest corners, wrapped around a soul, and squeezed until it was crushed.

Todd froze, then turned slowly to Francine. "There's something in front of me, touching me," he muttered hoarsely.

"No, there's not," she said, after peering hard all around them.

"I must be bloody mad," he muttered, shuddering visibly. He took out his cell phone and turned on the light, then took off down the corridor with unseemly haste. Francine walked as close to him as she could. There was something reassuring about his bulk that made the abandoned asylum marginally less frightening.

"We're in the right place for madness," she said, and the tight atmosphere lightened when Todd's chuckle rolled over her, then took on a life of its own and echoed down the buckled corridor. It came back to them with a blunt edge, all humor sucked from it.

Conversation was suppressed by the fetid air as they explored the high-ceilinged, echoing rooms on the ground floor, keeping close to each other, the light of the phone picking up relics from the days when the building had housed the criminally insane. Frames of metal beds chained to the walls, overturned wheelchairs, a series of rooms with equipment that looked like torture instruments, stinking communal bathrooms. The discovery of an office garnered a frisson of short-lived excitement, for there were no records, only a few scraps of paper.

A spiral staircase at the end of the corridor led both up and down. By tacit consent, the two went up. The dancing light from the phone cast shadows on the wall. Too many shadows; cavorting obscenely, closing in as they progressed up the twisted stairs, their footsteps loud in the dark. Footsteps that seemed to be following them.

When they reached the third floor, they saw nothing but another buckling corridor.

Skin crawling, Francine wasn't sure who was trying to walk closer to whom as she and Todd followed the light without saying a word for fear of releasing a scream that wouldn't stop.

But each room they entered was the same: vast and echoing, with rows of beds and leather restraints hanging from the walls. With her hands on her hips, Francine stopped in the final dormitory, which might have been a ballroom when the building had served a brighter purpose.

Todd watched her carefully, concern etched in the downward pull of his mouth. "Not what you were expecting?"

"No." She turned in a circle, hands to her cheeks, her breath coming hard and fast.

"What *were* you expecting?"

"Ghosts. Why can't I see them here?"

"Maybe there aren't any."

"In a place like this?" Francine snorted in disbelief. "At home I know them all. I've met them all frequently in the woods. I know their history and how they died. But here, where there should be ghosts everywhere, I haven't seen even one."

"I'm bloody glad we haven't," said Todd with feeling. "Let's finish off downstairs and get out of here."

They retraced their footsteps to the spiral staircase and down to the ground floor. There they paused, neither wishing to go down into the hell of what might be below the old asylum.

"Come on," said Todd, his reluctance a third person as he shone the torch down the narrow stairwell. "Let's get this over with."

Down they went, the cylindrical walls of the stairwell tightening around them as the staircase wound deeper and deeper into the stinking bowels of the wretched building.

They reached a narrow, windowless corridor that stretched left and right. On the remains of a swollen door just visible to the right, a sign reading *Staff Only* hung lopsided from a single screw. The floor was slimy and acid-green with mold as though diseased, and it stank of dank rot. Doorframes, minus their doors, lined the corridor.

Neither spoke as they turned left down the corridor, peering into the small rooms with walls covered in graffiti etched by desperate fingernails.

Todd hesitated in front of the swollen door. With a shudder he put his hand on the tacky handle. It stuck fast.

"It's not locked," he said after passing the torchlight between the door and the frame. "Move back." He handed the torch to Francine and put his shoulder to the door. It creaked under his assault, then grated ajar on his third attempt.

He was only able to open it halfway, and they squeezed through, almost gagging at the putrid stench that had been trapped for decades.

Metal filing cabinets and bookcases lay in twisted heaps amid torn boxes and scattered files, with paper everywhere, clinging damply to the moldy floor.

"Urgh!" muttered Francine, pulling her cardigan up to cover her nose as she picked her way through the debris and peered into a box marked X-Z on the side. She took out one of the files.

"Well?" said Todd.

"Patient files," she said. She glanced in another box marked with only a series of numbers, her heart sinking. "Hundreds of them."

His expression of dismay mirrored Francine's own. It would take ages to go through them all.

Todd rallied first. "They aren't going anywhere. We'll come back tomorrow and start going through them."

Without needing to voice their urgent desire for fresh air, they hurried up to the ground floor and sprinted along the buckling corridor.

"What's wrong?" said Francine, belatedly slowing her mad dash when she realized Todd wasn't beside her.

He swallowed and merely pointed, his eyes following a decrepit wheelchair limping, bow-legged, across the wide hallway behind them. It nudged the opposite wall before going backward again with an awful *thweak, thweak.*

"I really wish I hadn't seen that," he whispered.

"But nothing is pushing it!" cried Francine in frustration. "Why can't I see any ghosts here?"

Todd hurried up to her and took her arm. "Even if you could, ghosts won't help you find any answers."

Following the bobbing light, they made all haste to get out of Nonsuch Asylum. They ran through the ancient woodland, only slowing when Thwaite Manor appeared through the trees.

26 July, 1969

"There's my beautiful boy," crooned Father, words slurring. He lifted Monty up and smiled as he had never smiled at his daughters.

No responding giggle, no startled cry at being woken.

Cracking an eye open, Bree watched, confused, as her father slowly brought Monty closer to his face, mouth slack with shock.

"No," Father whispered, touching the small face with gentle fingers.

It was a dreadful, intimate thing to see another's dawning grief. That first moment when the face crumples as reality becomes nightmare. Even for one hated as Bree hated her father, she shared his grief.

For Monty wasn't sleeping. He was dead.

The burgeoning realization was slow to come. It was Father's face first: confusion and horror. A disbelieving shake of the head. Deep, vibrating breaths. With eyes squeezed shut, a wail of pure, feral anguish swept around the courtyard like an avenging angel as he clasped Monty's body to his chest.

Then came fury and blame.

Bree knew that look; a look all the Thwaite girls knew well. His face contorted in an instant, reddening so the tiny, broken veins in his cheeks turned purple, eyes narrowing to slits, lips pressed tight, tendons in his neck standing out, tense.

His enraged gaze settled on Bree. "You!" he hissed. "You've killed him!"

Feigning unconsciousness would get her nowhere now. Bree leapt to her feet and backed away towards the oak tree, hands raised defensively.

There was no time to deny or confirm the charge. In two long strides he was in front of Bree, even as she turned to make a wild dash to the oak tree and safety.

He grabbed her long red braids and pulled so hard her head snapped back until she peered up into his whiskery face upside-down. "I'll kill you!" he muttered.

Bree sobbed from the pain as she was yanked by her hair across the courtyard and into the kitchen.

"ELEANOR!" he bellowed. "ELEANOR! Get your scrawny arse down here. I'm going to kill her! I'm going to kill them all! She killed him . . . She killed Monty." The last was a choked whisper. He sank to his knees in front of the kitchen table where he had lain Monty and simply stared at the little boy as sobs wracked his body.

Bree struggled desperately, pushing at his shoulder to be free from his grip on her hair, but he seemed to have forgotten her as he crooned to Monty.

"George?" Mummy hurried into the kitchen and stopped short. Her green eyes flickered to Bree still struggling to be free, then to Monty. A hand to her chest, a single tear running down her prematurely lined cheek. She did not move, frozen in a time loop. She started shaking her head, even as her whole body shivered with an effort not to shriek and lament.

It seemed an eternity to Bree before Mum whispered, "What

have you done, George?" She stayed where she was in the doorway as though too scared to go to Monty, too scared to establish the truth with a cold touch.

George Thwaite whipped around so fast Bree fell over and was dragged across the floor like a forgotten ragdoll. "Me?" He shook Bree by her braids and pulled her to her feet roughly. "It was this little bitch of yours," he hissed. "I found her by the well with Monty . . . My Monty!"

Bree renewed her efforts, grabbing her braids and yanking them away from Father's now slack grip as he collapsed again in front of his son, wailing his name.

Mum's face mirrored her daughter's rictus of terror.

"I'm sorry, Mummy," Bree sobbed. "I'm so, so sorry. I don't know what happened. I'm so sorry."

Mum, who had been holding herself together with a fierce rigidity, sagged as the terrible horror hit her. "What have you done, Bree?" she whispered, tears forcing their way down her cheeks and left unstemmed. "What have you done?"

Bree shook her head, lips compressed tight against the words stuck in her throat.

Mum reached out to steady herself on a nearby chair and stared at her dead son. She made no move towards the little body, seemingly unable to comprehend the enormity of her world falling apart in the space of a few seconds.

Bree didn't know what to do. The evening had escalated into something far beyond anything she felt capable of dealing with, and she looked to her mum for help.

"I'm sorry, Mummy," Bree said again.

Mum swallowed against her unchecked tears, her eyes darting between her daughter and her wailing husband. She straightened, her expression wavering between her need to grieve and the need to protect her daughter from her husband's wrath.

"Mummy?"

Mum turned to Bree stiffly, "Get out and hide," she mouthed.

With a last glance at Monty, Bree darted past Mummy, who whispered, "And hide your sisters."

Bree nodded and ran into the foyer.

Taking the stairs two at a time, she yelped in fright when Agnes, Viola, and Rosina appeared at the top.

"What have you done, Bree?" said Agnes, hugging her tatty blue-and-white dog.

"Father's shouting," Rosina added, and ran down the steps to hug Bree tightly around her waist.

Bree shook her head, a hand on Rosie's hair, as fresh tears came. "Monty's dead," she whispered.

TWENTY-TWO

The next morning Francine and Todd stood in the asylum's vestibule, looking down the buckling corridor as the old building settled around them with skin-crawling intensity. The intermittent sunshine did not reach within these walls and did nothing to dissipate the fetid odor of madness that choked the air.

"This is going to be a mammoth task, Francine," said Todd. "All we have is the date that he came here. It's not a lot to go on."

"I know." Francine sighed, then smiled up at him, still a little floored that he had taken a few days off to help her go through the files they had found the night before. She had asked Madeleine to help too, but after her sister's look of horror, all she had got was a mumbled excuse. She hadn't seen Madeleine since.

Stiff with reluctance towards the job ahead, they made their way downstairs to the basement with twin expressions of dismay at the boxes of files in the light of the torch Todd had brought. Even though they were prepared for the diseased stench, if anything, it seemed more poisonous than it had the night before.

"Let's get cracking," said Todd when Francine made no move towards a file. With a grimace, he twisted his laced fingers inside out in preparation of getting his hands dirty. "We'll take these upstairs where there's some light. I'm not staying down here longer than I have to."

Setting up their base in the cleanest room they could find on the ground floor, the two brought up all the boxes from the basement and started going through the files with grim determination.

They fell into a process of elimination of what they knew of George, which amounted to little more than his age and date of admission. It didn't take long for them to realize that these were the files of the inmates who had never left Nonsuch; no one had cared enough to preserve them, and they had been left to moulder in the basement.

Minutes ticked by, then hours.

Todd looked up from a file. "Correct me if I'm wrong, but I seem to remember the police report saying George had red hair."

"It did and he did. The Thwaites have a strong family resemblance; we all had red hair."

"Your hair was red?" he said, eyebrows rising.

Francine smiled. "Very red."

"Oh," said Todd, nonplussed. Then he smiled. "I've always had a thing for redheads. That explains rather a lot."

It was Francine's turn to look nonplussed, while Todd just grinned at her.

But it was another small fact to help in their process of elimination, and the piles of files slowly moved from one side of the room to the other.

The asylum was not a silent place. It creaked and groaned

around them, with the occasional vile, taunting rustle creeping into the room that had Francine's head snapping up to stare into the dark corners.

Yet, for all the seeping misery around them, there was a macabre fascination in the lives of the inmates of Nonsuch Asylum, and a deep sadness for those who had been lost in their own heads as the world outside passed them by.

When day merged into night, they went back to Thwaite Manor, only to return early the next day. They grew accustomed to the noises and unnerving silences of the asylum. By the second day they no longer flinched when a fetid breeze ruffled loose pages before fleeing out into the buckling corridor.

Days passed. As their pile of files dwindled, so did their chance of finding George Thwaite. But neither voiced their concern aloud, not in that stifling tomb of sad lives, half lived.

It was late afternoon on the fourth day; Francine looked up when Todd grew quieter and quieter, forming a ballooning silence around them, punctured by the occasional flick of a page turning.

"You've found something?" she asked, not for the first time, always receiving a negative reply. So she was surprised when he nodded.

"It doesn't make for happy reading." He handed her the file.

"There's nothing happy about any of this," she grumped, then sat up straight when she read the first page. She had read it before. "This is the police report!"

Todd nodded. "Keep going. There's more."

There wasn't much in the file. Below the police report was a handwritten Statement of Particulars that was little more than a lined card:

> *Statement of Particulars*
> *If any particulars are not known, the fact is to be so*
>   *stated.*

(Where the patient is in the order described as an idiot, omit the particulars marked *.)

Name of patient: Unknown
Sex and age: Male, 40s to 50s
Description: Well nourished, red hair, hazel eyes.
*Married, single, or widowed: Unknown. Wedding ring is in evidence.
*Occupation: Unknown
*Religious persuasion: Unknown.
*Whether first attack: Unknown.
*Age on first attack: Unknown.
*Duration of existing attack: 48 hours, possibly longer.
*When and where previously under care and treatment as a lunatic, idiot, or person of unsound mind: Unknown.
On remand from Lancaster and Morecambe Constabulary until hearing before Magistrates. Believed to be of unsound mind, possible Confusional Insanity.

Francine turned the card over, but the back was blank. She turned to the next.

Admission Date: 5 August, 1969
Attending doctor: Dr Robert Lapino
Patient name: unknown.
Patient number: 37189
Diagnosis: Possible Confusional Insanity due to drugs or alcohol.

5 August, 1969—Patient 37189 placed in main ward on arrival and shackled to bed for fear of outburst of violence.

Sedated on arrival. Had little effect.

Patient displayed a wide range of symptoms: depression, wild rages, periodic vomiting, and complaints of headaches. Elevated blood pressure and rapid pulse.

6 August, 1969—Convulsions. Complaints of dizziness and dry mouth.

Mistrustful of staff. Will not eat, drinks little. Often violent and upset.

7 August, 1969—Constant demand for bag to be returned to him. Contacted Lancaster Station. Bag returned (Contents—couple of days' clothing (clean), stale food. No personal items). When questioned about bag, patient would not answer, curled into a ball, and said, "It is mine, and none shall take what is mine from me."

8 August, 1969—initial tests returned—traces of alcohol, but no drugs. Patient 37189 displaying deep degree of distress, often stating urgent desire to return home. When asked where home was, patient refused to divulge location. Possible flight risk: patient seen on balcony, bent on escape. Patient moved to ground floor.

9 August, 1969—Dr. Julian, after a number of sessions, has declared patient 37189 of unsound mind, pending further testing (Notes attached to file). Patient violent to staff. Placed in solitary confinement for observation.

10 August, 1969—Displaying symptoms of Confusional Insanity—delusions, hallucinations, and paranoia. Obsession with witches and devils. Seems convinced a witch has taken his home from him. Much talk of a pact with the devil (See log in file).

11 August, 1969—patient 37189 in weakened state and calm. Still refuses to eat but is drinking water.

Returned to ward, restrained to bed. Demanded his bag be given to him, ate what stale food remained therein.

After urgent call at 3 a.m., returned to Nonsuch. Arrived too late, patient 37189 had escaped after killing long-term patients Christopher Aldridge and Simon Newbury.

Spoke to patients and staff involved. It is believed the incident was triggered by patient 37189 discovering he was in Nonsuch, though it is not understood why this knowledge led to what occurred thereafter. Able to glean some information to what ensued (Accounts from patients (dictated) and Matron Adams' report in file).

Patient 37189 escaped restraints then broke into main ward on first floor and barricaded doors. Was in a wild rage and screaming for a Montgomery (which alerted Matron Adams to the situation). Patients within agree that patient 37189 displayed inhuman strength and threw beds and tables around the ward. He allegedly attacked Simon Newbury, throttling him, before Christopher Aldridge (Unsure of personality present at time), attempted to help. During the fracas, patient 37189 broke open the doors to the balcony and escaped by leaping from the first floor.

Unable to ascertain exact chain of events that led to the attack; accounts vary in coherency.

Police arrived shortly after self. Broke down the door.

After thorough search of the grounds and surrounding woods by the security staff, patient 37189 had not been found.

Nothing else was in the file. No other patient accounts or nurse records.

"What is it?" said Todd, alarmed by Francine's ashen face.

Shivering with cold understanding, she whispered, "A pact with the devil."

"Yes," said Todd slowly. "But the doctor does say he was delusional."

"No! Well, maybe . . . but I think George was talking about the marriage contract."

He frowned. "You've lost me. What contract?"

"Miss Cavendish—my mum's friend—told me about it. My grandfather had this obsession with continuing the Thwaite name. So he got George to marry my mum; George was a distant relation, but still a Thwaite."

"Why would either your mum or father agree to that?" asked Todd, horrified.

"For George it was a godsend; my grandfather added the clause that if my parents had a male heir then the manor would pass into George's name when the heir turned five. For my mother . . ." Francine shrugged. "Miss Cavendish said he was charming at first; perhaps she got caught up in his charm until it was too late."

"And Montgomery was that heir. So when he died . . ."

"George's chance of getting his hands on the manor died with him."

Todd gave a low whistle of incredulity. "That is seriously twisted." After a moment, he added, "Not to be callous, especially as your parents had lost their son, but why not have another one?"

"No, they hated each other too much."

"It's a dreadful irony, isn't it? That he was so close to home and didn't even know it. Must've been quite a shock when he realized he hadn't got away from the manor after all, especially with the hue and cry for him. It's a wonder the staff here didn't know who he was."

"Not really; this place always had a terrible stigma. The staff here were ostracized completely," said Francine. Then she frowned. "He hadn't known where he was," she murmured to herself. "Not until just before he esca—" A newborn unease grew to a queasy flutter in Francine's stomach as she read the report again, and her world fell away as she connected gleaned facts to half-baked theories. They meshed into one terrible certainty. "This is wrong," she whispered. "This has to be wrong."

"You don't think this is about your father?"

"No, I . . . yes, it's him, but it's wrong. George must have died here."

"Okay," said Todd slowly. "I'm not sure I'm following you."

Shaking her head, she read the report over and over, willing the words to change.

"Francine?" Todd's voice came from a long way off. "Have you any idea where he might have gone?"

She looked up at his concerned face without seeing him; she was only aware of the mantra running through her head . . . *wrong, wrong, wrong* . . . repressing what she knew to be true but simply couldn't admit to herself, even in the privacy of her own head. It wasn't possible. She couldn't, *wouldn't* believe it.

Her lips tightened. "It's wrong," she said again. "The doctor wasn't there. He didn't see what happened. He was relying on secondhand accounts from people who were . . ." She waved a wild hand around to encompass the madness that leached from the very fabric of the old building. "He got it wrong!"

Francine leapt to her feet, startling Todd, and dashed out the room and out of the asylum. She raced down the stairs into the wild garden and along the overgrown path to the forsaken graveyard.

Her heart bursting with a terrible dread, she hurried from cross to cross muttering, "37189 . . . 37189 . . . 37189."

"Francine!" cried Todd as he ran into the graveyard then stopped in astonishment. "What are you doing? George didn't die here. There's no point—"

"No!" Francine darted to the next cross, then the next. "He

must've died here. They made a mistake. They must've made a mistake. It's the only—" She choked on the words.

Todd grabbed Francine by the shoulders, forcing her to stop. "What does it matter if he died here or not?"

"You don't understand!" she cried. "I need him to have died here! He had to have died here!"

"It doesn't matter. He's dead. Nothing can change that."

She stared up at him wild-eyed. "No! It matters. It matters more than I can bear."

"We'll keep looking, Francine. We'll do everything we can to find him."

Shaking her head, she ripped away from him and ran from cross to cross, even as rain started to fall. Todd didn't try to stop her again. He stood on the edge of the graveyard and watched her, helpless and bewildered.

Francine sat on an ivy-clad bench in the garden of the asylum. She didn't notice the hissing rain or care that she was wet through, or that Todd sat beside her holding her hand.

"How are you feeling?" he asked after an age.

"Hollow," whispered Francine. "Just . . . hollow."

Silence stretched before Todd said, "Are you sure the records are wrong?"

It was an effort to crawl out of her gloomy reverie to shake her head. "No, it was . . . It was him. But it doesn't matter anymore." Her voice broke in an effort to hold back the tears that had been lodged in her throat since she'd read the report.

Todd squeezed her hand and smiled with a warmth that, at any other time, would have sent a blush to her cheeks. "We'll find out what happened to him," he promised. "Whatever it—" He was interrupted by the insistent tones of his cell phone ringing. He pulled out his phone, looked at the caller ID, and grimaced. "I need to take this. It's Keefe." He tapped the screen and put the phone to his ear.

A gabble filtered into the air. Todd didn't say much after the initial greeting but listened intently. "And no one was harmed?"

Something in his tone snapped Francine to attention. She frowned at him inquiringly.

"Very well, shore up the damage as best you can—" He broke off and listened, his expression changing from dismay to horror. "You found *what*?" He nodded a few times. "Don't do another thing except shore up. I'll be there in half an hour."

Todd disconnected and looked at Francine. "The gable end collapsed," he said, standing up. "We need to get back to the manor immediately."

"How bad is the damage?" she asked, her chest aching with a terrible anticipation.

"It sounds like the wall of the drawing room has collapsed, but I couldn't quite make out what Keefe was saying, he was crying so hard."

"I'm not surprised," she snapped. "He's just broken my house!"

Todd's face creased with sadness. "That's not why he was crying."

26 July, 1969

Death has little meaning for the young if never exposed to it. The Thwaite girls were not prepared for the death of a loved one, and none of them really comprehended that their world, already cracked and bloodied, had shattered.

But Bree understood a little more than her sisters. She had seen Monty's little body, noted the stillness, the paleness.

"What have you done, Bree?" Agnes demanded. "We're not getting a hiding for you. We won't!"

"Didn't you hear me?" Bree cried, tears streaming down her face. "Monty's dead. He fell down the well."

Agnes, being a little older, made the connections and assessed the possible repercussions for them all. She clutched her blue-and-white dog to her chest and sucked one of its ears.

"Mummy's shouting," said Rosina, her eyes flickering between her older sisters. She stuck her thumb into her mouth.

"Mummy never shouts," said Agnes. "Never." Her eyes grew round as she tried not to cry. "What do we do?"

"We hide. Outside. In the woods." Bree herded her sisters

downstairs, then stopped in the foyer. She automatically turned towards the kitchen, but Mummy and Father were still shouting at each other in there, blocking their exit. It was a violent roaring that scared the girls far more than any of their father's previous rants. Mum had always waged a silent war against their father; her weapons were distraction, a stiff calmness, and little retaliation to fuel his rage. The girls had never heard her fight back as she was now. Though they didn't understand it, she was fighting for them.

"To the front door," Bree whispered.

"We have a better one," said Rosina, talking around her thumb.

"Better what?"

"Hiding place."

Viola nodded. "We have the best one. No one will find us there."

"No, Vee!" hissed Agnes. "Don't tell her."

Ignoring Agnes, Viola took Bree's hand and led the way back upstairs, with Agnes and Rosina trailing behind them.

Viola led Bree right up to the third floor, then down the long gallery, following the crisscross of small footprints in the dust on the floor, for none of the family ventured up here often; it had become a tomblike, shrouded place over the last century.

"We're not allowed up here," said Bree.

"Hah," hissed Agnes. "Don't say you and Francine never come up here. We've seen your footprints."

Bree pulled a face at her sister, choosing to ignore the truth of the accusation, and hurried after Viola.

Viola stood up on tippy-toe and switched on the light. The library's elderly candelabra, cocooned in cobwebs from the colony of spiders that had thrived here for decades in peace, sent out soft, glowing fingers to brush against the bookcases encircling the walls from floor to ceiling. The books, their threaded spines splitting with age and lack of care, held little interest for the girls. A few cracked-leather wingbacks were grouped to one side on the age-blackened wooden floor.

Going to the bookcase abutting the single window, Viola jumped on one of the floorboards, then hopped onto the next.

"What are you doing?" whispered Bree with a fearful glance over her shoulder.

"Look." Rosina pointed at the board that had sunk in slightly.

Viola pushed at the sunken board until it slid under the other boards to reveal a small, empty cavity the shape and size of a coffin.

"How did you find this?" Bree was impressed and not a little peeved that she hadn't found such a good hiding place.

"It was Rosie," said Viola. "We were playing hopscotch in here when it was raining, and Rosie jumped on it."

"It's genius!" Bree hugged her little sister, who beamed at being singled out for praise. "Now, get inside and I'll close the boards over you."

"Shhh!" Agnes held a finger to her lips, then crept closer to Bree for protection as a heavy tread sounded on the staircase.

"Get your arses downstairs!" Father yelled, followed by a smash as he barreled into something. "When I get my hands on you, not even God will protect you!"

"Quickly! In," whispered Bree, pulling Rosina's arms away from around her waist.

The girls got in, squirming to fit inside the cavity, for it was a tight fit even for three small girls.

"Don't forget about Franny," said Viola.

Bree groaned. She had completely forgotten about Figjam in the panic of the past little while. "She'll still be outside . . . Now, don't make a sound. I'll let you out again when it's safe."

"You're not to tell Francine about our hiding place," said Agnes, wriggling until she was on her side with Viola behind her and Rosina spooned into her stomach, her stuffed dog under her head like a pillow.

Bree hesitated, for she had every intention of telling Figjam.

Agnes eyed Bree's indecision suspiciously. "Promise!" she demanded.

Bree scowled, then nodded. "Fine! I promise I won't tell Francine."

Satisfied, Agnes smirked, knowing Bree took promises seriously and wore them like a badge of honor.

"Don't forget about us," lisped Viola, her voice slightly muffled by her face pressed against Rosie's hair.

"I won't, I promise," said Bree.

She gripped the small rebate under the floorboard and pulled it over her sisters. It was heavy and dropped back into place with a dull thud.

Bree froze, tensed.

There were no running footsteps. No shouts of discovery.

Letting out the breath she'd been holding, she looked down at the floorboards in consternation. If she hadn't seen the girls open the cavity, she would never have known it was there. She counted the boards from the wall in case she forgot where the correct one was, then hurried out into the gallery.

Bree paused on the top of the staircase and listened intently. Heavy treads echoed up from the second floor.

Darting down both flights of stairs at breakneck speed, she scampered through the foyer and slipped into the kitchen.

Monty still lay on the kitchen table. He had been swaddled in the blanket Mummy had knitted for him, with the embroidered blue tractor on one corner.

And under the table was Mummy. She was curled up in the fetal position and lay very still. Too still.

Crouching down, tears springing into her eyes, Bree whispered, "Mummy?"

A careful shake of Mummy's shoulder.

"Mummy!" Bree said urgently, with a glance over her shoulder at a bellow from her father. He was coming downstairs. "Mummy!" she tried again, shaking Mum's shoulder harder.

Shutting her eyes tight, a great sob erupted from Bree. It came from the tight knot of panic that had been sitting in her stomach from the moment she had left the woods with Figjam. It forced its way up her throat in a choked wail.

"Bree?"

Her eyes snapped open. "Mum!" She stooped to cling to her mother, sobbing, "I thought you were dead!" into the crook of her shoulder.

"Is Monty . . . ?" said Mum, her voice muffled and hoarse.

Bree pulled back, her brow puckering in an effort to stop crying. "I'm so sorry, Mummy," she whispered, terrified by Mum's expression, for something had snapped and dulled her moss-green eyes to the greyness of sage. "It was my fault. If I hadn't angered Father . . ."

"Oh, Bree," said Mum. She put a gentle hand up to Bree's cheek. "This is not your fault, my flower. We have all lived in fear of that man for too long, and now it has come to this." She sat up slowly, felt her eye that was swollen shut, her brutalized mouth, her smashed cheekbone.

Mother and daughter flinched as another of Father's bellows shattered the otherwise sepulchral silence of the house.

Then Mum's eyes darkened to the sharp fury of emeralds. "We are Thwaites!" she hissed. "We shall no longer live like this . . . Go and hide your sisters."

Bree frowned in confusion. "I already have, like you told me to. But I can't find Francine . . . Mum?" she cried softly in alarm as Mum swayed, grimacing with pain.

Mum waved away Bree's helping hands. "It's nothing. Probably a concussion." She blinked and focused on Bree, then cupped her daughter's small face in her hands and whispered. "Go and find Fran, then hide. You are not to come out from hiding until I call you, no matter what you hear. Do you understand?"

Bree nodded, terrified by the fierceness of Mum's tone. She stood up, breathing heavily and looked down at Monty. Lips tight, anger boiling up with her grief, she gently picked him up.

She wasn't going to let Him have her brother, even in death. It was a small, spiteful revenge of sorts, and one that Mum understood, for she nodded her agreement as Bree clung to her brother's little body and scurried out the kitchen into the courtyard.

TWENTY-THREE

Madeleine rushed down from the porch where she had been waiting to fling her arms around Francine.

Francine stood stiff as a board within Madeleine's tight embrace. "It was horrible," she whispered. "I was so scared. There was this godawful crash and then we found . . . Oh, Franny. I think you'd better come and look."

Francine followed Madeleine and Todd into the house. Keefe was lurking in the foyer. He turned in relief at the sight of Todd.

"The worst of it is upstairs, on the third floor," said Keefe, not daring to look at Francine, and he turned to lead the way up the two flights of stairs and down the long gallery to the library.

Unable to bear the others' anxious expressions, Francine pushed past Keefe and made her way cautiously into the library, where the worst of the damage had occurred. The tattered silence enveloped her like a crippled moth, fluttering about the room in the echoes of lost words whispering from the pages of ripped books. The silence spoke to the anguish dogging Francine and the truth she had suspected in the asylum but even now didn't want to believe.

"Are you alright?" asked Madeleine anxiously.

Francine waved her away, eyes red-rimmed in an effort not to show any emotion. The outer wall had fallen inwards, taking the scaffold with it; blocks of old masonry lay tangled with metal poles and shattered bookcases. Books lay everywhere, their pages flapping like the broken wings of birds in the breeze gushing through the damaged wall. Any surviving furniture was covered in a thick layer of plaster and dust. The floorboards had been shoved up to reveal a gaping hole to the side of the single window.

"I'm sorry," said Keefe, shuffling his feet, barely able to meet Francine's gaze when it alighted on him.

"It wasn't your fault." She shook her head helplessly, unable to take in the enormity of the damage.

"We can still fix it," said Todd.

She shook her head again and stepped towards the hole in the floorboards.

It was small, large enough for a man to lie down flat, barely large enough for the three small skeletons curled together, ribs meshed with ribs, ulna across femur, three small skulls facing the same direction. Her lost sisters.

"All this time," she said, a hand to her mouth. She wanted to vomit even though there was no stench of decay. Their clothing had not survived the long stay under the floorboards. All that remained was a tatter on the smallest skeleton of Rosina, aged forever three—a scrap of material with faded red roses resting on the rib cage—and a toy animal under the largest skull of Agnes.

"We would never have found them unless we'd known where to look," said Todd from behind her. "A couple of the floorboards lift up, and a person could slide in. I think it's a priest hole. The joint was so cleverly wrought it would've been impossible to open it without knowing how." His face creased with a terrible sadness as he gazed down at the small skeletons. "It's no consolation, but they wouldn't have suffered." He hunkered down to touch a floorboard and ran his fingers over a small knot in the wood. "This was an air vent, but it's been blocked with debris. The girls would have run out of air fairly quickly. Within a couple of hours."

Francine nodded, barely hearing him. Her sisters: little Rosina; Viola at four; and Agnes, the eldest of the trio at six.

Sinking to her knees, she carefully removed the toy animal. It was a blue-and-white stuffed dog crisscrossed with sewn scars. The image it brought was quite clear in her mind of Agnes, scowling Agnes. Always so angry and quick to blame the others for the smallest wrongdoing. Just as desperate for their father's attention and seeking it in her own way, as a tell-tale to curry the favor she had never received. Agnes hugging her toy dog, sucking one of its floppy ears, standing at the top of the path leading to Hawkshead, waiting for Father to return to get in her stories before the rest of them could even get their versions worked out.

"They were above my bedroom all this time," she whispered.

Madeleine crouched beside her, put a hand on Francine's shoulder, then drew back when she flinched away. Throat dry, mind racing to catch the errant memory, Francine turned haunted eyes to her sister. "The morning that Bree and Monty drowned, Mum ran around the house trying to find them. There were others too, all searching. I remember . . ." Her voice caught in her throat. "I remember Mum so frantic, racing from room to room, calling for the girls . . . and I hid in my room with Bree, never suspecting the girls were right above me. Then everyone left that afternoon. The house was silent. It was unbearable. Mum . . ." She swallowed hard, dredging up the atmosphere and tense emotions she had sensed at the time. "Mum sat in the kitchen in the silence afterwards. She stared at the wall and didn't say a thing. Just stared at the wall."

"There was nothing you could've done, Franny," said Madeleine.

A warm breeze drifted into the library through the gaping hole. It swept around the room, ruffling the dust up into little puffs. It played around Keefe, who looked around wildly, before coming to stop over the three little skeletons. On the very edge of hearing came a small sob.

"Oh, Bree," said Francine, her heart breaking for the little ghost.

Madeleine gasped audibly, touching her face. "Bree?" she whispered. "She's touching my hair! She's never shown any interest in me."

"You're still sisters," said Francine. "We're all still sisters." She took Madeleine's hand and squeezed it as the breeze shivered and gusted up into a tower of dust. It drifted down, settling on Bree, and for a few precious seconds, her small form was visible.

Bree reached up a hand and touched Francine's face as though in benediction, then shook herself free of dust and blew out through the hole in the wall once more.

"Bree!" Francine cried, stepping through the broken library, ignoring Madeleine's alarmed cry, and hurrying down the stairs.

Once outside, she strode across the lawn that was now an old battlefield of dead plants and into Lonehowe Wood.

Agnes's toy dog was still clutched in her hand. She held it tightly, her heart breaking even as her skin crawled with the horror of her little sisters trapped under the floorboards.

Though her eyes prickled with fatigue, her mind wouldn't stop. Perhaps it was the recent knowledge of her family's terrible history, perhaps it was tiredness, but memories were coming back to her of that night fifty years ago. Nothing definite; a little clarity where before there had been a vacuum. Now, she no longer wanted the memories and desperately wished for her previous ignorance. And even more desperately, she needed to speak to Bree.

Late afternoon sunshine speared down through the trees when Francine reached the glade. It was unbearably silent. The birds did not call a startled greeting. The stream trickled down the hill, but that, too, seemed muted.

She crept between the boulders and sat down at one of the small rock chairs. Nothing had been disturbed since her last visit. All their childish treasures were on the rock table, just as she had left them.

"Bree?" she whispered. "Please speak to me."

Francine waited, sitting absolutely still.

Silence swirled around her. A heavy, sad silence of childish dreams lost. She sat in the cave for a long time, hoping Bree would come. The shafting sunlight moved across the rock walls, signaling the approach of night. Francine sat as the stars and a gibbous moon spun from west to east, and the chill in the small cave seeped into her bones until they ached. And with the cold came a clarity of thought as she listened to the gentle rush of the stream outside.

Eyes half closed, the lapping of water, so restful, lulling. It coiled around her, taking her to a place that was dark and quiet but for the gentle slosh of water on the walls and Bree's voice in her ear — *"Keep still . . . don't make a sound . . ."* Nothing more than a breathless whisper.

Frowning hard, Francine clung to the memory.

Montgomery, heavy in her arms as she hung onto the bucket in the well. He was cold, not from the water, but the coldness of death.

"Keep still . . . don't make a sound . . ."

The memory was vague, stretched, patchy. Shaking her head,

Francine concentrated, eyes shut tight to feel what she had felt fifty years ago.

It was cold in the well. There was a circle of purple sky above. No stars yet. The boughs of the oak tree visible to one side, the leaves dark green with summer foliage against the twilit sky . . . Twilight. It was twilight. Then night; dark and quiet, with only the water lapping against the bucket when she had shifted position . . .

"Keep still, Figjam. Don't make a sound . . ."

A cold hand brushed against her cheek and set Francine shivering. Bree's cold hand. Her arm had been wrapped around Francine and Monty. Bree had been dead. Bree had been dead for hours, but she had still been whispering her warnings in Francine's ear.

"Oh, Bree." Francine opened her eyes when the dim light in the small cave flickered as though a bird had flown over one of the holes in the ceiling.

An intangible softness touched Francine's hair, as light as a butterfly's wings.

"I've missed you," she said and smiled when Bree's caress moved to her shoulder. "There's so much I want to tell you, but I'm not sure where to begin." She paused and considered their dark family secrets. "I've been to the asylum. I found out about George. I know—" She swallowed the words, still not able to process her dreadful suspicions even to herself.

The air took on a still, expectant feel.

Francine swallowed a few times, her throat tight with the dreadful conclusions she'd made since her visit to the asylum. "I've been going over and over everything I've learned about the night you died." She hesitated, not certain how to phrase what she wanted to say. "And something occurred to me . . . That you stayed because you caused Monty's death," she whispered. Even with Bree's tickle around her neck, she knew the words were false as they left her mouth.

Unable to accept the alternative, Francine said, "What am I missing here, Bree? If it was only you and I with Monty, who else could it . . . ?" Though her mind and heart tried desperately to block it, the truth punched through the horrible silence that settled in that secret place. She clutched her stomach, gasping for breath.

A long moan rushed from Francine's lungs as though she had been holding her breath for years. "Me? Was it me, Bree?"

An infusion of despair filled the small cave, mingling with Francine's own heartbreak.

"I killed Monty." She shut her eyes as a tear trickled down her cheek. It dried in the breeze that gusted around her like gentle fingers. "How could I have forgotten?"

Dark gloom from Bree.

Francine stood abruptly. She needed air. Out of this cave. Away from Bree. She crawled out into the open, then stopped with the sudden rush of another memory. Barely daring to breathe lest it should vanish, she knelt beside the entrance, where one of the boulders had a small overhang at the bottom, like a tiny doorway.

"A fairy house," Francine whispered. She scrabbled about in the moist earth until her fingers brushed against a flat surface. She dug carefully around the small tin box that had been buried for fifty years.

Dusting the dirt off the lid, she opened it and murmured, "Oh, Bree." Clutching at the errant memory, she fingered the old pound notes and shilling coins. They weren't much in monetary value, but once they had been crucial in a childish plan to buy freedom.

With deep sadness, Francine replaced the box in its hiding place and covered it up again. As she stood, she looked back into the little cave. Bree was outlined in a shaft of moonlight. Transparent, indefinable, beautiful. A little girl. Her expression was one of infinite sadness, yet there was no accusation, only love.

"I'm sorry, Bree," Francine whispered, tears streaming down her cheeks. "I'm so sorry."

"Francine?" Todd stood on the other side of the stream, his face creased with concern.

"No! Go away!" Francine cried, backing away. She held up her hands to ward Todd off as he stepped across the stream. "Not here! No one is allowed here!"

He took her shoulders gently, making soft hushing noises.

Breaking away, she scrambled across the stream, tripping in her haste, wetting the hem of her skirt before turning to shout, "It was me!" The words burst from her, so big, so dreadful, they could not be contained inside.

"Okay," said Todd slowly. "Why don't we go back to the house, and you can tell me everything."

She shook her head frantically, the hell of the past flashing before her eyes. "All this time I've been blaming everyone else. Blaming Father, and Mum, even Bree. And all this time it was me." She glanced wildly at a horrified Todd. "It wasn't Bree!" she screamed. "It was me!"

She turned and ran. Back down the dappled path of forgotten memory, running towards her refuge, away from the awful truth stalking her.

Todd chased after her. But Francine knew these woods. She raced ahead of him. Then she was beyond the tree line and sprinting across her destroyed garden towards Thwaite Manor, which was ablaze with lights, like a signaling beacon. As she reached the courtyard, Todd caught up to her and blocked her way.

Gently, he took her face in his hands and sank with Francine as her knees collapsed beneath her beside the old well, the gates of memory open wide and releasing a deluge.

"Tell me, Francine," he murmured. "Tell me what happened."

She looked into his dark eyes as tears came into her own. The memories poured out of her in a dreadful, hoarse whisper.

She remembered running through the trees after Bree. Bree was looking over her shoulder and laughing. They were racing each other, but Francine knew Bree was faster. She had always been faster.

TWENTY-FOUR

❦

The memory was so clear, as though Francine's mind had kept it safe and untarnished by the distance of time.

Bree and Francine were running through the woods. It was one of those perfect days when the air was so clear it hurt just to breathe it.

Bree was laughing, looking back over her shoulder. Her red hair, tied into two long plaits, bounced off her back. And eyes so green, like Madeleine and Mum. Freckles scattered across her nose and cheeks, a faded bruise on one cheekbone. She was tall for her age of seven.

"Come on, Figjam!" Bree shouted.

Francine raced after her sister, grinning, wishing she were as tall, as strong, as brave as Bree.

They sped through the trees, their laughter captured by the high branches and thrown back at them like a secret echo. Their feet led them to their hideout. Their secret place where no one could harm them. No one shouted in a drunken stupor or hit them for some trifling misdemeanor. At least no one beat Bree there. For Bree always took the brunt of their father's anger.

She stood up to him, took the knocks for her sisters. As the oldest, she protected them as best she could.

It was late when they returned to the manor. Walking slowly, delaying the inevitable. Their father was at the pub, as was his custom each afternoon, but they knew to be back before he returned at twilight.

"Bree! Francine!"

Mummy stood in the garden, Monty on one hip, her thin, pale face anxiously scanning the woods. Relief then, with a heartfelt, "Girls!" as Bree and Francine burst from the trees and ran down the hill.

As the girls reached her, she said, "You're cutting it fine today. He'll be back any minute. Bree, round up your sisters and get them bathed. They were playing near the church . . . Not you, Francine," Mum added when Francine made to follow Bree.

"Aw, Mummy," moaned Francine. "I want to go with Bree."

"No, you come with me," said Mum, distracted as she glanced down the path leading to Hawkshead. "What are you still doing here, Bree? Get a move on, and we can all hope for a peaceful night."

Bree winked at Francine, mouthing, "I'll be back soon," before running around the side of the manor and down the hill towards St. Michael's church. Francine followed Mum into the courtyard.

A scream erupted from the second floor. Mum sighed. "Francine, you'll need to watch Monty while I go see to Maddie. She's been fretful all day." She put Monty down on the flagstones. "I won't be long, Fran. Don't let him go near the well."

"I won't, Mummy," Francine said, then took off after Monty, who headed across the courtyard at a fast, crooked crab crawl before plopping down on his padded bottom under the *Laburnum* trees.

Francine didn't take her eyes off him, knowing how fast he could move. She loved her little brother, she really did, but she couldn't understand why their father loved Monty more than his sisters just because he was a boy. Father played with him, tickled him until he screamed with laughter, did all the things Francine had seen other fathers do with their children. But if one of his daughters tried to join in, the game would instantly end with a hiding for no reason.

She did all she could to gain her father's approval. She never made a sound when he was around because he hated noise. She tidied up after herself because he hated mess. She always said please and thank you, knowing she would get a hiding if she didn't.

She didn't know what she was doing wrong, and still she kept trying.

Francine walked backwards to keep an eye on Monty, then glanced around the side of the house where she could see the church tower above the trees. Both paths were empty.

"Hurry," she muttered under her breath and hopped from foot to foot, urging her sisters on silently. She didn't want the shouting to start. Didn't want to hear the solid, dull thwack when knuckles connected with flesh. She hated the aftermath even more. Since she'd been able to walk, she had taken to climbing out of bed when everyone else was asleep to creep downstairs when Bree had taken a beating. Bree always hid in the oak tree afterwards, and their father left her there for the night as an additional punishment. It was always Francine who cajoled her sister down and snuck her back into the house.

With a last look down the hill, she turned back to the courtyard. "No, Monty!" she cried, and raced over to her brother, snatching away the *Laburnum* pod he was about to shove in his mouth. "It's very poisonous, you silly!" she said. "Urghh! And now I've touched it. Don't you move, Monty. I need to get a cloth, otherwise you'll get sick."

Monty looked up at her and smiled gummily, displaying his two new top teeth.

"Don't move!" Francine warned again and hurried into the kitchen. She grabbed a cloth, wet it quickly at the sink, and darted back into the courtyard.

"Monty?" she called. "Where are . . . Monty!" she shrieked. "Get away from there now!"

Monty pulled himself up against the well and swayed in the unsteady way of babies, stretching over the little stone wall to grab the chain attached to the bucket. He turned to Francine and laughed.

She leapt forward just as Monty toppled into the well, laughter cut off short, his head hitting the dangling bucket. Two seconds later, a splash.

"MONTY!" Francine shrieked. She stared around wildly, heart racing, tears on her cheeks. "Mummy!" she screamed.

Mummy didn't emerge from the kitchen, no call of, "I'm coming."

Francine burst into a fit of weeping and peered into the well. In the gloom she could just make out Monty floating on the water, face up. Rubbing the balls of her hands into her eyes, she took a deep, shuddering breath, conscious that at any moment Father would be home. He would see her here not yet bathed, and Monty down the well.

With a quick glance at the house, she cranked the handle, releasing the bucket.

Wiping her face on her sleeve, then her hands, now slippery with sweat and tears, on the back of her dress, she grabbed the chain and awkwardly climbed over the lip of the well.

It was cold and damp after the warm sunshine. Shivering and crying, Francine climbed down the chain, hand over hand, until her feet touched the bucket. A small splash and she was in the water, one arm around the bucket, spluttering, as she grabbed Monty.

His chubby face was a pale balloon in the dank gloom, mouth slightly open, lips a funny color. A mark where he'd hit his head on the bucket reddened in a line on his forehead.

Francine cradled her brother. "Wake up, Monty," she whispered with a fearful glance up at the circle of light above her, lest her whisper should travel and be heard beyond the safety of the well.

She didn't know what to do. Monty wouldn't wake up. Fresh tears leaked from her eyes. Father would be home any minute. If he found anything had happened to Monty . . .

Mummy. Mummy would know what to do. Quickly now, she carefully put Monty into the bucket.

"Figjam."

Relief flooded Francine. Bree would know what to do. She always knew what to do. "Down here," she called in a terrified whisper.

"Figjam!" Bree sounded farther away. "Are you up there?"

"No. I'm down here, in the well."

Francine heard the heavy fall of Father's footsteps, then Bree's faint voice saying, "If you're up there, then don't come down now. He's nearly here."

Nodding even though her sister couldn't see her, Francine obeyed the warning with implicit trust, the chain rattling as she tried to hide behind the bucket.

For a moment Bree's head shaded what little light came into the well. "Monty?" she cried. "How did you get down there?"

A creak of the well's handle echoed down the well, bouncing off the wall, masking Francine's desperately whispered, "Bree!" She watched in horror as the bucket rose, swaying above her, the chain clanking loudly with each crank of the handle.

Scrabbling about in the cold water, she felt along the old stones of the well. They were rounded from long years of water erosion. She found one that jutted out more than the rest and hugged it tight, then watched the quickly rising bucket with round eyes.

A shadow passed over the opening, eclipsing Bree like an ominous cloud.

Francine almost called out a warning. Father was looming over Bree. She could see them perfectly through the small, round window to the world above. His red hair stuck up in all directions, bloodshot eyes visible even from Francine's position.

"What are you doing out here?" He whipped Bree around, puce with rage. "How many times have I told you little brats to stay away from the well?" He faltered, fingers tight on Bree's arm. He stared, slack-jawed, at the little body clutched to his daughter's chest. "And with my boy!"

Francine shut her eyes and slid beneath the water when Father's hand came around in slow motion to slam against the side of Bree's face.

When she resurfaced, spluttering and coughing, there was only blessed silence.

26 July, 1969

    Bree hurried across the courtyard to her oak tree. She would wait out the storm up there, wait until Father had fallen asleep as he usually did. Then she would think what . . .

    "Bree!"

    Bree froze, clasping Monty tightly to her chest.

    "BREE!" The voice had an oddly echoey quality, as though shouted into the entrance of a cave.

    "Figjam?" Bree turned around, searching the courtyard, then looked up at the house. Every light was on, and she could hear Father coming down the stairs, muttering to himself.

    "Where are you?" Bree called as loudly as she dared.

    "Down here. In the well."

    With another fearful glance at the house, Bree darted to the well. And there was Figjam in the water at the bottom, clinging to a jutting stone.

    "Bree!" It was a small, heartfelt cry of relief. Figjam's face was a pale orb in the yawning darkness.

"What are you doing down there?" Bree's voice echoed back to her.

"I can't get out."

Bree went to the well's handle, then bit her lip when a bellow of, "Where the hell are you? Bree! Agnes!" ripped from the house.

She peered over the side of the well and said, "Can you hold on?"

"Yes," said Figjam. "I'm scared, Bree, and it's cold."

"ELEANOR!" Father's roar was so close, Bree jumped in fright.

A shadow passed across the kitchen window. She turned to her oak tree longingly. She wouldn't make it. A quick decision borne of necessity had Bree whispering, "I'm sending Monty down to you."

"Monty? He's alive?" Figjam's relief was a physical thing that made Bree frown, wondering just what her little sister had been up to. She placed her brother in the bucket and start turning the handle, wincing at each creak of the old mechanism.

A faint splash as the bucket hit the water.

Another bellow from the kitchen forced her to whisper, "I'm coming down." With her legs over the well wall, she grabbed the dangling chain with both hands before swinging over the deep void.

"What? No! I want to come up!"

"Shhh!" Hand over hand Bree slid down the chain, her heartbeat pounding in her ears. If Father heard the clanking they were done for.

"Eleanor!" Father shouted, his voice rising to a shriek. "Where is he?"

It seemed an age before Bree reached the bottom and slipped into the water. Leaving Monty in the bucket, she paddled to Figjam shivering against her stone and hugged her tight.

The sisters looked at each other, mirroring their shared horror.

Maybe tomorrow, Bree thought, *she would wake up and realize it wasn't real. A dream, perhaps. A horrible nightmare. But Figjam was real. In front of her, so close their breath mingled.*

"He broke your mouth," *said Figjam, lisping slightly through her missing front tooth.*

"I'm fine." *Bree felt her split lip with her tongue. She hadn't felt the pain until Figjam mentioned it; now, it hurt like the blazes. She smiled at her little sister.* "Everything's going to be alright. I'm here now. You, me, and Monty . . . What are you doing down here? What happened?"

Tears squeezed out the corners of Figjam's eyes. She reached across the short space to the bucket and touched her little brother's cold cheek, lips puckering on one side.

"It's my fault," *she whispered, voice choked.* "Mummy said I must watch him. He was at the Laburnum pods again, trying to eat one. I had to get a cloth and when I got back Monty was on the wall and he fell in." *She looked at her big sister with wide, frightened eyes.* "I killed him."

Bree was silent for a long moment, then sighed, unable to bear the rigid tightness she felt in Figjam's small body. "No, you didn't. It was an accident." *She shivered. The water was freezing; the well was so deep the summer sun never entered here.* "Get into the bucket with Monty. You'll catch your death in here," *she added, mimicking her mother's caution heard many times before.*

It was an awkward wriggle of arms and legs to get Figjam into the bucket, with Monty clasped tightly between her chest and the chain. Bree clung to the bucket in the water and shivered.

Silence. Long silence.

They stared up at the well opening, watching as twilight bled

*into night. Sounds came from the woods, an echo of the wind
blowing through the trees. The air in the well grew colder. Bree
shivered so hard her teeth chattered, yet she clung grimly to
Monty and Figjam. Her lifelines.*

"WHERE IS HE?"

*The girls turned wide eyes up to the small circle of night sky,
straining their ears.*

"ELEANOR!"

Indrawn breath. Heavy footsteps on the kitchen's flagstones.
"Where is Monty?"

Bree looked at Monty and smiled a vindictive little smile.

*A moan. A scraping. Creaking wood as a weight rested on it.
Then sobbing. Quiet, awful sobbing. Mummy.*

"What have you done with Monty?" *Father. Bewildered,
words slurred.*

*A long silence filled with dark emotions filtered down into
the well.*

"You will never see him again." *Mummy's voice was a hoarse,
painful hiss filled with wild venom.*

*Bree swallowed and raised a hand to her little brother's small,
cold face as the tears she hadn't allowed to fall squeezed from
her eyes. A terrible grief twisted her stomach; with Mum's
words, she only now comprehended what death meant. She
would never see Monty again. Never hear his belly laugh.
Never be irritated when he grabbed her hair to pull himself up
against her.*

"But . . . What . . . I left him here on the table." *Father's voice:
confused, lost.* "I need to give him a decent burial after I've
dealt with the others." *His brokenhearted sobbing filled the following silence.*

A chair pushed back. Light footsteps.

"You will not touch my daughters!" *Mum cried.* "You will
never touch me again. It is your fault Monty is dead. Your fault,
George!"

"*Get away with yourself, woman. I haven't done anything. It was that little bitch, Bree.*" *Vengeful silence. Then Father hissed,* "*Your precious Bree took my boy, and when I get my hands on her . . . her and the rest.*" *He laughed. A drunken laugh that bordered on the demented.* "*You and your little flowers, Eleanor,*" *he taunted through his mirth.* "*All your little flowers.*" *As suddenly as his laughter had erupted, so it stopped, and he started sobbing again.*

Tears welled in Figjam's eyes. "*He's going to kill us?*"

"*No. Everyone is safe, I promise. Agnes, Viola, and Rosie are in their hiding place. It's a good one . . . better than ours,*" *Bree added grudgingly through chattering teeth, keeping her promise to Agnes with difficulty. She could no longer feel her feet.* "*Mum knows they're hiding. I'll let them out when it's safe.*"

"*And Maddie?*"

"*Still in her room. She's alright . . . Shh!*"

The two girls, one in the bucket, one in the freezing water, raised their heads to the purple opening and listened intently.

"*I've always hated them,*" *said Father, his voice hoarse, clogged tight with emotion.* "*All these girls. Six girls for one boy. There's something wrong with you, Eleanor. You're a terrible wife to inflict girls on me. And now Monty's dead and gone.*"

"*Yes, he is dead.*" *A ragged sigh from Mummy. A tortured silence, then,* "*But I won't let you harm my girls. You have tainted my home for too long.*" *Her voice was quiet, controlled. Bree pictured her standing stiff and erect, as she did when she was holding herself together in the face of a crisis.* "*I should have sent you packing when my father died.*"

A low sneer of fury. "*Your father? He was the devil, and you are his spawn! I've paid my dues in bloody daughters and a witch for a wife. This house belongs to me.*"

"*No, it doesn't. With Monty dead, you have no claim.*"

Maniacal laughter. And in those few minutes, Bree truly be-

lieved her father was quite mad when he yelled, "Then you shall breed, Eleanor!"

"No! I shall never let you touch me again."

"Yes. You. Will! You shall give me another son, and another." His voice dropped to a gritted whisper of bitter hatred. "The manor is mine! I signed a pact with the devil, and I shall take what is due me with force if necessary."

A crash from the kitchen reverberated down into the well, causing Bree and Figjam to flinch and cling to each other in horror.

Mummy. A drawn-out shriek. It rose and rose, a horrible echo swirling around the girls ... Sounds of a struggle. Heavy versus light. A ripping of cloth. A grunting. A slamming door. Light, fleeing footsteps fading deep into the manor ...

"Eleanor!" A slurred yell. Wood creaking with weight. Hoarse sobbing ... then silence.

"Maybe we can get out now," said Figjam after a long while.

"No. We wait until He's asleep." Bree didn't want to leave the well. The well was safety, even if temporary.

Minutes stretched to hours. Faint sounds from deep within the manor. Father came into the courtyard a couple of times, roaring, laughing, or sobbing with that odd gravel that comes from crying and screaming for too long.

"Keep still, Figjam ... Don't make a sound," Bree whispered each time Francine started, her face lifting fearfully to their circular window to the world, now showing a couple of stars that slowly moved from one side to the other as the night deepened.

Bree clung to the bucket, her legs cramping with cold, then the cramps were replaced by an almost pleasant numbness so she couldn't feel her legs. Her head felt fuzzy, then drowsy.

Blinking each time, she looked up to where she could see a branch of her oak tree.

All through the night, whenever Francine's eyes began to

close or her grip on the chain slackened, Bree whispered, "Keep still, Figjam . . . I'm right here."

Even as her own grip loosened on the bucket and her body slid further into the water, she kept whispering, whispering, whispering, "Keep still, Figgie. I'll never leave you . . ."

Francine could no longer see Bree, but she could hear her . . .

Keep still . . .

Don't make a sound . . .

TWENTY-FIVE

It was the longest night of Francine's short life.

Bree's arms were slack around her, ice cold. Monty was just as cold, now stiff and heavy. And still Francine sat in the bucket down the well, trying hard to stay awake, shivering in the dreadful damp.

There was no way to tell the passing of time. Francine imagined the well was a small cave and, if she looked up at the night sky, the stars were the tips of hanging icicles.

Silence had been her companion for hours, the night so still that the slightest sound traveled on the air.

Francine started, thinking she must have fallen asleep. Muffled sounds filtered down to her. Cupboards banging, then bumping, like something being dragged down the stairs.

"Where've you been?" Father's voice slurred. A clink of a bottle against a glass. He was drinking again.

"I've packed your bag." Mummy. She sounded different, not the gentle voice Francine was used to. This was a different woman. Hard. Cold. Brittle.

"Why?"

"You are leaving."

"What? No!"

"You are leaving, George," Mum hissed, her tone hard with contempt. "I am going to call the police once you leave and tell them it was you who killed Monty."

"It was that little bitch, I tell you! Bree killed my Monty!"

"Bree did no such thing. It was you, and that is what I will tell the police when I call them."

"Do you think I'm a fool?" he snarled, voice stronger, trying to dominate, a note of cunning. "You have me coming and going. You always were a conniving witch. You did something, didn't you? You and your evil plants. Did something so we could only have girls, and then when we had a boy, *you* ensured he died."

Thwack!

Francine gasped, eyes round with shock. Had Mummy slapped Father?

"You have to leave. Now." No pity in Mum's voice, just ice. "If you stay, I shall kill you." Voice low, a venomous hiss. "Call me witch and so I shall be. Every time I put a plate in front of you, you'll never know if the first bite will kill you or the second or the third. You'll never know which poison I've slipped into your whisky so your nightmares become reality. You'll never know if I've put something on your pillow so you'll wake up with bleeding ears . . . If you do not leave, I will kill you, George Thwaite. I shall kill you slowly, and in the most agonizing manner I can."

A chair was pushed back, fell over.

"You wouldn't," said Father, fearful. "You wouldn't dare!"

"Yes, I would. And I will take pleasure in watching you die in agony."

"You're a witch," he hissed. "A witch!"

"So I am. Leave, George, and don't come back. There will be no welcome for you here." Mum's light, quick footsteps across the kitchen flagstones. "I shall call Sam Woodall when you've left . . . Take this with you."

"What is it?"

"Food. You'll need it." A pause. "It will keep you alive long enough." An odd note in Mum's voice. Like she was sharing a secret. A clinking of metal. "Here is all the money we have. Take it and get as far away as you can."

Francine strained to hear what was being said, desperate that her father would take the money and food and leave.

Heavy and light footsteps moved farther into the house.

Time passed slowly in the well after that. Occasionally Francine thought she heard a sound from the house, muted. Like someone calling, but so faint, she couldn't make out the words. She did not know if her father had left or not. Did not hear a door open and close to signal his departure. She clung to the chain and Monty. Bree's arms were no longer wrapped around her. But Bree was still there, whispering in Francine's ear, *"Don't move. Keep as still as you can. Don't let him find us. Not a sound, Figjam."*

Francine didn't move. Not when she heard her mother come out into the courtyard in the early hours calling her name, calling for Bree; not when she heard Madeleine cry and her mother hurrying up the stairs; not when she heard heavy boots and voices coming up the hill from Hawkshead; not when the voices spread into the woods.

She did not respond to her name being called again by different voices. She remained with her arms locked around Monty in a cold embrace. Numb and exhausted, her eyes fixed on the well's wall, she did not move a muscle.

Dawn arrived slowly. A lessening of the darkness first to grey, a red glow from above, then sunshine.

Voices again. Urgent voices. Tired voices. Hoarse voices. So many voices.

The chain rattling. Francine holding Monty in a vicelike grip as they rose in the bucket. Hands prying her arms away from her brother. Gasps of horror, and Eleanor's dreadful scream as Bree's body was pulled out of the well.

Bree and Monty laid out on the flagstones.

A moment of terror when Francine stared down at her sister, then quickly dispelled when she heard Bree's voice in her ear. *"I'm still here. I'm here, Figjam."* Bree was fine, right next to her. That wasn't Bree lying on the ground. A warm numbness spread through Francine. It was a relief to feel nothing.

Her mother wailing, then hugging Francine tight. A man leaning down to speak to her; he had blue eyes with huge eyebrows. He asked her how she felt. Francine just stared at his eyebrows, didn't respond. She had no words. She didn't really understand what was happening. Yesterday had been just another day, just another day.

People came running into the courtyard once word of their discovery got out, questions to the policeman and Eleanor, crowding around the bodies of Bree and Monty.

Francine recognized many of them. They all looked exhausted and dirty from tramping through the woods most of the night. Some looked relieved, others were crying. She saw Miss Cavendish running down from the woods, then stopping in horror, unable to believe what her eyes were seeing.

Francine held Mum's hand while she and the policeman spoke. Sympathy and pity on the surrounding faces watching Mum cry. The man with the eyebrows was talking to her again. Asking her where Agnes, Rosina, and Viola were. Francine stared back at him mutely; it was a silly question. Her sisters were in their hiding place.

Then Mum was kneeling in front of her, face drawn and desperate, begging to know where her sisters were.

Francine would've spoken then if she'd known the answer. But she didn't know. It was a secret only Bree knew.

The crowd dispersed to search again, for Viola, Rosina, and Agnes.

Francine had no idea how much later, but the sun was hot on her shoulders when she and Bree went upstairs and climbed into bed together.

On her knees with her arms wrapped tight around her stomach, Francine sobbed violently as the memories kept coming.

The hours afterwards ... People searching through the house, calling for the girls, then the calls moved out into the garden, into the woods. And Bree darting about her bedroom like a tiny whirlwind, knocking paintings off the wall, crashing around the bathroom. Agitated, yet unable to tell Francine why.

Then the activity had all stopped. The police and searchers left, and Eleanor had sat in the kitchen staring at the wall, wrapped in desperate silence.

Francine shook her head, trying to free herself from the memories, but they kept coming. Bree and Monty's funeral. A small affair, only four mourners: Francine, Madeleine, Eleanor, and Miss Cavendish. But only her mother had entered the graveyard. She had dug their graves and moved the small coffins herself. Francine had watched from the garden, holding Miss Cavendish's hand, while Madeleine slept in her pram.

The years of silence afterwards. Bree with her all the time. Her only friend. More real to her than the living. How could she have forgotten Bree was her sister?

And even those memories had faded. For three years Francine did not speak. She did not ask a single question about her father or what had occurred. In time, she had forgotten. Forgotten Bree, forgotten Monty, forgotten them all. And begun talking again.

"None of it would've happened if I had just kept my eye on Monty," she whispered to Todd, who crouched before her, not once taking his eyes off her face. "And I never asked Bree where they were. She knew. She told me she had hidden the girls. I could've asked her, but I didn't. I could've saved my sisters. They died because I didn't ask."

"You were five," said Todd. "You cannot blame yourself for what happened. You were a child."

They were hollow words. Guilt wracked Francine like a physical thing. It didn't matter that it had been an accident or that she had been only five. Her brother had died because of her, and three of her sisters had died indirectly because of her. If Bree had not come down the well and died, if Francine had died instead, if Francine had just kept an eye on her brother like she'd been told, if, if, if . . .

Francine Thwaite, who had always kept her emotion carefully in check, released the guilt she had been carrying for fifty years in a storm of tears. It blistered the air. Guilt that had tainted every emotion she had ever felt, laced together with all the suppressed rage of past snide remarks, all the grief at her mother's passing, all the happiness she had felt when in her garden. All those emotions she had never shown swelled within, a mash of sadness, grief, happiness, disappointment, and above all, guilt.

And Todd let her cry. An arm wrapped around her shoulders, he held her tight, absorbing each shudder of her grieving body.

She cried as she had never cried before. She cried for her dead. For the tragedy that had ripped her family apart fifty years before. She cried until there was nothing left.

Todd was quiet for a long time after Francine slumped into silence, spent of words and emotion.

"At least you know now that your mum didn't poison your father," he said softly. His face was grey in the gloom of night that had crept up on them without either being aware of the transition from light to dark.

"I thought she had." Francine's voice was hoarse from talking, her throat tight and painful. "I heard her threaten to kill him if he stayed, and I must've remembered the threat as though it had been carried out." She paused, running through her newly remembered memories in relation to all she had learned of her father's final week between leaving Thwaite Manor and his death. "I think she did poison him, but afterwards. She gave him food when he left, and his behavior in the asylum had all the symptoms of poison. She was trying to make sure he never came back."

"Your poor mum. To think she never knew the girls were dead, that they were buried in the manor, and she never knew."

"She thought George took them at first." Francine was struck hard by what had eluded her as a child but was starkly clear with the hindsight of adulthood. "But later she knew he hadn't because he came home," she whispered.

TWENTY-SIX

Todd frowned. "Who came home? Your father?"

"Yes . . . at the asylum I didn't want to believe. Couldn't believe . . ." Francine got to her feet slowly. The silhouette of the manor hunched against the night sky as though pained by the secrets it hid. Her eyes were drawn to the rhododendron maze. "I thought it was from before," she murmured.

"What was from before?" Todd said softly, fearing to raise his voice lest it stop Francine from talking.

"I—I—" She shook her head, her chest so tight she could barely breathe. She didn't want to remember, but the memory was already strengthening, filling in the blanks, unlocking the truth she had managed to bury for so long.

She suddenly darted out of the courtyard and ran down the ruined lawn to the rhododendrons.

"For Christ's—Francine!" Todd shouted after her, then ran to catch up as she slipped into the maze.

The towering tightly knit walls closed in around her. She didn't need light to guide her to the center. Darting left and right, she was vaguely aware of Todd's mild curses as he tried to follow.

Contoured in shadows, Neptune appeared above his dried-up fountain. But in Francine's mind the summer sun was hot on her back and the fountain's gentle drizzle was a background murmur.

"I thought it was from before Bree drowned," she said as Todd pulled up to a hard stop when he reached her. "But it was afterwards ... I've been getting this memory; I wasn't even sure it was real. It felt more like ... remembered atmosphere." Francine knelt and put her hand on the mossy flagstones, seeing the ring of white chrysanthemums, their petals ablaze in that long-ago sunshine. It was no longer a wisp of memory, but forceful and so vivid she could feel sweat trickling down her back, hear a blackbird fluting somewhere in the maze, and smell the peppery fragrance of the chrysanthemums. "Bree was here. She had seemed so real in those days afterwards. I don't think I understood even then that she was dead. She had had such an intense vitality when she was alive. I think that's what I retained; that vitality made her more real to me than I was. I was little more than a shadow then."

Smoothing the flagstones with gentle fingers, she whispered, "It was Agnes's birthday. We had a cake. We had a plan, Bree and I. We thought if we made Agnes's birthday extra special, she would come back. I wanted my sisters back ... Agnes, Viola, and Rosie. I missed them. Chrysanthemum was Agnes's flower, and we had collected all we could find in Mum's garden and made a chain around the fountain. Mum ..." She looked up as though trying to see the manor through the walls of rhododendron. "Mum didn't say anything. I'm not sure if she even noticed. I can't imagine what she was going through in those days afterwards. She was a ghost of her former self, and we—"

She cleared her throat, unable to bear the raw pain her mum had endured in those days—what they had all endured. "We heard footsteps on the driveway. It was a shock to hear it. The house had been so quiet for days, and Bree ..."

Francine stood up and dashed back into the maze with Todd on her heels. She followed the memory of Bree running ahead of her, her braids waving wildly behind her, to the entrance, and then pausing there with a finger to her lips. The manor rose above them, basking in the benign sunlight.

"We saw someone go into the house." She put a hand to her mouth, eyes darting frantically, connecting strands of memory into a symmetrical web.

"Who was it?" Todd whispered.

"Father." Her throat closed with her remembered five-year-old dread.

"Your father came home after he ran away from Nonsuch?" Todd clarified softly. "Are you sure?"

Francine nodded.

"Why? He was a wanted man. Why would he come home surely knowing your mum would've called the police? And it's not just that; your mum threatened to poison him. Why would he come back when your mum had made it clear he would never be welcome?"

"For the manor. It was always about the manor. All those years in a loveless marriage, only to have the prize snatched away when Monty died. He came back to claim what he felt was his by right."

With a shiver, she seized the unfurling thread of memory, stepping once more into the sunshine of fifty years before. "He went in through the front door. It struck me as odd at the time. No one used the front door except strangers. I don't think I knew who it was then. But Bree did. The door slammed and it-it scared me. But not Bree. She ran up to the house, and I did what I'd always done: I followed her."

Francine hurried across the lawn, opened the front door, and stopped in the foyer, squinting hard down the years. Todd closed the door quietly behind him, then stood beside her, watching her.

A murmuring crept into the foyer, dark and insidious. It swelled to a sly croon that rippled along the paneled walls. A hand to her chest, Francine turned in a slow circle, wide eyes on the susurrating walls. She wanted to run away. She didn't want to unlock anything further, wasn't sure her heart could break any more than it had tonight.

"What happened?" Todd whispered when Francine didn't continue. "What did you see?"

"It wasn't what I could see, but what I could hear. Mum's voice, and . . . and Father." She shut her eyes to better view herself standing with Bree in the foyer. The vile muttering crept around her and wrapped around her throat like sepulchral fingers, fretting together the past and the present.

She turned her head, following the rising murmur to the closed door of the drawing room. Mum's voice, soft yet ravaged, his voice, rough, uncertain.

Taking a step to the drawing room, then another, Francine put her hand on the door handle. "They were in here. Bree and I were listening at the door. They were arguing. Mum was angry. She was demanding to know where the girls were and shouting something about Bree, and Father was denying he'd taken them." She opened the door, steeling herself as she stepped into the room she hadn't entered in fifty years. "I can't remember everything they were saying, but I could feel . . ."

She tried to grasp the intense emotions she had felt in this room. The scent of tobacco hit her so hard she gasped. "I could feel hatred . . . and a terrible fury. I'm not sure what Mum was doing in here. This had always been Father's room." Her eyes flickered to the frayed Persian carpet, the corner of the hearth, the edge of the window. Then her eyes returned to the table, seeing the one thing that hadn't belonged in the room.

"Mum's sewing basket was on the table. It was odd because Mum never sewed in here; she always did it in the front parlor." Francine stepped back to the threshold and closed the door so she could only see a sliver of the drawing room, as she had fifty years before. A shivering took her as she whispered, "They were roaring at each other. Mum was desperate, convinced he'd taken the girls to spite her. There was a noise . . . I think he hit her."

A gasp broke the airlessness—her own. "Mum's dressmaking scissors were next to the basket. I was terrified of those scissors when I was small . . . She picked them up . . ."

Francine turned abruptly, watching Bree run into the kitchen. "We ran away, into the woods." She hurried after the memory of Bree, through the kitchen and out into the courtyard, with Todd following her. She ran up the incline to the woods, then stopped. "We stayed in the woods all day until long past our bedtime. I didn't understand, not then. I think even then I was blocking it from my mind." A wail broke from her as she collapsed to her knees. It fractured the night, twisting around her heart until she thought she would burst with the black despair swamping her.

She waved Todd away when he approached, not wanting all that was good about him to be tainted by the horror in her past.

"Your mum killed your father?" he murmured, stepping back warily.

Francine nodded. "It was the perfect murder," she said hoarsely. "Everyone thought he had run away. No one expected him to come home and then be killed. They were looking everywhere for him but here." Then she shut her eyes briefly and whispered, "And I know where she buried him."

"Not in the garden surely?" said Todd. "There's nothing left to dig up."

"No. She buried him in plain sight." She turned large, haunted eyes to Todd. "Where do you bury a body where no one would think to look?" It was a rhetorical question that meshed the final tangled threads of memories into coherence. "It's like the answer to a riddle, yet it's so simple . . . A graveyard. No one would think to look for a body in a graveyard. It's where the dead are supposed to be."

She stood up and whispered, "It was that night. It was almost dark when Bree and I finally came home." The image of her five-year-old self was strong in her mind, creeping across the lawn with the ghost of Bree beside her, holding her hand.

Her lips quirked into a sad smile. "I was worried that I'd get into trouble for staying out so late. I had worked myself up into a state. We crept into the house. I think even then I was expecting to see Father in the drawing room. But I was too scared to check." She glanced at the manor sagging under the weight of night and memories. "Maddie was whimpering. I went upstairs, thinking Mum was with her. But she wasn't. She wasn't in the house. I went outside. I wanted to tell Mum that Maddie was awake . . . That's when I heard the sounds of digging. I thought Mum might've been busy in the garden. She did that, gardened when she wanted. She was never governed by time."

Francine walked up to the Thwaite graveyard and opened the gate with none of her previous fear. "I got it all muddled up. I saw Mum digging in the graveyard. I thought she was digging Bree and Monty's graves, but she wasn't. They had already been buried. She was digging on the other side." She walked up the centuries of Thwaites until she reached the Victorians.

"Here," she said, pointing at the nameless grave shrouded in hate. "She buried my father here." She eyed the dark blooms with their message in shades of black, blue, white, and orange. "She must've really hated him," she whispered, grasping the dark significance. It was a dreadful, personal message, but it wasn't meant for her. "Mum left a message to my father."

She ran a hand over the blue, hooded racemes of monkshood. "I hate you . . ." she said before her eyes alighted on the overflowing lobelia that almost smothered the orange lilies, ". . . for your arrogance and spite . . ." A bush of black roses at one end of the grave. "I killed you . . . for your betrayal," her hand on the black dahlias. Across the grave, moonflower glowed brilliantly. "But I bloom in dark times," meshed around the thick twisted vines of Carolina jasmine. "Without you..." she picked out the thicket of blue irises "...I have hope."

Throat tight, though she had no tears left, Francine stared down at her mother's floral message to her husband. All that anger and hatred festering in the graveyard for all these years like a wound that seeped and seeped without cauterization.

"I don't blame her for killing him," said Todd. "None of this would've happened if you hadn't all lived in fear of your father. He created an environment of hatred and fear that had every chance of ending in tragedy as it did."

Francine nodded, still unable to really comprehend that the sweet, gentle woman she remembered had had it in her to kill someone in cold blood.

Todd mistook Francine's silence for shame in her mother's actions and said gently, "Don't think too harshly of your mum. She lost five children because of him, and she had to protect you and Madeleine. She had to kill him, otherwise she would never be rid of him. I would kill to protect my children for a lot less."

Francine didn't think harshly of her mum. If anything, she felt a vast empathy, for she remembered Eleanor in the days after she buried her husband, sweeping through the house like a dervish, searching through every nook and cranny. With hindsight, she realized Eleanor must've been aware that the girls had been hiding somewhere in the manor. But she would quickly have suspected they were dead, for they would've cried out if they'd heard her calling for them. She had been searching for their bodies... And while her mother had searched, she had cleaned every trace of Francine's father and her siblings from the house. Not a single photo or toy remained. They were all burned in the courtyard. A huge pyre, until only the ash of sad memories remained.

She could never tell anyone the truth that George hadn't taken the girls, couldn't ask anyone to help find her daughters' bodies; to do so would've drawn attention to the manor and her own crime would have been uncovered.

With a dry sob, Francine's heart swelled with sympathy for her mum, who'd had to live with the knowledge for the rest of her life that her little daughters' bodies were trapped somewhere in her home. It seemed too harsh a punishment for the crime she'd committed.

As those unbearable thoughts fluttered like feathers around her, so too they sent a trickle of foreboding down Francine's spine. She stood up and regarded the manor, her heart constricting with an aching love for the building. History was imprinted in every dark beam crisscrossing the white walls. It held so much sadness—not just for Francine, but for all those who had lived and died within. Yet even at a distance she sensed a change emanating from its higgledy-piggledy silhouette pinned against the night sky. A lessening of rigidity in the half-timbered walls, a new jauntiness to the angle of its many chimneys, a sheen of relief across its mullioned windows, as though the old building had been holding its breath for five decades, guarding its dark secrets, and was only now able to breathe freely with their liberation.

She found her hand in Todd's. Both gripping so hard Francine's knuckles rubbed together as a violent shiver ripped through Lonehowe Wood like a lament of torment. The shivering faded slowly into a silence that ballooned to fill the garden until it scraped against the walls of the manor, waiting for a single prick of sound to pop it.

A shriek burst the stifling silence as a ferocious gust of wind shot out of the woods and raced down the lawn towards the manor. Except it wasn't the wind, but a vast shadow. It moved fast, blotting out the stars as it passed. A high, keening screech fled before it like the wind before a tempest.

Too soon, it was upon Francine and Todd.

"He's here," she breathed. "George is here."

"Where?" Todd demanded, staring around wildly.

"All around us." Heart racing faster than the shadow that devoured the moonlight, in that moment Francine realized this was what she had been waiting for. She hadn't been sure if George Thwaite would reveal himself, but ghosts always returned to the place of their death, and George Thwaite had died in Thwaite Manor.

A scream pierced the shadow. A desperate scream.

"Maddie!" Francine cried, and ran down the lawn with Todd close on her heels.

A crash came from inside the manor, followed by a ripple of bangs as she and Todd tore through the courtyard and into the kitchen.

"It's coming from upstairs," said Todd, and the two rushed into the foyer, then froze in horror and watched a shadow flow over the wood-paneled walls of the staircase, then surge over the banister in a sinuous movement. From its depths rose a susurrus of two little words: *Eleanor's flowers.* They were repeated over and over, blending into each other in a spiteful croon filled with a persistent, decades-old loathing.

"What the hell is that?" whispered Todd.

Swallowing, Francine said, "My father."

Their attention was diverted to the landing when Madeleine appeared. She struggled futilely as she was dragged down the stairs by her hair clenched by an invisible fist, forcing her head back at an awkward angle. Keefe stumbled down after her, eyes wide and terrified, helpless, as he was kept at a distance against his own volition.

"George Thwaite!" Francine screamed. Her hatred of her father had obliterated her fear. "Leave Madeleine alone! She had nothing to do with Monty's death or yours."

Madeleine was instantly released. She stumbled down the

last few steps and fell to her knees, sobbing breathlessly. But as Francine rushed to pull her sister to her feet, the coiling darkness enveloped the sisters in a grasping, clawing, suffocating heaviness, and *Eleanor's flowers* swelled around them in a shadowy echo, creeping over their exposed skin with the same sour fear of hearing a serpent's hiss in long grass.

Pushed by the seething weight of George Thwaite's terrible hatred the sisters were forced to move, one resistant step at a time. The pressurized air beat against Francine's eardrums; she was distantly aware of Todd shouting as he and Keefe tried to battle their way through the cloying shadow. She felt Todd's fingers close around hers for a brief, solid moment, then she and Madeleine were forced across the threshold of the drawing room. Todd tried to follow, his eyes wide with bewildered horror, before a rush of swooping iciness flashed past Francine, hitting Todd and Keefe hard on their chests, and they flew back to smash into the opposite wall of the foyer. The drawing room's door was slammed so hard it shook the whole building.

Francine and Madeleine were suddenly released from the restrictive shadow and staggered against each other for support as George Thwaite gathered his darkness to himself, filling the drawing room like a suffocating cloud of vengeance. His hateful susurration rose to a fevered shriek that bypassed Francine's ears and hit every nerve attached to her spine, triggering remembered horror that the room had always represented. A screaming voice. Screaming at her five-year-old self. Screaming at Bree. Always raised in anger, never calm to take away the pain of a scrape, never a whisper of love. A hated voice. A feared voice.

Madeleine's hand wrapped around Francine's, her long nails digging into soft flesh. "George . . . Father . . ." Madeleine choked out. "Please . . ."

A hesitation, a wavering, and the shadow quivered into a shape from the memory of a five-year-old and the perceptions of height and girth remembered from that age. Then George Thwaite was standing before the sisters, staring at them with eyes that were fathomless holes.

Vile spectral fingers brushed against Francine's face, questing, seeking. Her breath hitched as she tried to lean away from her father's terrible touch. That creeping silkiness moved to Madeleine, drifting to her neck, then pressed down suddenly and hard.

Monty. Their little brother's name was a serenade to the agonies of loss. *You know, little flowers. You know . . .*

The words grated against Francine's scalp, as she futilely tried to pull at the shadowy hands around Madeleine's throat. "Madeleine had nothing to do with it," she cried. "She was a baby!"

George's grasp on Madeleine broke as a gush of warm air blasted out of the fireplace, and she fell to the floor. For a moment Francine became aware of pounding on the door and the muted shouts of Todd and Keefe through the dense wood. Then she screamed, "No, Bree! What are you doing?" But Bree was doing what she had always done. In a gust of warmth, she darted into the heart of George Thwaite's shadow and fought to protect her sisters. A tempest of indistinct shapes, hot and cold, hurtled around the drawing room.

Without thinking, Francine raced into the contained maelstrom. Faces blurred around her, first Bree—determined, twisted with a fear that broke Francine's heart—then George, contorted with hatred and fury. "Stop, Bree!" she cried, into the raging whirlwind. "You can't fight him anymore. He needs to know what happened to Monty!" The battle continued unabated around her until she took a deep breath and yelled, "Father! It wasn't Bree. It was me! It was my fault Montgomery died!"

A sudden twist and George flung Bree across the room to smash into the fireplace.

The little ghost's whimper was lost in the rush of swooping icy air that coiled around Francine, forcing her back as a keening, high-pitched wail filled her ears. All of a father's grief wrapped around her, squeezing the air from her lungs. Gasping, tears forced from her eyes, Francine was smothered in his hate-filled embrace. Driven to her knees, her back arched, her spine sheer, slow agony from the pressure exerted on her body.

You know, little flower, you know . . .

Francine stared up into her father's fathomless eyes when his face appeared above hers. "Yes," she gasped. "It was me . . . I took Montgomery away from you, from us. I am so sorry. For all of us. For all we lost."

Her father's expression changed from hatred to confusion, his shadow shimmering and fading at the edges like a midnight mirage. His grip on Francine loosened as the air behind him grew blacker than night; a primordial darkness the living could not enter, a blackness that went beyond color, for no color had ever existed in that dark place.

"It was no one's fault," whispered Francine as the vitality George Thwaite had clung to for fifty years started to diminish like a hated memory. "Monty died, and it was a dreadful, tragic accident, but no one is to blame. There is no vengeance for you amongst the living."

His fury simmered for a moment more, then ebbed until he stood broken before Francine, an amputated soul that didn't deserve pity. Yet, she did pity him. Pity was all she had left. Then the ghost of George Thwaite merged with the shadows and was gone.

It was a long moment before Francine struggled to her feet, waving away Madeleine's helping hand. There was no chance for the sisters to voice the horror they had witnessed before the door burst open and Todd and Keefe charged in, staring around the room wild-eyed.

"Are you two alright?" said Todd, once he'd ascertained they were alone.

"I—I think so," said Madeleine, touching her throat, which was already darkening with fingerprint bruises. "Franny?" she whispered when Francine didn't move or speak, keeping her distance as though fearful that a single touch would shatter something within her sister.

"Francine," said Todd, stepping towards her. "What just happened?" He dropped the hand he'd held out to her when she didn't take it. She couldn't bear his kindness, not in this moment. He stood beside Keefe, who was visibly shivering from delayed shock, and watched with concern as Francine walked out of the drawing room without uttering a word.

With tight apprehension she stopped in the foyer and listened to the manor: its ticks and hums, its little foibles that were so much a part of its background noise. She strained her ears for a murmur, a scratching. Nothing came. No muttering laden with the spite of hurtful secrets, no hate-filled fury to sour the tongue, no taint of a distantly remembered odor of tobacco. Instead, the manor wrapped around Francine with the warm comfort of a fleecy blanket on a cold winter's night.

"He's gone," said Francine, becoming aware of Todd standing in the drawing room's doorway, watching her.

She turned to the man who was the total opposite to her father in every way. Todd Constable, who had blown into her life one frosty evening, who didn't know her, yet in the past weeks had gained her trust in a way she had never felt with anyone else.

Francine's smile for him blazed. Then faltered. Her eyes twitched around the foyer.

"What is it?" he asked, frowning at Francine's colliding expressions of relief and renewed panic.

She shook her head to get rid of the dreadful buzzing in her ears with the enormity of terrible realization. Two ghosts from the past: George Thwaite, from whom she'd protected her home and mind, and Bree, whom she'd clung to for fifty years. If one was gone then . . .

"Bree!" she cried.

She rushed past Todd, through the kitchen and into the courtyard.

The well was a mere shadow, and over it the old oak tree swayed in a gentle breeze like an ancient guardian.

Trembling with bittersweet loss, Francine called desperately, "Bree? If you're still here, please show yourself."

A tickle started around her hair. The softest of touches. It danced along her shoulders, then brushed against her face.

A shimmer in the darkness and Bree stood before her. Bree, who would remain forever aged seven. Her face so dear to Francine, a face she remembered now with a vividness that hurt.

"I know why you stayed," she said, her heart aching for the brave little girl Bree had once been. "You stayed to tell me where Agnes, Viola, and Rosina were hidden, but I didn't understand. I'm so sorry, Bree. For everything."

Bree smiled and lifted a fading hand to Francine's cheek.

A breeze twisted around the sisters, caressing them in a moment bound in loss and love.

"I'll miss you," said Francine. There was no time for more. The pain of parting scored deep within her marrow and a piece of her soul died as she watched Bree growing fainter and fainter until she tattered like cobwebs into the breeze. One last time, the dancing air rustled up into the old oak tree, shivering the gnarled branches adorned in their spring finery. It curled and kinked, a gay whirlwind swaying hither and thither before darting across the garden, leaving nothing behind but memories.

Those memories were now fresh in Francine's mind, for though she had lost Bree's ghost, she had gained the girl; with the remembered horror came memories to treasure. Memories of her sisters and her little brother, of happier times.

But one memory would always be stronger than all the others: Bree running through the garden and up into the woods, always faster, always stronger, her laughter echoing back through the decades, making Francine smile.

Epilogue

❦

Moonlight gilded each leaf and newly dewed petal in pale gold when the two sisters stole into the garden at midnight. The air was alive with the sly fluttering of moths dipping into blooms and the strains of grasshoppers hiding in the lawn.

Francine no longer scattered her protection each night. There was nothing to fear from the remaining ghosts of Thwaite Manor and Lonehowe Wood. She saw them rarely now, except for Tibbles, who still slept on her bed each night. She had made a start to finding their reasons for remaining. The first had been the man in the top hat whom Francine had seen every night in her room. Only by chance did she discover that he was the late Jeremiah Thwaite, author of the Thwaite histories. For when she finished reading the dull tome, she never saw him again.

As was their wont on these moonlit nights, the sisters walked in silence up to the Thwaite graveyard.

Francine no longer feared the graveyard. It was her legacy and that of all the generations that had come before her. Now, it merely felt shrouded in sadness. She had buried the remains of Agnes, Viola, and Rosina in the small alcove beside Bree and

Montgomery. Five graves. So small. So senseless even now. The mystery of their disappearance laid to rest. When spring came the thousands of snowdrop bulbs Francine had planted on their graves would erupt in a carpet of simple purity echoing the shortness of those five lives.

George Thwaite's grave was no longer covered in hate. Francine had dug up all those dark plants with their terrible message. In their place, she had planted white tulips and purple hyacinths to signify forgiveness.

There was another grave beside that of Eleanor Thwaite. Miss Cavendish had died in her armchair almost a year ago, overlooking the fells she so loved. It had been a peaceful death. It was fitting that she be buried in the graveyard: a testament to her place in the Thwaite family through the strong bonds of friendship that had proved thicker than blood. There had been no rites, no rituals. Miss Cavendish had had *views* about religion, and she had been insistent in her last days that no fuss be made.

No words were needed as Madeleine took Francine's hand and led her away, down the path towards the greenhouse that shone silver in the reflected moonlight.

Change had come to Thwaite Manor after the discovery of their little sisters' remains. It was most noticeable in the garden, which was almost back to its original magnificence at the tail end of summer. Francine had replanted her poisonous plants, faithful to the garden's original design, and color exploded once more in the most unlikely places.

The manor itself had changed more slowly. The repairs had been completed months before. The clock tower no longer leaned, the gable end no longer bulged, the library had been restored to a glory not seen in this century and the central heating had been replaced so it no longer ticked and shrieked. But there were subtler changes: a lightening of the atmosphere, a tentative sense of hope.

It had been Madeleine who created the biggest change of all.

Francine had had little chance under the constant persuasion of both Madeleine and Todd to turn Thwaite Manor into a hotel. That had been six months ago, and under Madeleine's guidance, the place now echoed with voices. Voices of the living. Voices of those tourists Francine still secretly loathed, who came to Thwaite Manor in droves, attracted to a night spent in the most haunted house in Britain, complete with not one, but two priest holes.

And in that short time, Madeleine had blossomed into someone Francine barely recognized. She had given her sister the space and time to grow, hopeful that this new venture would make Madeleine feel secure enough to stay in Thwaite Manor and recognize it as her home, not a place to be feared.

"I've been thinking," said Madeleine as they approached the shed where the moonflowers were just unfurling to release their deadly perfume into the night air.

"Yes?" said Francine cautiously. While she never questioned Madeleine's wisdom when it came to running the hotel and dealing with their guests, in other matters Madeleine thinking was not always a good thing.

"Perhaps we should get a cat. I've always liked cats."

Francine glanced at her sister sideways. "It's something to think about certainly," she said, her head already filling with visions of hundreds of cats roaming Thwaite Manor—for she knew Madeleine would not stop at one—and herself being labeled the mad cat lady who lived up on the hill in the haunted house.

Madeleine suddenly hugged her. "It will be fun!" she cried in Francine's ear. "You and me and a cat called Marmaduke or Churchill."

"It might upset Tibbles," said Francine, her caution turning to alarm.

"Maybe it's what Tibbles needs. Maybe he thinks you need a cat about the house so he can rest."

Francine pondered this, then shrugged. "We can try it."

She let Madeleine prattle on, for these moonlit nights were one of the few times the sisters had the time to talk without interruption.

"So . . . looking forward to tomorrow?" said Madeleine, not even attempting guile.

Caught unawares, Francine blushed. Then she smiled a secret smile.

Change had come to Francine too. The dark secrets of her past had merged with a future of possibilities, filling her with a lightness of being she had never dared dream of. Tomorrow was Friday, and Todd would be home. It had taken a month to decide, but truly she had known what her answer would be from the moment he had asked.

It was on these moonlit nights, when the world was a blaze of monochromatic beauty, that Madeleine and Francine walked with the memory of ghosts. The ghosts of Eleanor Thwaite and her lost children. Though it was over a year since her sister's ghost had passed on in peace, the loss of Bree was still a constant ache. But the thread of memories no longer pulled taut as a garrotte; instead, they wrapped around Francine with the comfort of an old, knitted scarf.

Those comforting memories peopled the garden: Viola crouching at the edge of a flower bed, alive with excitement at some curiosity she had discovered; Agnes, not scowling for once, bent over a needle and thread as she sewed another scar into her tattered blue-and-white dog; Monty crawling across the lawn with that peculiar crab-crawl to Rosie, to pull her hair. And Mum lifting her head, smiling at little Rosie's belly laugh that hung on the air long after the memories faded. But it was Bree, dear Bree, who was remembered the most—running with her dress hitched into her knickers before disappearing into the labyrinth of rhododendron.

Author's Note

I am endlessly fascinated by language, but I'm especially drawn to secret languages that are not spoken at all yet are full of symbolism understood only by the initiated few. When I discovered Jean Marsh's lovely book *The Illuminated Language of Flowers*, I was instantly intrigued by the first line: "What a charming conceit it is to communicate through flowers instead of words."

That single line encapsulates everything I love about the language of flowers. The charm of someone spending time to pick specific flowers to send a particular message meant only for one other: a love letter in magnolia, gloxinia, and roses; the sorrow of yew weeping over the grave of a loved one; or a darker message of hatred for enemies with orange lilies or basil.

The language of flowers, though not known to many, dates back to the pharaohs. It has since evolved through the centuries, through many cultures, but gained the particular attention of the English during the Victorian period, who took the language to the level of art in their search for novel ways to express their feelings in an era where articulating emotion was frowned upon.

And who doesn't love a secret? There is conceit in secrets, a certain smugness of knowing what others don't, whether it be a gardenia as a token of secret love between lovers, a gauntlet of tansies thrown down in a clandestine war between rivals, or the devotion of violets between mother and child.

Taking my weird penchant for secrets and peculiar, invariably poisonous, plants, the language of flowers soon became a surprisingly important theme through the story, though shaped to suit the plot and characters.

Still on the subject of secrets, I would like to add a note about priest holes, which are a reminder of a dark and grim time in English history. I am always astonished by the lengths people will go to spread the word of their religion. This was particularly evidenced during Queen Elizabeth I's reign, who as a Protestant queen persecuted the Catholics, just as her Catholic sister, Bloody Queen Mary, had persecuted the Protestants. That was one seriously twisted family.

The Catholics, particularly wealthy families, refused to relinquish their religion and went to great lengths to keep a priest in their homes. When Elizabeth outlawed the priests, recusant Catholics built hiding places and escape routes behind walls and under floors, building false rooms into the fabric of their homes. These priest holes were often successful in hiding their occupants when the priest hunters came knocking.

One Jesuit priest, a carpenter called Nicholas Owen, spent much of his life designing priest holes so cleverly that they are still occasionally discovered in Elizabethan stately homes in England, a testament to his ingenuity. Owen saved many priests' lives, but was eventually caught in 1606, then tortured to death in the Tower of London. He was canonized in 1970.

Acknowledgments

Behind every book is a veritable population who've helped shape it in large or small fashion. *Her Little Flowers* was born and grown no differently. I feel rather guilty that these wonderful people get only a small mention at the very end, when their input, time, and enthusiasm has been invaluable for what really started as a gremlin of an idea one drunken evening many years ago.

Thanks to my husband, Anthony, my best friend and the only person who can still make me laugh so hard I get hiccups. Not bad going after twenty years.

And to my beautiful boys, Rory, Nathan, Owen, and Luke who delight and bedevil in equal measure. Thank you for not being offended when I'm locked inside my head and don't always hear you. It's not you, it's me.

Thanks to my mum, Zoë Fourie, who instilled a love of reading in me from a very young age, and who has loved everything I've written, even if it was dreadful.

While writers may have the support of family, writing is a lonely pursuit, and I would've been lost without my friends — some writers, some not. In no particular order, I owe thanks and gratitude to:

Melanie Michael for a friendship without judgement, and more recently for careering around Italy at my breakneck speed and crying at the beauty of Pitigliano. *HLF* was born on a gin-soaked night from one of your twisted pronouncements; look how far it has come.

Karen (K.K.) Edwards, my Michigan Goose, for your unfailing support, friendship, and encouragement through the years. You have penned so many wonderful stories of your own, both published and yet to be, and I can't wait to see them all on bookshelves so others can marvel at your genius as I do.

To the Tokens, Haaniem Smith, Nicole Clark, and Barbara Toich, for endless coffee, gossip, and laughter over the years. Even though we're spread across the globe I will always treasure our friendship.

A special thank you to Barbara Toich for reading various versions of *HLF* while battling breast cancer and coming out stronger and more beautiful on the other side. I am especially grateful for your many weird and unexpected talents, and always taking your enthusiasm one step further with sketches and visual ideas.

To Catherine Johnson for sitting on a dike overlooking the Wash in Norfolk and listening to me rabbit on for three hours about a plot hole, then coming up with a simple solution that had eluded me for months. You are such a special, unique person, allowing me to see the world anew through your eyes when mine had become too jaded.

To Jesse Q. Sutanto, who was there at the first written words of *HLF*, always beating me in word sprints during NaNoWriMo. I am so proud of the success you've had with your writing; so well deserved.

There are so many special people in the publishing world who rarely get the acknowledgment they richly deserve, people who put endless hours, dedication, and love into the creations of others, who are quite often strangers. For most writers the first step into this rather terrifying world is a literary agent, and I have the fortune to have Kaitlyn Katsoupis of Belcastro Agency as my rock star agent. I can't thank you enough for your attention to detail, your speed and knowledge of the business, and your patience when I ask endless dumb questions.

Another step into the publishing world is an editor, and I am so grateful for the kindness of Elizabeth Trout of Kensington Books, whose vision aligned so closely to mine and who never pushed me to accept something I didn't want to. She's very good at compromise! I'd also like to thank the people of Kensington whom I've never met or spoken to but who have in mysterious ways pushed *HLF* through the process to get it out into readers' hands.

Shannon Morgan

HER LITTLE FLOWERS

ABOUT THIS GUIDE

The suggested questions are included to enhance your group's
reading of Shannon Morgan's *Her Little Flowers*.

DISCUSSION QUESTIONS

1. A theme running through *Her Little Flowers* is the language of flowers. Did the novel pique your interest to read more about that? If so, what flower best represents you?

2. Tea-leaf reading is something Francine has done all her life. Have you ever had your tea leaves read? And if so, did any of the predictions come true?

3. Sisterhood and sibling relationships are major themes in *Her Little Flowers*. What were the differences between Francine and Madeleine's relationship and that of Francine and Bree (in both timelines)?

4. Do you enjoy stories where inanimate objects are personified? Does the manor's personification bring a richer, layered emotion to your understanding of the characters and the story? In what way?

5. Much of *Her Little Flowers* is about memories—some forgotten, some fickle, some fractured, some falsely remembered. Did you find this use of memory created an element of suspense, and did it keep the pace of the story moving forward?

6. Priest holes are an interesting element of the novel, and they are not well known. Had you heard or read of priest holes before? Do you know the history behind them? What are your thoughts on people so persecuted for their beliefs they are forced to hide in this way?

7. Ghosts are a fabulous literary device whether real or imagined in a story. What did you think of Bree as a ghost, then meeting her later as a real girl? Did you find knowing her as a real person gave you deeper empathy for her as a ghost?

8. *Her Little Flowers* is set in the Lake District of England, an extraordinarily beautiful area. Have you been there before? Did the descriptions make the area come alive for you? Did the setting suit the story? Did the setting enhance the story?

9. There's a lot of symbolism in *Her Little Flowers*, from the language of flowers, to tea leaf reading, to ghosts. Do you feel this gave a more layered story? If so, in what way?

10. *Her Little Flowers* is told in dual timelines. Did weaving the story in this way make the ending more satisfying? Do you feel the structure worked well for the novel?

11. If there was one thing you could change in the story, what would it be?

12. Francine is a traumatized woman, who had cut herself off from the world as best she could. Did you feel Todd Constable handled Francine with the gentleness she needed while also showing his interest in her without being pushy?

13. Which scene in the book has stuck with you the most?

14. Did you feel the title of the novel, *Her Little Flowers*, works well for the story?

Visit our website at
KensingtonBooks.com
to sign up for our newsletters, read
more from your favorite authors, see
books by series, view reading group
guides, and more!

BOOK **CLUB**
BETWEEN THE CHAPTERS

Become a Part of Our
Between the Chapters Book Club
Community and Join the Conversation

Betweenthechapters.net